The Angels' Footpath

Let's take this walk together...

Ronald R. Cooke

The Angels' Footpath is a work of fiction. The names, characters and events described herein are fictitious. Any similarity to actual events, or real persons, whether living or dead, is purely coincidental.

Copyright 2010 by Ronald R. Cooke
Auburn, CA.
All Rights Reserved

This book or parts thereof may not be reproduced in any form, stored in a retrieval system, or transmitted in any form by any means without prior written permission of the publisher, except as provided by United States of America copyright law.

International Standard Book Number: 978-0-615-36779-8
Library Of Congress Copyright TX 7-195-126

Published by Ronald R. Cooke
Auburn, CA.
2010

www.roncooke.blogspot.com
www.book3.blogspot.com

Original Cover Painting
"The Path"
by
Dwight H. Cooke
Owls Head, Maine

Cover design
by
Marianne Harris
mharrisgraphics.com

Text Edited
by
Several Wonderful Friends

Author's Biography

Ron graduated with an A.B. in Economics. He spent 43 years in corporate operations, marketing and business development.

As an avocation, Ron pursued the study of Cultural Economics, established a WEB site on economic topics, and authored two books on cultural/economic issues. He started his exploration of the spiritual in 2002. The result is this novel.

Foreword

My father, his father and his grandfather were all ministers. My Grandmother Anna was a missionary. Research into my family's colorful history revealed additional ministers and evangelists. I will admit to having been a (not very good) lay preacher, and if you carefully examine my brother's paintings you have to be impressed with their mystical quality. You might say, a passion for the spiritual runs in the family.

When I graduated from college with a degree in economics, I was determined to pursue a career in the business world. It has been my good fortune to spend 43 great years in corporate operations, marketing and business development, working with interesting people at companies of all sizes in 12 different nations. During this time, however, I was never far from the spiritual experience. I have always been fascinated by the wonderfully complex relationship we humans have with our cultural and economic environments, and our very human need to find personal relevance in an infinite cosmos.

Work on this book started when I retired in 2002. In the course of looking for a plot line, I stumbled upon oil depletion and took a literary detour to write two books on oil, economics, culture and political systems. But some power kept nudging me to get back to work on this project. Ever so gently it encouraged me to get started. Finally, unable to resist any longer, I immersed myself in a quest for spiritual enlightenment. I soon determined my discoveries could best be expressed in the form of a novel. It would be story of love, conflict, and faith. The plot had to be realistic. The characters had to be interesting.

I'm not entirely sure where this story originated. Was it from somewhere deep in my subconscious? Or somewhere else? I really don't know. In any event, it just seemed to flow as I wrote each paragraph.

Writing this novel has been a rewarding experience. It has strengthened my faith.

Ron

To Cynthia. We did this together.

Notes

Chapter 1   Innocence

Josue Vasquez leaned against the weathered doorway of his aging farmhouse. A gentle misty rain swirled about the yard. The cool night air was pungent with the smell of mud and farm animals. Nearby Putah Creek gurgled and splashed its way toward the valley. His eyes passed over the dark shadows of pens and sheds. But he really was not seeing anything. Not even the barely visible forms of his farm machinery. His mind was cluttered with the thoughts of the day. Mari telling him it was time. Calling for the mid-wife. Making up a bed. Boiling water. And now waiting. Just waiting. Straining to hear the sounds that would tell him he was a father.

Hours passed. To relieve the tension, Josue walked across the farmyard to the barn. Then he returned to the farmhouse. Back and forth. Maybe 30 times. Tracing a path through the mud and wet grass. The silence of the damp night air was broken only by the bleating of a lamb and the distant sound of highway traffic –all muted by the shroud of fog rising slowly from the creek.

Josue was a big man. Taller than most. Proud of his independence and his skills. Josue worked as a farm machinery mechanic in Winters. People said he could fix anything. There was a sense of satisfaction in that. Being really good at something. He and Mari worked their little farm in their spare time. They had three cows, some chickens, a pig for slaughter and – in the spring – rows of carefully tended vegetables.

Josue and Mari had tried many times to have a baby. They had prayed to the heavenly father for a child. And now this agonizing delay seemed to last forever. Just before midnight, the night sky began to clear, revealing the twinkling lights of a thousand stars. A gentle breeze brought the chill of cooler air . Josue shifted uneasily from one foot to the other.

Then – finally - the sound he was waiting for filled the house. The lusty cry of a new-born baby. Followed by much commotion as the mid-wife went about her chores. Suddenly, a very large woman appeared in the hallway behind him.

"Congratulations, Josue," she smiled. "You are a father. You have a beautiful son."

She carefully handed a bundle of blankets to him. Josue tenderly cradled the baby in his arms and unfolded the blanket just enough to see a very small pink face.

"My son, our life."

Tears filled his eyes as he looked upward at the stars.

"Thank you, Heavenly Father. Thank you for granting our wish."

***

In a nearby field a man reaches down into the damp grass to pick up a very small lamb. He hears the cry of a new born baby. It has happened. Josue and Mari have gotten their most cherished wish. Cuddling the lamb in his arms, an almost imperceptible smile traces its way across the man's weathered face. His eyes become moist with a private joy. Gently he strokes the lamb.

"It is done," he whispers.

***

News spreads quickly in a small town. By mid-morning the next day, neighbors were gathering at the door, anxious to get a look at the new baby. Hugs, kisses and heart-felt best wishes were accompanied by a nearly constant stream of animated chatter. And they brought gifts. Baby blankets, clothing, toys and incense. "Enhorabuena," they would say. "Dios esté con usted."

Although tired and still in pain from the delivery, Mari was radiant. She greeted each visitor with the quiet demeanor of a loving mother. She cradled her baby in her arms, still thrilled by the joy of her son's birth. As for Josue, there was never a man who had more pride or love for his wife. He ushered each visitor into the house. Talking in a hushed voice, they would tip-toe into the bedroom where Mari was propped up in the bed. And there was the baby. Wrapped in a blue blanket. Still a bit pink. Either sleeping or suckling at his mother's breast. It was a precious sight for all. A moment of reverence for a gift God had presented to these special people.

After the midwife brought a light supper that evening, the happy couple had a chance to relax from a busy day. Josue turned to his wife. "What shall we name our son?" he asked. Mari looked at him with a little smile on her face. They had picked out a name long ago. Even before she had become pregnant.

"Ricardo," she said. "Just as we planned."

Mari looked lovingly at the sleeping baby. "Ricardo Juan Sanchez Vasquez."

***

George and Abigail Mitchell were in their thirties before they were ready to start a family. George, an attorney in nearby Davis, had been preoccupied with building his practice. Abigail was a very busy software development supervisor at U. C. Davis. But as the clock of opportunity ticked down they reached a point where they either had to start their family, or forget birth parenting altogether. After much deliberation, the Mitchells made the decision to move from their apartment in Davis to a large parcel with a comfortable old house and huge barn in Winters. Soon thereafter, Abigail discovered she loved to ride horses and it was not long before they added a corral to their property.

Living in Winters proved productive. Their little girl, Neema, was born a short 10 months after the move. Josephine was born 18 months later. And then came Phillip, barely a year after Josephine. It was a bit more family than Abigail could handle by herself. What to do? The Mitchells decided to hire a nanny. After many unsuccessful interviews, they gratefully hired Mari.

***

By the age of two, Ricardo Juan Sanchez Vasquez had become a very bright, always outgoing, and irrepressibly happy little boy. He was also very lucky. Josue proved to be a firm but loving father. Hard working, thoughtful, and even tempered, he was destined to convey his demeanor to his son. His mother, Mari, was a slender, gentle and affectionate woman with a flair for baking wonderful treats. She almost always took Ricardo with her when she went to work and as a result he grew up with the Mitchell children. For Phillip Mitchell, Ricardo was a welcome playmate. The girls brought him into their home as a second brother. Neema, who became especially fond of Ricardo, gave him a nickname. He would be known as Rick for the rest of his life. Abigail and George took a special interest in Mari's little boy. He soon became one of the family.

***

The grim look on the Doctor's face told Mari and Josue that something was wrong. He led them into the clinic office, motioned for them to sit down, and sank with a heavy heart into the thick leather of his desk chair. The Doctor began to fidget with a manila folder. He hated this part of his job. "*What shall I tell them,*" he thought. "*Perhaps this is a good time to lie.*" He carefully evaluated Josue's face for a clue about his feelings. Josue, he decided, would be very upset. Mari seemed to be more composed. "*She will take it better*," the Doctor decided. Having made his evaluation, he reluctantly gave them the news.

"We have run many tests. The results, I am afraid, are not very encouraging. It does not appear you will be able to have another baby."

The Doctor leaned back in his chair to wait for a response. Josue spoke first, his eyes filled with disbelief and sorrow.

"Why not?"

"I could give you a technical explanation. But the simple answer is that Mari can no longer conceive."

"Is there anything we can do ? An operation? Some medicine?"

Josue was looking for answers. He had always dreamed of having a big family with Mari. Someday. Maybe 4 or 5 little ones. The Doctor shook his head.

"No. I'm sorry, there is no way to change the outcome."

Mari put her hand on Josue's shoulder. She tenderly rubbed the back of his neck.

"We have a fine son. Let us be thankful for what we have."

They talked with the Doctor for several more minutes. Then, having accepted the inevitable, they thanked the Doctor for his time and made their way out of the clinic.

In his heart Josue was not sure of the Doctor's explanation. But he decided the reason did not matter. Nothing would change their loss. He put his arm around the slender form of his beloved wife. He was more determined than ever.

"Ricardo will grow up to be a good man."

***

It was a childhood of innocence and joy. Hot dry summers and cool rain swept winters. It was a carefree life of work and play, love and learning, imagination and growing. Phillip and Rick became best friends, playing together almost every day. Always pretending. They could be wicked pirates, unstoppable heroes, or whatever else caught their imagination. Abigail made sure Rick had plenty of interesting books to read. George taught Phillip how to throw a football and the two boys loved to pretend they were pro-football champions. Mari spent countless hours with Rick in their garden, teaching him how to sow, weed and harvest the vegetables they grew each year. Josue would often take Rick with him when he went into town or to fix the farm machinery on one of the nearby farms.

For Mari and Josue, raising a boy was joy, sorrow, laughter, tears, satisfaction, frustration, discipline, chaos, and above all – very challenging. Rick quickly developed an irrepressible charm, frequently accompanied by a big smile and lots of energetic motion. By the age of 8 he could carry on a conversation with almost anyone he met. People loved him because he was so full of life.

On the other hand, Rick would occasionally experience periods of serious introspection and contemplation. It was as though he was trying to work through a new idea or solve a problem. Mari learned to handle both moods with her characteristic quiet demeanor. For his part, Josue would always be puzzled by these shifts of behavior. He wanted Rick to be like him all the time - solid, hard working and even tempered.

***

Phillip and Rick seldom got into trouble. But – well – they were boys. Abigail taught them how to ride and Phillip – who loved to work with the horses - would take Rick with him for treks along the trails of Putah Creek. On one occasion when Phillip was 10 and Rick was 9, they rode through the vacant fields next to Winters and actually made it all the way into town.

And so there they were. Proud as peacocks. Riding down Railroad Avenue. And they would have made it all the way to Main Street – a busy thoroughfare with many stores – had it not been for Officer Johnson. One can imagine his surprise when he looked up from writing a parking ticket to see two boys on horseback, riding down the middle of the road, big as life, followed by a string of impatient cars and trucks.

The Officer didn't quite know what to do. The only time horses were allowed on this street was during a celebration when the whole town would turn out for a parade. He pushed the ticket under the windshield wiper of the car and walked back to his police cruiser. Then he motioned the two boys over to a parking space behind his vehicle.

"Where on earth do you think you're going," he asked in a loud commanding voice.

Rick immediately flashed a great big disarming smile and said very brightly, "We're on a safari!"

Somewhat mollified by the innocence of the answer, Officer Johnson took the reins of Phillip's horse and led him to the curb. Still unsure what to do, he called dispatch to find his supervisor. Then he turned again to the two boys.

"What's your name?"

"Rick."

"Phillip Mitchell," the other boy said uneasily. He then turned to Rick. "You have to tell him your last name."

"How come?"

"Because I said."

Rick screwed up his face into a defiant look, but did as he was told.

"Ricardo Juan Sanchez Vasquez."

Officer Johnson smiled at the two boys. Perhaps they had done something wrong. But they weren't being bad. They were just being boys. Another patrol car arrived and pulled up behind them. It was Officer Johnson's supervisor. He went over to the vehicle. In a short time the two men were engaged in a very animated conversation. The supervisor knew Phillip's father from his work at County Court. He realized George Mitchell would appreciate a favor. They decided to escort the two boys safely back home.

***

It just happened that Abigail was working in her flower garden when she looked up to see a very strange parade coming down the county road. It was led by a police patrol car with red and blue flashing lights, followed by two boys riding single file on horse back, then another patrol car with flashing lights, and finally a long string of cars and trucks. The parade slowly made its way up the county road to the Mitchell house. When the patrol cars stopped by the front gate, the two boys rode into her yard, and the long string of cars and trucks went on by – horns honking, and people laughing. Officer Johnson responded with a quick blast of his siren.

"Phillip!" Abigail shrieked. "What have you been doing?"

"Nothing," Phillip responded sheepishly.

Rick was more positive. "We've been on a Safari," he said with a big happy smile. Then he pointed at the passing vehicles. "And look what we brought back!"

***

Coach Ramirez looked at the crestfallen faces of the boys slouched on the locker room benches. They had just lost their first game. He had to admit the truth. It was going to be a tough season of football. Small town teams usually lacked any depth. Although there were plenty of big boys to choose from, most of them were not great athletes. That meant he had to build his team from scratch. Teach them how to play. Turn raw strength into athletic contenders. And every four years he had to start all over again.

He said a few words of encouragement and then dismissed them. Ramirez washed his hands and wandered dejectedly out of the building. Only a handful of people remained on the playing field. He looked up and spotted the track coach sitting in the bleachers. Ramirez went over to join him. The man looked up.

"Tough start to the season," he said sympathetically.

"We could use a few more players with experience," Ramirez responded. "I'll have to do a better job of figuring out who can do what."

Ramirez looked absently over the field. "Why are you still here?"

"I'm just making a few notes for our track events next Saturday... Like you, I have a few holes to fill." The track coach smiled. "At least I have a few good runners."

Ramirez glanced at the man. "Do you have anyone who can run and catch a football?"

The track coach motioned toward the playing field. Two boys were passing a football back and forth as they trotted toward the sidelines. The taller of the two seemed to move effortlessly across the turf. The other boy was more muscular. A big kid for his age.

"You might try Phillip and Rick," he said. "Phillip throws a football really well and Rick is the fastest kid I've seen in a long time."

Ramirez looked at the two boys with a critical eye. "What's the catch?"

"Phillip's mother thinks football is barbaric. She won't let either of them play."

Coach Ramirez felt discouraged and despondent. "There is always an obstacle."

Then he looked up. Phillip and Rick were standing in front of the two men. Ramirez looked Phillip in the eye. "Can you throw that thing?"

Philip was taken back. Surprised at the question. "Sure!"

Then Ramirez looked at Rick. "And can you catch what he throws?"

Rick felt a bit awkward. No one had challenged him like this before. Then he flashed a big grin. "I can catch anything this dummy tosses."

"Show me." Ramirez challenged them with a toughness he really did not feel.

The two boys looked at each other with a mix of astonishment and playful pride. Well... Why not? Rick and Phillip ran to the middle of the field. They got down into an offensive stance, and then Phillip called, "hike!"

Rick ran a full 40 yards down the center of the field, and cut right. Phillip delivered a perfectly thrown pass right into his arms.

"Holy mother of God!" Ramirez exclaimed. "That kid is really fast."

The track coach looked amused. He couldn't help teasing Ramirez just a bit. "And he's got soft hands. Isn't that something you football people pray for?"

Ramirez ignored the track coach and stood up. "Try that again," he shouted.

***

Of course it took a lot of diplomacy, pleading and downright lies to get Abigail and George to let Phillip play football. Abigail had it in her mind that football was nothing more than a bunch of gladiators making war with grunts and farts. But she changed her mind when Coach Ramirez took her to a U. C. Davis football game. He patiently explained the strategy of each play. Ramirez emphasized the need for teamwork. That all appealed to Abigail. She was also impressed by the importance of self discipline and personal achievement. By the end of the game, she was certain football would be a good lesson for her son.

Mari and Josue were easier to convince. Rick decided that if Phillip was going to play football, he was going to play football. Period. And so with his irrepressible enthusiasm, he easily convinced his parents to let him play.

***

Neither the glare of the relentless sun, nor the heat of a dry September afternoon, seemed to have any effect on the noisy activity in the Winters High School stadium. The varsity football team was hard at work in the middle of the field. The cheerleader squad was shouting out the words and practicing the choreography of a new routine. The air was filled with calls and shouts, all intermixed with giggles and laughter.

When the cheerleader squad stopped for a break, Rosalinda Santiago Munoz and her friend Lydia sat down on the grass to watch the football team and share a coke. As the boys formed up a scrimmage line, she noticed a tall, good looking young man who lined up near her on the playing field. He looked a little nervous, perhaps unsure of his assignment. Coach Ramirez held up the play, gestured for him to come over to the quarterback, and gave both boys their instructions. As usual, the quarterback was Phillip Mitchell, and the other boy was his friend Rick. As the play resumed, Rick lined up as a wide receiver. When the ball was snapped, he moved skillfully through the pocket and looked downfield. Rick quickly ran past the linebacker, turned back toward the center of the field, and looked up. Phillip had already thrown the ball. Rick seemed to know exactly where it would be. That play, and that catch, was the first of many the two boys would make over the next two years.

Watching the two boys gave Rosalinda a rush of erotic excitement. She had seen Rick in class. Now, she decided, he was definitely someone special.

***

Cold winter rain poured down on the Mitchell house. Rick and Phillip were sitting at the kitchen table. Rick fiddled aimlessly with a glass of coke. Phillip was sprawled out on his chair, bored by a Saturday afternoon with nothing to do. They talked about football, last year's season, and their chances for next fall. It was a conversation they had many times. Then the front door flew open and Abigail struggled into the foyer. She took off her wet raincoat, shook her head so her hair would fall down around her shoulders, and put her coat into the hall closet. Then she came into the kitchen.

"Just the man I want to see," she said looking directly at Rick. "I have a book for you."

Abigail reached into a brown paper bag she was carrying, pulled out a black book, and handed it to Rick. He took the book and looked at the cover.

"It's a Bible," he said with some wonder.

"Yes, and it's for you to read... cover to cover."

"But I thought you were an atheist," he said.

Abigail sat down at the table and looked thoughtfully at the two boys. Then she turned to Rick.

"Phillip is interested in computers and software. He follows after me," Abigail said with some pride.

"But you seem to be more interested in philosophy and ideas. So here is a book for you to read... And I expect you to read it."

Although Rick had read parts of the Bible, he had not given it much thought. He was puzzled by Abigail's insistence he read the whole thing.

"OK... I'll read it... But you still didn't tell me why you... of all people... a strict atheist... want me to read the Bible."

Abigail looked at Rick with some determination in her eyes.

"If you are going to be a man of ideas... of philosophy... then you must read and understand this book.... it describes the greatest system of philosophy mankind has ever produced."

"But you don't believe this stuff...."

"The truths in this book are universal," Abigail said with some intensity. "I may choose not to believe in God... But nevertheless, the characters we meet in the Bible are dramatic and the drama is ageless. There are lessons of history. There is moral right and wrong, the best and worst of human behavior, and the experience of both pain and joy. The Bible's authors tell us about marriage, divorce, adultery, obedience, authority, honesty, parenting, nature, their concept of God, and much more. It presents us with real life stories of spiritual vision, high ideals, and great moral depth. No other book has had a greater influence on humanity because in its essence, this book is about us. We are the people in the Bible."

Philip looked over at his mother. "Do I have to read it?"

"Yes... as soon as Rick has finished, he can give it to you... And you can expect me to quiz you both about the content."

Phillip looked over at Rick and smiled with a certain resignation. His mother could be a woman of great determination.

***

Senior year. It was their last high school game. A final afternoon after a good season. Rick and Phillip were just having fun. Their senior year was filled with books, classes, football, academic tests, and love. Oh yes. Lots of romance. Neither boy had any trouble finding a date. Life was good.

"Rick," Phillip whispered in the huddle. "It's the fourth quarter. One more score and we can put this one away. Let's fake them out. Instead of going long like you usually do, pull up in the zone."

It was a good idea. Rick was playing wide receiver. Taking a pass in the zone would pull in the free safety. Rick looked up from the huddle at the young man he would have to deceive. He looked tired.

"I can fake him out," he grinned.

They broke for the scrimmage line, took their stance and Phillip made the calls. Then came a tumble of bodies pushing with all their might for position. Rick broke free and started down the field like he was on fire. The defense bought it. About 20 yards down he turned back up the field toward the scrimmage line. Unfortunately, Phillip was tackled just as he was throwing the ball and it threatened to sail over Rick's head. Jumping as high as he could, Rick was able to bring down the ball with one hand. He was running as soon as he hit the ground, dodging one player, breaking a tackle, and then running toward the open space ahead. Only the free safety stood between him and the goal posts. Rick faked left, pretended to turn right, and then broke left again. The free safety stumbled and fell. It was an easy run to the goal posts.

That last play was particularly impressive to two people. One was a scout from San Jose State University. The man looked at Rick, shook his head in admiration, and began to scribble a bunch of notes on a pad of paper. In two weeks, Rick would receive an invitation to attend a football training camp in San Jose. That would lead to a football scholarship, and a momentous change in his life.

The other person who watched Rick's every move that afternoon was Rosalinda Santiago Munoz, a slender and very cute cheerleader. Although they had never dated, she was absolutely sure she was in love with him.

***

After the game, players, students and parents collected into little groups on the playing field to experience the pleasure of victory. Lydia had watched Rosalinda's eyes as she followed the young man's every move on the playing field. Although it was the first time her friend had shown any real interest in a boy, the passion was unmistakable.

"Why don't you go out there and ask him for a date?" she teased.

Rosalinda looked at Lydia with a blank stare, as though contemplating a momentous decision.

Lydia could not help herself. She again playfully mocked Rosalinda.

"He'll never know you exist unless you smack him."

Normally a shy person, Rosalinda was more likely to act a bit saucy when she was wearing her red, white and black cheerleader uniform. Working out with the cheerleader squad seemed to give her a bolder persona. A smile crossed Lydia's face and she giggled. Rosalinda ignored her friend, stood up and walked out onto the playing field where Rick was talking with Phillip. She physically confronted Rick on the 40 yard line. Her determination caught Rick off guard.

Rosalinda looked intently into his eyes, a little playful smile crossed her lips. "How come you never asked me out?"

Rick could only stammer ,"uh, I dunno."

He was suddenly aware of her physical presence, the slender petite figure, her lovely brown eyes, the smell of her hair... A quivering sensation ran through his body. Although he had seen Rosalinda many times, he never thought she would have any interest in him. He could feel his heart racing for joy. At that moment, they were the only people in the world, everything else around them was dark and was silent. Phillip did not exist.

"*Oh God,*" he thought, "*how lame.*" He was being asked to fall in love with an angel and he had no idea what to say.

Rosalinda came to his rescue. "Call me," she said, "or meet me after class on Monday."

Rick struggled to regain his composure. "Sure… I'd like to do that."

With that, Rosalind abruptly turned around and walked back toward the sideline. She could feel his eyes on her. Watching her every step. So she put just a tiny bit more wiggle into her walk. Of course, it had the desired effect. Monday afternoon Rick would search for her, find her, and make her feel important. From then on they were inseparable. Best friends. Thoughtful companions. And intimate partners.

***

Although Phillip had purchased an old car before his senior year in high school, he was seldom able to drive it. Gasoline had become very expensive and just before Christmas there were fuel shortages throughout California. Even with ride sharing and public transportation, getting from Winters to Davis became a chore. In February, George and Abigail made a big decision. Although they would keep their home in Winters, they decided to move back to Davis in order to be closer to work. Phillip was devastated. He wanted to finish his high school year at Winters. Then Mari and Josue came to his rescue. They made room for him at their little house and he was able to bunk with Rick until his senior year was finished.

For Rick, the remainder of his senior year was one of change and growth. He and Phillip would hitchhike, take public transportation, or on rare occasions, drive Phillip's car into Davis to visit his parents. The University presented Rick with an almost unlimited access to any subject he wanted to study, and Abigail did everything she could to nourish his natural curiosity. She encouraged him to read books on religion and philosophy. Whenever she could, Abigail took both boys to lectures on history and culture.

Although both Rick and Phillip played computer games, it was Phillip who had the greatest interest in the software that made them work. He soon had all the computer toys and Abigail was able to enroll him in a U. C. Davis software class. Phillip was destined to be a talented programmer.

***

And then there was Rosalinda. Rick was not prepared for the sudden rush of emotions he would experience at the Senior Year dance. Phillip had managed to save enough gasoline to use his car for a date. They drove into Winters to pick up Rosalinda and her friend Lydia. As she walked to the car, Rosalinda looked radiant. Going to this dance was a dream for her, a sequence from a romantic movie, the very thing she had imagined for so long. But as she got into the seat beside Rick, she lost her cool.

"Do I look OK?" she stammered.

Rick wasn't sure what to say. The faint smell of her sweet perfume and the cleavage of her low cut gown had mesmerized him. He managed, somehow, self-consciously, to recover his composure.

"You are an angel," he said. "A pretty rose."

More confident with her appearance, Rosalinda sat back in the seat. Rick could not keep his eyes off her. His heart began to thump and a feeling of excitement coursed through his body.

***

It was the first dance. As if in a trance, eyes glazed, Rick guided Rosalinda onto the dance floor. Somewhere, from deep within, a new emotion swept over him. His heart began to pound and he felt just a little giddy. When he spoke, there was a slight tremor in his voice.

"Let's dance," was all he could manage to say.

He took Rosalinda in his arms and they began to move with the music. They began to flow with their feelings. Rosalinda placed her hand behind his neck, drew him close, and put her cheek on his chest. It was warm, it was wonderful, it was sensuous, and she smelled of lilac perfume. Although his eyes were open, Rick saw nothing but a swirl of shapes around him. The music seemed almost distant. They had created their own private world. Nothing could intrude.

But then Rick realized his manhood had arisen. Big time.

"*Oh hell, she'll hate me for this,*" he thought.

He carefully moved away from Rosalinda. Give her a little space. Be a gentleman. But Rosalinda looked up at him, gave him a sweet little smile, put her finger on his lips, and then drew him very close to her. She was not going to lose this moment. Rosalinda wanted Rick to know. He was her man.

***

Rick trudged up the well worn footpath to the ramshackle collection of old weathered buildings where he knew he would find Micah, his next door neighbor. And true enough, he found him stacking bales of hay in his barn. Standing on the hay wagon, covered with dust and sweat, Micah almost looked relieved to see Rick. He could, at last, take a break from his labor.

"Well … Good morning Rick. What brings you to my humble farm?"

"Oh, nothing … really," responded Rick.

He looked at the few remaining bales that needed to be stacked. "Can I help you?"

"Sure enough. You can start with that one over there."

Rick looked at a bale that had fallen off the wagon. He easily lifted the bale off the ground and placed it on the neatly arranged pile of bales. A puff of dust and bits of hay fell onto his shirt and face. Silently, he helped Micah finish stacking the bales of hay. Satisfied with their work, the two men sat down on the highest stack, feet dangling over the edge. Micah looked quizzically at the young man beside him.

"You should be leaving for San Jose soon. Have you already started football practice?"

"Yes. We started our drills three weeks ago. Classes start next week."

"Isn't this your Freshman year?"

Rick nodded in agreement. Micah could tell something was bothering Rick. "Are you ready for college?"

Rick stared off into space, collecting his thoughts before he answered the question.

"We don't have the money. Even with a football scholarship. I'll stay as long as I can, but when the money runs out, I'll probably just get married and settle down here."

Micah didn't like the answer he just heard. Rick had much too much promise to miss out on the opportunities a college education would offer. He looked out over the foothills that surrounded his farm, baked by the summer sun into a gray-brown landscape punctuated by patches of green where one could find the shade of a tree. Although he already knew the answer to his next question, he asked it anyway.

"Who's the girl?"

Rick smiled uneasily, and looked down at his feet. "*How did he know I have a girlfriend?*"

His mind swept over the events of his senior year. Rosalinda. Yearning to be near her. He was tempted to skip college and just get married. Rick felt a rush of emotion. He looked bashfully at Micah.

"Rosalinda. – Her name is Rosalinda Santiago Munoz."

Micah knew who she was. Shy, petite, very pretty, with almost jet black hair and lovely brown eyes. Like Micah and Rick, she was a member of the Catholic Church in town. Rick had almost stammered when mentioning her name. Micah looked again at Rick.

"Are you in love?"

Rick thought for a moment. "We are very much in love," he said with a little smile.

Micah gently prodded his young companion. "Are you sure it's not just lust?"

"No, no," Rick said defensively. "We have been in love a long time."

Micah's eyes wandered over the beams of the barn, the bales of dusty hay, and then at Rick.

"Do you know the difference between lust and love?"

Rick was uncertain how to answer. Embarrassed, his cheeks colored a bit.

"Lust is sex, love is …. more."

Micah looked away again at the gray-brown landscape around his farm. "It's important you know the difference, Rick. Lust is temporary. Love is forever."

Rick shifted his weight uneasily on the bale. No one had ever challenged him to explain his love for Rosalinda. Micah paused for a moment, and then quietly began to describe his convictions.

"Lust is a natural physical reaction to a contact we have made with another human. The excitement, passion and exhilaration we feel comes from deep within our physical being. It's all part of our physical self. Everything from our genes to our nervous system. Lust is the powerful inner energy that brings humans together for procreation. The problem is that we often confuse our natural physical reaction to someone with our equally natural desire to love, and be loved, in a physical way. But while lust is a physical reaction that stimulates our mind into action, love is an emotional reaction with far reaching spiritual implications."

Micah paused. Rick looked a bit confused, as though trying to sort out his feelings for Rosalinda. Micah smiled gently at his companion.

"Think of it this way. Lust is the way our body stimulates us into action. Sometimes for good. Sometimes for bad. But although the excitement of the activity may linger in our mind, lust is a physical thing. Love on the other hand, is more closely aligned with long term relationships. It is the feeling of friendship. Those we love we trust. We view them as companions with whom we can share our thoughts and dreams without fear of ridicule."

Micah paused again to organize his thoughts.

"When we lust for someone, it is usually a selfish act. We want to satisfy our physical need. The other person is an object to satisfy our physical desire. Love, by contrast, is an expression of giving - as well as receiving. Our need for love is fulfilled by making someone more content with our relationship. We want them to trust us. Be our companion. Share our thoughts. Engage with us on a spiritual level. That means true love is a commitment that lasts for a very long time, and it does not require us to perform a physical act. Remember, Jesus loved those with whom he traveled and the people that came to visit with him. Those relationships were spiritual in nature. He welcomed them as companions and friends. Love is for sharing. It is an act of caring"

Rick looked down at the floor of the barn, deep in thought. He appeared to understand Micah's words. The old man carefully slid off the bales and dropped onto the barn floor. He looked up at Rick.

"Well Rick. Is it lust or love you feel for Rosalinda?"

Rick looked intently at Micah. Slowly, solemnly, he said "both."

"Good answer," Micah responded. "A very honest answer."

Micah started to walk toward the hay wagon. Then he stopped. He turned to Rick and offered this thought.

"Just remember, a good marriage... a lasting marriage... is based on love. And if she loves you... she'll want you to finish college."

***

The years at San Jose State University passed very quickly. Football occupied most of his time from summer through winter. Tough courses in computer sciences and philosophy kept Rick busy most nights, and a part time job as a programmer for a local internet service provider took what little time he had left. Sporadic gasoline shortages and lousy public transportation limited personal travel to occasional trips home to see Mari and Josue. Although he looked for Rosalinda, he was only able to connect with her five or six times. She seemed to be reserved. Distant. The memory of senior dance gradually faded from his mind.

The only real distraction for him was a constant babble about the lousy economy. Neither political party could fix anything and unemployment seemed to be stuck at more than 9 percent. Jobs were scarce for college graduates and this contributed to a pall of gloom over the normally upbeat mood on campus. Beggars began to appear on the streets of San Jose. Sporadic protests erupted but did no good. People were increasingly frightened by the turn of events.

***

Because of his football success and easy-going personality, Rick was invited to a fraternity party in the spring of his Junior year. An easy mixer, he was soon involved in an intense conversation about San Jose's prospects for the coming football season. He was about to make a point when the young men in his little group all turned their eyes toward the patio door. There stood an incredibly beautiful woman, tall – almost regal in appearance. She seemed to be looking for someone. Her eyes swept the room and then, with a nod of recognition, she headed right for where Rick was standing. Her frilly blouse and tight skirt revealed an incredible figure. The faint smell of her perfume made her easy movement all the more sensuous. Rick was mesmerized.

She had come to talk to a young man standing next to Rick. From the conversation, he gathered she was his sister. He turned to Rick and made an introduction.

"This is my sister from Los Angeles. Her name is Hannah." he said politely. "Hannah Zane."

The young woman offered her hand to Rick with a slight smile. He reached out to her slowly, captivated by her flawless olive skin and penetrating green eyes.

"I'm very pleased to meet you," Rick responded. *"Oh God,"* he thought. *"What do I say next?"*

Self assured and very cool, Hannah immediately took control of the awkward conversation.

"My brother tells me you are a wide receiver for San Jose. When do you have to be back in San Jose for practice?"

Relieved she had asked a question he could answer, Rick gratefully responded. The conversation then drifted from football to summer break. Hannah, he found out, would graduate from USC in June with a degree in Political Science. She was in San Jose to spend a week with her mother and brother. The conversation was friendly, unassuming, and all too brief. In a few minutes she and her brother left the party. A feeling of passion swept over Rick as he watched her walk gracefully out the door. That first vision of Hannah would stay with him for the rest of his life.

***

John was a happy, round, not very tall, elf of a man with a shock of white hair and a rather ruddy complexion, all hiding behind a pair of large black rimmed glasses. A brilliant programmer, he had an absolute command of operating systems and internet software technology. Both he and Rick worked for a local Internet Service Provider (ISP). Despite the difference in their ages, they had become good friends.

As Rick took a seat beside him at a computer console, John could tell his friend was too distracted to do much useful work.

"A penny for your thoughts?" John asked. "Or maybe a $1.50?"

Rick responded with a sheepish smile. "I met a girl. A beautiful vision I can do nothing about."

"Why not? Can't you get a date with her?"

"I don't know anything about her, except her brother is a member of the fraternity where I met her."

"Oh come on, Rick. Don't you even have a name?"

"Hannah Zane. From Southern California. USC, I think."

John looked mischievously at Rick.

"I'll bet you a coke I can find out all about your Hannah," he grinned. Then he thought for a moment. The far away look on Rick's face meant the information would be worth more than a coke.

"No. make that a pizza," John added.

Rick nodded his agreement.

And so it was. In short order John looked up Hannah on My Space, found her again on Facebook, and checked out her family on Google. Satisfied, he turned triumphantly to Rick.

"Want the results?"

Rick could only look at John in wonder. Of course, he knew how to do all this stuff. But for John it was all so easy – almost effortless. Like a music conductor who knows the score for a thousand instruments.

"OK. Sock it to me," he said humorously.

"Hannah Zane was born in L.A. She will graduate with honors in Political Science this June. Her father and mother are divorced. He is a big deal in the entertainment business. That means she's rich. Would you like her mother's telephone number and address?"

Rick definitely wanted to see Hannah again. So John gave him a telephone number in upscale Los Altos, and after much prodding, Rick called to see if he could get a date with Hannah. To his surprise, Hannah answered the telephone and once again gently took control of the conversation. Of course, she would be delighted to meet him for lunch.

When he hung up the phone, John was laughing almost uncontrollably. "Rick, you are usually one smooth puppy. But that woman has you baffled."

***

Rick arrived at the restaurant early. The scent of a fresh breeze wafted in from the Bay and flirted with the window drapes. He wanted to make sure he did not screw up and miss Hannah. Rick was uneasy. He did not know what to expect. Then, right on time to the minute, a blue BMW convertible came up the restaurant driveway. And there she was. Elegant, regal, beautiful, and – he decided – way out of his class. Rick met her at the door. A very formal waiter escorted them to a table with a window that overlooked a small garden.

"*Perfect*," Rick thought. "*Very romantic. But now what?*"

Once again, it was easy to talk with Hannah. She seemed to know all the right words and Rick soon found himself discussing the high price of gasoline, the state of the economy, football and a bunch of other stuff he soon forgot. Hannah's delightful perfume and lovely persona held his attention. The waiter came by the table with two very large menus. So many delicious choices. Hannah was the first to order.

"I thought at first I would have the baked fish special, but I think the roast veal with wine sauce looks even better."

She paused. "And a glass of your best house white."

Rick looked at the menu. His heart almost skipped a beat when he saw the prices. All ala cart. Did he have enough money to pay for all this?

"I'll have the stew special and some ice tea, please"

The waiter nodded, and then – almost absently - poured two glasses of water.

Satisfied with his selection, Rick settled back to enjoy a short conversation with Hannah. They joked about the nutrition police, commented on the hot weather, and then – for a moment – their hands touched across the table. Rick felt a distinct thumping in his chest. But his romantic trance was broken by the waiter's sudden interruption when he abruptly returned with their selections. Except for a few brief words of conversation, they ate in silence. After lunch, Hannah went to the rest room to wash her hands. Rick watched her every lovely move as she disappeared through the doorway. A few moments later, the waiter reappeared. Rick summoned him for the bill.

"No, no, sir," he whispered. "The lady has already paid the bill."

Rick was crushed. He had invited her to lunch and then she had paid the bill. No. No. That was not right. He was so embarrassed by it all.

But when Hannah came back to the table, she dismissed the whole thing with a wave of her hand. They had one last sip of wine. Rick, trying to be the perfect gentleman, escorted Hannah to her car.

"This has been delightful," she smiled warmly. "We must do it again sometime."

Rick looked into her green eyes, searching for any sign of passion. In response, Hannah placed her hand around his neck and kissed him lightly on the cheek.

Then she was gone.

**

The next afternoon, after much anguish, Rick finally found the courage to call Hannah. The phone rang several times before an older woman's voice answered.

"Hello, this is Rick. Is Hannah there, please?"

"No. I'm afraid not," the woman responded. "Hannah has gone back to USC. She left this morning."

**

After the end of classes and exams, Rick went home to Winters for a short vacation. He was anxious to see Rosalinda again. In one more year, he would get his degree and be ready to settle down. Then he made a serious mistake. He told Phillip about his lunch with Hannah. That part was OK. But Phillip could not resist telling his sister Josephine, who - of course – couldn't wait to tell her friend, Rosalinda. As Josue was fond of saying, "that sure put some fire under the pot!"

**

Summer months in Winters can be very hot, especially when the wind blows the super-heated air of the Sacramento River valley to the south. Nevertheless, Rick felt a bit chilly when he picked up Rosalinda. She was polite. Smiled. Courteous. And made a point of refusing his kiss.

"*Uh, oh*," thought Rick. "*I'm sure in the dog house.*"

"And how was school?" she asked icily as they walked to the car he had borrowed from Phillip.

"It's going just great," Rick replied uneasily. "One more year and I'm through."

He opened the passenger door for her and noted she was being unusually careful with her skirt as she swung into her seat. He went around the car and settled into the driver's seat. Rick turned to Rosalinda who was sitting stiffly upright in her seat, as though waiting for something to happen.

"Look, Rosalinda. I'm sorry if I have done anything to upset you."

It was the wrong thing to say. Rosalinda looked straight ahead through the windshield when she replied.

"I've waited for you... Three years... I've been faithful." Her voice began to tremble. "You'd better believe I had plenty of offers."

Then, inexplicably, she put her head down and began to sob, her body shaking as the tears ran down her cheeks.

Rick was stunned by the heat of passion. He touched the back of her neck and felt the sweat beneath his finger tips. She angrily pushed his hand away.

"Don't touch me!" she screamed.

Rick had no idea what to do. All his life he had been surrounded by people who loved to have him around. Now one woman had chosen to ignore him, and this one was so angry she was crying hot tears.

Rosalinda turned and looked up at him. Her eyes were red with tears that streaked down her face. "And where is your new girlfriend?" she shouted sarcastically.

And then she began to sob again.

"She has gone to Washington," he stammered. "Her father got her a job with some political consulting outfit."

Rick felt a sense of desperation. He wanted Rosalinda to stop crying. The tension between them – half frustration and half sexual - was unbearable.

"And besides," he said firmly, "she was never my girlfriend."

Rick thought it best to just sit for a moment. Maybe this would all pass. He offered Rosalinda a handkerchief, which she took to blow her nose with great vigor. Moments passed. Neither of them said anything. Then Rosalinda looked up at him again, brushed the hair from her face with her fingers, and smiled tenderly.

"Rick," she said softly. "I love you."

And with that, Rosalinda planted a very long, very passionate, and definitely hot kiss on his lips. To which he responded with grateful relief and a welling passion of his own.

***

It was the first game of the season. His senior year. Rick had become a respected wide-receiver and was a key player for San Jose. The team was taken by bus from San Jose State to Stanford for an annual confrontation that brought out fans from all over the Bay area. On this particular afternoon, a constant drizzle made everything wet and cool. As the ancient bus drove onto the Stanford campus, the sweet-pungent smell of eucalyptus drifted through the open windows.

Because of gasoline shortages, about a third of the parking stalls were empty. Rather than use precious gasoline to go to the game, people either walked or took public transportation. Here and there a tent or tarp provided a minimum of cover for a tailgate party. Cold and wet football fans, some dressed in Stanford red, others in San Jose blue and gold, huddled under whatever shelter they could find. The misty rain would continue all afternoon.

Stanford played a tough game and by the forth quarter both teams were exhausted. In the huddle the quarterback motioned to Rick. "It's the forth quarter. One more score and we can put this one away. Let's fake them out. Instead of going long like you usually do, pull up in the zone." "*Somehow,*" Rick thought, "*that play sounds vaguely familiar.*"

As they went to the scrimmage line, Rick looked at the safeties. They were definitely much larger than the ones he had encountered in high school.

The ball was snapped and Rick got free. The pass was perfect. Rick took the ball and was turning up field when he got slammed very hard by a very large body. Everything turned black and he had the sensation of falling ... hearing voices ....

When he opened his eyes, he was flat on his back starring up into the face of a smiling Stanford player. "Hi," he grinned. "My name is George Kincade Taylor. I'm the free safety you forgot about."

After they determined nothing was broken, a coach and the team doctor got him onto his feet. At first he seemed to be all right, walking on his own toward the sideline. But then he stumbled and almost fell to the ground. Taylor was at his side instantly, helping him to his feet. The crowd stood up and clapped with approval as the Stanford player helped Rick off the field. It was a good display of sportsmanship.

***

June. His senior year. Rick was dressed in a dark blue suit that Mari and Josue had purchased for him as a graduation present. He sat uneasily in the stadium, waiting for his name to be called for a degree in Computer Sciences. Mari, Josue, George and Abigail drove down from Winters for the ceremony, and best of all – they brought Rosalinda with them.

June can be very hot in San Jose. But the heat did not seem to bother the crowd at the graduation ceremony. Spartan Stadium was filled to capacity. The air was electric with excitement and happy thoughts. And no one took more pride in the event than his parents. When they heard his name called, they cheered so enthusiastically that the other people in the stadium began to chuckle.

Mari and Josue had all the feelings of parents who had loved and watched over a little boy who grew up – perhaps all too soon – to become a man. Josue believed he could now hold his head up in any company. With much love and a firm hand, they had kept Rick out of the gangs that plagued the valley, avoided any experimentation with drugs, and supported his efforts to complete San Jose State University. In Josue's eyes, his son was a huge success!

And there was Rosalinda. Pretty as a picture. Fragrant with her delightful lilac perfume. After the ceremony, she squeezed Rick's hand while Josue and George took turns taking pictures. She felt wonderfully close to Rick. After the incident his Junior year, he had made it very clear. She was the only woman in his life. Two people in love. His graduation was a moment of triumph for them both.

***

It was a perfect evening for a picnic. Although a bit cooler than usual, the air carried the scent of newly mowed hay. Putah Creek gurgled and bubbled noisily past the picnic area. Rick had decided to ask Rosalinda to marry him. He had practiced his proposal several times. He wanted it to be perfect. Next Tuesday he planned to go with George to a jewelry store in Davis to pick out a ring. He would ask her to marry him next Saturday night. Rick had it all planned. Every step. A romantic dinner. Hands across the table. Then put the ring on her finger and make his carefully practiced speech.

It was a delightful picnic. Hamburgers and beans. Piles of potato chips and almonds. Several rounds of wine. Getting a little drunk. All followed by a piece of Mari's very sweet and sinful double chocolate cake. Rick could not be happier.

After the food and dishes had been put away, Rick and Rosalinda walked hand in hand along the creek to a grassy knoll. There they stood quietly in the moonlight, listening to the sounds of crickets and a lonely owl.

Rosalinda put her arms around his neck and drew him closer. She felt the heat of his pulsing, vibrant body against her. This was the man she loved. The only man she ever wanted. As he bent over to kiss her, she stopped him with a finger to his lips.

Rosalinda looked dreamily into his eyes and said "Let's get married."

Chapter 2   Independence

July. Although the weather was hot, a cool breeze carried the fresh scent of the bay into the office through an open window. Clyde Tattaersol was slouched in his office chair, absently fingering a letter opener. Clyde had started his Santa Clara Internet Service business 15 years ago. Although it had grown, he was unsatisfied with its progress. He needed to change the way he approached his business. Reassign personnel to new duties.

He hated confrontation. It gave him bilious indigestion. And he felt very uneasy about his meeting with Rick. Clyde was unsure how the young man would respond to bad news. He would most certainly be confused. Probably angry. Clyde gave a heavy sigh. It had to be done.

For Rick, it was supposed to be his first day of employment after graduation. For the last three years, he had worked as a part-time programmer and the income had been a welcome addition to his meager finances. He was looking forward to working on a full time basis. He wanted to build up his cash reserves. Then he and Rosalinda could get married and find a decent place to live. Rick had a song in his heart as he entered the building.

"Rick," Clyde called out gruffly when he saw Rick. "I need to talk to you."

Rick put down his backpack and entered Clyde's cluttered little office.

"Have a seat," Clyde gestured - almost reluctantly - to a solitary chair. He felt a sense of apprehension. "Rick," he said slowly, "I have some bad news and some good news."

Rick was taken back, almost uneasy. Clyde looked at him intently.

"I've watched you work for almost three years. You're a good programmer. But you are not a great programmer… and around here… I need great programmers… That means I can't use you to code software."

Rick looked a bit stunned as the news sank in. He was fresh out of college and suddenly unemployed. Where on earth was he going to find another job?

"But," Clyde continued, "that's the bad news. The good news is that I have also watched you with our customers. You have a very outgoing personality."

Clyde paused for a moment to let that idea sink in. Although puzzled, Rick seemed to understand.

"Are you sure you want to be a programmer?" Clyde continued. "If you enjoy dealing with customers, and you certainly have good… no let me say excellent… systems skills, then I can use you to help me build this business."

Clyde took a very deep breath and waited for a response. As Clyde had predicted, Rick was terribly confused. And perhaps a little angry. But he didn't reject the idea.

"You think I can sell our services?" he asked.

Clyde felt a sense of relief. "*Keep it positive,*" he thought.

"I have every faith you can be successful. I have people asking for help. Small businesses that need internet access, protection from hackers, new business systems, new operating systems, new applications, and lots of handholding."

Rick looked uncertain. He had seen them come through the office. Small business owners who needed help. And he had been able to help them. But doing sales and systems would mean changing all his plans. He would have to reorient his thinking. He felt apprehensive.

"Could I have a day or two to think it over?"

"Sure. And if you have any questions, just ask."

Then Clyde had an idea. He would sweeten the deal.

"If you decide to take this job, I'll give you a cut of every dollar you bring into the business."

Rick was confused. This was all new to him. He exchanged a few more words with Clyde and left the building. As he walked down the street, the cool bay breeze freshened his senses. In a few short moments, in a brief conversation, his life had been changed.

***

Rick walked for 3 hours. By noon, he had stumbled his way to a shopping center. Still confused by his conversation with Clyde, Rick wandered into a restaurant and made his way to a long mahogany bar. He ordered a beer and then stared at the face in the mirror behind a line of liquor bottles. "*Rick,*" he thought, "*You are not going to make a living as a programmer. Now what?*"

Resigned to his fate, Rick took a sip of his beer. He would take Clyde's offer. Jobs were tough to find. Any job was better than no job. And besides, who knows? Maybe he would be successful.

It was a good decision.

A vigorous voice interrupted his thoughts.

"By golly. Look who's here!"

Rick turned and found himself face to face with a smiling George Kincade Taylor, the very tall Free Safety who had tackled him at the Stanford game.

Rick felt a twinge of pain in his shoulder. He still got a backache from time to time, and he was sure it was a "trophy" from that game.

"Somehow you look different without your shoulder pads."

George chuckled. "I guess I do." Then he turned to a man standing beside him.

"This is Robert Wells. He just came up for the day from Orange County."

Rick shook hands with both men. Wells gestured to a nearby table.

"Por qué usted no nos ensambla?" he asked.

"Gracias," responded Rick. Distressed by his conversation with Clyde, he was thankful to have something different to think about. He looked at Wells.

"Are you fluent in Spanish?"

"My parents were bi-lingual and they insisted I do the same. Spanish seemed to be appropriate for a boy who lived in Southern California."

"I can't argue with that," Rick said as he turned to Taylor.

"Are you bi-lingual?"

"I'm afraid not. I took a shot at French but I can't claim to be fluent."

Taylor called over the waiter and ordered a round of beers. Then he turned again to Rick.

"Bob is working as a corporate attorney. His family and mine have been close for many years. He went to the University of Arizona. But," Taylor smiled, " we forgive him for that."

"And what are your plans?" Rick asked.

"We're starting an electronics company back in New Mexico where my family lives. I'm currently looking for electronic engineers." Taylor looked sharply at Rick. "You don't happen to have an engineering degree, do you?"

Rick blushed a little. "No. I'm a computer services kind of guy."

Taylor nodded. He felt at ease with Rick. They talked for several minutes about Stanford Football, and Taylor's plan to start his own company. Then Taylor stood up. "I think my wife has gone missing. He motioned to Wells. Why don't you two get to know each other while I go find her."

Just then a tall, very attractive, blond woman appeared in the bar doorway. She had a commanding appearance, and she was obviously very pregnant. Taylor motioned her to the table.

"This is my wife, Helen and ...." he grinned proudly, "our daughter to be."

"George," Helen looked at her husband, "you'll embarrass me yet."

Wells and Rick got up to re-arrange the chairs so Helen would have a place to sit down.

"Have you selected a name?" Rick asked politely.

"Amanda," Helen responded. We named her for my grandmother who was an early leader in women's liberation."

Taylor looked at Rick. "Are you into politics?"

"No. I've been too busy trying to make it through San Jose State."

Wells looked a bit surprised. "No demonstrations about high taxes, inflation, unemployment, fuel shortages, civil rights, and so on?"

Rick blushed again. "No. I didn't dare ignore my homework. And when I wasn't hitting the books, I was working to make sure I could eat."

Wells tended to be impetuous. He usually spoke with a certain passion. "We have become a polarized nation. Left and right. Christian versus liberal. You need to figure out where you stand on the issues of the day."

Rick suddenly felt very awkward. "Now that I'm starting my own family, I guess those things will become more important to me."

Taylor was more conciliatory. "You've done what you needed to do. That shows the ability to focus and a sense of independence. I'm sure you will do what's necessary to take care of those around you."

With that, Helen motioned to her husband. They had another appointment. The four of them stood up, shook hands all around, and were about to part when Helen leaned over to Rick and took his arm.

"If you make it to Albuquerque, please do stop and see us."

***

August. The old Priest walked slowly around the corner of his ornate desk, fingering his pendant and wondering what to tell these two young people. *"They shall ask for my blessing, which – of course – I shall give, but what advice can I give them that will make any difference?"* The Priest sat down into his leather office chair with a heavy thump, as though he would never get up again. He studied them intently – Rick and Rosalinda. *"Nice kids,"* he thought. Rosalinda had been steadfast in her attendance and respect for the Church. Rick, on the other hand, had been less dedicated to Catholic ritual. But, he decided, it didn't matter. Most of the young people he saw in his office were there because they were in some kind of trouble. Pregnancy, drugs, divorce, jail, family troubles… Asking for his blessing to get married was an act of respect. This was a good day for any priest.

The Priest's eyes drifted toward the ceiling, and then to the cross on the office wall. *"Rick is a good boy. Nice personality. He will make a good husband. Like his father. Solid, dependable, … a good provider."* He broke from his contemplation and gazed intently into Rosalinda's eyes. She looked away. A little embarrassed. Her cheeks rosy with a nervous blush.

"Rosalinda, why do you want to marry this man?"

At first, Rosalinda didn't know how to express her love for Rick. She had expected the question. It was all part of the pre-wedding ritual. But the Priest's question was blunt and direct.

"Father Michael. I have loved this man for more than 5 years. There is no one else…"

The Priest waved her to silence.

"Yes. Yes. I know you are in love. Every bridal candidate that comes in here is in love. But why Rick? Why not another young man?"

"Because Rick is not like any other man," Rosalinda said with impulsive passion. "He is kind, considerate, and fun to be with."

The Priest looked at Rick. "Are you sure this is the one?"

Rick was very calm, thoughtful, and deliberate with his answer.

"We select those we choose to love because they will be good friends, constant companions, and honest partners as we journey through life."

Rick flashed a friendly smile. "And of course, I think Rosalinda is very special."

The Priest was startled by the response. "*Good Lord,*" he thought, "*that's supposed to be my line. I'm the one who usually gives a speech about friendship, love and truth.*" He looked at Rick intently for a moment, as though trying to think of something important to say. But words escaped him. Rick was an unusual young man. He seemed to have a timeless wisdom. Briefly troubled by that thought, the Priest's gaze returned to Rosalinda. "*She will be a good wife,*" he decided. "*She will make him very happy and she will keep having babies until she has a boy.*" The Priest settled back in his chair. "*Yes. A boy,*" he concluded. "*A boy she can raise to be just like his father.*"

The Priest gave the couple a warm and reassuring smile. "You have my permission to get married .... and .... you have my blessing."

With those words the young couple quickly got up, thanked the Priest profusely for his blessing, and then - hand in hand - turned and rushed from the room as though escaping from an ordeal.

As they closed the door behind them, the Priest chuckled to himself. "*Perhaps they are afraid I will change my mind.*"

***

Their wedding was a rousing celebration of life. Rosalinda was radiant in her snow white dress. At 22 years of age, Rick was every inch the proud groom. It was a lively event with George and Abigail, Mari and Josue, Rosalinda's mother, twenty or so friends, and a bunch of very energetic children. With his imposing build and long ponytail, Phillip looked more like a bodyguard than a Best Man. And Lydia, bless her heart, wanted so much to look perfect. But alas, although she had been on a crash diet, her blue Maid of Honor gown was just a bit too small.

A captivating ceremony. Two people obviously very much in love. Words of commitment. A tender kiss. And then Father Michael pronounced them man and wife.

If it was a modest reception by expense, it was a boisterous party by fact. Rosalinda – always playful – had covered her bosom with a modesty panel during the ceremony. But after the festivities got underway, she removed it. Rick immediately noticed the revealing cleavage. For Rosalinda, that was a perfect response. She looked up tenderly at Rick.

"A preview of coming attractions," she whispered.

Rick looked a bit flustered. He wanted this woman. Waiting for days. The growing sense of passionate excitement ... Now in a few hours ...

They danced, were the subject of multiple toasts (not always in good taste), cut Mari's three tier wedding cake, kissed and shook hands with so many people it all became a blur of activity, and then - excused themselves for the long drive to Lake Tahoe.

They were soon off in an old car, tin cans tied to the bumper, marbles in the hub caps, and the words "JUST MARRIED" splashed in big white letters on the rear window.

Josue was elated. Tears of joy welled into Mari's eyes. They happily waved goodbye until the car was out of sight. Then Josue turned to Mari, gently enveloped her in his arms, and gave her a long, tender, and very loving kiss.

It was a perfect day.

***

The trip to the little cabin seemed to take hours. They pulled off the highway at Hutchison Drive and found a place where they could park long enough for Rick to remove the marbles from the hubcaps and tin cans from the bumper. They paused again at the rest stop east of Colfax so Rosalinda could freshen up. While she was occupied, Rick tried to wash off the JUST MARRIED lettering on the rear window. But he was only partially successful. People at the rest stop smiled knowingly at the young couple. A few wished them good luck.

They stopped again at the rest stop on Donner Pass summit. This time it was Rick who had to use the facilities. Rosalinda was a bit embarrassed by the looks of curiosity she got from other travelers. Again, some were bold enough to wish them luck. And then they were off. Down the steep grade to Truckee.

At last they arrived at the little cabin Rick had rented. As he stepped out of the car, Rick felt a welcome cool breeze that swept in from Lake Tahoe. They quickly unloaded the car, stored their groceries in the kitchen, and - somewhat self-consciously - opened their suitcases in the bedroom.

Rick opened a bottle of sparkling wine. Sitting on a very old couch in the living room, they drank a final toast to their happiness, talked almost absently about the day's events, held hands, looked into each other's eyes – and - it was time.

Rick was trembling with nervous excitement as he undressed. The bedroom was dark except for the light of a full moon that swept in through the window to give the room a soft radiance. Not sure what to do, he went into the little bathroom to wash his hands. He fumbled with the soap, and almost dropped the towel. He was aware that time seemed to be moving very slowly. Rick returned to the bedroom. He lay down on the bed with his back on the pillows, and waited for Rosalinda to appear.

Although it seemed he waited an hour, it was only a few minutes. Rosalinda had undressed in the living room. She wanted this moment to be perfect. Slowly, silently, she appeared in the bedroom doorway, her nightgown slung carelessly around her midriff. Soft moonlight bathed her face and breasts. Rosalinda was – at that moment – the most beautiful and erotic woman in the world.

***

Clyde Tattaersol was very pleased. His gamble with Rick had paid off. With his natural charisma and positive attitude, the young man easily made friends with prospective customers. His sincere demeanor and low key approach to selling created a sense of trust. Rick also turned out to have an instinctive ability to understand the complex systems problems that customers were trying to solve. He designed the systems. The programmers developed the software and installed the applications on the ISP's servers. Thanks to Rick, Clyde's Santa Clara Internet Service company had been able to establish a growing base of stable customers.

Rick had developed a warm and easy friendship with John, the company's senior programmer. The two could not be more different. Rick was tall and lean, almost athletic in appearance. John was about 20 years older, a round elf of a man with a shock of white hair and a rather ruddy complexion. With his happy demeanor and black rimmed glasses, John could have passed for Santa Claus.

The two men shared a great respect for each other. Rick understood how to turn business applications into working systems. John was incredibly good with operating systems and could manipulate Internet software with ease. Together, they were able to create a friendly working environment for themselves and the other programmers. Within two years, the Santa Clara Internet Service needed to add another programmer.

Rick recommended his friend, Phillip Mitchell.

***

Philip Mitchell was taking a blissful afternoon nap when the annoying ring tone of the telephone finally broke through his drowsy slumber. He arched his back, stretched his arms, and had a mighty yawn as he fumbled for the table. The sleeping form beside him moaned something unintelligible and pulled a pillow over her head. Phillip pushed the talk button and softly said, "Hello?"

Then he sat bolt upright, eyes wide awake. A smile crossed his face. It was Rick.

"Hey, how're doing?"

An animated voice responded over the telephone. Phillip happily listened to his friend and then the look on his face turned from a grin to a look of surprise.

"You want me to interview for a job with your company?" he asked. "Doing what?"

More animated conversation from the telephone. The woman next to him began to stir. She threw off her blanket, sat up, and put her arm around Phillip.

"Who is it?"

"Shush. It's Rick."

Lydia brushed a few strands of blond hair away from her eyes.

"Did he get you a job?" she happily gushed.

Phillip tried to ignore her. He was trying to pin down the details of a proposed interview with Clyde Tattaersol in Santa Clara. But Lydia – ever animated and talkative - would not be quiet.

"What's he saying?" she demanded.

Phillip pushed her gently away. It was a great moment. A joyous sense of relief coursed through his body.

"Sure. I'll be there. And thank you, Rick. You're a real friend."

And with that, he carefully – slowly - hung up the telephone.

"What's happening?" Lydia demanded.

"I'm going down to Santa Clara for a job interview with the ISP Rick has been with since graduation. He's in sales. Does systems work. They need a programmer analyst to help with user applications."

Phillip got out of bed and walked to the dresser. He fumbled for a comb, looked at the happy face in the mirror, and absently began to unsnarl the strands of his ponytail.

"Can I go with you?" Lydia asked.

"Sure."

Philip turned to look at the girl on the bed. He loved her too much to leave her out of his moment of triumph. She had stuck with him even though he was unable to get a job in Davis. Or Sacramento, for that matter. Too many programmers. Not enough work. It was a challenge to pay the rent. Yet she remained loyal to him as he struggled through a succession of contract programming jobs.

"Will your boss let you take a day off from your bookkeeping job?"

Lydia had a stable clerical job with a local insurance office. It didn't pay all that much, but having a regular paycheck had saved their butt several times.

"I have time coming," she said. "It will be great to see Rosalinda again."

And so they prepared for the big day. A chance for a steady job with a good company and an old friend. Phillip was euphoric. Lydia was relieved. Their future suddenly looked very promising.

***

Although he had been glad to bring Phillip down for an interview, Rick was actually preoccupied with an important event in his own life. Rosalinda was very pregnant. The baby was due any day. And of course, it all happened without any plan.

Rick came home from work about 6:30PM. Tired from the intense activity of the day, all he wanted to do was sit down and relax. Get his nerves calmed down. Rosalinda had prepared dinner. But she did not serve herself. Instead, she sat quietly upright on a chair in the kitchen, as though waiting for something to happen. Rick had just begun to eat when she called to him.

"Oh God."
"What's wrong?"
"My water just broke."

Rick was instantly nervous and joyous at the same time. He was about to become a father. He left his dinner on the table, walked over to Rosalinda, and tenderly took his wife's hand.

"I'll call the doctor.... and then we can get you to the hospital."

Rosalinda could only nod in agreement. She was beginning to feel very strange. Cramps began to tighten in her stomach. She felt nauseous.

Rick returned from the telephone and helped Rosalinda out the door to his car.

"I could only get the answering service," he said. "But they will find the doctor. She should be there soon after we get to the hospital."

It was only a short ride. But Rick was suddenly aware of every bump and every curve in the road. *"Oh God,"* he thought, *"what if she starts to deliver before we get there?"*

But of course, he need not have worried. They got to the hospital, checked in, and settled Rosalinda in a pre-delivery ward. Then the nurse took him to a room where he could wait for the baby to make its appearance. One hour. Two hours. Rick began to perspire. He was hungry and nervous. Maybe they should have waited. Rick was only 24. He was worried about Rosalinda. It seemed to take forever. This birthing thing. Is she OK?

After what seemed to be an incredibly long time, the doctor appeared in the waiting room door. She smiled at Rick.

"It's a girl."

***

They named their baby Adonica. Rosalinda was a calm and loving mother. Rick a proud and gentle father. It was a thrill for them both. Watching Adonica roll over by herself for the first time, the first tooth, learning to crawl, pulling herself up to stand with her hand on the coffee table, a first tentative step, and then her first birthday. By 18 months, the happy baby babble had become words, and words soon became short sentences. Adonica loved to talk.

***

It was a glorious sunny day. The air was cool, fresh and sweet. Spring was surely just around the corner. The warmth of the April sun lured Rosalinda out for an afternoon walk with Adonica. She strolled away from the apartment complex where they lived toward a local shopping center.

Adonica, wrapped in warm blankets and snuggly tucked into her stroller, was pointing to everything she saw.

"See, mommy?" Adonica would exclaim. Everything was so interesting to the little girl.

Rosalinda walked by the shops, stopping every so often to look at the merchandise in the display window. Then she turned to walk across the parking lot to the street. As she approached the sidewalk, a car pulled up behind her. At first, Rosalinda didn't notice the slowly moving vehicle. But Adonica was curious.

"See, mommy. Car."

Rosalinda turned to see what Adonica was talking about. She immediately saw the three men leering at her from the car as it pulled along side her. Rosalinda began to walk as fast as she could. Fear coursed through her body. The men rolled down the car windows and began to shout obscenities at her. They laughed at her fear. Tears filled Rosalinda's eyes. She looked straight ahead. Although the apartment complex was not very far from the shopping center, it now seemed to be miles away. Rosalinda crossed the street and with quick short steps headed for the door of the first floor apartment she shared with Rick. The car stopped. All three men got out and started up the sidewalk toward Rosalinda and Adonica. Rosalinda screamed.

"Rick!"

Inside the apartment Rick and Phillip were in the living room, watching a baseball game. Lydia was in the kitchen fixing a snack. Startled by Rosalinda's scream, Rick jumped up from the couch and ran to the door. When he opened it, he saw the three men walking toward his wife.

"Can I help you?"

Rick looked intently at the three men, and began to walk down the steps. They hesitated, and then looked up at the figure behind Rick. It was Phillip. A very tall and muscular Phillip with rather long hair tied into a pony tail. With his imposing build, Phillip looked like he could easily handle himself in a fight.

"Can I help you?" Rick calmly repeated. He looked straight into the eyes of the man nearest to him. The man stopped, uncertain.

"Uh. I think we have the wrong address," he scowled.

Phillip started to walk down the steps behind Rick. He too was calm and very firm in his demeanor. Rosalinda, sobbing with a mixture of relief and fright, grabbed Adonica from the stroller and fled by Rick and Phillip. Lydia was just coming out of the apartment door when Rosalinda rushed past her into the safety of the apartment. Lydia immediately knew what was happening. She glowered at the three men, and tuned to go into the apartment.

"I'll dial 911," she said in a very loud voice.

All three men turned around and walked back to their car. They got in, slamming the doors shut with great energy. As he was shifting into gear, the driver shouted another obscenity at Rick and Phillip, and then pushed down on the accelerator just as hard as he could. The car's rear tires left a log ribbon of black on the pavement as the car sped away.

Rick turned to Phillip.

"Thanks."

"Anytime."

Satisfied the danger was over, the two friends walked slowly into the apartment.

After the door was closed, there was much animated talk about what had happened. Tough economic times had encouraged lawless behavior. There was talk about the need for stricter law enforcement. But no one seemed to know what was going to happen next.

Rosalinda was able to dry her tears. Adonica, upset by all the commotion, wanted to be cuddled. Rick picked her up and held her in his arms. Then he leaned over and tenderly kissed his still shaking wife. Rosalinda slipped into his arms, pulled Adonica close, and held onto her man with all her strength.

Lydia suddenly felt weak, breathless, and afraid. She wanted a reassuring hug. Phillip tenderly drew her close and kissed her cheek.

That night, Rick and Rosalinda made hot passionate exhilarating love with an energy neither of them had ever experienced.

And Serafina was born exactly 9 months later.

***

Clyde Tattaersol was in his office, mumbling to himself. He knew he was no longer able to keep up with the million details of his ISP business. Clyde was frustrated by the constant barrage of senseless regulations from multiple government bureaucracies and an ever growing load of taxes. California was rated as one of the worst places to run a business in America, and the significance of that truth weighed heavily on him. It was time to make a decision. He picked up his telephone and punched the intercom button.

"Does anyone know where Rick is?"

No answer.

Impatient with the lack of response, Clyde eased his aching bones out of his chair and went into the programmer's office. Phillip looked up from his display.

"Rick went out to see a customer. He said he would be back around noon."

Disgruntled, but satisfied with the answer, Clyde turned to go back into his office. About an hour later, the front door opened and Rick walked into the building. Clyde came out of his office and eyed Rick solemnly.

"Rick, do you have a minute?"

Rick flashed a friendly smile and started for Clyde's office. Once inside, Clyde closed the door, walked slowly around the desk to his chair and sat down with a grunt. Rick began to fear something was wrong.

"Rick. You have done a great job," Clyde began, "and I am too old to keep up with all this software and business stuff."

Rick squirmed slightly in his chair, but said nothing.

"I have decided to create the position of General Manager," Clyde declared, "and you're it."

Rick was taken completely by surprise. Although he had gradually been taking over more and more of the day to day business decisions, he had been careful not to exceed his authority.

"What does a General Manager do around here?" he grinned.

"I want you to run this place," was the simple answer.

What followed was an intense 2 hour discussion of objectives, resources, people, facilities, and – finally – money. Rick was thrilled. Clyde was very generous.

*"It's a big responsibility for a 27 year old ki*d," he mused.

***

Phillip and Lydia threw a party in their apartment to celebrate the promotion. It was a typical California wine and cheese affair with side orders of dainty little goodies. Everyone came. John, James and Sarah from the programming staff, a new systems analyst by the name of Antonio, the bookkeeper, and Clyde. Everyone was in a festive mood. Rick and Rosalinda brought Adonica, now 3, and baby Serafina with them to the party. Adonica squealed with delight at all the attention she was getting from the adults. Serafina gurgled and smiled as she was passed from one person to another.

The party lasted for more than three hours. Then, one by one, the guests said goodbye. After they left, Lydia, Phillip, Rosalinda, Rick and the children remained in the living room. Adonica fell asleep in her mother's arms. Lydia found a blanket and a place for Serafina to nap. Phillip beckoned Rick into the kitchen for a private conversation.

"Will you have enough money to move out of here?"

Rick was taken back by the direct question. But after giving it some thought, he responded.

"This part of San Jose is too dangerous for a young family. Rosalinda wants to move down to the Almaden neighborhood. We will start looking at houses next week."

"What about the commute?" Phillip said. "Gasoline is expensive and not always available."

Rick had to admit, it was probably not the best time to be commuting from south San Jose to Santa Clara, but he felt he had no choice. This neighborhood was no place to raise a family.

"It's a tough decision. With California's economy in a chronic recession, there is much too much unemployment, and I have to wonder about the future of our business. On the other hand, gang thugs seem to roam the streets at will, and permissive behavior seems to have been institutionalized. Moving is the best defense we have against the tensions that are building all over California."

"Can you work from home at all?"

"I think I can do a lot of my account maintenance work by telephone and e-mail."

Phillip looked at Rick gravely.

"It's going to be tough. The Internet is routinely sabotaged by God knows who."

"Yes," Rick responded, "but that may give us an opportunity to establish private lines to our largest customers."

Uncomfortable with the conversation, Rick changed the subject.

"How come you and Lydia are not married by now? Aren't you happy with her?"

Phillip looked rather sheepish as he answered.

"I've asked her. But so far, she likes her freedom."

Rick nodded. "I believe commitment is the foundation of any worthwhile relationship. Maybe Rosalinda can help Lydia make up her mind."

And with that, the two friends walked out of the kitchen and into the thoroughly disorganized living room.

***

After the party Rick and Rosalinda went back to their apartment and had a long heart to heart conversation. They talked about the promotion, finding a house, moving, commuting, schools for Adonica and Serafina, and – then Rosalinda dropped the bombshell.

"I want to have another baby. I want a boy. I want a boy to grow up to be just like you."

Rick was reluctant to have more children. "I don't know. Things are so unsettled. We need to get our feet on the ground in a new home first. And I'm not sure what will happen to the business."

Rosalinda put her finger on his lips to silence him. She kissed his cheek lightly.

"A boy," she said with a sly sweet smile.

***

"I quit."

A startled Rick looked up from the papers on his desk. The ISP's bookkeeper stood resolutely before him, her hair in disarray.

"Why?"

"It's just too much for me. I can't handle the work anymore."

Rick decided to probe a little more into her reasoning.

"Have we treated you OK?"

"I suppose. But I want to do something else with my life."

"Have you thought through an alternative occupation?"

"My boyfriend says we can do better in Oregon, and that's where we are going."

Now the truth was out. She planned to flee to Oregon for what she hoped would be a better life. Rick could sense her mind was made up.

"We wish you well. Can we help you with anything?"

"No... I've cleaned out my desk... Only personal stuff... You can check if you like."

Rick got out of his chair and escorted the bookkeeper to her desk. She had indeed cleaned it out in anticipation of her departure. Rick arranged for her severance pay, and thanked her for helping them out. In a moment, she was gone.

"So we've lost our bookkeeper." It was Phillip.

"Yes," Rick responded, "and now I have to hire a new one."

"How about Lydia?" Phillip asked.

"I thought she wants to be an accountant."

"Unemployed people have to be flexible."

Rick looked gravely at his friend. Lydia, he decided, would be a good choice.

***

When Rick was 32, Rosalinda finally got her wish. Ramon was born in June. A big healthy baby with very bright eyes and a shock of brown hair. By then they had found a house in Almaden, moved, and had purchased the furniture, drapes, garden equipment, and other items that go with owning a home. The girls were delighted to have a little brother and Rick had to admit – he had a feeling of pride every time he came home and picked up his son. Ramon soon became a part of his daily routine. Most work days, Rick was able to be home by super time. As soon as he entered the door, Rosalinda would hand him a bottle and the baby. Rick would sit back in a chair, Ramon propped on his lap, and feed him the warm milk. The girls would gather around the chair and jabber about what they had done that day. Or maybe nothing at all. Whatever. For Rick and Rosalinda, it was a very happy time.

***

It was a chilly October morning. Fog covered the bay and most of San Jose. Rick was able to drive into work after the worst of the commute was over. As he entered the ISP, he immediately sensed something was wrong. John approached him first.

"We've been hit with malware. Phillip and James are working the problem."

Rick felt a sensation of dread. Malware is a blanket term used to describe software that is designed to infiltrate a PC or server without the owner's knowledge or consent. Disastrous forms include viruses, worms, Trojan horses, root kits, spy ware, dishonest ad ware, and malicious hacker attacks. For an ISP, an infiltration of malware can spell disaster. Files and applications are stolen, corrupted or destroyed. Operating systems and associated software are compromised. If unchecked, a successful attack would put his ISP out of business. Feeble international attempts to prevent the spread of malware had thus far proven to be useless. Rick immediately went into the programming office.

"Have we lost any customer files?"

Phillip spoke first.

"Not yet. We've been able to contain the infection on the Internet relay server. We are about to run our virus program to identify what is going on."

"What about our applications?"

James looked up from his screen.

"We haven't found anything yet. Once we isolate this guy, we can reboot our system."

Rick was relieved. It was bad, but not a disaster.

Phillip came over with a sheet of paper in his hand.

"John has contacted several of the other independent ISPs with a proposal to trap this malware when we identify its signature. We will work with the software protection companies until this gets resolved."

"What should I tell our customers?" Rick asked.

John shrugged and looked back at his computer screen.

"Sit tight."

Rick knew that was going to be a lousy answer for his customers. But he would have to deal with them later. Right now he had to make sure his software talent was focused on solving the problem that threatened the life blood of his company's business. He sat down at a terminal. James showed him how to go through the tedious business of sorting through the scripts. Rick knew it would be a long morning.

"*But somehow,*" he thought, "*we will get through this.*"

***

Houston, Texas means oil. And everything made from oil. The Houston Ship Channel is one of the busiest waterways in the world. It connects the interior of the continental United States with the Gulf of Mexico. It is lined with loading docks, grain bins, petrochemical refineries, and oil product storage tanks. Along this fifty mile waterway there are more petrochemicals, explosive materials, and toxic gases than anywhere else in the country.

One particularly beautiful fall day a series of terrifying explosions ripped open two refineries and sank a ship in the channel. Fire quickly spread to nearby storage tanks, leading to a series of additional explosions that could be felt all the way to Houston. The air was filled with toxic fumes and thick black smoke. It would take three days to bring the fires under control.

A key source of gasoline, diesel, propane, and jet fuels had been disrupted.

***

Rick was a happy man. Despite the very high price of gasoline and a growing rate of inflation, he was able to pay his bills. His girls were doing well in school. Under his leadership, the business was growing and profitable.

For no particular reason Phillip and Lydia threw a birthday party for him. Rick guessed it was just because they liked to party, and a birthday seemed like as good an excuse as any other. So on a cold December day, he and Rosalinda took the kids and made the journey up to San Jose. As they parked at the apartment complex, they saw a stack of moving boxes and two mattresses in the parking lot. Phillip and Lydia greeted them at the door. Rick turned and pointed to the boxes.

"Is someone moving in, or out?" he asked.

Phillip suddenly looked very somber.

"They're being evicted. Couldn't pay the rent and they have no place to go."

Phillip waved them inside, as though ashamed of the tragedy taking shape in the parking lot.

"They are an older couple. But with the collapse of Social Security they have no income."

"Didn't Congress promise a National Income Security program to help people like this?" Rick asked.

Phillip shrugged and looked down at the floor.

"Debt has crippled the economy. There's no money to fund it."

"Lots of promises but no action," Lydia added boldly.

"Haven't you been watching the news?" Phillip asked. "The economy is in the tank. The number of people living in poverty is soaring. The government seems to be paralyzed by all the debt we have accumulated. And to make matters worse…"

Phillip stopped talking long enough to help Rick and Rosalinda with their coats.

"There is a shortage of heating oil and propane."

Rick looked perplexed.

"Why?"

"A bunch of reasons. But the loss of the refining capacity in Houston was the final straw that broke the proverbial camel's back."

Although Lydia was usually upbeat and positive, she added a few words of her own in a very somber voice.

"Rick. Nationwide. Hunger, housing, poverty, and people freezing to death because they can't afford to heat their homes."

Rick looked at Rosalinda. Suddenly he felt very guilty. He had been so focused on the business and his family, he had ignored everything else. Yet these trends would soon affect them all.

"Nothing good can come from this. What do you have for heat?"

"We're lucky," Phillip said, "we have natural gas heat and so far, there is enough to go around."

"But who knows how long that will last," Lydia added.

Rosalinda looked very depressed. She suddenly felt very tired. Rosalinda had known things were not going well, but she too had ignored them. Seeing that stack of personal belongings in the parking lot had been a rude shock. She turned to Rick.

"Isn't there something we can do?"

"No," he said. "If the government is useless, then people must find a way to help themselves."

But Rick was sorry for what he had said almost before all the words were out of his mouth.

"I'm sorry. I have to think this through."

With that the four went into the living room to join the children who by now had found a video game to play. Rick looked at Rosalinda. He knew what she was thinking. How would they be able to protect their children?

The party was very quiet. Subdued. Not much fun for a 34th birthday.

As they were leaving to go home, Rick looked once again at the parking lot. To his surprise there was a large truck parked next to the now much smaller pile of personal belongings. Two men were helping an older man load the last boxes into the truck.

"Who is that?" he asked Phillip.

"I don't know. There are no markings on the truck. But someone is helping them out."

Lydia was a bit more nosey. She passed them on the steps and went over to an older woman who was standing beside an ancient car. The two talked quietly, almost in whispers, for a few moments. Then Lydia shook the woman's hands with both her own and returned to the two men.

"It's some kind of church group. They have a place for them somewhere in south San Jose."

Rosalinda joined them on the apartment steps.

"Thank God, someone cares and can do something."

Rick looked at his wife.

"Yes, for now. But where are these men from?"

Lydia shrugged.

"I think it's called … the San Jose Neighborhood Community."

As they drove away from the apartment complex, Rick struggled with what he had just witnessed. Deep down, somewhere in his soul, he felt a deep compassion for these people who had been impoverished through no fault of their own. But he felt powerless to do anything about it.

***

By spring Rick had established a routine for keeping up with current events. He set aside a half hour each day before he went to bed to scan the Internet for news and commentary. Sometimes he would read for an hour or more. With the coming of summer, shortages of heating oil and propane became a minor problem. Jet fuel shortages, on the other hand, were another story. Shortages drove up prices. The combination of shortages and high prices pushed several air carriers over the brink of bankruptcy.

***

The soft cool spring air from the bay drifted into the ISP's open windows. Antonio and Sarah left their programming chores long enough to have a cup of coffee in the ISP's tiny utility room. Antonio was developing a crush on Sarah. But he was too shy to let her know how he felt.

"I'll just wait for now. The right moment will come," he thought.

Antonio imagined himself escorting the slender, willowy Sarah to the movies. Or maybe dancing. Then he banished the fantasy from his mind.

"She will never go for a chunky guy like me."

Sarah carefully poured a cup of coffee for herself, and then poured another one for Antonio. With a sweet smile she handed him the hot cup.

"Are you going to the rally?"

"Which one?"

"The one for the Progressive Party. Michael John O'Brien is going to speak. He's probably going to get the nomination to run for President."

Antonio squirmed.

"Uh. I don't pay much attention to that stuff. They're all the same. These politicians. Lots of promises and not much else."

"But Michael is so dynamic. Charming. A really good speaker."

"Where does he get his money?"

"His family owns a mutual fund company. Michael works there when he's not playing at being a Senator."

"Rich and handsome. That should get him elected."

Sarah looked at Antonio with obvious disapproval.

"And Mary Rose will be with him."

Antonio had heard of Mary Rose Chartres O'Brien. Aggressive. Intelligent. Demanding. Pushy. Schemer. Belonged to a prominent New York family. Money from a firm of Anti - Corporate Attorneys.

"I hear she's smarter than he is," Antonio said.

"Probably. And she's better connected. An insider… and she has certainly done a good job of cultivating the Washington press corps."

"I don't trust her."

But as soon as he said the words, Antonio knew he had made a big mistake.

"What a way to impress a woman," he thought. *"Pick a fight with her."*

***

Antonio resolved to find out more about this couple from back east. Mary Rose had a reputation for rewarding her friends and demolishing her enemies. She actively raised money for favored candidates in state and federal elections, and she made sure they felt obligated to her for the support. She could be gregarious. She also threw the occasional temper tantrum and could be quite nasty. It was rumored her marriage to Michael John was a convenience, a sort of business partnership to enhance her political ambitions. In contrast to his affable charm, she could be deadly. Detractors on the Internet gossiped Mary Rose had a socialist-fascist philosophy, believed in using police power to support State policy, and was into social engineering.

In any event, Mary Rose was never very far from her husband's activities. When they came to San Jose, she was on the podium with him.

When Michael spoke he promised that he would, if elected, make sure there was enough fuel to keep America warm. And he promised to restore the vigor of the airline industry. He then went on to outline a very exciting program that would, if he were elected, end poverty in our lifetime. The audience cheered. Then he announced he would, if elected to be the party's candidate for President, choose Mary Rose to be his running mate as Vice President. The audience cheered again.

Mary Rose Chartres tried to smile. But her expression resolved into a sneer. She had engineered her way into a position of power. Just what she wanted.

***

As Rick climbed the stairs to the bedroom landing, he could hear Ramon's laughter and playful words. Rosalinda was giving him a bath. Rick stopped in the bathroom doorway to watch. Ramon was playing with a toy boat in the water, making motor sounds and occasionally calling "toot, toot". Rick smiled at the scene. Finished with the bath, Rosalinda picked Ramon up and walked over to a chair. She sat down, spread a towel over her lap, and placed Ramon on the towel. Then she carefully dried his face, head, arms, legs and tummy. When she dried his toes, she playfully tugged at each one. Ramon laughed and squealed with delight. Then Rosalinda carefully wrapped the towel around Ramon and tenderly hugged him. Ramon loved to be cuddled. He would forever remember the warmth of his mother's gentle love.

Watching his wife with the children brought joy to Rick's heart. She could be playful. She could be firm. She was always full of love and compassion. Adonica looked to her mother for advice. Serafina was given an extra helping of affection. Ramon was never far from her side. It was clear to Rick that Rosalinda was having a strong positive influence on their behavior.

Rosalinda was also a loving wife, friend, companion and partner. Before bed each night, they would have a quiet talk about the day's events, the children, Rick's work, or whatever seemed to be important at the time. They were both very happy.

***

In August it was announced that the Department of Homeland Security would be replaced by the Department of Personal and Private Security. It was not simply a change of name. The new agency was given sweeping powers over all of the other intelligence and law enforcement agencies. There would be new rules of evidence, surveillance, and detention.

In November Michael O'Brien was elected as President. He took office the following January. As expected, a triumphant Mary Rose was installed as Vice President.

***

For Rosalinda and Rick, San Jose's Cinco de Mayo celebration offered a chance to experience the excitement and fun of a family outing. There would be a colorful and noisy parade, strolling musicians, dancers, acres of craft shops, and an endless number of food vendors. Although Cinco de Mayo was originally intended to celebrate Mexican freedom from the French, it had become a demonstration of solidarity among Mexican and Latino immigrants to the USA.

Sunday morning they took a light rail train into the city, and began to wander among the many booths that lined the sidewalks. By mid-morning they could hear the marching bands on Market Street. Rosalinda took Adonica and Serafina by the hand, Rick picked up Ramon, and they quickly walked to a spot where they could see the parade. It was all very exciting for the children. Lots of noise and music. Rick hoisted 35 month old Ramon onto his shoulders so he could have a better view of the parade. Each time a band passed, Adonica and Serafina would dance to the music, laughing with delight.

After the parade was over, they again began to wander among the many vendor stalls. There were treats for them all at the food booths. Rick purchased a tooled leather belt for himself and a pendant rose for

Rosalinda. They bought a silver necklace for Adonica, and a pendant cross for Serafina. Ramon was more interested in the food. He ate everything that his father gave to him, and asked for more.

By mid-afternoon they were all very tired. Rick guided them to a station where they boarded a light rail car for the ride to Almaden. It had been a good day. Fun. Rick looked at his children with pride.

"*Which one,*" he thought, "*is my favorite?*"

He immediately scolded himself for having such a thought.

"*I love all my children equally.*"

Still, he could not help but worry about Serafina. She always seemed to be more vulnerable then Adonica or Ramon. There she was, quietly holding onto her mother's hand. A pretty 8 year old girl. Stoically waiting for the light rail car to reach its destination.

His eyes shifted to Ramon. There he was, gazing intently out the window, taking in every mile of track with irrepressible wonder.

"*I wonder what he will want for his 4th birthday? ... Maybe a fire engine, or a train.... Perhaps a baseball glove... NO. I never liked baseball... I'll teach him to play football. ... Maybe he will become a big name wide receiver like his father.*"

Rick paused with his thoughts to look more closely at the stocky build of his son.

"*Hmmm. More likely a full back.*"

Rick turned to look at Adonica. She was carefully studying each passenger as though she wanted to discover what they were thinking. Adonica was doing very well in school. She routinely downloaded lessons from the Internet Learning for Kids website and devoured them with ease.

"*She's probably smarter than anyone else in the family. Maybe she will become a programmer.*"

Rick smiled at the thought. He shifted his weight on the uncomfortable plastic rail car seat. He could not resist the pride that swelled up within him.

"*Adonica will probably be a better programmer than her old man.*"

The rail car lurched a little as they rounded a bend in the track. Rosalinda grasped his arm and leaned her head on his shoulder. Rick looked at her briefly. Rosalinda had matured into a lovely woman. A tender look crossed his face.

"*My lady,*" he said to himself, "*more beautiful than ever.*"

He squeezed her arm with affection. She looked up at him, and gave him a little kiss on the cheek. She adjusted herself on the car seat.

"Is your back bothering you again?" Rick asked.

"Umm.. and I have too much gas in my tummy. It must be the enchiladas."

Rick carefully examined her face. Rosalinda seemed to be more tired than usual. Rick resolved to help her with the chores when they reached home.

***

In July of that year the O'Brien administration announced the formation of the National Security Service as a division of the Department of Personal and Private Security. It would have broad police powers to track down terrorists and dissidents. Party faithful and media pundits wrote enthusiastic articles of support for this positive step in national security. By fall, the NSS was hiring thousands of new agents. For a nation in chronic recession, the added employment opportunities were most welcome.

***

Adonica was a slender 11 year old girl when her father introduced her to football. He would playfully throw the ball to her and she soon got the hang of catching it. It was a glorious October day when they played their first game of touch football. Rick coaxed Rosalinda, Serafina, and Adonica into the backyard. He and Serafina would play against Rosalinda and Adonica. It was great fun. Adonica loved these games. Her father would usually tickle her when he caught her, tickle her until she giggled and laughed. Serafina would squeal with delight as she ran with the ball until her father lifted her off the ground and gave her a loving kiss on the neck. He was even more affectionate with Rosalinda. Sometimes Rick would interrupt the game just to give her mother a passionate hug. Adonica's little 3 year old brother would usually run around and around them, laughing and trying to steal the ball. It was all great fun. Adonica loved her father, adored her mother, was good friends with her sister, and playful with her brother.

As the winds of fall began to turn into the chill of winter, Rosalinda decided her back hurt too much to play any more. Although that stopped the games, Adonica and her father were still able to play catch once in awhile. With great determination, Serafina learned how to catch the ball and to Rick's amazement, soon demonstrated she had a better throwing arm than her sister.

***

The first week of November, Rosalinda asked Adonica to spend more time with Ramon. A very active little boy, he needed more attention than Rosalinda could give to him. Adonica was soon helping him to dress in the morning, washing his face and hands when he got dirty (which was often), collecting his toys to put them away, making sure he ate all his vegetables at dinner, and a hundred other chores. Adonica became a second mother to Ramon, and they developed a tight bond.

Rosalinda was only too glad to have the help. At her husband's insistence, she called for an appointment with her doctor. The busy clinic staff could not schedule an appointment until late November. When she went to the clinic almost four weeks later, the doctor ordered some tests. The Doctor finally received the test results in late December. She made arrangements for Rosalinda to see a specialist.

***

New Years Day. Rick was pleased. Despite the lousy economy, the Santa Clara Internet Service company continued to do reasonably well. Several of their smaller accounts had simply turned all of their computing needs over to his ISP. The added work was welcome.

The staff of the Santa Clara Internet Service company worked together as a team. It was, Rick thought, like a family business. Clyde Tattaersol was the patron saint, more like a godfather to them all. At 36, Rick had assumed the role of father. Phillip, James, John, Antonio, Sarah, and Lydia were family.

Rick was very pleased with his life. Rosalinda was in good spirits. He had three wonderful kids, a nice home, and a great job. Rick was looking forward to a good year.

***

Winter was unusually cold. Snow clogged the roads of the Sierra Nevada mountains until March. When it finally came, spring was especially welcome to the residents of Santa Clara County. They had struggled through five months of soggy chilly days and wet cold nights. Route 17 over the coastal range had been closed by snow and ice several times. Although natural gas had been plentiful and less expensive than the prior winter, families in the hills that surround the valley had to rely on propane for heat. Some could not afford the high cost. They struggled with the cold by burning wood.

By May, however, the gray haze from a few lingering wood stove fires had cleared from the air. Spring had arrived. Each day a playful breeze from the Bay would moderate the warmth of the sun.

Rick had just finished lunch when the telephone rang. It was Rosalinda. She was obviously sobbing.

"Please come home. Please come home... I need you."

Stunned by the emotion, Rick stammered a response.

"Wha ..what's wrong? Are the kids OK? Are you OK?"

"Just come. Just come home NOW!" Rosalinda shouted over the telephone. Then she began to sob uncontrollably.

Rick was alarmed by the tone of Rosalinda's words.

"I'll be home as soon as I can."

Rick hung up the telephone. He cursed under his breath. He had taken the light rail system to work. The trip home would take forever. Then he had an idea.

"Phillip. Did you drive today?"

Phillip's cheerful face appeared in the doorway.

"Sure did."

"Can I borrow your car, please. I have to go home right away. It's an emergency."

Phillip looked both puzzled and alarmed.

"Sure. I'll get you the keys."

Rick grabbed his coat, picked up the car keys from Phillip, and ran to the parking lot. In a few moments he was on Highway 101 headed south. Thankfully, traffic was light and in 20 minutes he arrived home. Rick bounded up the steps and went in. Rosalinda was sitting on the living room couch, her eyes red with tears. Rick sat down beside her and took her hands.

"What is the matter?"

Rosalinda, pale and thin, sobbed once or twice and then looked up at him. Rick sensed her fear. Her voice trembled with emotion.

"The doctor wants to see us .... together."

She paused for a long moment.

"I just know it's bad news."

***

At the appointed hour a week later Rick escorted Rosalinda into the doctor's office. It smelled of disinfectant and rosemary. The doctor looked up from his cluttered desk and studied them intently.

"*What to say. How do I explain this?*" he thought.

He pulled a file from the pile of papers on his desk, and thumbed absentmindedly through a few pages. The first appointment last November. The results didn't come back until late December. Government approval to see a specialist didn't come through until March. He was too busy to see her until April. The tests he ordered weren't completed until last week. Almost 6 months to confirm a diagnosis. "*In the old days,*" he thought "*the whole process would have taken 30 days. But government health care is bureaucratic health care... and a bureaucracy moves very slowly. Everyone worries about forms, rules and procedures. Endless paperwork... Lousy results*" The doctor mumbled a few unintelligible words to himself and threw the file on his desk. Carefully, slowly, he folded his hands, sat back in his chair, and looked intently at Rosalinda.

"Rosalinda, you are one of the prettiest girls on this planet. I wish I could give you years of good health..... But I cannot."

The doctor paused for what seemed to be an eternity.

"You have a pancreatic carcinoma, better known as cancer of the pancreas. I think, with treatment, you may have 3 ... no ... maybe 6 months to live."

Rosalinda and Rick were both stunned by the news. Rick was completely overwhelmed with grief. He began to shake. Tears again welled up into Rosalinda's eyes.

"What happens next?" she said softly.

"We cannot remove the tumor. It has metastasized to your liver and your lymph nodes and .... God only knows where else. I'm sorry, but it's too late for an operation. We can apply for a series of chemotherapy treatments if you wish. Maybe we can get the government health care system to approve them."

"What can I do to help my wife?" Rick pleaded.

The doctor ignored him for the moment, preferring to talk directly to Rosalinda.

"The big challenge now is to manage the pain and other symptoms of cancer. I'll prescribe a regimen for you, and I will also give you a contact at Hospice... They can be a lot of help with pain management and psychological support."

The doctor paused to let Rosalinda and Rick absorb the information. Then he leaned forward and spoke again.

"Do expect to lose weight, Rosalinda..... And you will have more infections and liver problems. That can't be helped..... But your husband can help you with the feeling of depression."

With that, the doctor sat back for the inevitable questions. Why had Rosalinda gotten cancer? Where had it come from? Why hadn't they known sooner? If they had known last November, would earlier detection have saved her life? Deep in his soul, the Doctor felt a wave of disgust. He had no satisfactory answers. *"Damn it,"* he thought, *"why does this have to happen?"*

***

Rick knew he had a long list of things to do. Find day care for the children, call the Hospice people, call the pharmacy and get the prescriptions, learn a lot more about how to manage the pain, and - figure out how to take loving care of his lady. Tears came to his eyes. He was devastated. She was only 35 years old. A feeling of dread spread over him.

That evening he looked wistfully at his wife. Although she seemed to have accepted her fate, Rick knew she was still in shock. He looked at her tenderly, and slipped his hand around her waist.

"I can't live without you," he said.

Rosalinda looked up at him with great sadness in her eyes.

"I'm sorry for you.... This should never have happened... I worry about Adonica, Serafina and Ramon... I'm totally lost.... What should I do?"

Rick tried to console his wife. But he failed. He could not find the words. Nothing he could say would help her... This young girl who stole his heart... This blushing bride who gave herself to him... This mother who gave him a wonderful family... This woman he deeply loved... Rick felt incredibly helpless.... and suddenly alone.

Rosalinda died 67 days later.

Chapter 3   Change

A very large black van pulled up beside the house. Two men got out and knocked on the door. One of them was carrying a big black bag. The other man had a pair of long sticks wrapped in a plastic sheath. Ramon scampered to the door to let them in.
"Hi. Is your daddy here?"
"He's upstairs with mommy."
The two men hesitated, looked at each other.
"Could you get him please?"
"Sure!"
And with that, four year old Ramon bounded upstairs to the master bedroom. His father stopped him at the door.
"You can't go in," he said softly, almost in tears.
Ramon looked at his father. Bewildered. Something really bad was happening. He suddenly felt frightened. Apprehensive. "*Where's mommy?*" he thought.
Rick looked intently at his son. A feeling of deep sorrow enveloped his whole body. He wanted to distract Ramon's attention.
"Did the men come?"
"Yes, they're downstairs."
"Go get them."
Ramon turned and bounded downstairs again.
"Daddy says come on up!"
The two men climbed the stairs and went into the bedroom.
Ramon parked himself on the living room couch. In a few minutes the two men reappeared carrying the black bag on a stretcher. As they disappeared out the door, his father came into the room. He looked very depressed. Tears welled in his eyes.
"I have to go out for awhile. I'm going to take Adonica and Serafina with me. The lady from Hospice will stay with you until we come back." Rick paused. "Is that OK?"
Ramon nodded. He wondered where they were going. His sisters followed their father into the living room, and then went to the hall closet to get raincoats. The conversation between them was muffled, serious. Serafina had tears in her eyes. Adonica looked very sad. After putting on their raincoats, the three of them left, trooping out the back door and down the steps into the cold rain.
Ramon sat on the couch and played with his truck. The lady from the Hospice went into the kitchen to make a cup of tea. Ramon continued to play with his truck for a few moments. Then he got up and quietly went upstairs to the master bedroom. There was no one there. The bedding was rumpled and damp.
"Mommy?" he called softly. No answer.
Ramon went into the bathroom and called again.
"Mommy?"

Still no answer. Puzzled, Ramon went back down stairs. The woman from the Hospice came into the living room, a hot cup of tea in her hand. She immediately understood what was happening. She carefully put the cup down on a table, knelt on her knees, and held her arms out to Ramon. He walked slowly over to her and put his arms around her neck. The woman was very gentle.

"Your mommy has gone away."

"Is she coming back?"

A long pause .... then "no."

Ramon began to cry. He pushed the woman away and went over to the couch. He climbed up on his knees, placed his elbows on the back of the couch, and looked out the big window that overlooked the back entry where the men had come into the house. It was a dreary, cold day. A light rain fell from a slate gray sky. Ramon was determined to wait for his father to return. An hour passed. The woman from the Hospice tried to interest him in a game on her laptop computer. But he ignored her. Another hour passed. Still the rain drizzled down. The chill of the air seemed to penetrate every room in the house. Ramon refused to leave the couch. His eyes scanned every inch of the wet porch. Then he heard a car door slam. Adonica and Serafina walked quickly onto the porch, holding an umbrella over their heads. Rick followed and helped them open the door. Ramon jumped off the couch and ran to greet them. He looked at each face, searching for reassurance. Then he looked beyond his sisters to the driveway. Nothing. No sweet familiar face. ... And then he screamed.

"Where's mommy?"

Adonica and Serafina stopped in the doorway. Rick knelt down before his son. Ramon screamed again, this time with tears in his eyes.

"Where's mommy?"

Rick tried to hug Ramon but the little boy would have none of that. He peered out onto the wet porch again, wishing with all his heart he could see Rosalinda. But there was nothing but the cold rain and dreary slate gray sky. Rick tried to console Ramon.

"Mommy has gone away....."

But Ramon refused to believe his father. He desperately wanted his mother to come up the sidewalk. Like she always did. He was grief-stricken and terrified at the same time.

Just then a little white kitten appeared on the door step. No one has ever known where it came from, or how it got there. But Adonica saw the kitten and immediately had an idea. She carefully picked it up.

"Here," she said as she placed the kitten in Ramon's arms. "This little kitten needs someone to love, and he needs to be loved. ..... Can you do that?"

Ramon took the kitten and tenderly cuddled it in his arms. He walked slowly back to the couch. Rick closed the door. He and the girls took off their raincoats.

Ramon gently rubbed the kitten's fur. The kitten, having decided being warm and dry was much better than being cold and wet, began to purr. He contentedly settled back into Ramon's arms. Ramon began to

55

understand what had happened. Sobbing quietly, he continued to stroke the kitten. He felt lost, alone, afraid, and very hurt. But he could love this little furry kitten.

And from that day forward, Ramon and the little white kitten were inseparable.

***

Rick decided to take Ramon and the girls to the funeral. Most of his staff came from the ISP. Although Clyde Tattaersol was suffering from gout, he managed to hobble into the funeral home just as Mari and Josue arrived. There were whispers and muffled conversations. The funeral home had arranged several bouquets of flowers around the coffin. Soothing organ music filled the room. One by one, the guests walked solemnly up to the coffin to pay their last respects. The funeral home had meticulously prepared Rosalinda for the viewing. She looked lovely, serene, her head cradled on a white satin pillow.

When it was the family's turn to view Rosalinda, they filed up to the open coffin one by one. Adonica paused and looked at her mother with sorrow and resignation. She had stoically accepted the loss of her mother. Serafina was obviously bewildered and frightened. Rosalinda had been an anchor for her. Someone to rely on for compassion and support. Now she was gone. Ramon stepped slowly up to the coffin and peered in. Tears filled his eyes as he looked at Rosalinda's beautiful face. He only said one word, … very softly … "Mommy."

Rick was exhausted by the loss, the grief of his family, and the deep sorrow that ached through his body. He took one last look at Rosalinda… closed his eyes… and whispered… "I love you." Rick carefully closed the coffin, and walked with the children to the pew. Although they participated in the brief service, they were mentally far away, emotionally numb to everything that was going on around them.

***

Little boys need their mother. And so do little girls. Where else are they going to experience the bliss of warm affection? How else will they learn the difference between love and lust, compassion and passion, respect and insolence? Despite Adonica's best efforts to be a substitute mother, Ramon withdrew into himself, ever lonely and defensive. Serafina seemed to be lost, unsure, fearful of all that occurred around her. Adonica internalized her pain. She bravely faced each day with a grim determination.

His family's distress was not lost on Rick. He was frustrated because he didn't know what to do. Establishing a daily routine, assigning chores, spending time with each of his children - these things were only a mask for the deep emotional crisis that erupted after Rosalinda died.

Occasionally, he would drink until he was numb. Then he could pretend it didn't matter. He could convince himself that everything was OK. But it all flooded back when he sobered up. Rick was lost in time and space. He craved Rosalinda's touch, her smile, her playful flirting, her words, her love for him.

It was all gone. There was no one beside him in bed. There was no one in the kitchen. There was no sound of laughter in his house. He kept torturing himself with the same question, *"Did I take too much for granted?"*

***

The hot winds of August blew swirls of dust and trash across First Street in south San Jose. City blocks alternated between newer commercial buildings and seedy neighborhoods of run down structures. The glare of the bright sun was relentless as Rick squinted at the passing signs to find the building materials company. Then he spotted the yard's gravel driveway and drove into the parking area. The yard was enclosed with a 12 foot fence topped with rings of intimidating barb wire. The ramshackle retail sales building had obviously seen better days.

Rick had driven into the city with Ramon to buy materials for a tool shed he was building in the back yard. Although the girls were at home alone, he believed they would be able to take care of themselves during his brief trip into the city.

He helped Ramon unbuckle his car seat, lifted him out of the car, and took him by the hand as they walked into the yard office. Ramon was instantly mesmerized by all of the tools and building materials that lined the isles. He pointed to several items and demanded Rick explain how they were used. Rick patiently described each item. To his surprise Ramon never lost interest. He seemed particularly intrigued by the tools he picked up.

Rick looked thoughtfully at his son. *"Just like his grandfather."*

After much discussion with Ramon, Rick was able to pick out what he needed. He walked hand in hand with Ramon to the counter, paid the clerk, and went outside to his car. After loading his purchases into the car, he buckled Ramon into his car seat, and climbed into the vehicle. As they were driving out of the yard, Rick had a sudden inspiration. Instead of going home, he turned north on First Street, looking for a sign that would direct him to the San Jose Neighborhood Community. Although he drove all the way to the freeway underpass, he didn't see anything useful. Rick drove around a short block and headed south again on First Street. As he passed a row of storage units, he spotted a rumpled old man standing by the curb who looked vaguely familiar. Rick pulled the car over to the curb and called to him. Rick recognized him as he walked over to the car. It was the old man who had been evicted from his apartment.

***

No one can explain why Rick had the sudden urge to find the San Jose Neighborhood Community, or why at that precise time and place the old man was standing on a curb next to First Street, or even why Rick recognized him. But it happened. The old man's name was Fred. He was very friendly, talkative, and anxious to be helpful. Fred directed Rick to a side street and described the building that was home to the San Jose Neighborhood Community. When Rick offered to give Fred a ride to the NC, he quickly accepted.

As they rode toward their destination, Rick asked "What does a neighborhood community do?"

Fred thought for a moment, as though searching for just the right words.

"They provide shelter, food, and clothing to people like us. Sometimes they help us to find work. Father Giovanni runs the place. He is both a spiritual leader and a manager.

"Father Giovanni?" Rick was puzzled. He didn't think the NC was connected to the Catholic Church.

Fred smiled mischievously.

"Oh, he's not a real priest. We call him that because he's so mystical. He's actually just a very gracious human being. I'll introduce you."

Rick pulled the car into the driveway of a very large old warehouse. Badly in need of paint and repairs, it looked like it could use a lot of tender loving care. Fred smiled at the frown on Rick's face.

"This is what you get for free," he quipped.

They got out of the car. Rick took Ramon by the hand, and they walked into the building. The warehouse had been divided into a series of rooms. Some were used for sleeping, and some appeared to be common areas for families. There was a large hall in the center with a kitchen area and several long dining tables. A round, short, energetic man with white hair and thin rim spectacles was talking to a woman in the kitchen while he cleared a table and washed down the plastic table cloth. Rick decided Father Giovanni could be a double for John. Fred called to Father Giovanni, and the man came over. Although he didn't recognize Rick, he greeted him like an old friend.

"Can I get you a cup of coffee?"

Rick shook his head.

"How about some orange punch for this guy?" Father Giovanni gave Ramon a warm smile. "And maybe a chocolate cookie."

Rick nodded in agreement and moved forward to shake hands with Father Giovanni. But the man held back, intently examining Rick's face. Then he clasped his arms around Rick and gave him a bear hug. Startled and surprised by the greeting, Rick could only mumble, "I'm pleased to meet you."

Father Giovanni waved him off and took Ramon by the hand.

"Come on, let's see what we can find for you in the kitchen."

Fred chuckled.

"That's just the way he is."

Fred and Rick followed Father Giovanni and Ramon to a small table in the kitchen. Ramon was soon contentedly chewing on a cookie and sipping orange punch. Father Giovanni looked at Fred.

"Would you mind if I spend a few moments with Rick alone?"

Fred nodded it was fine with him and went off to find his wife. Father Giovanni took Rick to a long table in the dining room. Rick was again startled by this man's direct manner.

"I don't usually hug strangers," he said. "But you look like hell. You need help."

Rick was aware he probably didn't look all that well. In truth he had dark circles under two very red eyes, and the haggard look on his face was an indication of emotional exhaustion. Father Giovanni smiled as he continued.

"A friendly hug can do wonders for the tattered soul."

Rick looked with wonder at Father Giovanni. Losing Rosalinda had drained him emotionally, and he was always tired. The two men talked for a few minutes about nothing important. The NC could accommodate up to 17 families. At the moment there were 12 adults and 33 children. Some of the children, Father Giovanni told him, were homeless kids from the streets of San Jose. They had no place else to go. If they stayed on the streets they would not get enough to eat. Most were abused and many did not know much about their parents.

Rick began to feel more comfortable with this man. Father Giovanni seemed to be a competent manager and genuinely concerned about the welfare of his "extended family." He was talking about the children when he suddenly paused, looked intently at Rick, and asked with great compassion "What's wrong?"

Rick desperately needed some form of relief from his distress. He had kept it bottled up ever since the funeral. He spoke with deep emotion.

"I just lost my wife. ..... last month ..... pancreatic cancer .... I don't know what to do .... I can't live without her."

Father Giovanni reached across the table and placed his hand on the trembling fingers of a man who obviously needed help.

"Tell me about it. Tell me everything." He was obviously sincere.

With that invitation, the emotional flood gates opened. A sense of relief swept over Rick as he talked about his first fears for Rosalinda's health, the doctor's visit, the tests, the agonizing wait to receive permission to see a specialist, the final tests, and then the shock of learning she would die. Rick talked about the funeral and his family. Then he abruptly stopped.

"I'm sorry, I have taken too much of your time," he said quietly.

"Not at all," Father Giovanni said. "I think we have just begun."

Rick sat back in his chair. He looked at Father Giovanni as though expecting some kind of absolution. He was not disappointed.

"And so now you blame yourself. You think it would have turned out differently if you had acted sooner. You blame yourself for her death. You worry you took too much for granted."

Father Giovanni paused to let his words penetrate the guilt Rick was feeling.

"Life is not perfect... We make choices... We have to live with the consequences... You have done nothing wrong. But you are in danger. If you let this loss eat at your conscience, you risk screwing up the lives of your children."

Rick could only nod his head in agreement. He was very uneasy about managing a family with no mother at home.

"Focus Rick, focus on the job ahead. Focus on the responsibility you have for those you love"

Although Rick nodded in agreement, he still didn't know what to do. Father Giovanni understood his dilemma.

"I don't know what religion you belong to.... or even if you believe in God... But at a time like this, prayer can be a big help. It connects you with the spiritual .... and the spiritual can be a great source of comfort and inspiration."

Just then Ramon came over to the table.

"I want to go home." He was very insistent.

Rick looked affectionately at his son.

"Yes. It's time for us to go."

He stood up and shook Father Giovanni's hand.

"Thank you for your help. You are a good listener."

"I want you to come back," Father Giovanni said. "I want you to come back with your whole family. Your children can play with our children, and I will put you to work. There is much to do here."

Rick smiled as he looked around the large hall. "OK... I guess I owe you a return visit."

He took Ramon's hand and together the two of them made their way to the door. Father Giovanni smiled gently at them as they left and said to himself, *"Good luck and God bless."*

***

It was a sunny Saturday in September. Adonica, Serafina and Ramon were playing down the street with several neighborhood kids. Rick sat down at his desk to open the mail. An envelope bearing the official seal of the United States Government caught his eye. He opened the envelope, and took out what looked like some kind of form. He carefully unfolded the paper. It was from the Department of National Health, Medical Services Agency, Division of Procedure Approvals. It was addressed to Rosalinda.

"Reference your request for treatment # 45592H9N, dated May 30. We regret to inform you that your application for chemotherapy has been denied."

A wave of furious anger swept over him. He jumped to his feet, pounded his fist on the desk, and screamed several obscenities at the useless health care system, government indifference, and a brainless callous bureaucracy.

***

Serafina loved her father, felt sorry for her little brother, and was jealous of her sister. Adonica always appeared to be in control, unflustered by anything that happened, and incredibly smart. At age 12, Adonica was also functioning as a part time mother. This responsibility gave her an excuse to be bossy. Serafina felt lost, lonely, depressed, and inferior. And when Adonica dominated her sister, Serafina became angry and resentful. Still, she said nothing. Serafina hid behind a mask of cooperative obedience. She smiled when she was supposed to, and managed to suppress the urge to cry. Serafina seldom giggled or laughed outright.

By October, the household routine had been established. A nanny came four days a week to look after the children. Rick would arrange his schedule so that he could work from home on the fifth workday, and on the weekend. Although her approach to the task was a bit haphazard, Adonica did a reasonable job of caring for Ramon. Serafina stoically did her assigned chores each day. Ramon appeared to be an active, inquisitive, and occasionally boisterous little boy. No one understood how much his heart ached over the loss of his mother's love.

***

In December, Rick turned 37. He decided to accept Father Giovanni's invitation to spend most of Christmas Day at the NC. Christmas morning, Adonica seemed to be more annoyed than usual with Ramon. She was very uptight as she picked out a dress to wear to the NC and laid it out on the bed. Serafina, who was also getting ready to go, accidentally sat on the dress. Adonica exploded with rage.

"Watch out! You'll wrinkle my dress you clumsy bitch."

Serafina was terrified by the sudden outburst. Tears welled in her eyes as she got up and walked to her bed. But Adonica was still angry. She shouted at Serafina.

"Every time I try to do something, you get in the way!"

Serafina cowered on her bed. She began to shake with emotion. Then she decided, impulsively, to fight back.

"I do not get in the way! You have big feet!" she screamed.

Adonica lunged at her sister and the two wrestled on Serafina's bed. The bedroom door flew open as Rick entered.

"Stop that. Stop that right now!"

Rick separated the two girls. He put Adonica on her own bed and sat down beside Serafina. Both girls were sobbing large tears.

"Ok. What is this all about?" he demanded loudly. Both girls babbled an explanation, blaming the other for their quarrel. Rick listened patiently until they ran out of words. Then, he forced himself to speak with a quiet reassurance he did not feel.

"Adonica, this is not like you. Serafina has always been very helpful."

Adonica would not look at her father. Instead she looked at the floor, then out the window, tears in her eyes. She was clearly distressed. Rick stood up, gave Serafina a loving hug, and kissed her on the cheek.

"Let's go downstairs, Adonica. We can talk in the kitchen."

Rick took Adonica's hand and led her out of the room. They walked downstairs to the kitchen and sat down across from each other at the kitchen table. He carefully brushed her disheveled hair from her face and looked at her intently.

"Now then. Tell me all about it."

"I'm sorry, Daddy, I just got upset."

"Why are you upset? This should be a fun day for all of us."

"I .... I have something wrong with me... like Mommy"

Rick felt a thump of dread in his chest. He gently took her hand in his.

"You are a perfectly healthy little girl."

Rick abruptly stopped. He was embarrassed by his assertion.

"I mean," he paused for a moment, "you are becoming a lovely young lady."

Adonica looked at him for the first time since the fight with her sister.

"Daddy, I have stuff coming out of me. It's on my underwear."

Rick was not prepared for this. He was unsure what to say. He could talk to total strangers, discuss complex business problems with his staff, carry on a conversation in almost any situation. But this?

"What kind of stuff?"

Adonica looked down at the floor. "Kind of gooey."

Rick looked at his daughter with wonder and affection. He had a sudden inspiration.

"Let's call grandma and ask for her advice."

He picked up the telephone and dialed a familiar number. To his relief, Mari answered. After the usual greetings and inconsequential comments, he asked Mari to talk to Adonica about her discharge. Mari was immediately apprehensive.

"Put her on the phone. Let me talk to her."

Rick handed the phone to Adonica, and walked out of the kitchen so his daughter could have some privacy. After a few minutes, Adonica called to him.

"Grandma wants to talk to you."

Rick took the phone. The voice on the other end was reassuring, informative and helpful. Mari understood the situation between father and daughter.

"Your little girl is growing up. It's nothing to worry about. In a few months she'll start her period."

Rick was immediately relieved. He asked a few questions and hung up the telephone. Then he felt a wave of self-conscious doubt sweep over him. His face turned a bit red with embarrassment. Rick looked at his daughter.

"Ok?" was all he could manage to say.

"Ok, Dad." Adonica gave her father a big smile. Rick was grateful for her response.

"Go upstairs and apologize to your sister."

Adonica, obviously relieved and happy, left the kitchen to find Serafina.

Rick slumped back in the chair, closed his tired eyes, and whispered softly: "Rosalinda, I need you."

He remained in the chair with his eyes closed for several moments. Then he detected the faint scent of lilac perfume. He drew more air through his nose. The scent was unmistakable. It was Rosalinda's favorite perfume. Then Rick felt a hand on his shoulder. He was afraid to open his eyes, afraid of what he might see.... yet he desperately wanted to see her so much.

"You're doing the right thing," her voice said. "Our children are growing up. You are a good father. It will all work out."

Tears formed in Rick's eyes. He was sure it was Rosalinda.

"But I need you..."

"I'll be here until you no longer need me," she said. "All you have to do is pray... spend a few quiet moments alone with your thoughts... and I will come."

"But where are you?"

"You would call it heaven... you will learn to call it the Spiritual Universe."

"What?... I don't understand."

"You will... All in good time... Now remember... a few quiet moments and I will come."

Rick was sure he felt a light kiss on his cheek. Then he felt her hand lift from his shoulder, and she was gone. Rick began to sob with joy, sadness and love... all at once.

Serafina came into the kitchen. As soon as she saw her father, she knew what happened.

"Mommy was here," she said quietly.

"Yes..."

"She is with God, isn't she?"

"She told me she is in heaven."

Serafina came to her father and gave him a big hug.

"And I can talk to her whenever I need to... and so can you."

***

The following Monday Rick called Lydia into his office. Coffee cup in one hand and a bagel in the other, Lydia was having her second breakfast.

"Hi. What's up?"

Rick hesitated for a moment. He could not look directly at Lydia.

"I have a problem with ... Adonica."

Lydia's response was guarded. "What's the matter?"

Again Rick hesitated, and then he murmured... "she's getting ready for her period."

A broad smile flashed across Lydia's face. It was, for her, rather humorous to see Rick so unsure of himself. He was usually in command. Almost charismatic. She took a sip of coffee.

"Have you talked to Adonica about the birds and the bees?"

"No."

"Did Rosalinda talk to her?"

"I don't think so."

Lydia chuckled. "And so you're up a rope. Someone needs to talk to Adonica.... but you're not it. Am I right?"

"I guess so," sighed Rick. He forced himself to look at Lydia in the eye. She was still amused at his predicament. Then she became more compassionate.

"Bring her up... bring all the kids up... this weekend. I'll take a walk with Adonica, or maybe we can have some quiet time in my bedroom."

Rick was grateful. "Thank you, Lydia. Do you think you can handle her questions?"

Rick was immediately sorry he doubted Lydia's capabilities. Big, brassy Lydia. She could handle most anything. Talking about sex would not phase her in the least.

But to his surprise, a serious look crossed Lydia's face. "I will give her better information than they dish out at school."

Rick agreed with her. He arranged to bring his children up to see Lydia and Phillip the very next weekend. Lydia had come to the rescue. Rick could relax. Later in the day, Phillip playfully nudged Rick.

"There are times I'm glad I'm not a father," he grinned.

***

Rick took the light rail train to work the next day. As the cars lurched and shuddered their way north, he made an early New Year's resolution.

"I will give each of my children a loving hug at least once every day."

***

The tools for a National Security Database have existed since the 1990s. When the National Security Service (NSS) decided to track all suspicious Americans and aliens, it issued a Request For Quotation to Oracle, IBM, Hewlett Packard and RBQSC. For political reasons, and despite vehement protests, foreign database vendors were not allowed to participate in the bidding process. Although Oracle, IBM and Hewlett Packard were qualified vendors, they only made a half hearted effort to win the business. Insiders knew RBQSC was already wired to win. Questions about the poor quality and inherent vulnerability of RBQSC software were ignored.

Although various government agencies already had massive surveillance databases, the NSS wanted to tie them all together with a composite file that could be used to identify, track and watch everyone. Newer cell phones, pagers, and other devices were equipped to receive location information from GPS navigation satellites. This location information can be stored on the device and then collected by the network whenever the device was active. All cell phones could be tracked by the location of the cellular network towers. Credit card, ATM, and other point of sale appliances would automatically activate the consumer identification and location system which recorded all transactions. Radio Frequency Identification tags, and other types of identification chips, embedded in clothing, consumer products and under the skin, would activate a network of surveillance sensors. Agency computers already recorded e-mails, blogs, social networking, search request, and other Internet WEB sites to create a record of written thoughts. Voice calls over cell phones, telephone lines and other devices were being captured and stored for reference.

It would be an enormous data base. Most of the stored information would be useless. A high percentage would be inaccurate. Hackers would be able to tamper with individual records. But for the NSS, it would give the agency the personal information it needed to carry out its mission. The NSS wanted to know who you are, where you are, what you are doing, and what you think. People who are politically incorrect can be identified, tracked, arrested and confined for questioning.

***

The torrential rains of March had morphed into the blustery showers of April. Rick was in his office when Clyde Tattaersol arrived at the ISP, dripping wet and shivering from the cold. He took off his raincoat and shook the droplets of water onto the floor of the entrance lobby. Then he went into the utility room to find a towel so he could dry his face and hands. A few moments later he walked into Rick's office.

"Damn, it's cold out there."

Rick looked up from the papers on his desk. "It sure is. The light rail train I took to work was full of wet and cold people. The weather service says April has been about 7 degrees cooler than normal this year."

"Do you believe them?" Clyde retorted. "I think it's colder than that."

Rick sat back in his seat. "I don't know. It's certainly colder and wetter than I can remember for this time of year."

Clyde sat down in a comfortable old easy chair Rick kept in his office.

"Well, it's too cold and wet for me. I've decided to move to my condo in Hawaii. Give it all up here. I'm too old for this weather. Hawaii may be wet, but at least it's warmer than Santa Clara County."

Rick had heard this all before. Clyde was always threatening to get out of California.

"But what about your company, your computer service business?"

Clyde didn't answer right away. Instead he looked thoughtfully at Rick, as though trying to find just the right words. Finally he spoke.

"Why don't you buy it? All of it. You run it anyway."

Rick was astonished by Clyde's offer. Same old Clyde. Always direct and full of surprises. A thousand questions rushed into his mind.

"Do you mean it? Are you really ready to throw in the towel?"

"Yes. ... I'm serious. I want to be in Hawaii by June first."

"But I don't have enough money to buy you out, and the banks aren't interested in making loans to small businesses like ours."

Clyde studied the younger man's face for a moment.

"Rick, look at me. I'm pushing 80. I ache in the morning and I hurt at night. My knees are bad and I have arthritis in my feet. I can't stay awake all day. You know I take a nap almost everyday after lunch. Let's face it. It's almost over for me. I have no relatives. No one to give the business too. All I want is some extra income until I die."

Rick started to protest. Clyde was a good manager, a rock of stability upon which he had leaned several times. But Clyde waved him off again.

"You need this business. And so do the people who work here. Jobs are tough to find. Most of them pay lousy wages. If I close the doors, where do you all go?"

Clyde had a point. California – actually all of America – was suffering from chronic recession. Unemployment was a constant threat. These people, his team, needed this business to thrive, else they would be looking for work in a very unfriendly world.

"So. OK. What do you want me to do?" Rick asked.

"Pay me 3 percent of the revenue until I die or a maximum of $300,000, whichever comes first."

It was a generous offer. The business was already paying Clyde a salary. Rick would have to add another person to help with sales and systems development. But the added expense should be manageable.

"How do you know you are getting your fair share of the revenue?" Rick asked.

"Rick. Of all the people I have ever known, you're the only one I would trust without reservation. It's not just a matter of honesty. I also trust your judgment and your character."

Rick was both pleased and embarrassed by the reply. But with that said, the two men launched into a discussion of the details, shook hands on the deal, and went out into the big office to tell the staff.

***

As planned, Clyde was gone by June first. He sent a "Wish you were here" card from Hawaii. When Rick pinned it on the bulletin board, everyone had an affectionate chuckle. They would miss Clyde's gruff voice and fondness for afternoon naps.

Rick called his staff together one afternoon for punch and cookies. He needed to find an analyst who could help with sales. He asked them for a recommendation. Phillip suggested a man named Peter Bachman, whom he knew through his work with other Internet ISPs. As it turned out, Peter's employer had just gone out of business and he was looking for a job. Rick nodded in agreement and took a telephone number from Phillip.

Peter came in for an interview in late June. Rick had him meet and talk with everyone else in a series of brief individual meetings before bringing him into his office.

A tall man of medium build, brown hair and blue eyes, Peter looked to be in his early 50s. He had a quiet spiritual quality about him that immediately put Rick at ease.

"Welcome to the Santa Clara Internet Service company," Rick said as Peter entered the office.

"Thank you. This appears to be a thriving business. How have you been able to survive the recession?"

"By working hard and sticking together as a team. Have you met everyone?"

"I think so. Even the cat in the utility room."

Rick smiled. They had adopted a stray cat last year. Once inside, he never left. By now, the cat was definitely one of the family.

"Tell me about your background."

Peter told Rick about his career, the work he had done, and the positions he had held. Peter had been an operations supervisor in his last job, and had also been responsible for customer service. The two men exchanged information and Rick, after briefly consulting with Phillip, decided to hire Peter. There was additional discussion about responsibilities and money. Peter appeared to be pleased with the offer. Rick decided not only did he have a good employee, he had a new friend.

***

Gangs and gang warfare had been a threat to San Jose's peace for some time. In mid-June there was another drive-by shooting that killed three teenagers. Rumors swirled around the neighborhood that kids from the street where Rick lived were involved.

On a cool June night, Rick noticed two sedans cruising down his street. Inside there looked to be three teenagers and two older men. Rick concluded, correctly, they were looking for trouble. Ramon, who had just had his fifth birthday, came running up the street from the corner. Rick was alarmed his son was so far from home. He was about to scold Ramon when he heard two shots. Ramon screamed and rushed to hug his father. The two cars sped down the street and disappeared around the corner.

When the police came they took statements. Everyone in the target house played dumb. They insisted no one had been hurt. The police went away. Rick was stunned by the trouble that had occurred so close to home.

Josue called that night. He and Mari had seen a report about the shooting on television news. They knew it was the street where Rick lived. Josue was calm, firm, and very caring. After a few words about what he had seen on TV, he asked Rick a question.

"Rick, why don't you let the kids come up for a visit this summer? We'd love to have them. They will have a safe place to play and we can take them over to see Abigail and George once in awhile to ride horses …. just like you and Phillip used to do."

"But these are three very active children. You'll never keep up with them."

"Oh. We'll have a little help from Neema Mitchell. She moved in with her parents last year."

Rick remembered George and Abigail had both retired and moved back to their little ranch near Winters. He hadn't seen Neema since his marriage to Rosalinda.

"How old is George?"

"He and Abigail are both a very active 73."

Josue paused briefly. Then he said with quiet assurance "Don't worry, we can handle everything."

"Well … OK… how about a two week vacation. Then we'll see how you feel about a longer stay."

"Fine. You should be able to send them on the train to Davis. We can pick them up there."

And so the arrangements were made. The kids were very excited about the prospect of a train ride by themselves. Very grown up. And they loved Mari and Josue. Rick was thankful for the offer. Perhaps the gang warfare would be resolved before the kids came back.

***

June soon became July. The kids were in no hurry to come home, and Mari insisted they were no problem. So July became August, and things were still going well. In early September, Rick decided to take a short vacation with his parents in Winters. Because there was no room for him at home, he booked into a rooming house on Main Street. Each morning he was able to have a quiet breakfast at the Putah Creek Café before going out to see his family. The second night of his vacation he took Neema and the kids to the Buckhorn Steak and Roadhouse. Neema was dressed in a baggy pant suit, had her hair tied back in a bun, and wore no makeup. Rick noticed she would occasionally look at him as though trying to make up her mind about something.

"*Mysterious woman,*" Rick thought.

The kids were thrilled to eat in a real restaurant, and a very large waitress lavished her affectionate attention on them. It soon became clear to him that Neema had taken a special interest in his children, and she appeared to be especially close to Serafina. As they ate, Neema fussed with Ramon's dinner, talked easily with Adonica, and exchanged playful nonsense with Serafina. Rick was content Neema could be a good friend to his children.

After dinner the third night, Mari and Josue asked Rick if he would like to take a stroll through the historic district to the old Vaca Valley Railroad trestle pathway. They left Adonica, Serafina and Ramon with Neema. As they walked through the park, they talked.

"The kids seem very happy," said Rick. "I'm really impressed with Serafina. …. Neema seems to have encouraged her to blossom."

"Serafina needed someone to love, someone she could attach too," Mari said quietly.

Rick was startled by Mari's assertion. But Mari continued to speak.

"I know you love Serafina. And she loves you. She talks about you a lot. But she misses her mother. When Rosalinda died, something broke in that child's heart."

"And Neema is doing a great repair job," Josue added.

Rick smiled to himself. Leave it to his father, a man who could fix any vehicle ever manufactured by man, to think of Neema as a mechanic for the heart. The more he thought about it, however, the more he was convinced it was a good description.

"And what about Ramon?"

Josue answered. "He's a rascal. Just like you. Rides a horse like he was born on one."

"And he misses his mother more than you can imagine… His heart aches for her touch. I can see it in his eyes," Mari added.

"And Adonica?"

Mari responded. "She's growing up. A teenager. Struggling to manage her hormones." Mari hesitated, slightly embarrassed. … But her son had to be told.

"Adonica has started her periods."

Although Rick expected this event would happen, he was still a bit flustered by Mari's announcement. Dealing with a teenage girl, periods, boys and gang threats were suddenly an overwhelming challenge.

"How bad are the gangs in Winters?"

"Not bad," Josue responded. "At least for now."

Mari knew what Rick was thinking.

"Adonica will be better off here than in San Jose. We can provide a good home. I know our house is not as fancy ......"

But Rick interrupted her.

"It's the home I grew up in. It's the home I love.... and the people I love."

Josue looked very pleased with himself. Mari turned and gave her son a gentle hug.

"We can take care of them. You can come up to see them every week if you like. Please Rick. These are the girls I always wanted, and Ramon is just another version of you."

"Besides," said Josue, "Ramon takes after me. He loves to take things apart. All I have to do...." Josue stopped to chuckle, "is teach him how to put them together again."

Rick looked at his parents. How old were they? Sixty? Three kids could be too much.

"I'd like to talk with Neema before I make a decision. You're going to need her help."

Then Rick changed the subject. He noticed Mari looked a little disappointed. But she said nothing more about the children.

***

His meeting with Neema, Rick decided, would be short and to the point. Would she be able to take the kids once in awhile in order to give Mari and Josue a break? That's all he wanted to know. He didn't want to leave his children in Winters unless his parents had some help. He could pay for the expense of raising three children. Take the kids back if things got out of hand. But first he needed to have a short conversation with Neema. He called her that night.

Neema readily agreed to have a private conversation with him. She insisted, however, they spend more time together. If Rick was going to leave his children in Winters, they needed to talk about schools, schedules, and many other details. Neema suggested they meet in town for a walk and a cocktail. Although he hesitated at first, Rick agreed to see her the next evening.

When they met in town, the sun was just setting over the coastal range, giving the pale blue sky a pink tint to the west. Cool air swept up from the Bay to create a very pleasant evening for walking. Rick had borrowed his father's car and drove to the parking lot next to the Winters Community Theatre. He got out and leaned back on the car to wait. Five minutes passed. Then ten. Finally Neema's CR-V appeared and she drove into the space next to him. She gracefully got out of her car and closed the door. She was wearing a white dress with a pink bosom sash. For her second meeting with Rick, Neema had skillfully applied a light touch of makeup and combed her hair so that it tumbled down to her shoulders. Rick suddenly realized Neema was a very attractive woman, about 3 years older than he was, and perhaps a little taller than Rosalinda. She walked and carried herself with a quiet assurance that most men found fascinating. As she approached Rick, she let the sash drop away.

"*Good Lord. She has a stunning figure,*" he thought to himself.

As Neema drew closer, Rick caught the scent of her delightful perfume. For the first time since Rosalinda's death, a woman was stimulating his senses. A feeling of excitement surged through his body. Rick tried to look calm. Nonchalant. But he failed to fool Neema. She knew how she was affecting Rick. And it was just what she wanted.

"It's nice we can spend some time together," Neema said as she extended her hand to Rick.

Somewhat confused by her appearance and the scent of her perfume, Rick forced himself to be very formal as he shook her hand.

" Yes. I wanted to talk with you about the children, my parents, and what kind of life ...."

Neema interrupted him and squeezed his hand. "Let's walk to the bridge," she said softly.

Surprised by her demeanor, Rick turned and started down the path. Neema slipped her arm into his arm and drew close to his side. Rick was captivated by her sensual intimacy. He was aware of the light scent of her perfume, and aroused by her erotic allure. She started the conversation.

"My parents are really too old to care for the ranch, but they won't give it up. It's who they are. I'm sure they want to die with their boots on. As for me, I was married for 12 years. My husband turned into a drunk. He killed himself when his car ran off the road and hit a bridge abutment. So last year I came to live with my parents. I'll care for them until they die."

Neema paused briefly to let Rick absorb all she had said.

"I never had any children. That turned out to be a good thing. Otherwise I would be a single mom."

They entered the old Vaca Valley Railroad trestle pathway. Rick was walking more slowly now, enjoying the stroll, the air, the evening ... and this lovely woman. Neema tugged gently on his arm.

"Although Adonica seems to be relatively independent, Serafina and Ramon need a woman's touch. They still miss Rosalinda ..."

Neema wondered if she should have mentioned Rosalinda's name. Would it make Rick defensive? Reluctant to come closer to her? Neema looked up at the tall, rather handsome man beside her. Despite a slight paunch at his belt line, he still had a slender build. His eyes were steady, unflinching – except when he glanced at her bosom. A little smile crossed her face. "*He still looks. He can't be totally disinterested in other women.*" She smiled sweetly up at Rick, but he didn't appear to notice. Undeterred, Neema continued.

" Your parents can be there for them when they come home from school. I can take them ... I want to take them... on the weekends for a few hours each day. I can bring them to my parent's house. Ramon loves to ride. I give them all a turn on our old mare. It's perfectly safe."

Rick was still not convinced. He loved his children. Whenever he thought about them, which was several times a day, he would get this nagging ache in the pit of his stomach. Neema seemed to know what he was thinking.

"You can come up every weekend if you wish. Or more often. I'll pick you up at the train station in Davis if you decide not to drive."

Gasoline was expensive and there were occasional shortages. Rick was cautious.

"Do you think you'll have enough gasoline?"

"I'll save up... and they now have a bus that goes from Railroad Avenue in Winters to the train station in Davis. ... But I'd rather pick you up. The kids love to go into Davis. I bribe them with ice-cream." Neema gave Rick a little wicked smile. This time he noticed her expression and chuckled at her scheme.

"And what about gangs?"

"Sure. We have some trouble. But people around here keep pretty close watch on their kids, and the police have a no tolerance policy. It's not perfect, but I'll bet it's a better situation for your children than what is going on in San Jose."

Rick decided she had a point. Things were going down hill in all of California's larger cities and towns. He wanted to protect his children from gang activity.

"So OK... And what do I need to do?"

"Your parents need more bedrooms and another bathroom. They could add on a wing, but you can't ask them to pay for it. I don't think they have the money."

Rick pictured his parents house in his mind. It would be easy to renovate the kitchen, extend the hall, and add a bedroom wing. Once again, Neema knew what he was thinking.

"And Josue knows how to build anything."

Rick began to waver. Maybe Neema was right.

They quietly walked along the bridge footpath. Neema's thoughts wandered back in time to the dinner she had with Rick and his children at the Buckhorn. Here was a man who desperately needed a woman's love. After watching him at dinner, Neema had decided she wanted to be that woman. But she did not press him any further. Neema wanted to make sure Rick knew she would be there for him and that she cared for him. Perhaps in time he would learn to love her.

"Let's walk back to the Buckhorn. I hear they have a country music singer and his band for entertainment."

Rick was relieved to put aside the troubling question of his children. As they walked, Neema would occasionally squeeze his arm. It felt good - comforting and exciting - all at the same time. They could hear the music of a band that was playing on the street in front of the Buckhorn long before they turned the corner. The restaurant was packed with a boisterous crowd. They found a place at the bar, sat down, and ordered two beers. Rick noticed most of the men would occasionally look over to eye Neema, and that only served to increase his excitement.

After an hour or so they left the Buckhorn and walked back to the parking lot. This time Neema did not take his arm. But as they walked, her hand brushed his. Almost instinctively, he grasped her hand and gave it a little squeeze. She responded by grasping his fingers, and they walked hand in hand to their cars. Once there, she turned to him.

"Well …. what about it? Can we have the kids for awhile longer?"

"If you will care for them, love them the way I do, then I guess it's all for the best."

Neema lifted up her face, placed her arms around his neck, and gave Rick a long, warm, gentle kiss. He eagerly responded, the passion coursing through his whole body. It had been over 14 months since he kissed a woman, and Neema was a lovely companion.

***

As the train back to San Jose swayed, lurched and rumbled across the Benicia – Martinez bridge, Rick experienced a moment of guilt. He had agreed to leave his children with his parents. But what would happen if Neema didn't live up to her part of the bargain?

Rick starred out of the window at the ripples of gray water, and then up the channel to the idle ships. "*It is for the best*," he told himself. "*It will be a better life than I can provide as a single parent father, and they will be safer in Winters.*" Then he thought about Neema. "*And I'll have an excuse to see Neema.*" A faint smile crossed his face. Life was improving.

When the train stopped in Oakland's Jack London Square, several children gathered around the passengers as they left the train. Rick watched them from the train window as they begged for money. They had learned to be very insistent. They followed the passengers, hands extended, pleading as they walked, until the passengers left the platform. He wondered if they were street children, like the ones he had met at the San Jose Neighborhood Community. He looked intently at their faces. They were mostly dirty, sullen, and desperate. Somewhere from within his gut a feeling of pity welled up within him. There were thousands of these children in America. Perhaps millions. They needed love, compassion and a decent home. Else they would be forced to join a street gang. Rick shuddered. Once in a gang, they would either perish or become like angry animals. Drugs, disease, and mutilation. A life of fear, anger, hatred and misery followed by callous death. As the train accelerated away from Jack London Square, Rick knew he had made the right choice for his children.

***

By October Rick was able to sell his house in San Jose. He quickly moved into an apartment in Santa Clara. With the money he received from the sale he was able to pay off his mortgage, and loan his father enough money to build the addition he discussed with both of his parents. Mari had been very pleased with the thought of remodeling her ancient kitchen. They both were grateful for the chance to add some extra room to their house.

Rick would go up to Winters four or five times a month to see his children. Neema, true to her word, was always anxious to see him. That made the experience all the more exhilarating.

***

Hackers are able to get into a user's PC and copy user identification information from the user's PC files, including e-mail addresses, the operating system identification number, and any credit card, access codes, passwords, and social security numbers the user has entered. This data can then be sent to the hacker's computer. The National Security Service used these same techniques to collect information for its massive data base. Every time a user logged on to the Internet, the software authenticated the user's identification. It then launched a tracking program it stored on the user's PC that would record everything the user was doing on the Internet. Every time the user closed a browser session, a copy of the collected data would be sent to the NSS data center. Hackers soon learned how to monitor these activities. Copies of the NSS files could then be transferred to the hacker's own computer system.

Internet security disintegrated. The first serious threat came in November.

The telephone was rigged to automatically increase the volume of the ring tone each time it rang. At first, Rick encountered the ring tone in a dream. People were asking him to answer the telephone. Although he stretched out his arms as far as he could, the telephone was always too far away. The ring kept getting louder and louder until it penetrated through the haze of sleep. Rick awoke with a start. No one had ever called him at night. He rubbed his eyes and struggled to find the annoying telephone. Rick finally grasped the handle of the handset and pulled it toward his ear. The telephone base fell onto the floor with a loud thump, and the receiver started making a screeching noise. Rick was suddenly very awake. He sat up and spoke brusquely into the handset.

"Hello?"

"Rick, this is Phillip," said a voice from out of nowhere. "We have a problem."

Rick was alarmed at the harsh sound of Phillip's voice.

"What's happened?"

"The Internet is down. All our servers are locked out. I can't seem to get any response from the network system. It's spam, ... or maybe a denial of service attack. I've called John and James. They are on their way to the office."

Rick was stunned. Hackers. Viruses. Spyware. Trojans. Worms. Constant threats that could paralyze his business. But none had ever knocked them off the air. This was a serious breach of security.

"Call Sarah and Antonio. We'll need all the help we can get....." Rick struggled to free himself from the bed sheets. "And bring in Peter."

He hastily hung up the telephone and went looking for something to wear. For some reason he couldn't find his shoes. He looked under the bed and shuffled through the mess in his closet. Then he remembered he left them in the living room. He ran into the room, found them, put them on without tying the laces, and raced out the front door.

Rick had purchased a very small electric car to use for transportation. It wasn't much of a vehicle, but it got him to work and back again. He prayed it had been plugged in long enough to give the batteries the charge they would need to get him to work. He unplugged the cord and got in. When he switched on the lights, the power meter needle climbed slowly into the yellow zone. Rick cursed under his breath. A few years ago he would have had a real car, with a real gasoline engine. "What the hell, I'll go as far as this thing will go, and then I'll walk the rest of the way," he muttered.

Small or not. The little electric car had great acceleration. Rick sped out of the apartment complex parking lot and headed for the office. Although it was very cold, he turned off the heater to save his batteries. It began to rain again. "*Great*," he thought. "*Now I'm going to be cold and wet.*"

The little car's lights penetrated through the rain and fog, briefly revealing familiar street signs and lane markers as they suddenly appeared and then rushed by in the gloom of night. Now and then a blinking red or yellow light marked an intersection as Rick sped through the streets of Santa Clara. His luck held. Rick made it all the way to the ISP. He parked the car and went inside. Phillip was intently scanning his computer screen and furiously typing software instructions on his keyboard. John was checking all of the network cable connections to make sure this wasn't a simple screw up.

"Who else is here," Rick demanded.

Phillip continued to focus on his computer screen. "Just us.... so far."

John appeared in the office doorway. "Everything is up. It's definitely a software problem."

James and Sarah stumbled into the office. A loud noise in the parking lot signaled another person had just arrived. To his surprise, it was Lydia. She soon barged into the office, took off her coat and started toward the utility room.

"You're going to need lots of coffee. Sarah looks like she's still asleep."

"I didn't call Lydia," Phillip said. "She probably couldn't get back to sleep after the monitor alarm went off."

Phillip had rigged a monitor alarm on the Internet server. It sent a constant stream of status information to another computer. If the server failed, the data stream stopped, and that would trigger the other computer to send out an alarm over a separate telephone link to Phillip's bedroom. When the Internet crashed, the monitor software sent out the alarm.

Rick took command. "Ok everyone. Let's get busy."

A few minutes later, Antonio arrived. Rick immediately put him to work on the backup server. Lydia popped her head out of the utility room.

"Can we get some heat in here?"

Rick was abruptly aware the office was very cold and damp. He went into the ISP storage room to turn up the thermostat. When he returned, the smell of fresh coffee had begun to filter out of the utility room. Lydia soon had coffee for everyone.

Peter suggested they contact other ISPs and network hub operators to see what they were experiencing. Rick put him in charge of that effort. An hour passed. Then another hour. The first faint gray light of dawn began to seep into the office. By then Phillip and John had traced the disruption to a particularly nasty zombie attack. John called Rick over to look at the code on his screen.

"This is a massive denial of service attack. I can stop it from infecting our servers, but only for a few seconds. There must be thousands of computers involved."

Phillip joined them. "Other ISPs are having the same problem. The Internet is flooded with crap."

John looked perplexed. "There is a repetitive code flowing through these strings that doesn't appear to be connected with the zombie assault. It's as though someone is using the attack to cover up something else." He paused for a moment. "And look at this, each time that string comes through, it has a different target address."

Peter joined them. "I've seen this before. The zombie attack essentially paralyzes the security software on any target computer connected to the Internet. By using a timing algorithm, hackers can access a Trojan horse to manipulate the computer's files and software."

"But they don't need to do this to bring down a server or PC," James interjected.

John had an inspiration. "But they could use it to cover up a transfer of data into or out of a target machine."

"Can we tell who owns the target computers?" Peter asked.

John began to capture the errant strings of data. He then got James to match them to a file he kept on another computer. James suddenly gave a shout.

"Every other one is a bank or other financial institution!"

John got up from his desk and went over to peer at the data on the screen. Phillip and Sarah joined the two men. Sarah looked puzzled, then her eyes lit up with excitement.

"They are doing bank transfers. There're moving money from one bank to another!"

What followed was a very animated discussion. Everyone talking at once. Someone was using the zombie attack to cover up a massive theft of user financial accounts. Banks, insurance companies, and stock brokers.

The thief was using IDs, passwords, and account numbers previously stolen from user PCs to loot their accounts.

"But we can stop them!" John exclaimed. "We can capture a hundred or so strings and send our own version of spam back to the crook's computer. That should knock him off the air."

"But we would need the help of several ISPs and institutions," Peter added. "We need to create a coordinated attack from multiple computers."

A plan began to form in John's mind. "The financial service computer people on the East coast must be open by now, let's ask them to help."

The whole staff was soon busy contacting computer programmers they knew. Although some were reluctant to become involved, they rounded up enough help to try John's plan. He had them make their own copies of the errant data strings, and faxed them the necessary spam code. When all was ready, John set a time for all participants to simultaneously interject their code into the thief's data string. They were ready by mid-morning. Everyone at the ISP had a PC attached to the Internet. They waited for the office clock to reach 9AM. Then they all began to transmit their code strings. They waited for the result. Several minutes passed, then Phillip jumped up from his seat and yelled "Eureka!"

John's plan had worked. The hacker's computer had been sabotaged. Everyone looked relieved and rather pleased with their efforts. Rick sent Lydia and Antonio out for donuts. Rick went into his office and rubbed his eyes. It had been a tough night. Peter looked into his office.

"John's still hard at work. He thinks he has something. Come see."

Rick got up and walked into the programmer's office area. John was indeed feverously typing on his keyboard.

"You'll never guess where this all started."

"Romania, Russia, somewhere else in Eastern Europe?"

John looked up and flashed a very small sly smile, "Virginia."

"Won't this make the newswires hum!" Peter exclaimed.

It would be another three hours before the Internet was running without an error, and another two hours before the staff had cleared and restored all of their accounts. They were all exhausted and Rick sent them home for some well deserved rest. But before he left, John wanted to talk to Rick. He came into the office and sat down in the big easy chair. John looked like he could fall asleep right then and there. But he had a serious look on his face.

"The newswires are raising hell about this breach of financial account security. They're saying the Internet isn't safe anymore. It can no longer be a trusted link for any financial information. That's going to hurt us if our accounts lose their financial service customers."

Rick nodded in agreement.

"And another thing," John went on, "If they ... the crooks ... find out we are the ones who screwed up their spam attack, they will retaliate. They could really hurt us."

Rick looked at John for a few moments. "We have to take things as they come. ... But you're right. Let's not advertise our role in this. ... Some victories are best if they are not celebrated. I'll warn the staff."

John nodded in agreement. "I do have some interesting news ..... I think I have found a sort of back door to the Internet, a way to send packets without being detected. I can misdirect packets... fake a DNS server ID. I'm going to play around with the software in my spare time. Being able to send information to the Internet without detection might come in handy some day."

"John. Thank you for all you have done. Now go home and get some sleep."

Rick got up, stretched, yawned, and decided to go home. When he went out to the little electric car, it was fully charged. Thanking God for little favors, Rick drove back to his apartment.

***

The cold December wind whipped down the dusty street and across the parking lot as Rick made his way to the office. The morning news had warned of possible snow showers before Christmas. Although an occasional snow shower was not unusual for the San Francisco bay area, they were normally confined to the higher elevations of the coastal and valley ranges that ring the bay. These snow showers, the weather man promised, would blanket the valley floor with white stuff. Since most California drivers have no useful experience with ice and snow, skidding cars and accidents would make the roads virtually impassable. That worried Rick. He was planning to visit his children in Winters over the holidays. Snow showers would make travel more difficult.

As he walked through the door of his ISP, the programmers began to cheer and hoot. Then Phillip marched up to him, took his hand, and raised it above his head.

"Here he is folks," Phillip announced in a very loud jovial voice. "Here is the man who is dating my old sister."

Everyone began to laugh. Rick was flustered beyond words. His face turned red with embarrassment. Phillip didn't let up.

"I was unsure what to do about Neema. She was just getting older with no man in her life. But Rick – gallant man that he is – came to her rescue."

Rick began to smile. A rather sheepish kind of grin. He still didn't know what to say, so he just said "Thank you, thank you all for your support." To which there was another round of laughter. Rick managed to slip from Phillip's hand and shuffled into his office. As he took off his coat, Peter and Phillip poked their heads into his office.

"Are you going to make an honest woman of her?" he asked with a smile.

Rick looked at the two men. He had regained enough of his composure to respond.

"Neema and I are just good friends. She has been wonderful with the children. I really appreciate all she is doing for me... and yes... I'll be seeing her Christmas week."

Phillip became more serious. "She really cares for you, Rick. I could tell from the tone of her voice when she called last night."

"You'll both be in Winters for Christmas," Peter observed. "It will be a chance for you and Phillip to take your girls to dinner."

"We shall see," Rick responded.

Phillip left to go back to work. Rick sat down in his office chair, but he paused a moment before plunging into the pile of papers on his desk. "I'm a lucky man, Peter. We are a team."

Peter looked at his boss with compassion. "They respect you, Rick. They look to you as their leader and they want you to be happy."

***

Two days after Christmas Phillip picked up Rick at the rooming house to go to dinner. He had Lydia and Neema in the car with him. Neema was in the back of the car, and when Rick opened the rear door to get in, she motioned for him to sit with her. Neema was wearing a black fur coat and a stunning black dress with a black lace modesty panel that actually accentuated the cleavage of her bosom. As soon as he settled into his seat, she moved over to be next to him. Neema's delightful perfume instantly captivated Rick, and when he turned to look at her, she gave him a lovely smile.

Phillip put the car in gear, maneuvered out of the driveway, and started down the road toward Winters. Every so often he would look in the rear view mirror at Rick and his sister. As they passed under a street light near Main Street, he noticed Rick seemed to be unable to take his eyes off Neema – including her black lace modesty panel. Phillip laughed outright. Lydia, who was half turned to talk with Neema, playfully punched him on the arm.

"Stop that. Leave them alone."

Rick could feel the warmth of Neema's leg against his. Her hand crept up his arm and gave it a little squeeze.

Rick managed to recover his cool by the time they reached the restaurant. He escorted Neema into the building and helped her with her coat. He managed – somehow – to keep his eyes off her black lace modesty panel. They found a cozy table, ordered dinner, and then waited for the food to arrive. Phillip and Lydia were in an amiable mood. The chit chat was pleasant. Nothing about the recession, or the business. Dinner was delicious. After dinner they ordered dessert and coffee. They began to talk about Christmas and the children. Neema and Rick were soon holding hands under the table, as though to hide an indiscretion. Of course, Lydia noticed right away. She winked at Rick, and gave him a little smile.

Although she and Rosalinda had been best friends, she knew it was time for Rick to move on.

As the car threaded its way through the black of night to the rooming house where Rick was staying, all four occupants were preoccupied with their own thoughts. Neema leaned against Rick. He put his arm around her shoulders. She snuggled closer. Rick was captivated by the delicate scent of her perfume and the sensuous warmth of her body.

"Will he kiss me goodnight?" Neema wondered. *"Or will Phillip ruin everything."*

Phillip stopped the car at the curb in front of the rooming house.

As Rick got out of the car, he turned to give Neema a little kiss on the cheek. She put her finger to his lips, as though to stop him. Then she gently placed one hand on each side of his head, drew him close, and gave him a long, warm, exhilarating kiss.

Phillip began to laugh. "No tongue, you two!"

Mortified by her brother's boisterous remark, Neema let Rick go. Embarrassed, Rick backed away and carefully closed the car door. As the car sped off into the night, Rick watched the vanishing taillights and heaved a big sigh.

He was developing a special place in his heart for Neema.

***

Normally, Neema projected a composed, quiet, and courteous persona. Very much in control of her emotions. But as the car pulled into the driveway of their parent's home, Neema was experiencing an incredible surge of anger. Brother or no brother, she was going to confront Phillip and castrate him for his crude behavior. They all got out of the car and went into the house. Phillip was walking a few feet in front of Neema. As he turned to go into the living room, Neema grabbed him by the shoulder and furiously pulled him backward. Totally surprised, Phillip turned to face his raging sister. Before he could speak, she tore into him.

"Don't you ever do that again!" she screamed. "You acted like a stupid teenager."

Neema's face had turned a bright red. Hot tears began to pour down her cheeks.

"Rick's children have more manners than you do... and they're smarter!"

Neema began to beat her fists on Phillip's chest. Although Neema was not really hurting him, her sudden rage and sobbing totally bewildered him. To make matters worse, his father appeared at the top of the stairs. He was visibly upset at the commotion.

"What's going on?" George demanded.

With that, Neema turned and rushed for the stairs. Half way up, she turned and shouted at her brother. "Phillip.... grow up!"

Phillip, still bewildered, turned to Lydia. But she was no help.

"Sometimes you can be such a moron," she sputtered.
"But ... but.... " Phillip stammered.
Lydia looked at him with anger in her eyes.
"She's in love with him, you dope."
Then Lydia turned and went upstairs to join Neema for some girl talk.

George, sensing the whole thing was beyond comprehension, threw up his hands in mock surrender and went back into his bedroom.

Perplexed, Phillip tried to understand what had just happened. He looked at the man in the hall mirror. He was puzzled. A little lost. Then a mischievous smile crossed his face.

"She's in love with him!" he exclaimed.

***

After a terrible Christmas season, e-commerce revenue continued to plummet. Because of last November's banking fiasco, consumers were increasingly reluctant to make any credit or debit card transactions over the Internet. Several of the ISP's accounts were in financial trouble and by late February, three were forced to close their doors. The lost revenue took its toll on the ISP. New accounts – the ones that could pay their bills - were increasingly hard to find. America was unable to shake the problems of chronic recession. Bay Area news media told gory stories of unemployed people committing suicide. Theft, burglary and murders increased. Gangs brazenly competed for territory. Although Rick was determined to hold his team together, he was beginning to fear the worst for his little company.

***

It was a clear, cold, windy and bone chilling February day in Northern California. More snow had fallen in the hills that surround the Bay Area. Travel over the Route 17 summit between San Jose and Santa Cruz was described as treacherous. Phillip burst through the door of the Santa Clara Internet Service company, accompanied by a blast of cold air that quickly chilled the office.

"Man, it's cold out there!" he exclaimed to no one in particular.

Phillip took off his leather coat and wool hat, rubbed his hands together to warm them up, and headed for the utility room where he found Antonio and Sarah who were making a fresh pot of coffee. Peter was at his desk, scanning the Internet for news when he found an announcement on Google from the Department of Public and Personal Safety. After he read it, he scowled and sat back in his chair.

"Phillip, come and take a look at this," he called into the utility room.

Antonio, Sarah and Phillip appeared at the utility room door and walked over to Peter's desk. Peter pointed to the text on the screen:

"The Department of Public and Personal Safety is pleased to announce the formation of a new agency to combat false and misleading information. The newly formed Department of Public Information will take over the news reporting responsibilities of the O'Brien Administration, the United States Congress, and all Federal agencies. In order to assure public access to news and information on a timely basis, and in an effort to encourage greater Federal information transparency, the Department of Public Information will actively encourage further consolidation of America's news and media companies. A common editorial policy will promote a more efficient distribution of information, and cause less confusion among voters."

Phillip sighed softly. "They've created a propaganda mill for politically correct thinking."

"The Department of Public and Personal Safety has also proposed we all carry a National Identification Card," Peter intoned in an almost inaudible voice. "And there is a move to make big corporations an extension of government police power."

"That's logical," Phillip added. " They already are being used to implement State economic and social policy."

Sarah looked worried. "Will these measures mean we have to be careful what we say in public?"

Peter and Phillip looked gravely at Sara and nodded in agreement.

"I don't think it's going to affect us much," Peter said. "But I'd better tell the boss about this when he comes in."

"Where is Rick?" asked Antonio.

"He's at a customer, probably trying to get us paid," Phillip responded. "I sure hope he's successful."

***

By April the weather was much improved. Although the rain swept hills were shrouded in low clouds almost every day, valley temperatures were in the low forties at night and occasionally climbed into the low sixties by mid-afternoon. Rick was complaining about the ISP's heating bill because it had become a major expense item for the business.

As the Department of Public Information had promised, government reports were reasonably uniform from one news service to the other. Party politicians hailed the agency's progress as beneficial to national welfare. Only radical Internet opposition sites dared publish unapproved information.

In March it had been reported that President Michael John O'Brien was ill and confined to bed. Proper notices of respect and best wishes for a swift recovery had been issued by all of the primary government agencies. In order to protect his privacy, the news wires published little about President O'Brien's health. It was rumored, and then officially denied, he had some kind of heart condition. His wife, and now Vice President Mary

Rose Chartres, began to appear more often in well choreographed news conferences and public events.

By mid-April, the news wires were reporting O'Brien's health had deteriorated. On April 24, it was announced he had passed away in his sleep. A week of mourning and respect was ordered by Mary Rose. Flags flew at half mast. The funeral was a very formal affair.

Then in May Internet buzz began to speculate on the real cause of O'Brien's death. It was rumored he had been murdered. Mary Rose Chartres issued a vehement denial and condemned Internet radicals for causing so much confusion.

***

As had become his custom, Peter scanned the Internet for news and information every morning during his coffee break. By late May, speculation and rumors about O'Brien's death had reached a fever pitch. Many sites published reports that Mary Rose had engineered a conspiracy to murder her husband so she could become President. Few doubted this woman's ambition. She was known for her outbursts of irrational and vindictive remarks.

On this particular May morning, Peter saw another item that shocked him. Almost as an aside in a news conference, the Public Relations Officer of the Department of Public Information casually announced the Federal Government, in an attempt to quell the spread of unauthorized and vicious information, was going to take over the Internet. Strict rules of access and use would be imposed on American users. All American ISPs and Internet communication companies would become Federally Chartered Government Sponsored Enterprises. Internet users would all be moved to the National Internet Service.

Peter jumped out of his chair and ran to find Rick. He found him with John and Phillip.

"Do you know what the government is going to do to us?" he asked breathlessly.

The three men looked up in amusement. Peter was so excited, his face had turned red and he was out of breath. This was a very rare display of emotion for a man who usually had an almost serene demeanor.

"No," responded Rick. "What are they up to now?"

"THEY!" Peter almost shouted, "are going to take us over. WE are going to become a Government Sponsored Enterprise."

The three men were dumbfounded by Peter's announcement.

"How can they do that?" Phillip retorted.

"Why?" Rick asked with a puzzled look on his face.

Peter didn't have an answer for either question. Instead, he motioned the three men over to his computer screen to read the announcement for themselves. After they had done so, Rick looked dejected, beaten, a man who suddenly realized he had lost everything.

"Well, I suppose that will help with payroll," he said with a lame attempt at gallows humor.

***

By mid-July the weather was delightfully warm. Fog blocked the rays of the sun almost every day until late morning, cooling the valley. Occasional rainstorms would rush through the area as they headed up the delta to Sacramento. Although many farmers groused the rain ruined their summer crops, most people were just glad the winds and freezing temperatures of winter had been replaced by shirtsleeve weather.

Rick still came to work at least five days a week. But he had no energy. Rick knew – everybody at his little company knew – that the ISP's days were numbered. Antonio and Sarah planned to apply for a new job with the GSE that took over the Santa Clara Internet Service Company's accounts. Phillip, John, James and Peter were not as sure of their plans. Everything seemed to be unsettled. Insecure. It was therefore a surprise to all when Congresswoman Belle Gunness called and told Rick she would be in to see him the next week. Rick was puzzled. He could not figure out why she would have any interest in his business. But he made the requested appointment.

When she came, Lydia announced the congresswoman's arrival, and ushered her into Rick's office. He stood up to greet her, hand extended to shake her hand. She refused to acknowledge his gesture and sat down with a self-important thump on the easy chair.

"I see you have a nice little business here," she said. "I've heard good things about you and your people."

"Thank you for the compliment," Rick said warily. "How can we help you?"

Rick sat down. He felt uneasy. Belle was a large woman, maybe as tall as he was, and she probably outweighed him. Her manner raised a red flag. *"Better be cautious. She wants something."*

Belle came right to the point. "As you undoubtedly know, the Federal Government has decided to take over all of America's Internet companies. The Department of Public and Personal Safety has given the job of implementation to the Department of Public Information. They are converting existing Internet companies into Government Sponsored Enterprises as we speak. Since they started with the large suppliers, little businesses like yours will not be targeted until later this fall."

Belle stopped to let her words sink in. She looked at Rick disdainfully, as though he were not worthy of her time. She continued: "If it's decided to convert your business to a GSE, then you can stay and retain all your employees. You will all become government employees with benefits and pay suitable for your civil service grade."

Rick knew what that meant. A pay cut. For everyone. The GSE's paid lousy wages. Barely above poverty. Belle seemed to know what he was thinking.

"We can not allow anyone to take an unfair share of America's wealth. Equal compensation for equal work is the rule, and managers...." Belle stopped and stared at Rick with obvious scorn. "Managers can not expect to receive excessive compensation."

Although Rick had expected this speech, he was still unprepared for the incredibly cruel presentation. Anger began to well in his chest and gut. This last month he had cut his own pay to the minimum – just enough to pay the rent and to buy food – in order to have enough money to meet payroll. Sacrifice. Hard work. This woman could care less. To her everyone was a peon. People were supposed to be manipulated by elitist government politicians. And what did they want? Political power and money. Insider privilege. Rick was disgusted with it all. But he wisely held his tongue. Rick tried to look inquisitive, friendly and perhaps a bit meek. What did this woman want? "*She didn't have to come here to tell me this,*" he thought. "*She could have sent a government lackey to give me the bad news.*"

Again Belle didn't waste words. "I can fix it so you can keep your business. Even all your employees."

She stopped and looked intently at Rick, waiting for him to respond.

"And how could you do that?"

A very faint smile crossed Belle's face. "I have friends... people who will cooperate with me. You don't have to know any more."

Belle thrust her chin up with a look of domination. She was, Rick decided, a thoroughly nasty human being. And she was lying. Belle Gunness was a "freshman" member of Congress. New to the job. At this point she didn't know anything or anyone. She could not be of any help even if she were an honest person. Rick gave Belle a serious, almost hostile look.

"And why would you be willing to help us?"

"It's called campaign money. I have to pay my bills from the last election. Running for Congress costs money, you know."

Rick grunted his agreement. He spoke slowly and carefully.

"And how much of a campaign contribution would you expect from us?"

Belle sensed a victory. She smiled condescendingly at Rick.

"I'll have my office call you with the figure after my accountant has gone over your books. We should be able to reach a suitable agreement."

Rick glowered at the woman. He again spoke slowly and carefully.

"I will not pay a penny. Not to you. Not to your party. Not to your campaign. And do you know why? Because you are a crook. This is extortion. And God help us, I think what you have just done is still illegal in America." Rick stood up, as tall as he could. "I'll have Lydia show you the door."

Rick called Lydia into his office. Lydia, being Lydia, had heard almost all of the conversation by positioning her chair just outside the office door.

And Lydia, being Lydia, was prepared to strong arm Belle out the door if she had to.

Belle got up. Her being was enveloped in hatred. Here eyes narrowed. "You'll be sorry."

She brushed Lydia's arm away from her and stormed out the front door. Lydia came back into the office and smiled at Rick.

"I'm proud of you."

***

True to his word, Rick continued to make the increasingly arduous trip from Santa Clara to Davis 3 or 4 weekends a month. Neema would pick him up and drive him to Winters. If the children were not engaged in a school or community activity, she would bring them with her to the railroad station. Neema always managed to make the trip to Davis an adventure for Ramon. "We are going to see a train!" she would exclaim. Ramon loved the big engines and shiny rail cars. The conductors got to know him and would take the time to say hello. Ramon was thrilled. Although Adonica and Serafina were more blasé about going to pick up their father, they were always eager to see him.

Rick was grateful for the unlimited love and attention this woman showered on his children. She seemed to be able to turn each trip to Winters into a family outing. But after the bribery incident with Belle Gunness, he knew his company was existing on borrowed time.

***

When he went up to Winters the second week of August, he vowed to have a discussion with Neema about his clouded future. The train ride from Santa Clara had been a grueling experience. The air conditioning didn't work, the crowded cars were dirty, and the train – as usual – was late. Still, it was the only practical way for Rick to make the trip to see his children. Gasoline shortages and government regulation limited the use of personal vehicles. His little electric car could not go that far on one charge, and Rick – like many of his peers – had decided a gasoline vehicle was out of the question. Neema still had her old gasoline powered Honda CR-V, but her trips were limited by the availability of rationed gasoline. Somehow she managed to save up enough credits to buy the gasoline she needed to make the short trip to Davis and back each time Rick came up for a visit. Rick often wondered how long she would be able to keep up this routine.

Nevertheless, when the train finally shuddered to a stop in Davis, there was Neema with Ramon and Serafina on the platform. Ramon, who was by now an active 6 year old, immediately sought out the friendly conductor. Serafina ran to give her father a lingering hug. Rick shook Neema's hand, and gave her a little kiss on the cheek. Serafina smiled with unrestrained happiness. As far as she was concerned, she had a loving mother and a gallant father.

Neema, however, was troubled. There was something bothering Rick. Her brother had told her about the bribery incident. In a later call, Lydia had added the details about the precarious state of the business. So she put a question to Rick.

"Do we need to talk?"

"Yes. I'm afraid so. Things don't look good. I think the Department of Public Information will shut down our company as soon as they get around to it.... Maybe tonight we can spend some time alone.... We can take a walk."

Neema squeezed his hand as though to assure him. Then they collected Ramon and started toward the railroad station parking lot.

"Where's Adonica?" asked Rick.

"She's at the dentist!" chirped Serafina. "Adonica has a bad tooth. They have to fill it with magic cement."

Rick looked at Neema for a better explanation.

"I took her in for a checkup. The dentist found a cavity. Abigail took her to the dentist this afternoon to get it fixed. She should be home by the time we get there."

"Is she OK?"

"Sure. No problem. It's just one of those things we all go through."

"How do I pay the dentist?"

Neema took his arm and gave it an affectionate squeeze. "Don't worry, I've already arranged to pay her."

"The Dentist?"

"Yes."

Rick let her explanation go for the moment. He wanted to focus on having a lively conversation with Ramon and Serafina. His son had a new toy truck that Josue made for him from scraps of wood. Serafina bubbled on about the coming school year. She would be going into sixth grade and in another year, she told Rick, she would be a big girl.

"Do you need anything for school?" asked Rick

"No. Neema and I went to the store with Ramon. He's going to be in the first grade."

"And what about Adonica?"

"Grandma took her to the store. She's so picky. Thinks she's special just because she's going to be in High School."

Rick looked at Neema, who was driving. "Do I detect a little jealousy?"

"It comes and goes. Sibling rivalry. It comes with having children."

She smiled at her thoughts. "Actually they are very close .... most of the time."

"I forgot about all this school preparation stuff. I guess I owe you a bunch of money to cover the cost."

"No. .... You don't owe me a thing," Neema responded. A serious look crossed her face. "We can talk about it later."

Rick was puzzled, then worried. Had he sent enough money to Mari and Josue to cover the cost of raising his children? And what was Neema doing?

Neema steered the CR-V into his parent's driveway. The little farm had not changed much. Same fields of feed, a big garden, and a big old barn. It was home. Only the house had changed. The new wing Josue built for his grandchildren dwarfed the original structure. Three bedrooms, a bathroom, a family room, and a sunroom where Mari could fuss with her plants.

The front door was open, as usual. Anyone could walk right in. But that was Josue and Mari. Always open and friendly. As they got out of the CR-V, Mari appeared in the doorway. Ramon and Serafina ran up to give her a hug and then rushed by her into the house. Rick looked at his mother, as though appraising her total being. She was a serene, confident, compassionate woman. In his eyes, still lovely at sixty one.

"Where's Dad?" Rick asked.

"He's still at work. There's plenty to do during the summer. Always something breaking. Farming this soil is tough on the machines."

Rick nodded in agreement. He would see his father later.

"How's Adonica doing?"

"A bit woozy from the Novocain. I gave her some aspirin. She's in her bedroom. You should go in and say hello."

Rick gave his mother a little kiss on the cheek, and walked into the house to find his daughter. After he left, Mari turned to Neema.

"Have you told him yet?" Mari asked.

"Not yet. We need to spend some time together."

"Land sakes, Neema. It's about time he knows how you feel."

***

August is normally hot in Winters. The winds that blow south through the valley only serve to bring hot air from miles of semi arid plain. When they blow north, the air is sometimes heavy with moisture from the delta. It was one of the warm, sticky kind of nights when Neema picked up Rick at his parent's house. She wore a loose-fitting dress to help wick away her perspiration. Rick had on shorts and a t-shirt. It was, she decided, a bad night to have a serious discussion. The heat would make them both uncomfortable. But it happened anyway.

It started as they walked over Putah Creek on the old Vaca Valley Railroad trestle. They stopped in the middle to look down at the water as it slowly eddied and swirled under the bridge. Neither wanted an argument. Not tonight. Especially Rick, he had something to say.

"Let's talk about money .... I don't want you to be spending your money on the children. They're my responsibility and ...."

Neema interrupted. "And they are my responsibility now. Just as much as you."

Rick was taken back by her comment. "How do you figure that?"

"You entrusted them to your parents. And they are doing a great job. Adonica is doing very well in school. Serafina is a sweet little girl, and Roman is all boy. It should be just as you want."

"Yes. But ...."

Neema interrupted him again. "And you also entrusted your children to me. Haven't I done a good job?"

"Of course. You're a jewel. A princess. A good .... mother," Rick stammered out the word. He was bewildered. Rick suddenly realized Neema had become his children's mother.

"But what about the money?" He took Neema's hand and turned her so she had to face him.

"I can't ask you to spend your money on my responsibility."

"Yes you can. .... and I will," Neema retorted.

"But wait just a minute ...."

Neema put her fingers on his lips, as she had done before. Rick knew it would be wise to shut up. She smiled gently at him, very confident of herself.

"My husband was a drunk when he died. But he was a rich drunk. He made his money playing stock market futures contracts. He used to boast how good he was. Actually, I think he had it wired for insider information. But now we shall never know how he did it. .... The point is, when he died, he left me everything. .... I have money, Rick. .... and if I choose to spend it on three little people I love, that's my business."

Rick was stunned. He was - unusual for him - at a loss for words. Then he shrugged his shoulders in resignation. Neema was relieved. She had made her little speech. But what happened next was a total surprise. Rick turned to her.... standing in the middle of the old Vaca Valley Railroad trestle... and enveloped her in his arms. His husky voice wavered just a bit.

"I love you Neema."

Tears came to her face. Tears of joy and relief. The words she wanted to hear. For so long. Neema threw her arms around his neck. They embraced in a very long and passionate kiss. Two men jogged passed them and smiled at their embrace. A woman jogger, pushing a three wheeled baby stroller, trotted by them going in the opposite direction. She too smiled at the lovers.

It was, all things considered, a wonderful evening.

***

The winds and chill of fall swept across the valley in October. No more shirt sleeve weather for this year. The weatherman tried to be helpful. "Another early winter," he predicted. Rick knew he was right. Each winter seemed to be colder than the last. The dreary gray of October would last until April. Maybe later. The planting season was getting shorter. No one had a credible explanation for the climate change. But it was undeniable.

Perhaps the only good thing was the rain. In the past the valley had usually dried out by April. Little rain would fall until the next October. Now it seemed to rain almost every week. Mostly showers that seemed to come in with the fog. There was no shortage of water.

Rick had been expecting the worst to happen. It was only a matter of time. And then in the early morning of October 14th, it did. As he pulled into the parking lot of his ISP, Rick saw three men and one woman standing at the door of his company. One was a cop from the county. The woman looked like a lawyer. The other two men, he decided, were flunkies.

He was right. The woman was a lawyer from the Department of Public Information. She approached Rick as he walked up the steps to the building.

"Mr. Vasquez?" she asked. "Mr. Ricardo Juan Sanchez Vasquez?"

Rick nodded. The two flunkies bared his way to the door.

"I have an order for you to turn over your business to the National Internet Service."

Rick knew it was useless to resist. That's what the cop was for. If he laid a hand on the woman, or either of the two men, he would be arrested for assault. Rick knew other small business owners had tried to resist. One could hardly blame them. All their hard work, all their income, it was all gone in a moment. But resistance was useless. Protestors were given a mock trial. They were always guilty. Then came public derision. The protestor would be sentenced to prison or maybe a "re-education camp". The carefully controlled media always scorned anyone who dared to complain about government policy.

Rick looked at the woman inquisitively. "What do you want me to do?"

"Mr. Bird," she pointed to one of the flunkies, "is an auditor. He will value your company. Mr. Esposito is a software expert. He will start the process of shifting your accounts to the NIS. All we need from you is your complete cooperation."

The anger began to well in his chest. His muscles tensed. Rick felt the same frustration and rage he had experienced when the Congresswoman asked for a bribe. The lawyer saw his anger. She had seen it many times before. She didn't care. Get this guy out of the way so they could close down his business. That's what she did. Day after day. It was a monotonous job.

Rick looked at her with obvious disgust. "I'll show you what you need to look at. After that, you're on your own."

The cop stepped forward as though to intervene. But the lawyer waved him away. "OK. ... Let's go inside."

After they entered the ISP, Rick saw Peter. Then he saw Phillip and Lydia. In a surreal fog of recognition, James, John, Sarah and Antonio came to him. Sarah was weeping. Lydia looked like she wanted to throw a punch. Rick took her hand and squeezed it. "Not now."

The handover was mercifully quick. Everyone was told to clean out their desks and to leave the building. They stumbled through the exercise of cleaning out their desks. Then they reluctantly left the building, one by one. Rick was the last one to leave the ISP. As he walked away from the building, Rick turned and looked with sorrow at the faded sign "Santa Clara Internet Service". He had shared good times and tough times with these people. His team had worked together to build a business. They shared a certain pride in their accomplishments.

Now they had nothing. No job. No pride. Nothing.

Rick turned, walked to his little electric car, and got in. He turned the start key. The charge needle crept slowly into the yellow zone.

Rick uttered a single word, "Damn."

Chapter 4   Gift

Although she was on the long end of her 74th year, Abigail Mitchell could have passed for a woman of 60. "It's in my genes," she was fond of joking. Of course her continuing youthful appearance was not lost on George, who both loved and depended on his wife of more than 50 years. They had a wonderfully affectionate relationship.

When the Department of Public Information closed down the Santa Clara ISP, they knew Rick would soon be in financial trouble. His plight was the subject of their conversation at breakfast in late October. George put down his coffee cup, pushed away from the table, and folded his hands in his lap.

"So OK...... What's next for Rick?"

"I just don't know," Abigail responded. "He has been mostly quiet about it all.... He has to find something else to do."

"Rick should be damn angry. He put his heart and soul into that company. Assembled a team of good people. I don't think it was ever a booming success.... financially. But it was his.... No... It was theirs. That business belonged to all of them. That's what Lydia says. Rick was the leader of a team. They were in it together."

"And now it's gone," Abigail interjected.

"He should be furious," George fumed. "There's plenty of small business owners who resisted .... even tried to keep the NSS out of their building."

"Yes, ... and they all lost. Branded as terrorists by the Department of Public Information."

"Damned propaganda machine. Everything is orchestrated to make the government look good....... There's talk of a revolution, you know."

"Hush, George. You can be arrested for even mentioning that word."

George was clearly upset. "To think we voted for these people. We thought they would fix all the problems in Washington ... and Sacramento. And now what do we have?"

"Fuel shortages, high prices and no jobs," Abigail responded with a vigor that surprised her.

"And a government that closes down small businesses, Abigail. They've ruined our economy."

"Now George, they are just trying to make sure all Americans have an equal share of the wealth." Abigail smiled. But her heart was full of remorse. Millions of Americans were out of work. The government controlled all the jobs. Things were getting steadily worse.

George was still grumpy. "What really irritates me is the constant spying. I can't go anywhere without being monitored. It's like they want to be in my pants all the time."

Abigail ignored his complaint. Her eyes wandered wistfully over the kitchen and through the window to her garden. *"How things have changed,"* she thought.

"But ... what do you think will happen to Rick?" she asked. "And what about Neema?"

George frowned. "Haven't they consummated their relationship yet?"

"I don't think so."

"Well .. what's holding them up? He's OK, isn't he?"

"Neema says he is a gentle man, very thoughtful, compassionate ... sometimes even spiritual."

George looked quizzically at his wife. He didn't understand the relationship between Neema and Rick. But she seemed to be very devoted to him and his kids.

"Listen, I like Rick. .... But Neema seems to be in love with a man who will soon be broke and hasn't got enough hormones to ....."

"George!" Abigail interjected. "That's enough!"

George knew he better stop. His wife was getting angry with him. George decided to let nature take its course. Neema and Rick would eventually get it together. Hopefully. Then he had an idea.

"How about we give them our house for a weekend? ... We could go into Davis and ..."

"George!"

And that ended the conversation.

***

In November, they held a wake for the ISP. Rick invited them to come to his apartment in Santa Clara. Everyone was there. And everyone was out of work. There was a little booze, some wine, but mostly they just wanted to talk. Lydia, ever assertive, told them she had been turned down for three jobs. That started the conversation in earnest. Peter related his job hunting misadventures. Sarah, Antonio, James and John all had similar stories to tell. One failure after another. Because Phillip and Rick had not started a job search, they could only listen with a sense of doom to the dreary conversation. Then Lydia mentioned something about her last interview that got everyone's attention.

"I don't know what was going on," she began. "But my last interview was for a government job. Things were going pretty well until the interviewer looked at the profile he had from the NSS. Then he seemed to freeze, looked warily at me, and said the interview was over."

"Do you think there was something in the file that sabotaged your interview?" Peter asked.

"I don't know. Maybe I should have demanded a copy to review."

Sarah looked puzzled. "The same thing happened to me at both interviews. We were getting along OK until the interviewer looked at my NSS profile."

"Can we get a copy of our profile?" Peter asked.

Lydia nodded. "They have to give you one if you request it. It's the law."

"Then OK. Let's all request a copy the next time we apply for employment," Peter said. "Then let's compare notes."

Antonio suddenly stood up. "Wait a minute. I have mine in my backpack. The interviewer gave it to me. I remember her saying I should look it over."

Antonio picked up his frayed and tattered backpack, rummaged around in it for a moment, and then produced a single sheet of paper. He shared it with Peter and Lydia. After they had read it over, all three shook their heads.

"I can't see any problem," Peter said.

Rick spoke up. "May I look at it, please?"

Antonio handed him the profile. Rick looked intently at each entry. Toward the bottom there was an employment code tagged with a "U". Rick looked up at Peter.

"What does this mean?"

Peter looked puzzled. "I don't know. It appears to be some sort of score or ranking. I don't know who puts it there or how it's generated."

Antonio joined the conversation. "I think I could ask the woman who interviewed me. She seemed to want to be helpful."

Peter frowned. "Call her. She should still be at work. See if she will tell you."

Antonio took the paper from Peter and flipped open his cell phone. They were all tense with anticipation as they waited for the interviewer to answer. After four rings, a female voice answered. "Human Resources. This is Jennifer."

Antonio introduced himself, thanked Jennifer for the interview, and then asked if she knew the meaning of the employment codes on the NSS profile. The woman hesitated before giving him a response.

"I don't think I should do that. Divulging that information could get me into trouble."

Antonio tried to persuade Jennifer to help him, but she remained unwilling to cooperate. Then she asked him a question.

"Where are you now?"

Antonio started to give her the address of the apartment complex where Rick lived, but suddenly stopped.

"Thank you for trying to help me, goodbye." And with that, he pressed the stop button on his cell phone.

"Why did you do that?" Lydia demanded.

"I don't really know. Something weird was happening. I had the feeling she knew the call was being monitored."

Resigned to the loss of information and suspicious of the call, they all sat down again. Peter, however, was undeterred.

"John, how about the Internet. Do you think you can find a source for this information?"

John nodded, and went over to pick up his lap top. He instantly made a WiFi connection and began to furiously type a string of commands. Rick groaned. He didn't like what was happening. Not at all. Then John exclaimed with great satisfaction "I'm in!"

It took a few more minutes to search for the right files, and pull up a list of employment codes. He stared at the screen, dumbfounded by what he saw.

"They have a code that tells anyone who uses this information whether or not the NSS approves of their employment. A code of U means that person is unacceptable to the government because they may be a terrorist or a criminal."

Everyone was shocked at the revelation. Then the confusion gave way to anger. Everyone was wondering the same thing. How did this happen?

Rick began to sense the situation. He spoke up. "Antonio. That woman. Jennifer. She was afraid to speak to you. In a different circumstance, she would have helped you. Next week, try to see if you can contact her outside her building. Maybe she will talk to you there."

Just then, John gave out a very loud "Uh Oh."

Rick was alarmed by the look of fear on John's face. "What's the matter!"

"The NSS is trying to track me." He began to type furiously on the keyboard. "I'd better get lost."

Everyone else in the room stared at John with great apprehension. They would all be arrested if he was unsuccessful. In a moment, John sighed "Thank god," and closed his laptop. Everyone breathed a little easier.

Rick spoke again. "John. Phillip. Can we alter those records? Could we put in a good code to replace the 'U' that's there now?"

Phillip and John looked at each other. Questioning.

"We can try," said Phillip. "Antonio, we need to know what that woman – Jennifer – can tell us about the codes and how they get there. Maybe we can submit a new form that will alter the NSS record without them becoming aware of what we are doing."

Antonio nodded. It would be dangerous. If they were caught, they would all be arrested. But Antonio decided he had no choice. As long as the NSS profile contained damaging information, he could not get a job. Nor could anyone else.

**

Rick was particularly upset about the closure of the ISP, and the tragic consequences for his employees. They had been a team, and he wanted desperately to bring them together again. Rick was tempted to let his emotions overcome his common sense. He had a recurring dream where he planted a bomb at NSS headquarters and killed all the agents. But he knew that would only get him into more trouble than he could handle, and if he was in jail, the children would suffer the consequences – Neema or no Neema.

Although Rosalinda never appeared again, he could sense her spirit. She was, he decided, never far away from him or the children. Her presence had given him increased confidence. In his prayers he often talked about the children and the interaction with a spiritual being gave him inner strength. But as time went on, he began to feel guilty about his growing affection for Neema. Rick was falling in love with her. She was fulfilling his need for an erotic attraction, and she was definitely assuming the role of mother for his children.

As it turned out, Rosalinda solved that dilemma when she appeared to him one more time. It was late November. Thanksgiving. He was packing his bag for a trip to Winters when Rick suddenly felt lightheaded. He sat down on the bed to clear his head. But his condition did not improve. He could not focus his eyes. Everything was hazy – like a dream. And then into his dream state came a figure. He immediately detected the scent of lilac perfume. The petite figure that appeared before him was definitely Rosalinda.

"My task is done," she said. "You don't need me anymore."

Rick felt incredibly guilty. He was uneasy. He worried his thoughts about Neema were making him unfaithful. Rosalinda understood his conflict.

"There are things you need in the physical universe," she said. "One of them is a person to love, a person you can touch and feel. That's perfectly understandable. The children also need to experience the physical affection of a woman who can be their mother. God has provided you with a perfect solution. Neema will be a good mother and the wife you so desperately need. Go to her... Go to her with my blessing."

And then she disappeared. Rick's vision slowly began to clear. Although he continued to feel lightheaded, he knew he had the answer to his conflict. Rosalinda had just performed the ultimate act of love.

***

Thanksgiving is a time for families, friends, animated conversations, quiet talks, a fire in the wood stove, the wonderful smell of Thanksgiving dinner, and demonstrations of affection. For Rick, Thanksgiving with Mari and Josue had always been a day of joy and sharing. Before dinner, Josue would always give thanks for the blessings they shared.

Despite the empty feeling in the pit of his stomach, and the incessant subconscious anger that was throbbing away in his thoughts, Rick was determined to ignore the loss of his business. He wanted to create a loving affectionate experience for Adonica, Serafina and Ramon. He wanted to be - needed to be - close to his parents - and Neema.

When Mari opened the door of the kitchen stove, the unmistakable smell of turkey wafted through the kitchen and into the dining room. Adonica and Ramon ran excitedly into the kitchen to inspect the steaming hot bird that almost overflowed the cooking pan.

Rick heard the doorbell and got up to see who had come for a visit. It was Neema, looking very attractive in her light brown fuzzy sweater and dark brown skirt. And she was wearing that sensuous perfume. Rick was instantly beguiled by her appearance. He gave her a gentle kiss on the lips before he led her into the living room. Serafina came over and gave Neema a long affectionate hug. Josue, Mari, Adonica and Ramon crowded into the kitchen doorway, all talking at once, greeting Neema with arms outstretched. More hugs all around. Then Neema disappeared into the kitchen to help Mari with the turkey.

Josue announced he would say grace. Just as he had always done for many years. After everyone was seated at the long dining room table, he had them join hands. Josue then gave the blessing:

"Father. Bless this food to our use and us to thy service. On this day of thanks, let us dwell on those things that are good in our life, and put from our minds the problems of yesterday."

Everyone murmured, "Amen."

Josue surveyed the table. He saw a wonderful family.

"*There is love in this house and that is good*," he decided.

Then he looked at his son. Rick seemed to be very relaxed, content to be with Neema. Josue caught Rick looking at Neema's sweater. He chuckled to himself.

"*Neema has made her point*," he thought. "*And why not. Our families have been friends for almost 40 years. Neema is as much a part of our family as Rick.*"

Josue picked up a plate of turkey, took two pieces for himself, and passed it on to his wife.

"*Leave it to God to heal all wounds and bring peace to a battered soul.*"

The room was soon silent. Seven hungry people had all they could eat, and eat they did. After he had cleaned his plate, Neema helped Ramon with more turkey and vegetables. Serafina, usually a dainty eater, took only a small portion of turkey. Adonica – who was a freshman in High School - said "No thank you" to seconds. Neema could only smile at Adonica's refusal.

"*History repeats itself*," she thought. "*I was just like that as a freshman. Always worried about my weight.*"

A little wine to make him drowsy, eating seconds of warm turkey and vegetables all topped with gravy and cranberry sauce, animated chatter with his children (all talking at once), a big piece of Mari's delicious pumpkin pie for dessert, and for a moment – at least for a little while – Rick could forget the cold outside world and its devastating disappointments. He was also acutely aware of Neema's soft fuzzy brown sweater. A soft, gentle, passion was growing within him. She caught him looking at her. Although Neema pretended to ignore him, the almost imperceptible smile that briefly crossed her face gave her thoughts away.

After dinner Neema and Rick helped Mari clear away the dishes. Then it took about a half hour to clean up the kitchen. Every so often. Mari would give Neema a knowing look.

"*What do these women have planned?*" Rick thought.

Neema was being very coy. She brushed up against him two or three times, as though to make sure Rick was aware of her presence. She needn't have worried. Rick was totally entranced. A captive of her feminine allure. Everything about her fascinated him.

Then they all retired to the living room. Adonica, Serafina and Ramon were quietly playing a card game. Mari and Josue relaxed in their overstuffed chairs, making idle conversation with Neema and Rick who were sitting on the couch. Rick was beginning to feel drowsy again when he felt Neema's warm hand on his.

"Could you take me home?" she asked. "I don't feel like driving tonight."

Startled by her request, Rick could only respond "Sure. When would you like to go?"

"As soon as I say goodbye to the children."

Neema stood up and went over to where the children were playing. She kissed each one on the cheek, and gave Serafina a special hug. Then she turned to Josue and Mari.

"Thank you for inviting me. It was a wonderful treat."

Mari and Josue stood up and smiled with obvious affection. Neema and Mari talked about their plans for the weekend. Rick chatted with his father about the Winter's High School football team. Then Neema gave Josue a little hug and a kiss on the cheek, hugged Mari goodbye, and turned to Rick.

"Let's go."

Rick said goodbye to his children and his parents, helped Neema with her coat, and opened the front door. They walked hand in hand down the walk to Neema's Honda, got in, fastened their seatbelts, and waved goodbye as the CR-V disappeared down the driveway.

"Is he coming back?" Josue asked Mari.

"I don't think so. …. Not tonight," Mari said with a mischievous smile.

***

Neema guided Rick toward town. But instead of turning onto the road where her parents lived, Neema directed him toward Main Street. Rick followed her directions, puzzled by her quiet but firm voice. He attempted to start a conversation.

"I really like Winters. Perhaps I should settle down here. Find a job. Raise my kids. Buy a farm....."

But Neema interrupted him.

"The traffic light is turning red."

Rick stopped the CR-V for the traffic light at Railroad Avenue. After it changed to green again, they continued past the Rotary Park Bandstand on East Main Street to an apartment complex. Neema motioned to a driveway on the right side of the street.

"Pull into that parking area."

Rick maneuvered her Honda into a parking space, and turned off the motor. Neema motioned for him to follow her. Unsure of what was happening, Rick walked behind Neema to an apartment building next to Putah Creek. She walked up to the door of an apartment, inserted her key, and opened it for Rick to enter. The room was inviting and warm. Neema turned on the lights, closed the door behind her, and turned the lock.

"Welcome to our new home," she said quietly.

***

Neema awoke with a wonderful feeling of peace and contentment. She stretched and yawned, pulled the bed sheets and blankets up around her shoulders, and rolled over to look at Rick. She propped herself up on one elbow so she could study his face.

"*He's a good man,*" she reasoned. "*People respect him. They want to believe in what he has to say..... Phillip would do anything for Rick. .... I'm a lucky woman.*"

Neema fell backward onto the soft silky sheets. Rick had been a considerate lover, carefully controlling his passion until she had been fulfilled. Neema began to fanaticize about the experience. The memories were erotic and exciting.

But Rick interrupted her thoughts. He rolled over, stretched and look at her. Neema gave him a warm, gentle kiss. Then Rick threw off his blankets and sheets.

"Nature calls," he said.

Neema carefully studied his buttocks as he walked into the bathroom. Then she lay back and began to fanaticize again about the warmth and sensuous joy of last night.

"*I wonder if he would like a little playful wrestling,*" she said to herself.

***

Father Giovanni looked up from the disorganized pile of papers spread out before him on his desk to see who was coming through the Neighborhood Community's big oak doors. It was Rick, walking toward him with a large box in his arms.

"Where should I put these toys," he asked.

Father Giovanni gave Rick a big smile. This man had worked tirelessly for several days, collecting food and clothing donations for his residents. Now he had talked some of the downtown merchants into giving them several boxes of toys for the NC's children. Father Giovanni motioned to a nearby doorway, and followed Rick into the room.

"Bless you, Rick. The children will be thrilled. It will be a great Christmas for all."

"Despite the lousy economy," Rick responded, "Most of the merchants in San Jose are still human. They care about our little community. One even told me he thinks he has a little boy that has taken refuge from the cold in his store. He hides in the racks during the day. The merchant plans to find him before closing tonight. If the little boy is homeless, the merchant will bring him down to be with us ... and give us a donation for the boy's care. I trust that's OK with you."

Father Giovanni nodded in assent. Somehow, they would find a way to make room. Several street children had already died from exposure. Night after night in the freezing cold. Most of them were malnourished and sick. Although he was doing everything he could to help them, Father Giovanni knew it was not enough. With a heavy heart, he turned to Rick.

"Come on. I'll buy you a cup of coffee. You must be freezing from the cold spell we're having."

Rick shook the snow from his coat as he took it off. San Jose had never seen this much snow in its history. People were talking about the possibility of some bigger storms in January. Hot coffee would be most welcome. Rick laid the coat over a chair.

"I'll take you up on that offer."

The two men made their way to the ramshackle kitchen. Father Giovanni poured two cups of steaming hot coffee and motioned Rick to a nearby table. After they had taken a few sips of their coffee, Father Giovanni looked at Rick intently and asked a question.

"You seem happier than at any time since you started coming to us. Something good has happened to your life. Am I right?"

Rick thought about the question for a moment.

"Yes. There are good things to be thankful for. I count my blessings each day."

"But still no job?"

"The NSS has labeled all our personal files with a vicious do not hire code. We can not be hired for a job... Me... All of my employees. With that code in the file, no one dares hire us. The NSS won't let us get a job."

"Why not," Father Giovanni asked in surprise.

"Because I would not give our local Congressional Representative a bribe."

"Belle Gunness?"

"Yes. I'm sure she is behind this. Otherwise the NSS had no reason to hurt us.... except ...."

"Except what?"

"Some months back. ...Remember the day the Internet was sabotaged with spam?"

"Sure. I couldn't send any e-mails."

"Well John and Phillip... two of my employees ... found a way to stop the spam. They worked with other ISPs to clean up the problem. Afterward, it became apparent someone was using the spam attack to hide their real purpose. During the confusion, crooks were looting money from consumer financial accounts."

"You did our country a service," said Father Giovanni. "The government should have given you a medal."

"Unless it was the government that was doing the looting," Rick said with a very serious expression on his face.

Father Giovanni was shocked at the allegation.

"Do you have any proof?"

"No. And even if we did. Who would we tell? The NSS is not going to do anything to embarrass another agency unless they are told to do so by a political leader. Neither will the Department of Justice, or the FBI. This was a classified job by some well connected insiders."

"You seem very positive."

"Maybe I'm wrong. But either Belle or the NSS took it upon themselves to screw us."

Father Giovanni was half inclined to believe Rick. He was having his own problems with Government corruption.

"How do you still smile? The National Health system bungled your wife's diagnosis. If they had been on the ball, she might still be alive."

Rick looked upset, but said nothing. Father Giovanni spoke more slowly.

"Then they shut down your business..... and .... now they won't let you get a job."

"That about sums it up," Rick responded glumly. "And there is nothing I can do about it."

"But you came here today with a smile."

Rick suddenly looked more relaxed. He leaned back in his seat and toyed with his cup.

"I have a woman in my life. A woman who loves me without reservation. .... I have three great kids. ... And two great parents and several nice people I can call friends.... including you .... I guess it's the people in my life that make all the difference..... And that is why I can still smile."

***

Phillip called Rick to invite him to an informal party in his apartment. When Rick arrived, he was surprised to see all of his former employees gathered in the living room. After greetings and handshakes all around, Phillip called everyone to pay attention. He had an announcement.

"After several days and nights of hard work, John figured out how to hack into the NSS personal files. He found a profile for each of us, and has altered the hiring code to something more appropriate than that dreaded "U" for unfit. We should be able to get jobs. We can pass the NSS screen for employment."

Everyone clapped and cheered with enthusiasm. Money was getting tight. They desperately needed to find work.

"There is more," Phillip continued. "Antonio has an announcement."

Antonio, somewhat embarrassed by all the sudden attention, stammered at first. But he finally found his voice.

"I was able to have a secret meeting with Jennifer, the woman in Human Resources we talked to the last time we were together. She has confirmed the codes have been changed on our personal profile files, and she agrees it was the NSS that marked us as unemployable."

"But who told the NSS to do that?" Lydia demanded.

"No one knows …. and I sure as hell don't dare to ask," Antonio responded.

Rick took the lead in the conversation. He questioned each person where they were looking for work and how things were looking.

Sarah already had a job.

"It's not much," she said. "But I can pay the rent and have a decent meal now and then."

Everyone was relieved. Then the conversation turned to Rick.

"Are you looking, Rick?" John asked.

"Not really. But with the NSS codes changed, I think I will start looking in earnest."

Phillip chuckled. "Rick has been preoccupied ….. with my sister!"

Everyone had a good natured laugh. The mood of the party changed to light hearted banter.

**

Because of his participation and volunteer work, Father Giovanni prevailed on Rick to join with the residents of the NC to celebrate Christmas Eve. When he walked through the big oak doors Rick was greeted with a rousing cheer. There were handshakes and a few affectionate hugs from men, women and children as Rick made his way to the table where Father Giovanni was seated. Rick was especially delighted to see the children were genuinely happy. Father Giovanni stood up and greeted Rick with a firm handshake.

"Tonight, we celebrate the birth of Christ," he said in a loud voice to everyone in the room. "And we have one more celebration."

Father Giovanni made a broad sweeping motion with his hand toward the piano player. She started to play a familiar theme. Everyone began to sing a very loud and somewhat boisterous rendition of Happy Birthday! It ended with:

"Happy Birthday Dear Rick, Happy Birthday to you!"

Rick was at once embarrassed by the attention and delighted with the honor. He smiled and waved to the throng gathered around the piano. His heart filled with joy. This was a moment he would remember.

Father Giovanni quickly found a knife to cut the birthday cake. After cutting a piece for Rick, he gave the knife to his assistant.

"Well Rick, another birthday." Father Giovanni paused for a moment. "You must be 39. Am I right?"

"Yes," Rick answered. "39 and still counting."

Several women busied themselves cutting the cake and dishing it out with scoops of ice-cream. The piano player launched vigorously into a series of Christmas carols. The singing, perhaps off-key from time to time, was nonetheless enthusiastic in both joy and warmth. Rick felt a tear or two well in his eyes as he surveyed the faces in the room. These people had nothing. Absolutely nothing. But they still had their faith, and it was powerful enough to sustain their outlook on life. It gave them the inner strength they needed to survive with a large measure of human dignity. The cloak of goodwill and love enveloped Rick. He could only wonder at the magnificent feeling it gave him.

Father Giovanni could see the expression on the face of this man he had known for only a short time, but who was definitely someone special. After making sure everyone was served and satisfied, Father Giovanni motioned Rick to a quiet area in the big dining room. He looked at his watch.

"Rick, you have only an hour before the train leaves for Davis. You need to get going."

Rick nodded in agreement. On the other hand, he dreaded going out into the frigid cold and howling wind. It would be a long walk to the San Jose railroad station. Once there, it would probably not be open. He would have to brave the raw cold on a wind swept platform until the train arrived. He shuddered at the thought.

"I'm not looking forward to this trip. But, I know I'll be glad to get there."

Father Giovanni smiled with great serenity and placed his hand over Rick's hand.

"When you first came here," he began. "You were both lost and angry. Your wife and family were your life. She was your woman. And you had lost her under questionable circumstances."

Rick nodded his agreement.

"But now," Father Giovanni continued, "I see a look of passion and determination in your eyes. God speed your success.... and Merry Christmas."

Father Giovanni stood up, shook Rick's hand, and turned away to administer the festivities of the evening. Rick pushed back his chair and went to look for his overcoat. One of the women residents helped him to sort through the pile of coats in the entry. She held it out for him.

"Thank you for your help..... Merry Christmas and God bless you," she whispered in his ear. Rick carefully took both her hands in his. He instantly experienced a surge of thoughts and images. She was bewildered by the loss of her home and the hunger of her children. He sensed her grief, felt her fear. This woman was afraid - uncertain - and very tired. She was desperately reaching out to him for help. Rick was unprepared for this show of deep emotion. He spoke the first words that came into his thoughts.

"May God give you the strength to endure."

He lightly squeezed her hands and turned again toward the big oak doors. Then he stopped, turned back to her, and took her right hand in both of his hands. He closed his eyes and prayed for a way to give her strength. Rick began to sense a flow of energy that swept from his whole being to the woman's hand. She began to smile. Wonder filled her eyes. The flow of energy continued to increase until it reached a climax and began to gradually subside. A genuine feeling of relief swept across her face. Rick let her hand go.

"Go. Give this strength to those who need it most."

Then he slowly opened the big oak doors and left.

***

As he battled his way through the cold and wind to the railroad station, his experience with the woman at the NC haunted him. His act had been impulsive. Yet he could not shake the wonder of the energy he felt when he touched her hand, or the fact he seemed to know what she was thinking. It had been a spiritual and a physical experience of great compassion. Helping her had given him a tremendous feeling of satisfaction. He began to wonder if he had some kind of gift. Then he shook his head.

"*It was very nice... what you did... But it won't happen again... It was a fluke... an accident.*"

But as he neared the railroad station, he realized his experience at the NC was something far greater than a mere coincidence. Something was happening to him. Something wonderful.

There were only three other people on the platform. They were all bundled up, hands stuffed in their pockets, plumes of moist air coming out of their mouths as they breathed. They looked at Rick warily, as though he might be a threat. But he smiled at them and looked down the track for the train. He continued to think about the meaning of his experience.

He had often been able to take a few moments of quiet time to pray. He was reaching out to a God he never knew. It was a curious experience. At first he was hesitant and insecure. He felt a little foolish, trying to connect with something he could not see. But after several sessions, he began to feel a greater sense of fulfillment. He discovered he could ask God questions. Then at night, perhaps in a dream, or the next morning as he was bathing, the answers would suddenly come to him. He also became aware that God – or something – was pushing him toward a greater religious experience.

Rick sighed with resignation. Somewhere in all this there was a purpose. He was destined to do something. Rick had no idea what it might be, but he was content to let it happen. He believed all would be revealed to him in good time.

***

As Rick expected, it was a miserable ride to Davis. The train was late, the heat was woefully inadequate, and the dirty rail car was littered with trash. He was desperately glad to see Neema at the station in Davis, and to his amazement she had all three of his children with her. Although sleepy, cold, and somewhat stiff from waiting in the CR-V, they ran across the platform to greet him. Rick hugged each one in turn, listened patiently to their happy chatter, and then stood up to give Neema a long hug and a warm kiss.

"Merry Christmas," she said in a soft voice. "I have a present for you."
"What is it?'
"You'll have to wait..... ."
Neema gave Rick a mischievous smile and took his hand. Rick took Adonica's hand as they walked across the wind swept parking lot to Neema's CR-V. Ramon and Serafina ran ahead to the car, each claiming to have reached it first.
"I got here first!" exclaimed Ramon.
"Did not!" shouted Serafina.
"Hush .. hush you two," Neema commanded. "You'll wake up Santa Claus."
Adonica and Serafina wrinkled up their noses at Neema's suggestion. Ramon looked uncertainly at Neema, as though he was trying to decide just where Santa Claus would be at that time of night.

***

Rick was happy to be home. Christmas day at his parent's house was one long celebration with plenty of food, laughter and love. The delightful smell of the fir tree, the warmth of the fire, and the soft sound of Christmas music penetrated into every corner of the house. They opened presents. Laughed together. Shared many happy comments. By eleven in the morning they had opened all the presents and removed every item from the children's stockings. Although it was unusually cold outside, Adonica, Serafina and Ramon insisted on going out to feed Josue's animals. After bundling up in warm coats and mittens, they hurried out the door and headed for the barn. That gave Rick a chance to talk with his father and Mari.

Josue was reassuring. Although the farm machinery business he worked for was struggling, Josue believed it would survive the chronic recession that was crushing America. Mari was spending one or two days a week helping the Mitchells with household chores. With that income, plus what Rick could contribute, they would be able to pay their bills.

These last thoughts bothered Rick. He had no income and his savings would not last much longer. He told Josue about his problems with the NSS and the personal file alteration John had been able to make. Although Josue was troubled by what he heard, Rick was able to assure him that it would be easier to find a job after the first of the year.

Their conversation was interrupted by three very cold children who bounded into the living room and ran to warm themselves by the wood stove. Rick looked solemnly at his mother and father.

"Let's keep this from them for as long as we can."

Mari affectionately squeezed his arm. "Of course, … as best we can."

***

Although Rick stayed with his parents until after New Year's day, he alternated nights with Neema and took her to a dinner dance on New Year's Eve. He helped his father with the chores each day, and had a glass of wine with him in the evening. Rick also drank copious quantities of Mari's coffee, and ate enough of her baking to gain three pounds. He happily spent many hours with his children. They played games on the computer, took short walks around the farm, and went downtown to see the lights.

Rick was also able to have several quiet conversations with his children. They obviously loved Neema and encouraged him to do the same. Ramon was the most direct.

"Why don't you get married?" he asked. The girls giggled. Rick became a bit red in the face from his embarrassment.

"Maybe I will. Do you think she'll have me?"

More giggles from the girls.

"Why not?" Ramon responded with great vigor.

***

On the Thursday morning before New Years Eve, Josue urged Rick to go next door for a visit with their neighbor, Micah. As a teenager, Rick had visited with Micah many times, listening to the man's wisdom with rapt attention. But he had not seen Micah for several years, and was a bit timid about barging in on him. Josue insisted. He even made a call to be sure Micah would be home. So Rick put on his overcoat, wool hat and leather gloves, bid his mother and father goodbye, and trudged the eighth mile to Micah's farmhouse.

"*When we were kids,*" he thought, "*Phillip and I would cut through the woods and get to Micah's house in no time. Now I have to walk the long way around. Kids have it easy.*"

In a few minutes he was at the door of Micah's old weathered farmhouse. Face flushed and feet numb from the cold, he knocked on the door. He could hear footsteps shuffling inside the house. Then the door opened and Rick found himself staring at the rumpled appearance of a gray haired old man.

"Good morning," Micah said in a firm voice. "Please come inside from the cold."

Rick was only to glad to be inside the farm house. He took off his hat, coat and gloves.

"We can put them on that chair," Micah said with a smile. "And then come on into the kitchen. I have the wood stove going." He chuckled softly. "Except I'm burning coal."

Although Rick had heard many people were burning coal to keep warm, this was the first house where he knew the owner. It was, of course, a breach of the clean air laws. But few towns enforced the code. For low income people, propane had become prohibitively expensive. The alternative was either to strip nearby forests for wood fires, or subsidize the use of propane. Since most towns or cities had only enough money for basic services, few had any propane allowance money. The use of coal as a replacement for propane, heating oil, and kerosene was increasing all over America. The Department of Public Information issued regular denials, claiming the use of coal for heating and cooking was isolated to a few rogue citizens. Although approved media outlets published the obligatory stories in support of the Department's reports, rumor had it that over 170 thousand American homes had switched to coal. There was a story, hotly denied by the Department of Public Information, that citizens in Boston had rioted when a train load of coal was held up by the NSS.

Once in the kitchen, Micah poured two cups of steaming hot coffee. He handed one to Rick and motioned him to a kitchen table chair. Rick took a cautious sip of the coffee, not wanting to burn his lips or tongue. Micah sat down across the kitchen table with his coffee cup in hand.

"I hear you have had a rough time these last few years. My sympathy for your loss and my condolences for your run in with the NSS."

"Where did you hear all that...."

"From your father. We talk from time to time. He worries about you.... just like any loving parent."

Rick cautiously acknowledged Micah's remarks, and took another sip of his coffee.

"It's true I have had a run of bad luck..... But my former employees will be OK. ... And I'm confident I will find something soon."

"In the meantime, you've been working with Father Giovanni at the Neighborhood Community in San Jose."

Micah took a long sip of his coffee, as though waiting for Rick to respond. But Rick said nothing. He merely shook his head in agreement.

Undeterred by the silence of his visitor, Micah continued with his thoughts.

"Father Giovanni is a good man... Honest... Honorable... A good manager... And very compassionate."

Micah sat back in the rickety kitchen chair, appraising his young visitor. "Is Father Giovanni a good teacher?"

"Yes.... I suppose he is." Although Rick had never thought of Father Giovanni as a teacher, he suddenly realized he had learned much for him. But Rick was puzzled.

"How do you know Father Giovanni?"

"We met some years ago," Micah responded. "We keep in touch. You might say we are in the same business."

Micah abruptly changed the subject.

"You and I have had many conversations over the years. Especially when you were a teenager. I enjoyed our talks. You always seemed genuinely eager to learn."

"I guess we did. You and Josue were good to me."

Rick thought of himself as being close to Micah, Josue and George Mitchell. These three men shaped his outlook on life. Then there was his mother Mari and Abigail Mitchell. He loved both women for their compassion, and it was Abigail who encouraged him to apply for San Jose State. He was lucky, he decided, to have grown up surrounded by people who really cared about him.

Then his mind wandered to the incident with the woman at the Neighborhood Community.

Micah looked intently at Rick. It was as though he knew what Rick was thinking.

"As you were leaving the NC for the railroad station in San Jose, you had an unusual experience with the woman who helped you find your coat."

"How did you know about that!" Rick exclaimed.

Micah responded with a quiet smile. "Someday, I will tell you.... But for now, I want to know how that experience made you feel."

Rick was bewildered by the revelation of his conversation with Micah. His curiosity aroused, he wanted to know how this gentle old man could have known about the incident. But he decided not to argue the point. There would be enough opportunity to question Micah later. Instead, he sat back in his chair, toyed with his now empty cup, and allowed his thoughts to concentrate on the incident with the woman at the NC.

"I felt a sudden urge to help her. Something deep within me wanted to connect with her in a spiritual way. I guess.... I guess I just said whatever words came to mind.... without much thought. The words just seemed to flow."

Micah seemed to understand what had happened. He spoke in a manner that conveyed both a deep sense of understanding and a spirit of unlimited compassion.

"Many people have the ability to sense what others around them are feeling. A good salesman will often be aware of your thoughts before you have fully formed them. A minister or priest soon learns how to sense human emotions. Mothers are often aware their children have gotten into a dangerous situation even though they are in the next room. A good detective can sense if you are telling the truth. Twins can sometimes sense what the other twin is feeling, even though they may be miles apart. The list of incidents where people are able to tap into the non-physical dimension goes on and on."

"But what does that have to do with me?" Rick asked.

"Think, Rick. When you touched that woman, took her by the hands, what did you feel?"

Rick responded with great care. "There was a connection. My mind and her thoughts. I experienced her pain, her fear, her desperation ...."

"You sensed what she was thinking?"

"Yes. And then, ... I don't know why... I took her hand, ... held it in my hands, ... and prayed."

Micah waited patiently for Rick to pull his thoughts together.

"And you prayed?"

Rick looked thoughtfully at Micah.

"I have never been one for prayer. Not since I was a little boy. But it just came to me."

"And then how did you feel."

"Relieved..... A sort of inner peace came over me. The woman... She seemed to be much happier."

"That's good, Rick." Micah placed his elbows on the table and looked intently at Rick.

"I've known you since you were a baby... Actually since the day you were born.... And I have always believed that one day you would have the experience you just shared with me. You have within you the ability to sense what others are thinking.... experiencing... their emotions.... happiness... pain... whether they are telling the truth or lying. It is a great gift many people have. But you... you are something special.... You have a gift beyond all others."

Micah leaned over the table and looked directly into Rick's eyes.

"Do not be afraid to use your gift... Use it wisely... Always to help others."

Rick was puzzled, almost afraid of what he had just heard. But, Micah did not stop.

"Rick. Look at me. You must learn to pray... with deep intellectual honesty and unlimited compassion... I know you can do it... You will do it. You have it within you to do a greater good for all the people you meet... and even those who only hear about you."

Rick was uneasy. *"This is crazy,"* he thought. *"Micah has always given me good advice. Been a good friend. But this .... is unbelievable."*

Without thinking, Rick blurted out a simple question. "Why me?"

A warm smile slowly brightened Micah's face. "Rick, you look to be a bit confused. I can not give you an answer to every question. There are some things you must discover for yourself. But you must do one thing for me.... for yourself."

"What's that?"

"Don't fight it. This gift you have. Learn to use it wisely. Never act in haste."

"How did you know I would have this... gift"

"I could see it in you when you first came to visit with me. You and Phillip. There has never been any doubt in my mind. It was just a matter of time. You would eventually discover your gift and the use of prayer to help others."

Rick was at a loss for words. He wanted to believe Micah. He respected this intelligent and philosophical man. Yet he was thoroughly bewildered by what he had heard.

"Can I get you another cup of coffee?" Micah asked.

Rick managed to smile. "No thank you.... I guess I've had enough coffee for today."

Rick slowly rose from the kitchen table, deep in thought. Micah got up, shuffled over to the chair where he had put Rick's coat, and picked it up. Micah held the coat for Rick as he put it on.

"You have a great gift, Rick. Use it wisely... and always use it to help others."

Rick turned and shook Micah's hand.

"You have always given me much to think about, Micah. But this conversation will take time to sort out."

Micah smiled broadly for the first time.

"I have faith in you Rick... Absolute faith."

***

January. Each work day was the same. Rick would get up in the morning, spend an hour or two making telephone calls to prospective employers, scanning the Internet for job openings, and preparing resumes to mail on his way to the NC. Then he would get into his little electric car to make the 15 minute drive from Santa Clara to the NC in San Jose. Even though it was a cold and uncomfortable ride, he was glad he had an electric car. On many mornings there were long lines of cars and trucks at the gasoline stations he passed. Because of oil shortages and refinery restrictions, gasoline and diesel fuel deliveries were often sporadic. In order to get a few gallons of precious fuel, drivers frequently had to compete with other drivers for a better position in a long line of cars and trucks. Tempers were short. Fights between drivers were common.

Despite reassuring words from federal and state politicians, the chronic recession dragged on and on. Day after day of ever higher prices and increasing unemployment. Jobs were not only scarce, but even if he was lucky enough to find one, Rick knew it would not pay much. That was the reality. Declining wages and higher prices. A sort of anguished desperation had settled over Santa Clara County.

Rick drove his little car into the NC parking lot and parked it as close to the entrance as possible. Icy cold air stung his face as soon as he opened the car door. Rick stumbled to the front of the vehicle, found the electric plug, and connected it to an outlet. Fingers numb from the effort, he stuffed his hands into the pockets of his overcoat as he walked the few steps to the entrance. He opened and closed the big oak doors as quickly as he could in order to conserve what little heat the NC was able to afford. Once inside, he immediately smelled the wonderfully sweet odor of freshly baked bread and hot coffee. Father Giovanni was stocking a wood stove in the kitchen with scraps of lumber. He looked up from his task as Rick approached.

"Good morning," Father Giovanni said with a smile. "I trust you had no problem with your morning commute."

"Rick looked at his watch. It was 10:30. "Not at this time of day. Most people are either at work or waiting in line for gasoline."

He shivered involuntarily, as though the energy of his shaking would somehow make him warmer. Rick took off his overcoat, moved closer to the hot stove, and shook hands with Father Giovanni. *"Here is a man of great compassion, a man who has a genuine interest in those about him,"* Rick thought.

"I'll do the honors," Father Giovanni said. He went over to the big stainless steel coffee urn and poured a cup of hot coffee for Rick. "Perhaps you can help me with the books..... I'm not very good at keeping records. .... or paying bills."

Rick took the cup from Father Giovanni. "Sure. Where are they?"

"In my office. Come, I'll show you."

Father Giovanni guided Rick into a tiny office. There were piles of paper stacked everywhere. Bills, order forms, receipts, shopping lists, files for each resident, bank statements, and an assortment of government notices.

"Can you do something with this mess?" he asked.

"I'll try," Rick said a bit bewildered by the mountain of paperwork. "But you have to promise I can come up for air once in awhile."

Father Giovanni flashed a broad grin, eyes sparkling. "I'm letting you have a look at our most inner secrets. Income. Expenses. Money. Profit and loss."

Then Father Giovanni began to chuckle. "Come to think of it..... mostly loss. I think we may have a few unpaid bills.... I used to have the time to keep it all straight. But not now. Too many people are coming to us for help."

Rick nodded and began to sort through the stacks of paper. The first thing to do was to organized the mountain of paper into stacks that he could then process. Father Giovanni, satisfied Rick would fix the paperwork, left the office to find the cook. It was time to prepare for lunch.

Rick busied himself with the seemingly endless piles of paperwork. He concentrated on the bills, making a list of unpaid balances by due date. Father Giovanni was right. The NC was seriously behind in its payments to vendors. Food and fuel were the most important. No one made a salary at the NC. In exchange for shelter, one man had assumed the duties of head cook, another did building maintenance, and still another took charge of cleaning. One woman made sure the children were fed, sent off to school and kept out of trouble. Another woman was in charge of the dining room. People working together. To stay alive.

At 12:30 Rick took a break to eat lunch with Father Giovanni. It was a simple meal of vegetable soup, fresh bread, and a cookie still hot from the oven. Father Giovanni looked expectantly at Rick.

"Anything interesting in all that paper?"

"Mostly routine stuff," Rick responded. "We could use a few more cash donations."

"Always," Father Giovanni responded with a gentle smile. "And the notices?"

Rick was disturbed by what he had read thus far. Federal, state and county bureaucrats had all sent notices to the Neighborhood Community, demanding the NC comply with government regulations. There were too many people in the building, it violated the fire code, and it was not zoned for residential use. The Department of Human Services objected to the provision of shelter and food to homeless children. The Department of Education was sure the children were not getting a government approved education. The EPA had warned Father Giovanni the NC could not use wood or coal for heat. The Department of Health was concerned about the cleanliness of the kitchen and the quality of food. The Department of Child Welfare wanted the NC to hire a social worker, a nurse, and a licensed care giver. The list of government notices went on and on. A total of eleven agencies, all wanting to put the NC out of business. None offered to be of any help to the desperately poor people who lived there. They were effectively demanding they all be turned out into the bitter cold of winter. Let them freeze to death. Just so long as the NC didn't break any government rules. That's all they cared about. Bureaucratic procedures. Oppressive rules. Filling out forms. Processing paper. Then using the police power of the State to force their will on these helpless people.

Rick was disgusted. Life was cruel enough. The State deliberately made things worse. He looked at Father Giovanni. "They have to justify their existence, these government bureaucrats..... They can be so arrogant, vindictive, and incredibly pompous .... Fortunately for us they are also lazy."

"Or they would have shut us down long ago," added Father Giovanni. "It is the way of government regulation.... Dream up ways to say no..... Create more restrictions.... Block innovation.... and strangle opportunity."

Father Giovanni sighed. "This is why America is mired in a chronic recession. No one is allowed to take the initiative. Everyone is subordinate to the State. But the State does not know how to create wealth for the people."

Rick was surprised at Father Giovanni's comments. This was the first time this man had said anything remotely critical of the government.

"Be careful, Father Giovanni," Rick joked half heartedly. "The Department of Public Information thought police will be after you."

The two men lapsed into a period of quiet thought. Rick was about to get up when the woman who managed the dining hall approached them. She shook Rick's hand with a smile and then turned to father Giovanni. They were soon engrossed in a discussion of tables and chairs. As they went off to work on the problem, Rick was aware that even with that brief encounter, he knew what the woman was thinking.... feeling. *"Her name is Clarise. She is very loyal... Devoted to her job... It gives her a sense of self-worth. And she adores Father Giovanni."*

Rick was not sure how to handle the thoughts that had come to him.

***

It rained almost every day in February. Cheerless gray clouds covered the Bay Area as they made their way to the Western foothills of the Sierra Mountains. Periodic showers of cold rain and gusty winds swept through Santa Clara. It was miserable, bone chilling weather. Few people were willing to venture out for any length of time. Nevertheless Rick was somewhat elated by the letter he received. A government agency wanted him to call for a job interview as a section manager. The letter described the position. All very formal. Grade so and so. Low pay, but a chance for advancement, plus a government health plan and a retirement plan that would be – as the letter described it – very generous. He made the requested call right away. The voice on the other end of the line, however, seemed to hesitate. She was not sure what to do. Rick patiently waited until another voice came on the line. A man asked Rick to verify who he was. A few more moments of hesitation. Then the man suggested he come to the agency office in Sunnyvale the following Friday. Happy to have a job interview at long last, Rick agreed with the time and place of the appointment.

But after he hung up, Rick was aware of an uneasy feeling that welled up from somewhere within his gut. The woman seemed to be afraid of the call, insecure, distant.... as though she did not want to be involved. Rick wondered if perhaps the man had a mysterious motive for making the appointment.

***

Rick was cleaning up the last of the disorganized NC paperwork when he heard a familiar voice coming from the dining room. It was Antonio. Smiling and elated, Rick immediately got up and walked out into the dining room to greet his former employee.

"Antonio! Welcome to our humble Neighborhood Community."

Antonio grinned happily as he approached Rick. As the two men shook hands, Rick detected a feeling of happiness in Antonio's heart. Here was a genuine, easy going, human being. There wasn't a malicious bone in his body, and he was really glad to see Rick.

"I have a new job," he gushed. "And so do John and Sarah."

The two men sat down at one of the long dining tables.

"And I think Peter may have an offer."

Rick was very pleased. His former employees were finding jobs. John's little change to the NSS files had done some good after all. Antonio guessed what Rick was thinking.

"After John infiltrated the NSS files and changed our personal records, it was suddenly easier to get interviews.... Well at least a little better.... The economy still stinks."

Rick uneasily looked at Antonio. "You must never say that again, Antonio... People will get the wrong idea about us."

"OK. I understand," Antonio said. Then he looked nervously around and spotted Father Giovanni. "Is he OK?"

"That's Father Giovanni. He's one of the good ones. And Antonio... if you ever need help. Come here."

Rick stood up and motioned Father Giovanni over to the table.

"Antonio.... Meet Father Giovanni."

***

As it turned out, the address for the interview was located on Moffett Federal Airfield in Sunnyvale. As Rick approached the facility, he began to get an uneasy feeling about his appointment. Something was just not right. He took a circular road out toward the shore of the Bay. In the distance, shrouded in damp, cold fog, were three cheerless slate gray single story buildings. They were almost lost in the thick cover of gray clouds that had moved into the Bay Area from the South. Rick slowed his electric car and stopped to read a shabby sign at the entrance to the parking lot. The bold letters increased his apprehension: Department of Personal and Private Security, Department of Public Information, and National Security Service. Rick pondered for a moment. He could turn around and flee. But that would do no good. If he failed to show up for the "interview", the NSS would come to get him anyway. Then they would presume he was guilty of something because he didn't show up as requested. Resigned to his fate, Rick drove into the fenced compound where the buildings were located. He sensed he was being watched. At least two video surveillance cameras were following his every move.

Rick got out of his car. A cold mist fell on his coat as he walked to the building entrance. Once inside, he walked to a security checkpoint. The officer told him to take off his overcoat and loosen his pants. Rick did as he was told. The officer carefully checked him with a metal detector and peered into his pants. He then grunted for Rick to follow him to a machine that "sniffed" for explosives. That completed, he motioned Rick to a waiting room. In a few moments, a woman came out, asked him who he was, and took his identity papers. Rick waited for half an hour before she reappeared, handed him his identity papers, and asked him to follow her into the office area.

"*She is a cog,*" Rick decided. "*A nameless clerk who only knows how to follow orders and rules.*"

Rick followed the woman into the office area. There were several rows of dirty green and silver desks occupied by a sea of lethargic clerks. He counted three conference rooms filled with more clerks and a few managers, all intently following someone's boring PowerPoint presentation. The musty air in the office area seemed stale and cold. Rick shivered and stuffed his hands into the pockets of his overcoat.

He walked behind the woman for almost the full length of the office area. Rick could not help but notice that some of the clerks were looking at computer screens. Others were wearing earphones as though listening to conversations. It took a moment to sink in, but suddenly Rick realized this was some sort of surveillance center. Then he could only wonder. "*Who are they watching? Whose telephone conversation are they following? Do they have listening devices planted everywhere*?"

The woman looked at him and smiled with a nasty smirk. "This is one of our centers for monitoring illegal activities against the people of the United States. If we wish, we can locate where you are at any time…. day or night. We know what you say. We know what you write. We know what you buy….. We even know when you pee…. and how much."

She turned a corner and went into a small conference room. It had a single table in the middle of the room and two chairs on opposite sides of the table. A dark mirrored window was set into the middle of one wall. The woman motioned for Rick to sit down, and then left the room. As she left, she made a point of closing the door with a loud "thump". The latch clicked as it closed.

Rick waited by himself in the barren little room for about 30 minutes before someone finally knocked on the door. He couldn't be sure, but he thought he heard voices in the next room. Then a short plump man entered, followed by a tall thin man. The shorter man obviously thought he was very important. He talked non-stop, and very fast, energetically waving his arms in the air as though to punctuate his words. He had some kind of communication device inserted into his right ear. The other man leaned against the wall, arms folded. The acerbic look on his ashen face conveyed a feeling of doom. Neither man introduced himself.

"Vasquez, Ricardo Juan Sanchez," the talkative man said. "Thank you for coming in."

Rick felt uneasy at the words "coming in." They sounded less like an interview and more like the setup for an interrogation.

"You were the proprietor of the Santa Clara Internet Service, were you not?"

Rick nodded.

"Born in Winters. Grade School. High School," …. his voice trailed off until it was inaudible as he read the file. Rick decided he was actually an interrogator for the NSS. The tall man leaning against the wall was some sort of security agent. Rick relaxed. He would play word games with the little man seated across the table. The little man spoke up.

"You people played a key role in shutting down that awful disruption of the Internet, didn't you?"

"You're too kind," Rick responded. "We merely helped when we could. Everyone was scrambling to recover from the spam attack."

"But didn't the code everyone used come from your ISP?"

"We copied some code. I really don't know much about it. It was all handled by my software people."

"But didn't you approve the use of the code?" the little man persisted.

"I only told my software people to cooperate with the other ISPs. Wasn't that the right thing to do?" Rick gave the little man a friendly smile.

The little man scowled at Rick, obviously unconvinced. But instead of pressing the point, he went to a different subject.

"Your NSS personal file looks good ..... but .... of course you know that...."

Rick looked intently at the man in front of him. Then he leaned across the table and gave the man another big smile.

"Of course my file looks good. We have always been very helpful to the hard working agents of the DPPS."

There was some sort of scuffle and conversation in the room behind the window. The little man jumped. Someone was talking to him in a loud voice over the communication device in his ear. Then the little man looked crestfallen. Like a dog who has been whipped for being bad. He took a deep breath to regain his composure. He pulled out a very worn sheet of paper from his folder.

"This job is with the Department of Personal and Private Security," he said as he held up the piece of paper. Do you have any objections to working for the government?"

"Oh no. Not at all," Rick replied. "Do you have a job description?"

The little man obviously disliked Rick. But Rick ignored his smirk. And that made the man all the more upset. This man probably didn't like anyone, and he was so obnoxious it was likely no one liked him. He stuffed the sheet of paper back into his file case.

"I only have this copy. I'll make up a new one and send it to you by mail. If you want the job, we can have you come back to interview with your potential manager."

And with that, the little man stood up, motioned to the security guard, and left the room. The security guard leered at Rick as he walked to the door. In a few moments the woman who had escorted him into the office came to take him back to the front entrance.

As he walked to his car, Rick stopped long enough to turn and wave at the video surveillance camera. He gave whoever was watching a big smile.

***

Of course, no job description would ever come from the DPPS. Rick decided it would be wise if he didn't ask why. The whole thing was a sham. The NSS was bringing people into their offices for interrogation on the pretense of interviewing them for a job. Then an interrogator would grill them for information. Since the little man was obviously an inept interrogator, someone in the next room had been very angry with him. Rick was relieved he had been able to get through the interrogation without revealing anything useful.

Instead of driving back to his apartment, Rick made his way through the misty rain to see Phillip and Lydia. He pulled into the parking lot and made his way to the familiar door. Lydia answered his knock.

"Rick," she exclaimed. "What a pleasant surprise. Come on in!"

She gave Rick a little hug and went to find Phillip. He came into the little apartment's living room from the back.

"Caught me," he said. "Just taking out the trash."

Rick smiled and shook Phillip's hand. "I have a job for you."

Phillip looked surprised. "I already have an offer. Probably start next month..... on the first."

"It's not that kind of job," Rick responded. "We have a problem with the NSS."

Phillip was immediately both serious and apprehensive.

"What's up?"

"I just left the NSS office in Sunnyvale. They brought me in on the pretext of giving me a job interview. Actually it was an interrogation. Luckily for me, the interrogator was totally inept and the interview was a short one. But here's the problem....."

Rick paused for a moment. Lydia motioned for him to sit down.

"They know, or at least think they know, that we are the ones who foiled the spam attack on the Internet. Apparently, they are very unhappy we did that... and... I think they know we hacked into the NSS computer database to fix our personal files."

Both Lydia and Phillip were shocked by what they heard. This was serious business. If the NSS pressed on with its investigation, they could all go to jail.

"Are you sure?" asked Lydia.

"Yes. The little man I met mentioned both events at our meeting. Then someone gave him hell over his earphone for bungling the interrogation. I learned more from him than he learned from me."

Lydia was perplexed by what she had heard.

"Why should the NSS care about our work on the spam attack?"

Rick could only shrug. He had not given it much thought. Then he had an idea.

"Perhaps the NSS is somehow involved."

Phillip was uneasy. He spoke very slowly.

"What do you want me to do?"

"I can not be seen visiting with all our former employees. The NSS is watching me. But you can still move with relative freedom. Throw one of your parties, or stop by and see them one at a time. But no matter how you do it, you must find a way to tell everyone about the NSS investigation. Warn them to keep their mouths shut."

Phillip looked at Lydia. She nodded in agreement. It was a chore they had to do.

"OK," Phillip said. "I'll figure out a way to see everyone as soon as I can. A party is out. You'd have to be here and that would tip off the NSS. I'll do it another way."

Rick looked relieved. "Thank you, Phillip. You are a real friend."

"Can I get you something to eat?" Lydia asked.

"No... Thank you very much. But the shorter my visit, the safer it will be for both of you."

Rick stood up and began to button his overcoat. Both Lydia and Phillip gave him a warm hug. Rick knew he could count on them. They shared a mutual affection for each other and a level of trust only really good friends can establish.

"Rick," Phillip interjected. "I'll find a way for us to communicate without an actual meeting. It will be safer if we keep in touch at least once a week."

Rick nodded his agreement.

"Goodbye you two.... Keep the faith."

Rick forced himself to smile as he walked to the door. But deep inside, he knew his life – and the lives of his former employees – were destined to become more difficult.

***

Rick was sitting on the edge of his bed, sorting through the day's mail. He mentally made a note of each bill, added them together, and sighed with resignation. His rent would soon be due for March. He was running out of money. He knew he had to reduce his expenses.

Rick scooped up the bills he had just opened and took them to the desk he kept in the living room. He checked his arithmetic.

"*I can't afford to stay here,*" he thought. "*No job. No money.*"

Rick looked mournfully at the stack of rejection letters he had gotten from multiple companies and government agencies.

"*Not much demand for an ex ISP manager,*" he groaned. "*And my programming skills are out of date.*"

He decided he would rent a van to take his furniture up to Winters. Rick was sure Josue would let him store it in the barn. Since he was spending two or three days a week with Neema and his children in Winters, he only needed a place to sleep for the rest of the week in San Jose.

Rick felt a little lost, discouraged. Things were really going downhill. The phony interview at the NSS office. No job prospects. His future didn't look all that good.

***

Father Giovanni made room for him in a tiny little room off the NC kitchen. Rick didn't mind the limited space, or the communal bathing. The building was reasonably warm. He had food to eat. He worked each day with Father Giovanni. There was always so much to do. By the time the day's chores were done, he was so exhausted he gladly sought out the refuge of his bed and would quickly fall into a deep sleep.

Although there were several days of partly cloudy weather in March, the gusty winds and frigid temperatures encouraged most people to stay indoors. Several people at the NC got terrible colds, and for awhile it looked as though they might have to deal with an epidemic of flu. But fortunately for the 37 adults and 53 children at the NC, the threat passed without a major incident by the end of the month.

***

On Good Friday Rick and Neema took the children for a walk to visit the stores in Winters. Ramon needed new shoes. Serafina wanted a new winter coat, and Adonica – who was becoming a young lady – insisted emphatically she had nothing to wear for spring.... If it ever came.

By now, they were a family. Perfectly relaxed with each other. They shared moments of affectionate teasing, a constant flow of chatter, and lots of laughter. Rick parked Neema's CR-V in a parking lot on Railroad Avenue. As they walked hand in hand down the Main Street sidewalk from Railroad Avenue toward 4th Street, Ramon was vigorously describing his need for a horse of his own. Apparently, George Mitchell had been giving him rides on his old mare and Ramon - thrilled by the experience – was convinced he loved horses. Neither Adonica nor Serafina thought much of the idea, and they were thinking of as many reasons as they could to cast doubt on Ramon's plan. Neema and Rick smiled happily at the children's prattle. Despite the raw cold of the day, there was warmth in their hearts.

Then Rick looked up the street and his heart almost stopped beating. A lump formed in his chest. A uniformed policeman was walking toward them. On his arm he had a green band with gold letters that identified him as an agent of the NSS. He stopped in front of Rick, looked briefly at Neema and the children, and then at Rick.

"May I see your National Identification Card?"

"Sure." Rick reached for his wallet. Then his heart sank. He had taken his NID card out of his wallet the night before to show it to Josue. The card was on the kitchen table at his parent's home. He fumbled for his wallet, opened it, and looked up at the officer.

"I'm sorry. But I think I left it at my parent's house."

"Do you have your card?" the officer looked intently at Neema. "And how about your children?"

Neema quickly produced her NID card from her purse and showed it to the officer. Then she helped the children to show the officer their NID cards. He studied each one, comparing the picture on the card with each face. Satisfied with Neema and the children, he turned to scowl at Rick.

"You know what the penalty is for being in public without proper identification, don't you?"

"Yes Sir, I do," Rick responded. "But I do have one. I'll be glad to go home and get it to show to you."

"I should arrest you on the spot," he growled.

Adonica and Serafina were terrified. They had been taught in school to fear and respect the NSS. Whatever the NSS did, it was the law. Ramon was more defiant.

"My Daddy is telling the truth!"

The officer looked more thoughtfully at Rick.

"Is your name Vasquez?"

"Yes... and these are my children."

Rick began to examine the officer's face. *This man is well over 50,* he thought. *Checking for NID cards is a part time job. He doesn't want to arrest me. Not in front of the children.*

Rick changed the conversation.

"Didn't you work for the county?" he asked.

The officer was uncertain how to respond. Then a look of recognition changed the demeanor of his face to one of conciliation.

"Aren't you the kid on the horse? The one we had to escort out of town? You and Phillip Mitchell?"

Rick instantly remembered the officer.

"Officer Johnson," he responded. "You're Officer Johnson!"

At that the officer relaxed and then began to laugh. He turned to Neema.

"You should have seen these two. Proud as peacocks they were. Oblivious to the traffic jam they were creating...."

Then he paused.... looked carefully at Neema.

"And you're Phillip's sister, aren't you?"

Neema gave the officer her most alluring and affectionate look.

"Why – yes," she said sweetly.

Totally disarmed and glad he could let them go, Officer Johnson looked intently at Rick.

"Look.... I have to stop at least 20 people a day to check them for valid NID cards. ... 20 people at random... Adults and kids. You better make sure you keep it on you at all times or you'll be in big trouble... "

Then Officer Johnson paused, pondered what he was thinking for a moment and took Rick by the arm. He led Rick a little way down the sidewalk so they could talk without being overheard.

"Can you keep a secret?" he whispered.

"For you, I will be silent," Rick responded.

Rick felt a huge sense of relief. He knew the officer was going to let him go. But what the man said next was extremely distressing.

Officer Johnson seemed to be genuinely concerned.

"A day or two ago I was going through the suspected offenders list. Your name was on it. Something about possible theft of NSS data. You'd better be careful. I think they are trying to make a case against you."

"I have already been interviewed by the NSS. They have nothing."

Officer Johnson took Rick by the hand. He was trying to be helpful. Friendly. He was an honest man who sometimes hated his job - or rather what it had become.

"They really don't need any evidence to arrest you. Sometimes I think they arrest people just to prove they have the power of life and death."

Rick could only nod in agreement. The brutality of NSS tactics were well known. Officer Johnson looked worried.

"I never talked to you... OK?"

Rick again nodded his agreement. But Officer Johnson wanted to drive home his point.

"You know what will happen to me if they every find out I talked to you."

Rick clasped Officer Johnson's hand with warm appreciation.

"We never talked.... and I found my NID card."

The two men turned back to Neema and the thoroughly frightened children. Officer Johnson left them and walked briskly on up the street.

"What was that all about?" Neema asked, obviously very troubled.

"Nothing. Just a friendly reprimand," Rick responded. Then he changed the subject.

"Let's find Serafina a nice winter coat," he said with a light hearted tone in his voice.

The children were relieved. Neema hid the uneasiness that was in her heart.

***

March and April passed without further incident. Phillip and John devised a way to encrypt hidden messages in the e-mails they exchanged, and they tried to keep in touch at least once a week. Antonio, Peter, James and Phillip all found work, and by the end of April even Lydia had an offer. Rick was relieved and happy that all of his former employees had jobs. Unfortunately for him, however, his employment prospects had gone from bad to worse. He was running out of places to look for work.

"Maybe you need a new line of work," Father Giovanni quipped one day. "Your work here has been excellent."

Chapter 5   NSS

By May the sun had returned to the Bay Area. Warm breezes laden with the scent of spring flowers were a welcome relief from the cold winds of a very wet winter. The buds of a new crop of green leaves made their appearance. Brown and yellow grass suddenly turned a rich green and soon needed mowing. Despite the continuing chronic recession, people appeared to be in a better mood. The tensions of winter gave way to a more easy-going social environment.

Phillip found work at a small grocery distributor in San Jose. Since most of trucks were loaded between 5 and 7 in the morning, he had to be at work by 5AM just to be sure there were no problems with the computerized material loading system. After the trucks left to make their daily rounds, he could take time to have something for breakfast.

It was a Thursday. Phillip had just finished his breakfast when two men entered the building and marched with great purpose to the manager's office. Although somewhat curious, Phillip didn't think much about them. He put his trash into the refuse bin and started to walk toward his cubicle. As he passed the manager's office, one of the men pointed at him. Phillip heard his boss utter several words of protest, and then he too pointed at Phillip. The two men immediately came out of the manager's office and accosted Phillip in the hall. They were wearing the green arm bands of the NSS.

"Phillip Mitchell?" the heavier of the two men demanded.

"Yes," Phillip stammered. He was bewildered by the question.

"You are under arrest," the NSS agent growled. He quickly produced a pair of handcuffs, roughly pulled Phillip's hands behind him, and snapped them shut. The cold steel of the handcuffs bit painfully into Phillips wrists.

"What for?" Phillip protested.

"You'll know soon enough," said the second man. He stepped in front of Phillip as though to force a confrontation.

"Are you coming peacefully or do we have to drag you out?"

He grinned at Phillip with a sick smirk. He was anxious to have some sadistic fun. He leered at Phillip, hoping he would resist. But Phillip meekly complied and turned to walk with them out the door. That didn't stop the NSS agent from giving him a brutal fist to his back. Phillip staggered, but kept on going. He knew he was defenseless.

They shoved Phillip into the back seat of a big black SUV, locked the door, and got into the vehicle. They drove him up to Moffett Field in Sunnyvale. As the SUV rounded a bend in the road, Philip could see the three cheerless slate gray single story buildings Rick had described when he went in for his "interview". Phillip could only hope he got the same inept interrogator.

But Phillip was not that lucky. The two NSS agents took him to a ramshackle building located behind the first three buildings. Surrounded by a high fence of barbed wire, and secured by two steel fence gates, it looked ominously threatening. The SUV pulled up to the first gate. The NSS agent on the passenger side got out, inserted a key in the lock, and opened it. The driver let the SUV coast into a secure area between the two gates. After closing the first gate, the NSS agent opened the second gate. The SUV entered the interior of the compound and stopped. They dragged Phillip from the vehicle by his pony tail and took him inside.

They led Phillip to a barren, cheerless room with nothing on the walls except a picture of President Mary Rose Chartres O'Brien, and a green plaque with the gold NSS insignia. Bold letters across the bottom of the plaque proclaimed "To Protect America". There were two metal chairs and a small table in the center of the room. The NSS agents pushed Phillip onto one of the chairs, and then stood motionless behind him. A few moments later, a pale thin man with long gray hair and rimless spectacles came into the room. He looked with contempt at Phillip, sat down, and began to shuffle through a file of papers. He would be, Phillip decided, a skilled interrogator. He spoke to Phillip with a quiet, almost inaudible, voice that projected an aura of dread.

"We closed down your illegal ISP, did we not?"

"The government did, yes," Phillip responded. "But I'm not aware we ever did anything illegal...."

"Silence!" The interrogator barked. "Just answer the questions.... understand?"

Phillip decided to remain silent unless he had a clear understanding of the question.

"And after we closed you down, you and your fellow employees were still able to get jobs."

Phillip nodded in agreement.

"How was that possible?"

"We all started to look for other work... and ..."

"Explain how you were able to find work.... You know the NSS disqualified you... Don't you? ... All of you were prohibited from being approved for further employment."

The interrogator motioned to one of the NSS agents.

The man slapped Phillip on the ear with the palm of his hand. The force of the blow knocked Phillip's head sideways. The second agent pulled him upright in the chair.

The interrogator stared into Phillip's eyes, unblinking, ominous, sadistically pleased with his power over the helpless man in front of him.

"Now then.... let us see if we can get some correct answers."

***

The NSS grilled Phillip for over two hours. Then the two agents drove him to his apartment complex, pulled him by his pony tail from the SUV, took off his handcuffs, and pushed him toward the building. They got into the SUV. But before they drove away, one of the agents rolled down the passenger window and leered at Phillip. "Till we meet again."

Although the blood had dried on his face, Phillip was still dizzy from the repeated blows to his ear. He staggered up to the door of his apartment, fumbled with the key, grasped the latch with shaking hands, and somehow managed to stumble inside. He went to the bathroom to wash his battered face. The image he saw in the mirror was terrifying. Cheeks swollen, blood on the right side of his face, blood on his shirt, hair matted and pony tail disheveled, he was a mess. Phillip gingerly moved his head from right to left, and then front to back. The NSS agent had used Phillip's pony tail like a handle, yanking his head backward and from side to side whenever the interrogator was dissatisfied with his answer. He knew the aching muscles in his neck would get much worse as they tightened from the abuse.

Phillip took a shower, cautiously washing his face, neck and hair. Afterward he called his employer. The obviously frightened voice on the other end of the line told Phillip not to come to work... ever... not ever again. The voice told him he would send Phillip a check for back wages, and then the line abruptly went dead.

Philip went to the kitchen, found a bottle of bourbon, and poured himself a stiff drink. The anger began to well inside him. The more he thought about his interrogation, the more frustrated and upset he became. There was no recourse. No one to go to. The NSS could do anything they wanted without fear of reprisal or prosecution. That's what President O'Brien wanted and that's what Congress had passed. It was the law. The protests that erupted after the bill was passed quickly faded away. People were afraid for their safety and O'Brien promised the NSS would protect America from terrorist harm.

The latch on the front door of the apartment rattled noisily. Lydia let herself into the living room and put down her handbag. Then she saw Phillip and screamed.

"Oh My God!"

She instantly began to sob. Hot tears ran down her face as she ran to Phillip's side. Lydia threw her arms around him and began to moan.

"What have they done to you?.... Who did this?.... What happened?"

They embraced for several minutes. Two people who deeply cared for each other. Two people who were stunned by something they could not control. Phillip waited for Lydia to regain her composure before revealing the events of the day, his interrogation, and the loss of his job.

"They know we hacked into their files... The NSS... They want to know how we did it and they want to punish us for the intrusion."

"But the government has no right to take away our jobs," Lydia exclaimed.

"This government has no right to do most of the things it is doing."

"Can't we stop them?"

"Not without a revolution..... We can't be the only ones the NSS has persecuted..... The more they clamp down, the greater the resentment."

Just then Lydia's cell phone rang. She picked it up.

"It's my Boss," she said.
The voice on the call was firm. The call was short. Then Lydia hung up.
"I've been fired."
"Why…. what for?"
"She won't say…. She refused to say… I will get a separation check in the mail. My job is over"
Lydia and Phillip looked at each other with disbelief. In one day their lives had been shattered. Maybe forever. There was no way out.
Lydia came over to where Phillip was sitting on the living room couch and sat down next to him. She carefully took his arm and placed it around her shoulders. Then she snuggled up. Tears welled in her eyes.
"What are we going to do?"
"I'm too tired to think. Tomorrow. After breakfast. We can talk."
There was a loud knock on the front door. Suspicious of what or who it might be, Phillip quietly tiptoed to the door and looked through the peep hole. It was John, and he was holding a finger to his lips. Puzzled, Phillip opened the door. John immediately stepped into the room, his finger still giving the sign of silence – first to Phillip and then to Lydia. Then John tip toed quietly across the room. In his right hand he held what looked like a wand. It was connected to a small gray box he held in his left hand. Slowly, deliberately, he began to sweep the room. The box gave out a low pitched tone. John motioned for Phillip and Lydia to come and look at what he had found. John carefully picked up a lamp and turned it over. Attached to the bottom was a small black rectangular box with a small antenna protruding from the top. John whispered in Phillip's ear.
"Bug."
John then repeated the word to Lydia. Phillip sat down on the couch and slumped over, his head between his hands. Totally discouraged by the events of the day – and now this. Obviously the NSS had been listening to them for some time. John carefully put the lamp down and went on with his search. In a few moments he reappeared from the bedroom, motioned for Phillip to come with him, and turned around toward the bed. There, under the night stand, was another small black box with a protruding antenna. Phillip and Lydia nodded their acknowledgement.
Although John searched the whole apartment for listening devices, he didn't find any more. Then he spoke up in a loud voice.
"Phillip, you're a mess. Let's go down to the corner and get you some healing cream."
Phillip was about to say no when Lydia spoke up. "Can I come too?"
"Sure," said John. "Let's all go to the store."
Lydia gently pushed Phillip toward the front door, opened it, and waited for the two men to leave the apartment. The three of them walked slowly toward the corner shopping center. Phillip was still a bit lightheaded. He stumbled several times on the sidewalk. After John made sure the coast was clear, he spoke again in a low voice.
"Leave the bugs. Just remember. Only tell them what you want them to hear."

Phillip and Lydia understood the strategy. Then John spoke again.

"I accidentally found a bug in my apartment while I was cleaning up a coffee spill on my desk. The same kind of bug you have in your apartment. I got out this old signal detection device and ran a sweep of my apartment. Apparently, I'm not as important as you are. Only one bug."

John grinned. But the humor was lost.

"How about the others?" Phillip asked.

"I've been to see James, Antonio, Sarah and Peter. They seem to be clean. I'm still trying to think of an excuse to go down to San Jose to see Rick."

"He's got to be warned!" Lydia exclaimed.

"I'll do it," Phillip said. "Can you teach me how to use that thing? I think I can sweep where Rick works without raising any suspicion."

John looked at Phillip with a very grave expression on his face.

"Antonio can do it. He's already been to the NC. Going again won't raise much suspicion. Phillip... you're in so much trouble, you're almost radioactive."

"Serves me right," Phillip murmured. "You do the hacking and I get the blame."

They walked to the drug store and purchased a tube of antiseptic cream. It would help to prevent infection and keep Phillip's skin soft during the healing process. After they returned to the apartment complex, John said goodbye and got into his car. He waved to them as he drove out of the parking lot. Phillip was about to turn toward the apartment building when he noticed a black sedan parked across the street. The woman in it appeared to be doing nothing... Just staring down the street. His suspicions aroused, Phillip hurried Lydia into the apartment.

***

They made up a story. Lydia and Phillip. They would move to Arizona where Phillip proclaimed (to the bug) he could get a construction job. Lydia actually seemed to enjoy making things up to fool the NSS. They talked about packing, renting a moving van, and how many days it would take to reach Phoenix. Then they actually packed, rented a van, and moved from the apartment. Phillip even made a pretense of driving down to Los Angeles on Interstate 5. But when they reached the Interstate 5 cloverleaf, he turned the van northward, toward Winters.

Somehow, the nearer they came to Winters, the greater the feeling of freedom they both felt. Phillip began to talk about his determination to resist the NSS. They discussed politics and religion. Lydia was amazed at Phillip's knowledge. Phillip was elated with her interest. As the miles went by, they became far more aware of their common interests. It was a precious time of sharing. When Phillip finally turned off the freeway at Winters, he had only one more thing to say.

"Lydia. I love you."

Despite the dreadful events of the last week, Lydia had a brief moment of deep affection and joy for the man she loved.

***

Abigail and George Mitchell were totally surprised when the van pulled up in the driveway of their ranch. Phillip had kept their coming a secret because he didn't want to let the NSS know what he was going to do. But if Abigail and George were surprised when the van pulled up in front of their house, they were shocked when they say Phillip's face.

"What on earth... What happened to you?" Abigail exclaimed.

"All in good time mother... Besides... you should have seen me last week. I'm really much better now."

Abigail hugged her son, and then hugged Lydia. She sensed something momentous was happening. Phillip hugged his father and encouraged Lydia to do the same.

"I have to get this stuff under cover as soon as possible. Is that OK?" Philip asked.

Although George was thoroughly puzzled by Phillip's sudden appearance, he quickly agreed to help unload the van. Some of the furniture they put in Phillip's old room. The rest they put in the barn. There were clothes to unpack and incidental items to sort through. It took almost two hours. When they finished, Philip announced he had to take the van back to San Jose. He figured that would confuse the NSS. He gave Lydia a very emotional kiss. Then Phillip thanked his parents for their help and climbed into the van. He backed up all the way to the county road, and roared off into the dusk. Lydia stood in the driveway with his parents, watching the taillights disappear as the van vanished from view. Unable to contain herself any longer, Abigail turned to Lydia.

"OK. .... NOW you can tell us what is happening."

"And why," groused George.

***

Phillip returned the next morning on the first train from San Jose. He called Lydia from the railroad station in Davis and said one word.

"Come."

Lydia's heart leapt with the joy of knowing he was safe. She borrowed George's old car and went to Davis. Phillip was standing on the 1st Street sidewalk about a block away from the station. As soon as she stopped the car, he got in and said one word, "Go."

Lydia drove quickly away from the area, her heart pounding with excitement. Phillip's hand crept up her skirt and squeezed her thigh.

"You're a good accomplice, Lydia... a regular gangster doll."

Lydia giggled and pushed his hand away. The "getaway" from Davis was about all the excitement she could handle for the moment.

***

When they got to the house, they discovered Abigail and George had gone somewhere. A note on the kitchen counter explained they were visiting Josue and Mari. They would return after dinner. It was an opportunity they had both wanted since leaving Santa Clara.

"Go upstairs and take a shower," Lydia order. "I'll see you when you are done."

Phillip did as he was told. He showered and shaved, carefully combed his hair, and went into the bedroom. He threw himself on the big bed and snuggled up with the pillow. Phillip was very tired. The events of the last two days had drained him both emotionally and physically. His eyes closed and he began to feel drowsy. Phillip soon fell into a deep sleep.

A few moments later, Lydia came into the room. She looked tenderly at her man. Then she undressed and slipped into bed with him. She fell into a troubled sleep looking at his battered face.

***

Exhausted by a long day, Rick was in a deep sleep at the NC. A scuffle outside his little room was followed by a sharp knock on the door.

"Rick," a voice called. "Rick.... come quick."

The caller knocked again. Rick slowly became conscious of the caller and the knock on his door. He flailed in the bed, trying to orient himself.

"Yes..... Just a minute."

Rick struggled to find his pants and a shirt, fumbled for his shoes, and stumbled to the door. He opened it slowly, and found himself looking at one of the women residents.

"It's Alice," the woman said. "She's dying."

Although the news was expected, Rick was nevertheless startled by the revelation. Alice had cancer. It had metastasized. The doctor said it was just a matter of time before she died.

"Where's Father Giovanni," he asked.

"He's with her.... He asked for you to come."

Rick walked with the woman to one of the small bedrooms in the back of the building. When he entered, he saw Father Giovanni holding the hands of a frail gray haired woman. Her back was propped up by two pillows stacked against the back of the bed so she could breath more easily. Rick immediately went to her side. Father Giovanni took the woman's hands and placed them gently on the blanket.

"Here, take her hands in your own. Maybe you can bring her more comfort than I can."

Rick did as he was instructed. He sensed the woman's pain. Her breathing was erratic. She was struggling to fill her lungs with air. Each breath seemed more difficult than the last. Rick gently massaged each hand in turn, and then held them in his own. There was nothing to do but to wait for Alice to die. He wished he had the power to give her life, but he knew he did not. After several minutes, Father Giovanni placed his hand on Rick's shoulder.

"Let's leave them alone together."

He signaled the woman's husband to the side of the bed. Rick stood up and shook his head.

"I can do nothing. What happens next is up to God."

He grasped the man's hand, felt a flow of grief that was consuming the man's entire being, and left the room.

An hour later Father Giovanni came to the dining room table where Rick had gone for a cup of tea.

"She has passed on," he said. "Let's go to her room and say a prayer."

Rick followed Father Giovanni to the barren bedroom. The woman's husband was sitting on the lone wooden chair, sobbing and whispering.

"I've failed her," he whispered to Rick. "I promised her the moon and I only gave her ...this..."

He thrust out his shaking hand and pointed to the ceiling.

Rick looked at Alice, carefully examining her ashen face and withered arms. She looked as though she had died in agony, her face contorted by the struggle to breath, her sunken eyes desperate for hope. He helped Father Giovanni pull the sheet up around her shoulders. Rick carefully slid his fingers over her eyes to close them. Then the two men led Alice's husband out of the bedroom.

"I'll call 911," Rick said.

Father Giovanni nodded his agreement. He escorted Alice's husband into the dining room, got him a glass of juice, and sat down to console the man as best he could. Rick soon returned from making his call.

"They said it would be a few minutes. The rescue crews have other calls."

The three men sat together, quietly talking about Alice, her wonderful spirit, her ready smile, and the devotion she lavished on her family. A feeling of deep compassion and sympathy swept over Rick. This simple man had been victimized by circumstances he could not control, or even fully understand. They had only been at the NC for a short time. Street people had referred them to Father Giovanni. Rick, somewhat ashamed he did not know the man's name, finally asked him the question.

"I'm really sorry... but I do not know your name."

The man quickly turned to look at Rick. "Harry..... Harry Kieslowski."

Rick shook Harry's hand.

"If there is anything I can do...."

His words were interrupted by a joyful shout from the back of the NC. A woman's voice rang out.

"Father Giovanni! ... Come quick!"

Unsure of what to expect, Father Giovanni, Harry and Rick hurried to the bedroom. Alice was still propped up on the pillows. But the look of terrible agony was gone. Instead her face conveyed an expression that was relaxed, almost angelic, with a wisp of a smile on her lips.

Harry rushed to the side of his wife, knelt beside the bed, and bowed his head.

"Finally.... you have found the peace you were looking for... the happiness I had promised... God bless you Alice.... I will be with you... as soon as God tells me it's OK."

Harry began to sob again, his head and arms on the blanket.

"This often happens," murmured Father Giovanni.

"What?" asked Rick. He was very curious about what he had just witnessed.

"When people die... and I mean good people like Alice and Harry... death is a physical thing. It is an agony within the physical universe. Then... after some time... they usually pass into another place. They are certainly no longer here in this world. Their expression, their whole being is that of a person who is somewhere else."

Father Giovanni paused long enough to start walking with Rick back to the dining room.

"I call it the Spiritual Universe," he said as they walked. "We move our life energy from the physical universe to the Spiritual Universe.... The body stays behind, ... the spirit moves on.... and there we find peace."

***

Over the course of the next few days, Rick spent several hours with Harry. Here was a man who had been a successful retail shop owner. Over 27 years at the same location, selling shoes and leather goods. But like many small businesses, he had been caught without enough cash when the economy turned down. Then, as he struggled to regain his financial security, local government bureaucrats began to pester him about building violations, and the state issued a warning his business was not in compliance with the California Business Code. One thing after another. Oppressive rules and regulations. Then he received a shipment of defective boots from China. He didn't have enough cash to recover. It was the incident that killed his business. Strapped for cash, he and Alice were forced out of their little house by the bank when he missed three mortgage payments. With nowhere to go, Harry and Alice had been grateful there was room at the NC.

A week went by. Each day Rick visited several local markets, shops and restaurants, looking for surplus food and clothing. He had been doing his rounds since January. By now, most of the managers and owners knew who he was, and a few went out of their way to be helpful. Some days were good. He would be able to fill his little car with bags of merchandise. And on other days, he came back to the NC with little or nothing.

May had turned into a beautiful month with mostly clear skies and gentle breezes. The third Monday of the month, he went once again on his rounds, traveling in his little car from store to shop, talking at length to the people he met. He was encouraged by the upbeat mood of the people he met on his rounds. There was even talk of a better economy.

Finished for the day, he turned his little electric car onto First Street and headed South toward the NC. About three blocks from the building, he saw a man frantically waving his arms at him from the sidewalk. Rick pulled over to the curb and recognized the man. It was Harry. He rushed over to the car and yanked open the door. Excited and agitated, he began to speak so fast Rick had to slow him down.

"What's happening?" Rick asked. He was still in a good mood because the car was full of donated groceries.

"It's the NSS. They are watching the NC. Two tough looking agents. When I approached their SUV, one of them asked if I knew you... I played dumb."

Rick was instantly alarmed. He didn't know what to do. If the NSS was looking for him, it was because they wanted to arrest him. Rick had heard about Phillip's interrogation from Antonio. He turned to Harry who was leaning on the car door.

"Get lost. Walk away. Pretend I don't exist..... and thank you."

But Harry protested. "Maybe I can find out if they want to arrest you or something."

"No... Just go."

Harry started to walk away, and then turned back to Rick again. Harry was determined to help in any way he could.

"I'll call you on your cell phone. If I say the word GO, that means you leave the car here with the keys in it and disappear."

Before Rick could object, Harry was on his way down the street. Rick's heart sank. Harry was placing himself in mortal danger. The NSS would be furious with him if he interfered with their activity – no matter what it was.

Rick carefully pulled his car into an empty parking space next to a warehouse. Although he would be almost hidden from the street, he would still be able to watch the traffic. Minutes went by. Rick became agitated. More minutes passed. Then abruptly, his cell phone rang. Rick quickly answered. It was Father Giovanni.

"I don't know what the hell is going on," he said nervously. "The NSS were just here. They were looking for you and they arrested Harry."

Rick was shocked. His heart began to thump in his chest. The prickly sensation of fear welled up within him. Father Giovanni continued in hushed tones.

"They searched your room. Tore it up really bad. They must hate you something awful."

Rick had to assume the call was being monitored. Father Giovanni was endangering himself by making this call. Rick had to hang up. He wanted to protect Father Giovanni as best he could. It would take a few minutes for the monitor in Sunnyvale to contact the NSS agents about the call. It would take a few more minutes to locate him using the GPS system. Rick had to act fast. Then his heart stopped. A black SUV passed the lot where he was parked. He could clearly see the two agents staring intently ahead. They were looking for him on the street and sidewalks.

"Father Giovanni. You're mistaken. They couldn't possibly be looking for me..... I have to say goodbye now. Tell Janice goodbye and tell her to carefully look both ways when she crosses a street."

"Wait!" Father Giovanni exclaimed. "Before they hauled him off, Harry told me to tell you - Go".

"I think Harry must be confused," Rick whispered into the cell phone... Goodbye."

Then Rick clicked the "Off" button. Janice was a resident at the NC. She walked by his hiding place everyday. If she was looking for his car, she would see it. Rick got out, left the keys under the mat, and closed the door. He could only hope Father Giovanni would give Janice his message.

He began to walk up First Street toward San Jose. They would be looking for the GPS location of his call. He hoped they would leave the car alone. The NC desperately needed the groceries he had collected. Rick began to walk a little faster. He needed to get away from this spot as quickly as possible. He crossed the street and headed for the 2nd Street freeway undercrossing. Once on the other side of the freeway, he headed for a ramshackle building where he had previously met the driver of a Sacramento Distributor's truck. As he neared the building, he scanned the street for the truck. His heart leapt with relief when he saw it parked on the next block. Without hesitation he got in and crouched down on the passenger seat. Minutes ticked by. Then the driver opened the truck door and gave a short startled shout "Jesus!"

Rick held his finger to his lips as a sign to be silent.

The driver got in and looked at Rick.

"You're the guy that collects stuff for that place on First Street."

"The same," said Rick. "But, I'm in trouble. The NSS is looking for me. Can you take me to Sacramento?"

Rick had talked to the driver several times. He knew the man hated the NSS. He was hoping the driver would help him out. He was not disappointed.

"Hey. For you. Anything," he grinned.

He was obviously pleased he had a chance to stick it to the NSS, despite the danger.

"Just keep low.... Crouch in your seat until I get out of San Jose."

The driver started the truck's motor, shifted into gear and drove toward the First Street freeway ramp. He had to stop for a traffic light on First Street. A black SUV pulled up along side. The driver gave the NSS agents a big smile. Then, as the SUV pulled away, he flipped them the bird.

It was an easy trip on the freeway to Sacramento. The traffic was light and the roads were clear. Rick had the driver drop him off in Davis at the Richards Boulevard interchange. After thanking the driver, he walked into town, found a pay phone, and called Neema. Startled by his unexpected call, but happy he would be home, she agreed to pick him up. About an hour later, her CR-V came down the street and stopped by the bench where Rick was sitting.

"Need a ride, stranger?"

Rick gratefully got into the passenger seat, gave Neema a quick kiss, and put on his seat belt. It would be good to get home. Obviously he could not go back to San Jose. But Winters may not be a safe place either. It was only a matter of time before the NSS sent someone to look for him. Troubled by his thoughts, Rick began to reveal the events of the day to Neema. By the time they reached her apartment in Winters, they were both worried.

What would happen next? What should they do?

***

It was a typical morning at the NC. Everyone pitched in and helped to get the chores done. Several women were busy with the children. Father Giovanni was hard at work, cleaning the dining room floor with the help of two residents. In the kitchen, three women were making fruit salads and baking fresh bread. Two men were busily repairing dining room tables.

Around 10:30 the big oak doors suddenly swung open and hit the wall stops with a loud bang. An unkempt figure of a man stumbled into the NC, dried blood on his badly bruised face, and angry red marks on his wrists.

It was Antonio.

Slowly, painfully, he made his way into the dining room. Father Giovanni gasped and ran to Antonio's side.

"What happened? .... Did you have an accident? .... Get run over by a car?"

Antonio sat down on a chair and looked up at Father Giovanni with very tired eyes.

"I've been a guest of the NSS," he said gasping for air.... "Rick said to come here if I ever got into trouble."

Antonio slumped down and then fell forward. Father Giovanni could not move fast enough to save Antonio from falling out of the chair onto the floor. He lay there like a pile of rags, fresh blood streaming from his nose.

"Damn.... Clarise ! .... Bring hot water and towels!" Father Giovanni commanded. Then he placed his hand under Antonio's head until Clarise brought a towel to use as a pillow. Together, they rearranged the battered body so that Antonio was lying on his back.

"I don't know how he made it here," Father Giovanni said in a low voice.

Antonio moaned. A woman resident began to gently wash his face and hands with warm water. Antonio stirred and tried to open his eyes.

"They know we hacked into their files.... They want to know how.... I didn't know.... It was John and Phillip who figured it all out..... They beat me for an answer..... But I couldn't explain how we did it.... so they beat me some more."

Antonio's eyes suddenly opened and he looked at Father Giovanni with fear.

"They plan to find Sarah next. They figure she's vulnerable and will tell them what they want to know... You've got to warn her."

Antonio moaned again, obviously in pain.

"I'll do it," Father Giovanni said.

"NO!... I'll do it," Clarise interrupted. "You'll just get into trouble."

Clarise bent over Antonio. "How can I find her.... contact her?"

Antonio whispered a few words in her ear. Clarise stood up.

"Do we still have Rick's car?"

"Yes," Father Giovanni replied. "It's in the back lot. It should be charged up..... Where are you going?"

"None of your business," Clarise said solemnly. "I'll find her and warn her."

Father Giovanni had learned not to argue with Clarise. Besides, she was right. The less he knew the better.

"Come on, Antonio. Let's get you up and to a bed. You can sleep where Rick used to sleep. I don't think he had any really bad infections..."

It was a half hearted attempt at a little humor. Anything to defuse the growing tension in the dining room. With the help of another man, he carefully took Antonio to the little room where Rick had slept. One of the women went into the kitchen for another pan of warm water. She soon returned and began to tenderly bath Antonio, her eyes wet with tears.

"Can we hide him here?" she asked.

Father Giovanni shuffled out of the little room and went to the dining room. His eyes swept over the 15 or 20 adults and children that had gathered next to the kitchen.

"Can we hide him here?" he asked them.

Father Giovanni solemnly looked each one in the eye. One by one. They all understood the risk they were taking. But they all agreed. Father Giovanni made his decision.

"We will hide him here until we can find a way to slip him out of San Jose."

***

Father Giovanni left the building and walked down First Street to a pay phone at a nearby gas station. He called his old friend Micah in Winters and told him about Antonio's "intense" interrogation. He asked Micah to tell Rick and Phillip. The voice on the other end of the line was very troubled.

"What can we do?"

Father Giovanni paused, and then said firmly "We need to move him out of San Jose."

134 The Angels' Footpath

"Bring him here," Micah responded.

The two men exchanged ideas about how to move Antonio to Winters without being caught by the NSS. After they agreed on a plan, Father Giovanni hung up the telephone and walked back to the NC. As he turned the corner to climb the steps to the big oak doors, the reflection of a windshield caught his eye. Parked up the street was a big black SUV.

***

After he hung up the telephone, Micah sat down in a big stuffed easy chair and rubbed his chin thoughtfully. Things were heating up. Moving faster than he had planned. He needed to spend more time with Rick... And soon.

***

Rick stayed in Neema's apartment for the next three days. He was a man in hiding. Rick never used the phone. He seldom looked out of the apartment windows. On Sunday, Neema coaxed him to visit his parents. Upset and fearful for their son, they wanted the comfort of being able to talk to him. She even brought her CR-V close to the apartment entrance so he could get in without being noticed. Although it was a short drive to his parent's house, every mile seemed to take forever. When they pulled into the driveway, he saw the Mitchell's old car parked beside the house. Neema tooted the CR-V's horn. In a moment, Phillip and Lydia came bursting out the door and ran to the car. Everybody was talking at once with great excitement. There were hugs all around. Mari and Josue emerged from the house, both shaking with relief. Their son was OK.

Rick walked up to the steps and hugged Mari. Tears welled in her eyes. She was, he decided, the most beautiful and loving mother he had ever known. Although she was deeply concerned about him, she bravely pretended nothing was wrong. Rick turned and shook hands with his father. Then on a sudden impulse, they embraced. Father and son.

After they went inside Rick began to tell his story. Working with Father Giovanni at the NC. The woman who had died. His arrest and subsequent escape from San Jose. Then Rick asked Phillip to tell about his confrontation with the NSS. After both men had finished, Mari and Josue were even more worried for the safety of their son and his friends. Josue was the first to speak.

"What will you do now? ... Both of you... and Lydia... Aren't you fugitives?"

Rick shrugged his shoulders.

"I think only the NSS wants us. The local police have never hassled me. They could have, ... but they didn't."

"We need to lay low for one or two weeks," Phillip added. "We need time to get organized."

The telephone rang. The sudden intrusion of the telephone's insistent ring startled everyone in the room. They all fell silent while Josue picked up the instrument.

"Hello," he said softly.

The voice on the other end of the line spoke in brisk tones for almost a minute. Josue looked apprehensively at Rick and Phillip. Then he hung up with only a short "Goodbye."

"That was Micah. He has some bad news. He wants you both to come over right away."

Rick was mystified. "Did he say why?"

"No.... but it sounds very serious."

***

Rick and Philip took the same shortcut to Micah's house they had used as kids. Walking through the woods on the familiar footpath brought back many memories of a far happier time. Micah opened the door of his house just as they turned up the walk.

"Come in," he smiled broadly. "It is nice to see you are safe and sound."

They walked through the living room and into the kitchen. Just like they had done so many times when they were kids. But instead of cookies and milk, Micah gave them a cup of steaming hot coffee. When they had settled into their kitchen chairs, Micah looked gravely at Rick.

"Antonio has been beaten and questioned by the NSS."

Rick was shocked. Phillip was stunned.

"Fortunately, you told him to go to Father Giovanni, and he did..... That may have saved his life."

Micah shifted his gaze, back and forth, between Rick and Phillip.

"Antonio heard them saying they would pick up Sarah next.... because she would be more vulnerable than John or Peter."

"Can we do anything?" Phillip asked.

Micah sat back in his chair, and took a long sip of his coffee.

"I've arranged with," Micah paused.... "You must promise to keep this a secret between us and only us."

Rick and Phillip nodded in agreement.

"I've arranged with Father Giovanni to smuggle Antonio out of San Jose. He can stay here with me until things get sorted out."

"But how..." Rick interrupted.

"The less you know, the better for you and Phillip."

"That's not what I was asking," Rick interjected. "I'm surprised you know Father Giovanni."

Micah flashed a gentle smile.

"Father Giovanni and I go back many, many years. We met at the seminary in Los Altos. I was a handyman. He was studying to be a priest. When they closed the seminary, we went our separate ways. That's when I bought this place."

"Father Giovanni was studying to be a priest!" Rick exclaimed.

"Yes," Micah mused with a gentle grin. "Until they kicked him out."

Micah looked intently at Rick. He wanted to change the subject.

"Rick, have you had any more experiences with your sense of touch... your sixth sense?"

Rick stopped a moment to consider his answer. He hadn't noticed anything special. No distinct sensations when he shook hands or hugged someone. But he always seemed to be able to connect with people's inner thoughts. It all seemed very natural to him. And that's what he told Micah.

Phillip was puzzled.

"What's this all about? he asked. "Does my buddy have a special talent I don't know about?"

"Yes he does," replied Micah. "I have a special favor to ask of you, Phillip."

Puzzled, Phillip could only think to ask "What favor?"

"You two have been friends since you were little boys. Two men have seldom had an easy going relationship of the quality you two have enjoyed for more than 35 years. Am I right?"

Philip was somewhat embarrassed by Micah's assertion. But after thinking about it, he decided Micah was right.

"OK. I agree. .. Rick and I have been friends since forever.... Now what does that have to do with his special talents?"

Micah pointed his finger at Rick.

"His special talents... gifts if you will... are still evolving. They will become stronger over time. Eventually you will both understand them. I can not explain everything to you just yet.... To you or to Rick.... That will come later. But in the meantime, Rick is going to need the friendship of a companion who will be willing to help him at any time...."

Micah looked intently at Phillip.

"Can you be that friend?"

"Of course!" Phillip responded.

But this whole conversation was strange. Upsetting. He wondered what the hell was going on. Then he looked at Rick. His friend seemed to be at peace with the world. Serene. It was as though he understood everything Micah was saying. Phillip turned back to Micah.

"We can work it out. Whatever lies ahead."

"Are you sure?" asked Micah.

"Yes. I'm sure."

***

As the two friends walked back to the farmhouse, each man was engrossed in his own thoughts. For Phillip, the conversation had been unsettling. The news about Antonio and Sarah. The exchange about Rick and his special talents. Phillip had to fight off the feeling of bewilderment.

Rick sensed and understood Phillip's confusion. But Rick was certain Phillip would remain his steadfast companion. And he had received a special message - sensed it - from Micah. The special gift he was developing. How it could be used. All of a sudden, he understood what was happening to him. His whole being seemed to fill with joy. A passion was building within him, a passion for life. A passion for his mission.

***

After a light lunch with Josue and Mari, Neema drove Rick back to her apartment. She wanted to drop him off before 2:30PM. Then she would have enough time to pick up Adonica, Serafina and Ramon from school. As they turned onto Main Street, a siren sounded behind them. A police car with flashing lights was following them. Resigned to being pulled over, but fearful for Rick, Neema stopped the CR-V next to the curb and waited for the policeman to come to the window. They were in luck. It was Officer Johnson.

"Neema ... and Rick. What a surprise!"

Neema nervously said "Hello." Rick only nodded.

"Actually, I have been following you for a couple blocks. I have a message for Rick."

"Are you going to arrest him?" Neema protested with alarm.

"No... at least not today. I wanted to tell you Rick... The Sacramento office of the NSS has nothing on you that I can find in the police report file."

Rick was puzzled. "What does that matter? Can't the San Jose office order my arrest?"

Officer Johnson chuckled softly.

"That's not how the system works, son..... The Sacramento Office is a big bureaucracy. The San Jose Office is a big bureaucracy. They don't get along. Some kind of competition for political power. Sacramento will ignore anything San Jose sends them unless it is politically expedient for them to act."

"Can't San Jose come here and arrest us?"

"Technically... they can not. Winters is outside their jurisdiction. If they show up here, it would just piss off Sacramento..... Cause a big fuss... And besides... they are probably too lazy to make the trip."

"What about you... and the police?" Rick asked.

"Again, you got to understand the system, son..... I didn't want to cause you any trouble when I caught you without your NID card. I don't want to cause you any trouble now. When the report of your escape from San Jose came into our computer, I started checking. Unless you did something really wrong, I figured it would be better to just help you out. You see, us local police have been marginalized by the NSS. Yeah sure, there are some gung hoe people in the police department who will cooperate with the NSS. Make a big show of muscle. But most of us are more likely to help the people who live in our neighborhoods... We got to live here too."

Neema looked relieved. "You mean you're not going to arrest us?"

Officer Johnson chuckled again.

"Not unless I catch you going 50 in a 35 mile zone.... again"

And with that, he walked back to his police car.

Neema looked at Rick, tears of relief in her eyes. She took his face in her hands, and gave him a long joyful kiss.

***

It was a delightful June morning, complete with a cloudless blue sky, the fresh scent of spring flowers, and a cool breeze to playfully stir the living room curtains of Neema's apartment. Rick had finished breakfast and was scanning his e-mail for coded messages. Although there was only one this particular morning, the content was rather ominous. It was from Sarah who was hiding from the NSS at a friend's apartment. She had learned from Anika, Peter's niece, that John, James and Peter had been arrested by the NSS. Rick immediately replied to Sarah's e-mail with instructions to see if she could contact Peter's wife Jocelyn for more information. In about an hour, Sarah replied that Jocelyn only knew they had taken Peter to somewhere in Sunnyvale. Jocelyn was terrified for her husband's safety.

Rick knew what he had to do. He must go down to San Jose, get himself arrested, and hope the NSS would put him in a cell near his friends. Rick went into the kitchen where Neema was sorting out the laundry.

"I have to go down to San Jose. Maybe then to Sunnyvale. James, John and Peter have been picked up by the NSS. I have to do something, ... anything I can, ... to rescue them."

"You can't rescue them!" exclaimed Neema. "They have a tight lock on Santa Clara County. You'll only manage to get yourself arrested."

Rick thought about Neema's words. She was right. But Rick was determined to stand by his friends. If he was arrested, he could claim he was responsible for whatever the hell the NSS was so upset about. That would take the pressure off his friends.

"Can I borrow your CR-V?"

Neema's face turned ashen. She knew there was no way to stop Rick. He would at least be able to confuse the NSS. Maybe avoid the same kind of "intense" interrogation Antonio had suffered. Neema shuddered at the thought of Antonio's beating. Tears welled up in her eyes.

"Please, Rick... you can't help them.... Why do you have to stand up to the NSS?"

"I have to go. We got into this mess together..... I can't let them take the blame alone."

Neema slipped herself into Rick's arms and gave him a warm tearful hug.

"Oh Rick... please stay here... for us... for the children."

Rick quietly hugged Neema and then began to stroke her hair.

"I don't know where this will lead, Neema.... What tomorrow will bring... But it has to be done."

***

Borrowing Neema's CR-V was the easy part. Finding enough gasoline to make a round trip to San Jose was more difficult. She had only 5 gallons left in her CR-V. Rick was able to get 6 more from Josue. Then Phillip and Lydia actually drained 3 more from their car. It took more than 2 hours to pack, scrounge enough gasoline for the trip, and say goodbye to a tearful Neema. But by 2 PM. he was on his way to the South Bay. It was a quick trip. Because of the gasoline shortages, the traffic was almost non-existent. The only challenge was to avoid the thousands of potholes and cracks in the freeway surface. They forced him to slow down several times. He drove straight through without stopping. It seemed fate was making it much too easy to put himself within the cruel clutches of the NSS. Each passing mile seemed to plunge him deeper into danger.

When he arrived at the 7th Street ramp to get off the freeway, Rick was startled to see smoke rising from downtown San Jose. A few very angry men were running toward the center of the city. Some of them had clubs in their hands. Rick was careful to smile as he drove past them. He didn't want to become a victim of whatever was happening.

Just before 4PM he pulled into a parking spot at Father Giovanni's NC. As he emerged from the CR-V, he could hear sirens in the distance. Were they fire trucks? Ambulances? The police? Perhaps the NSS? He looked toward the source of the noise and saw thick black smoke billowing upward into the clear blue sky from somewhere in the downtown area. Apprehensive for his safety, he quickly entered the building.

***

She was a tough woman with a very unfriendly face. Because of her deeply rooted unhappiness, she relished the chance to be nasty. She wore the lifeless gray uniform of the NSS prison guards with arrogant pride. It gave her status, authority and permission to treat her prisoners with sadistic pleasure. As they walked down the cold, damp, hallway toward the cell, she squeezed the arm of her prisoner so hard her fingers left brutal red marks on the girl's skin. She opened the cell door and roughly shoved the girl inside. The girl staggered and fell to the cold cement floor.

"I'll be back," the guard leered at the helpless figure. Then she turned and walked away.

A firm but gentle voice spoke from somewhere in the darkness.

"Welcome to the NSS Resort By The Bay."

The girl struggled to her feet. Shaking and bewildered she looked for the source of the voice. It spoke again. This time with a note of compassion.

"I'm Christina Leung. ... Let me help you."

The voice in the darkness morphed into the slender figure of an attractive Chinese woman. She put her hand out to the thoroughly frightened girl.

"And who are you?"

The girl trembled when she spoke, unsure of what to expect.

"My name is Sarah."

Christina helped Sarah to a wood bench set against the concrete wall of the cell. She fished out a handkerchief from the pocket of her skirt and handed it to Sarah.

"Here.... have a good blow.... and then tell me why you're here."

Sarah unfolded the handkerchief and blew her nose. When she had finished, she looked with a mixture of bewilderment and fear at Christina.

"I don't know.... I think they picked us all up... My three co-workers.... They want us for questioning."

Then Sarah began to tremble uncontrollably. She knew what had happened to Antonio. The brutal interrogation that had left him scared. Maybe for life. What would they do to her? A woman?

Christina put her arm around Sarah's shoulders, waited for a few moments, and then spoke.

"Were you in a gang?... What did you do?"

Sarah thought about her answer for several more moments.

"We worked at an Internet Service Company in Santa Clara. The NIS shut us down.... I don't know why.... Then the NSS sabotaged our personal records.... It's all so confusing."

"They probably won't do much to you... A few questions... They probably are more interested in the men .... Just be strong and don't lie."

The sharp crack clang crack of an aluminum stick being dragged back and forth on the bars of the cell door interrupted their conversation. Startled by the intrusion, both woman looked up to see the leering face of the female guard.

"Are we comfortable? .... Come here to the cell door so I can look at you."

Sarah cowered on the bench where she was seated. The guard spoke again ever so softly.

"Perhaps you would like something to eat.... A warm cup of tea... It gets cold here at night... and so lonely."

She unlocked the cell door and entered the cell. Christina stood up and confronted the guard.

"I'll keep her warm and she's too tired to eat.... But I'd like a cup of tea."

She looked the guard in the eyes, never blinked, and let her hand drop to fumble with the woman's uniform. The guard stepped back in surprise. Christina became more aggressive.

"You don't want her. She might be important tomorrow. How will it look to your superiors if she's all messed up..... She wouldn't be any help at all... and they would blame you."

Christina kept pushing her body closer to the woman.

"Take me for tea.... I'm of no consequence... Tomorrow they plan to transfer me to the San Francisco district."

The guard roughly pushed Christina away.

"I don't take no China dolls," she said savagely.

The guard abruptly turned away, and left the cell. She slammed the steel door shut and strutted off down the hall.

Christina sighed with relief and sat down beside Sarah.

"We are safe for tonight," she said.

The two women talked for an hour. Christina was the only daughter of a wealthy San Francisco importer. A tough, smart lady with strong opinions, her assertive style of dealing with others often gave way to reveal a more gentle and compassionate persona. Sarah told her about her work, her search for the perfect man to marry, and then – she talked at length about Antonio. Just before they drifted off to sleep, Christina summed it all up for Sarah.

"You have been looking for the perfect man. That's the same fantasy I had. He doesn't exist, Sarah.... and even if he did you probably would not recognize him."

Sarah lay back in her dirty bunk. Still thoroughly frightened, she blocked out the day's events by thinking of her affection for Antonio.

***

When the big oak doors of the NC closed behind him, Rick felt more at ease. He was home. This was a place he could share with others. They were all family. His feelings were even more elated when Harry saw him and walked briskly to his side.

"Rick!" he exclaimed. The two men shook hands. Harry called across the dining room to a short, round, energetic man with white hair and thin rim spectacles. It was, of course, Father Giovanni. He looked up, and when he spotted Rick, he gave out a shout of welcome. If anything were true about Father Giovanni, it was the simple fact that he was a genuinely affectionate human being. He loved people. And he had a special place in his heart for Rick. The two men embraced and began to talk with such enthusiasm no one else could possibly have interrupted them. Harry only smiled and listened to the conversation. But then Rick's face became very serious. He told Father Giovanni about the arrest of James, John and Peter. Father Giovanni's face grew somber.

"What do you plan to do?"

"Tomorrow, I plan to get arrested.... If all goes well, the NSS will interrogate me alongside the others. I hope to deflect any blame from them to myself."

Father Giovanni looked attentively at his friend for several moments.

"You're a good man, Rick. Not many would do what you plan for the sake of a friendship."

"But I am," Rick responded. "And I will. It is as Micah has said. I am responsible for those around me. ... May I stay here tonight?"

"Of course.... and after dinner we can have a good talk."

"I'd like to spend some time with you. You appear to be in a philosophical mood."

***

By 9 PM most of the younger children were tucked in bed, the dinner dishes were done, and Father Giovanni could take a well earned break from his hectic routine. He brought two cups of tea to the kitchen table where he and Rick could sit to have a private conversation. When Rick put the cup to his lips, he was surprised it was filled with crushed ice and a liquid that looked like tea. He was even more surprised to discover it was bourbon.

"The best tea for a late evening repast," Father Giovanni smiled.

Rick swallowed a sip of bourbon and returned an impish grin.

"In cups.... so the children won't know.... right?"

Father Giovanni grinned openly, his eyes beaming with merriment over his thin rim spectacles.

"And it will help to free up our thought processes.... I can be quite eloquent with one of these under my belt."

The thought of Father Giovanni being a philosopher with the help of a bourbon amused Rick. He looked at his companion in the eye and said with a great pretense at being serious:

"What shall we talk about?"

"Truth.... we shall talk about truth... But first, I have a question."

"OK."

"Did you see the fires in San Jose?"

"Yes, just as I was leaving the freeway.... and again from the parking lot.. What's going on?"

"Riots.... People are unhappy.... There's not enough gasoline, diesel or propane fuels to go around... Rumor has it things are going to get worse.... much worse.... People can't get to work, can't go to the store to buy groceries, get their kids to school or anything else.... and as for propane....

many of those who don't have natural gas had to burn wood last winter to keep warm.... The misery just keeps growing"

Rick immediately had a vision of Micah and his coal stove.

"Is that why people are starting to burn coal for heat and cooking?"

"If they can get it."

Father Giovanni sat back in his chair.

"For you however, shortages are a blessing."

Rick was completely surprised by Father Giovanni's words.

"Why?"

"Because shortages mean riots, and riots mean the NSS will have their hands full keeping track of riot leaders and events. Your indiscretion will soon become small potatoes. The bureaucracy will be so busy with other things they won't have the time to bother you."

"I hadn't thought of that.... I hope you're right."

Father Giovanni took a long sip of his "tea".

"What do you plan to tell the NSS tomorrow?"

"The truth.... I want to end this as soon as I can."

"And what is truth?"

Rick started to stammer a response but he stopped. He knew Father Giovanni wanted to answer his own question.

"Truth is reality..... But unfortunately.... Truth is unpopular.... You want to tell the truth but the NSS won't like it.... My residents want to know the truth about their future, but they don't want to know the answer unless it's what they want to hear. Our politicians routinely ignore the truth if it conflicts with their quest for political power. The list of denials goes on and on. We humans have a long history of denying truth and since truth is reality, I suppose that means we humans frequently refuse to accept reality."

Rick sipped his "tea" and waited for Father Giovanni to speak. He became most eloquent.

"What is truth? Truth is reality. It is the right answer. It describes how things really work. It is the ultimate understanding of the Cosmos. It is the perfection of knowledge. If truth is unpopular, it is because truth often conflicts with prior belief. How many times have we been forced to change our mind because we found out our beliefs were in error? It is a natural process, one which God has ordained for us when we were given the intelligence to discover and reason. We should be willing to recognize the path to truth – and understanding reality – often requires we discard or modify prior knowledge."

Rick began to fidget with his cup. He wondered why Father Giovanni had launched into this philosophical discussion. Father Giovanni guessed what Rick was thinking.

"Truth may not be evident. It must always be discovered. One can not reject God on the basis of known observation or calculation, because man's understanding of physical reality keeps changing. Today's knowledge is often tomorrow's ignorance. It will always be possible, for example, ... that God exists in a form most humans have not experienced."

Father Giovanni paused for a moment, and then pressed on with his dissertation.

"The discovery of truth encounters a paradox. For many questions, absolute truth is unknowable. One can only hope to discover that which is highly probable. We are not absolutely sure what happened during the creation of our physical universe. We do have explanations. But they rely on the acceptance of theory. And theory is not absolute fact. Theory is belief. Does it not follow that if truth is an expression of belief, and these perceptions of reality keep changing, then is it not possible to develop both materialistic and non-materialistic explanations of the Cosmos that are equally valid?"

"When we speak of going to heaven, we are really talking about the transformation of our energy – our Life Force - from one universe to the other. Science has often denied there is any evidence of this transformation, or a Spiritual Universe. But to those who doubt I ask a simple question: have you looked? ... Think about it.... Just over 100 years ago our best scientists did not believe atoms existed... But they found them... Many scientists denied the existence of protons, electrons, neutrons, neutrinos, quarks and a long list of theoretical bits and pieces to the puzzle that is energy and matter.... But today, science believes it has found them."

Rick was puzzled... "Why did they find them?"

Father Giovanni's response was both eloquent and simple.

"Because they looked....."

Rick looked a bit uncertain. Father Giovanni continued to press his point.

"Your people found a job because they looked for one..... You found our NC today because you were looking for it.... If you want to find God, you must look for God.... Seek him out.... It is interesting to note how many people have described their coming to God as a journey, a search, a quest, or a footpath to spiritual salvation. Rick, ... they found God... because they looked for God."

Rick nodded his head in agreement. He had already sensed he was on such a journey. He was seeking a better understanding of spiritual truth. Father Giovanni looked intently at Rick. He knew Rick was undergoing a transformation, and so he continued his message.

"We humans have developed our religious theologies in an attempt to understand our relationship to our natural world, our universe and our Cosmos. It is impossible to exist without trying to comprehend the meaning of this relationship. This effort leads to the essence of religious experience. It may come as a personal sensory awareness, or it may be the result of our participation in an institutional service. But our view of the Cosmos is a critical component of self realization.

The idea that all things we observe are separate one from the other is an illusion of our perception. We sense energy and matter. But that which we sense does not exist by itself. It acts and reacts with all other energy and matter. Although we may not be aware of this action and reaction, that failure is merely an illustration of our limited senses. The realities of energy and matter continue to exist, even if they evade our perception. The physical universe exists in ways we can not experience… That is reality. The Spiritual Universe also exists in ways we can not experience…. That too is reality. We humans should have learned from science that many things exist… even if our senses are too limited to experience them. And that is the paradox of truth. Absolute truth is unknowable. Although we humans do not have the ability to understand all reality, …. it exists.

"Just remember. Despite the chaos we may observe, there is an orderly harmony in the Cosmos. We are all interconnected with this reality, …this unity, …this interaction of the physical with the spiritual, and this interaction has become central to all the great religions found on our planet, however it may be expressed."

Father Giovanni drained the last of the liquid from his cup. And then he challenged Rick.

"Do you know why I am telling you all this?"

"I confess, Father. I do not," Rick smiled. It had been an unusually long dissertation.

"Because understanding the nature of truth is a fundamental pillar of what you are about to experience……"

"What do you mean… what I am about to experience?"

"You have started on your journey, Rick. I know and you know it has begun. You will have many experiences… and hear many conflicting thoughts…. You will need to measure them against your understanding of truth and reality, and your comprehension of how the physical interacts with the spiritual."

***

It was hard to fall asleep. He kept imagining the confrontation with the NSS. Getting arrested. Interrogation. Humiliation. Perhaps torture. Rick went over and over his responses to the NSS interrogator. Finally he said to himself… "*This fear of tomorrow is doing me no good. I need to sleep. I need to be fresh and alert in the morning.*"

He tried to doze off. Bits of conversation with his team and images of the NSS interrogation drifted through his semi-conscious state. The health and safety of several people were in his hands. He could not fail. He must not fail. The fear of failure began to dominate his dream state. Horrible images of his friends pleading for mercy. Splatters of blood and hideous screams. NSS agents leering at helpless victims. Bodies consumed by fire. He struggled to help them, but he could not. They were always out of his reach. In his dream, he was paralyzed. He could only watch the same vile scene over and over again with terrifying anguish.

Then a matter of fact voice said to him: "Now you know where Hell is… It's here… On this earth…. Hell is a human invention."

Rick awakened with a start from his dream. His bed was damp with sweat. He needed to think of something else. Rick turned to God for help.

He began to pray by thanking God for his blessings. He thought about Neema and his children. Rick pictured them in his mind, one by one. Next he prayed for Father Giovanni and the people at the NC. Then he thanked God for the friendship of his team members and asked the inevitable questions about tomorrow. "How will all this turn out? ... "What should I do? ... And how can I protect my friends?" He asked again for God's help and drifted off into a troubled sleep.

The next morning he received his answers. After he had finished breakfast, Father Giovanni came to his table and sat down.

"Everything is going to be OK," he said reassuringly. "Be yourself... Be a leader.... Be friendly and firm... Show the NSS people they have better things to do than pursue your little team."

With that, Father Giovanni got up, flashed a broad smile, shook Rick's hand, and walked away. Rick felt a tingling sensation in his hand and a surge of energy flow through his entire being. He suddenly felt more confident. Father Giovanni had come to his rescue and given him strength.

"I can do this," he muttered to himself.

***

It was not hard to get arrested. All Rick had to do is drive Neema's CR-V into the visitor's parking lot at the NSS compound in Sunnyvale, walk over to the guard house, and announce who he was. The startled guards immediately whisked him into a big black SUV. In less than five minutes Rick was walking down a damp cheerless hall to the interrogation room. As he entered, he was surprised to see Sarah and a Chinese woman in the room with James, John and Peter. They were equally surprised to see him. Rick shook hands with each of them. Then he turned to Sarah.

"Why did they pick you up?"

"I don't know. I can only guess they wanted to get all of us in the same room at the same time."

"But who is this?" Rick asked as he turned to Christina Leung.

Sarah moved closer to her new friend.

"When the guards came to escort me here, they insisted on bringing Christina to the party..... Christina Leung, meet Ricardo Vasquez..... We all call him Rick."

Rick shook the woman's hand. Although Christina had decided to say nothing, she gave Rick a tentative smile. He sensed her apprehension, and then immediately knew what she was thinking.

"Let me do the talking.... I'll tell them you're not one of us."

Christina looked at Rick with curiosity. Even though he only shook her hand, she felt a warmth in his demeanor that made her feel at ease.

One of the guards rattled a metal chair.

"Sit down.... all of you," he ordered.

They took their seats and waited for the interrogator to appear. When Peter tried to whisper to Rick, a burly guard shouted at them, "Silence!"

A thin blond woman appeared at the doorway. She appeared to be very agitated, as though this whole interrogation was a waste of her time. She peered slowly at each person in the room, and then took a seat directly across from Rick. She carefully sorted through the files. Then she looked at Christina.

"Who is she?" the woman snapped. "I don't have a file on her."

Christina responded slowly and deliberately.

"I'm Christina Leung. The NSS is holding me for the San Francisco district. They are supposed to pick me up today to take me up the peninsula."

"Do you know these people?"

"Only Sarah. She and I shared a cell last night."

The blond woman looked very unhappy.

"Obviously a screw-up…. Guard … find me this woman's file."

One of the guards scurried off to find the errant paper folder. The interrogator continued to fidget with the files on the desk. She was not prepared for this interrogation, and she was obviously confused by all the paper work. Finally, after much groaning and frustration, she looked at Rick.

"All I can see is that you did something the NSS didn't like. You and your people."

She absently waved her hand at the others in the room.

"I can't find any specific charges that you broke any laws except hacking into the NSS files. We could charge you all with a felony for that, either directly or as accomplices."

Then she leaned back in her chair and contemplated the anxious faces before her.

"But there are extenuating circumstances….. If you agree to tell me the truth and cooperate… I'll drop the charges."

A collective sigh of relief swept the room. Rick relaxed in his chair.

"We will help the NSS… Of course we will…. But why don't you let me clarify things for you on behalf of the whole group."

Rick didn't trust this woman. Not at all. But he decided it was worth playing her little game to see what would happen. What the interrogator said next, however, was astonishing.

"As you know, the NSS has the responsibility to monitor anyone in government …. federal, state, or local…. to make sure they aren't disrupting the processes of governing."

Rick looked at Peter. "Disrupting" was a code word the NSS liked to use when it was after anyone who was out of line with government policy or propaganda. The interrogator continued her explanation.

"We have had some complaints against Congresswoman Belle Gunness…. I'll not go into them… But according to her file Belle was responsible for closing your ISP and putting you all out of work… Is that true?"

Rick thought about his answer for a minute. Should he be cautious, or lead this woman down the path she obviously wanted to go? His little business was of no real interest to the NSS, and it was likely they had already patched the software to prevent anyone from duplicating John's hack. No. This woman was looking for a bigger fish to catch, probably so she could make a name for herself. He decided to tell her the truth, or at least the truth as he understood it. A trace of a smile crossed his face. He remembered last night's conversation with Father Giovanni about truth and reality.

"We are not sure. But it would appear Belle used her NSS contacts to cause our personal files to be modified with a code that shows we cannot... should not... be employed. Our crime, as you have deducted, was to change those codes so we could get jobs to support ourselves and our families.... and that's all we did."

"What about closing down your business?" the interrogator demanded.

"Belle did ask me for a contribution to her re-election fund... I refused."

"Did the Department of Public Information close down your business soon after that?"

"Yes... but I really don't know if there is a connection."

The interrogator looked very pleased with herself. Apparently she was building a case against the Congresswoman. She looked at the others.

"Do you have anything to add?"

Rick's friends all shook their heads. No one said a word. The woman closed the files on the desk and looked thoughtfully at Rick.

"I could nail you for hacking into our system. I probably should. But I have more important things to do and I don't have the time. I'll close this case.... and put a code in your NSS personal files that will let you get a job with smaller companies.... Even start your own business... But you won't be allowed to work for a large corporation or any agency of the government.... You people are obviously security risks."

The interrogator stood up and prepared to leave the room. She waved her hand at them and murmured to the guard. "Let them go."

Another guard suddenly appeared with a file in his hand.

"Here's the file on Leung," he mumbled.

The interrogator grunted something unpleasant and pushed him aside as she walked off down the hall. The guard looked uncertain as to what he should do with the file. Christina walked up to him with a big smile and took the folder from him.

"I'll take care of this," she said sweetly.

***

It was all over in a few minutes. They all checked out with the exit desk, were escorted to an NSS bus in the parking lot, and were driven to the Santa Clara rail station. It wasn't where they wanted to go. But that is where the NSS bus was supposed to stop. And so it did. Rick chuckled. Then he just shook his head in disbelief.

"I guess I'll have to go back to the NSS compound to get Neema's CR-V.... I left it in the visitor's parking lot.... But first, let's have a little talk."

Rick waited for them to find a seat on the platform benches.

"We've been lucky. If they had nothing better to do, they would have crucified us.... just for the pleasure of being nasty... But they are busy.... Too busy for us."

Rick's hand swept over the horizon toward San Jose. A thick cloud of black smoke was still billowing up from last night's riots. His companions were shocked by what they saw.

"Peter... you, James, Sarah and John have to leave San Jose before they change their mind. You can come up to Winters, but we need to find something more permanent to do.... something that makes money."

Peter spoke up. "The President has told everyone she wants to put America back to work... Congress has created another jobs bill... I saw an item on the Internet about the National Internet Service... They have decided to farm out rural ISPs to local entrepreneurs.... The NIS wants to claim it is creating new jobs... That will make the President look good."

"I saw that item," John added. "They are even willing to grant money to ISPs under a Federally Chartered Government Sponsored Enterprises program."

Rick looked at Peter. "Will you see if we can get a rural license.... and some money?"

Peter nodded. "I'll get my niece Anika to help... and my wife. We can blanket the NIS with calls until we find the right person to talk to, someone like the interrogator this morning, ... someone who wants to be politically correct."

Rick looked hopeful. If Peter was successful, they would be back in business. He knew they would never be rich, but at least they would be able to survive. He turned to the group.

"Let's just hope the left hand doesn't know what the right hand is doing. The NSS would be dead set against our starting another ISP.... not after what we did with our Internet service the last time. We have to make a deal with the National Internet Service with as little notice as possible. Hopefully we'll be up and running in another part of the state before the National Security Service finds out we've been funded by a different government agency."

Then he turned to a wide-eyed Christina.

"And what are we going to do with you?"

Although a tough lady, Christina Leung could not help but blush. She was very impressed with these people, especially Ricardo.

"I'd like to join your little band of merry men and women... I really don't have many other choices just now... and you people seem unbelievably lucky."

Christina glanced over at Sarah. "Can I stay with you?"

***

Although two very different people, Sarah and Christina soon became good friends. Christina's always practical assertive style contrasted with Sarah's gentle, spiritual demeanor. The two would learn from each other. Sarah would learn to be more assertive. Christina would become more comfortable with her role as a compassionate friend. Sarah learned her programming skills at San Jose State, tended to be liberal in her views, and came from a family with limited financial resources. Christina graduated with a degree in Economics from Stanford, leaned toward a conservative ideology, and came from a very wealthy family. Given these differences, they decided that sometimes it would be better if they did not talk about politics.

Christina didn't dare go back to San Francisco because the NSS was probably still looking for her. She, along with some students at San Francisco State University, had been involved in a fuel shortage demonstration that got out of control. The NSS was questioning anyone they thought may have instigated the ensuing confrontations. So she limited her public appearances while helping Sarah to pack for the trip to Winters.

Peter, his wife Jocelyn, and his niece Anika spent the next two weeks making inquiries about rural ISP licenses and grants. In the evenings Peter and his wife began to pack their belongings for a move they wanted to avoid, but knew they had to make. They were glad their children were grown and out of the house. That made uprooting their home, saying goodbye to their friends, and moving a little easier. Anika still had her job and would be safe in San Jose.

James and his wife Renita were going through the same trauma. Although they didn't want to leave Santa Clara, they knew it was inevitable. Like Peter and Jocelyn, they needed a steady source of income in a place where the NSS was unlikely to bother them.

John, dear John, he took it all in stride and made no preparations to move. He spent his day time hours cruising the Internet and exploring system software and applications. Most evenings would find him occupied with multiplayer games. John's activity on the Internet placed him in the upper echelon of network software experts. His interest in multiplayer games brought him closer to game designers. Over the years he built up a long list of contacts. Software experts who respected his programming capability. He often exchanged tips with them, and several speculated he could use a "backdoor" to access the Internet undetected.

***

The third week of June Sarah and Christina rented a van and moved Sarah's belongings to the Mitchells' home in Winters. When they arrived, Abigail and George greeted them with great empathy for the disruption of moving. They quickly found a place in the barn for most of Sarah's furniture, boxes and trunks. By the end of the day Sarah and Christina were settled in their new temporary home, glad the move was over, and a bit apprehensive about what would happen to them next.

After dinner the three women cleared the table and did the dishes. George went out onto the porch, sat down in his favorite rocking chair, and began to hum happily to himself as the sun began to disappear behind the hills. The women came out to join him, and soon all were engaged in a quiet conversation about San Jose, the NSS, and the day's events. As dusk began to settle over the farm, the headlights of a car appeared on the road to town. It slowed down, turned into the driveway, and came to a stop about 70 feet from the house. Three occupants emerged and started toward the porch. It was Phillip, Lydia and Antonio.

When Sarah realized it was Antonio, her heart began to pound. She drew a long deep breath. Sarah got up hesitantly from her chair and walked slowly down the steps. Eyes focused on Antonio, she was only aware of his image. No one else mattered. As he drew closer to her, she was sickened by the scars on his face. He seemed to walk with a slight limp. Sarah knew he was still suffering from the NSS beating.

Impulsively, Sarah ran the last few steps to him and threw her arms around his neck. She hugged him with all the energy she could command, and began to cry softly into his collar. The astonished Antonio returned her hug, and gratefully immersed himself in the warmth of her trembling body. He was suddenly very glad Lydia had insisted he come with them to visit with George and Abigail. Finding Sarah was a wonderful surprise.

Up on the porch, Christina looked at the spontaneous show of obvious affection. She smiled at the couple, a feeling of delight growing within her, *"Sarah, you've found Mr. Right. He was there all the time... Just waiting for you to find out who you are."*

Chapter 6   Transformation

The third week of June was characterized by cool mornings, hot days and warm nights. Area farmers, who had battled unusually cold weather all winter and spring, were glad they could work the land in familiar ways. Rick had gotten into the habit of taking a morning walk into Winters, strolling down Main Street and then returning by Edwards Street or Grant Avenue. In the cool breezes of the fresh morning air, there would always be a mixture of wonderful fragrances: flowers and new mown grass, intermixed with the aroma of donuts, cakes, breads, and other treats in the shops he passed.

On this particular morning he noticed the door of St. Anthony's Church was open and – on an impulse – walked into the parish hall. He was immediately greeted by the smell of polished wood and burning candles. He went over to the candle stand, made a small contribution to the box, lit a candle, and placed it in one of the glass holders. He wandered around the hall, looking at the windows, the alter, and the cross. The images of a suffering Jesus filled his mind as he drew nearer to the cross. Rick knelt down and began to pray. At first he was uncertain. Why was he suddenly so passionate about connecting with the cross? His mind was full of conflicting images. Although he tried to focus his attention on one central theme, he could not seem to organize his thoughts.

But as he searched for a focus, he became more tranquil, almost serene as he let his thoughts drift from image to image. Neema. Adonica. Serafina. Ramon. John. James. Peter. Phillip and Lydia. His parents. Antonio's scars. Sarah's arrival. Meeting Christina. The NSS. San Jose. There seemed no limit to the images that filled his thoughts. Then he felt a gentle hand on his shoulder. Rick turned and looked up. It was Father Michael, the old Priest who performed the ceremony when Rick married Rosalinda. Rick looked at him in astonishment. He hadn't seen Father Michael for years.

"Good Morning, Ricardo," Father Michael said with a kind smile and affectionate voice.

Rick stood up and shook the old Priest's hand. Father Michael motioned him to a church pew. The two men sat down and studied each other for a few moments. Then Father Michael spoke.

"I hear your life has been disrupted by a series of events. ... "I'm truly sorry to hear about Rosalinda... may God give her grace."

Father Michael took Rick's hand and covered it with his own. Rick could feel a surge of compassionate energy flowing into his body from the Priest's hand. He was suddenly completely at peace. Calm. Joyful to be alive.

"Yes... I loved her very much."

"Rosalinda is in a better place. She still loves you, and the children. You can be at peace. Fear not about where she is. Her spirit lives on in the Spiritual Universe."

"The Spiritual Universe?"

"Yes, Rick..... there is such a place.... where she has energy and joy."

"I've heard that term before. Where is the Spiritual Universe?"

"An explanation of its location would take us more time than I have... unfortunately... but you need to know the Cosmos includes multiple universes... There are several kinds.... and in one of them Rosalinda dwells at peace."

Rick wasn't satisfied with Father Michael's answer.

"Tell me more," he demanded in perhaps a louder voice than he really wanted to use.

Father Michael again smiled with the care of a sympathetic father.

"Over these last several months, have you not experienced an increasing spiritual awareness?"

"Yes.... but I thought it was just a greater sensitivity to those with whom I come in contact."

"Of course... many people have the same experience... the same ability... We connect with the spiritual because we open ourselves to the possibility it actually exists.... But for you, it is far more than that."

Rick settled back into the pew. He decided to let Father Michael make his points without interruption. Father Michael continued.

"We humans are able to experience the physical dimension... the physical universe... with the senses God gave us... We can see, hear, smell, taste and touch the world around us. We can extend our sensual perception with scientific instruments to see the very small... an atom for example... or the very large... as we do when we study the stars. But our ability to sense our environment... the Cosmos around us... doesn't stop there. Our Cosmos includes both physical things and the energy that flows through them. In fact, even the physical things we can see or touch are really concentrated forms of energy. Billions of atoms that happen to be in the same place at the same time, all energetically interacting with each other. A piece of steel. A fresh breeze. The water in the ocean. These are all forms of energy. When we develop a true spiritual awareness, we learn how to tap into this energy... feel its presence... and when that happens we open the possibility we can experience the Spiritual Dimension."

Father Michael paused for a moment before continuing. Rick was having trouble absorbing all he had heard, but he didn't want Farther Michael to stop.

"We are spiritually aware when we connect to the Spiritual Dimension. It is the energy that flows throughout the Cosmos. We can experience that energy.... and from there we can enter the Spiritual Universe. That is what happened to Rosalinda. It will happen to you... someday."

"Explain the dimensions," Rick asked in a low voice.

"There are three dimensions of space in our known physical universe. Up/down, backward/forward, right/left. For many scientists, time constitutes a forth dimension because at an given instant of time, all things in space are at a specific place. Where we are is always relative to the time we are there. Some scientists believe there are additional dimensions of time and space. You do not need to understand the complex physics and mathematics of these probabilities. What you do need to realize is that the energy of the Cosmos permeates all of these dimensions... and Rick... one of these is the Spiritual Dimension. We can not experience the Spiritual Dimension with our five physical senses, but our spiritual self is able to make the transformation. When we enter this dimension we are able to experience the Spiritual Universe. It is there, Rick. Just follow the Angels' Footpath. That is where you will find God."

Rick was troubled. He had many questions to ask. But Father Michael slowly rose from the pew and stretched his arms, as though he needed a nap.

"I must go now. I know you have much to think about. But don't worry. It will all come to you.... I promise."

With those words, Father Michael walked toward the alter, turned to give the sign of the cross, and disappeared through a door. Rick felt a sensation welling up within him. A sense of mission. He would care for everyone with whom he came in contact. He would assemble his friends, get them settled in a new location where they could be safe, and then reach out to others with the message that was gradually taking form in his mind. Rick stood up and then bowed his head before the cross. A surge of energy flowed through him. He shook his head at the wonder of it all.

"*Why me?*" he thought.

Rick slowly walked up the aisle toward the open church door. A man appeared in the doorway, saw Rick, and waited patiently for him in the vestibule. It was a young Priest. A nice looking man of about 35.

"Have you had a fruitful encounter with God?" he asked.

"Yes... I have," said Rick thoughtfully. "And a very challenging conversation with Father Michael.

The Priest looked carefully at Rick, obviously puzzled.

"That's wonderful..." he said as Rick shook his hand.

Rick smiled and went on out the door. He sensed the Priest's confusion. As he was walking down the sidewalk, the Priest called out to him in a very uncertain voice.

"Father Michael passed away over 10 years ago."

***

By the end of June, Christina's parents were able to smuggle her clothes and essential possessions out of San Francisco and up to Winters. George managed to find additional storage space in the barn for multiple boxes and several pieces of furniture. "I hope we don't get any more guests," he quipped. "I'll have to build another barn."

On the last day of the month, Phillip took Lydia for a late evening walk around the Mitchell property. The barn's loft was stuffed with a new crop of hay that gave off a pleasant pungent-sweet odor. They fed the horses some grain, played with the dogs, and laughed at the antics of

Abigail's newborn kittens. Then, as they turned to go back to the house, Lydia began to talk about jobs, income and finding a place of their own. Phillip found himself playing the role of a positive and reassuring husband. Then on an impulse he stopped and turned to face her. The words just tumbled out of his mouth.

"Lydia... will you marry me?"

Lydia smiled and reached up to playfully pull on his pony tail.

"Not unless you get rid of this..."

"But ...but ...," Philip began to protest.

Lydia grinned. She actually liked the pony tail. It was part of Phillip's character. Standing on her tip-toes, she looked him right in the eye.

"Of course.... it's time we tied the knot."

***

Harry Kieslowski was happy to help Father Giovanni with the daily chores. Busy activity helped him to suppress the heartbreaking pain he felt from the loss of his beloved Alice. He could at least pretend she was working elsewhere in the NC, ready to come to him at dinner time. But night time was pure agony. He could not make believe she was there beside him. Her spot in the bed was always empty. His pillow was always soaked with sweat.

July began with pleasant weather. Cloudless blue skies. Warm days that always gave way to cool nights. Despite their hardship, the residents at the NC were unusually upbeat, hoping for a break that would help them to get their lives back together. But things at the NC were about to get worse. Much worse.

On the sixth of July a caravan of two cars and two moving vans pulled up in front of the NC. Four well dressed men and women emerged from the vehicles. As they started toward the big oak doors, a police car came into the parking lot. Two uniformed officers got out and followed them into the building. Father Giovanni was working in the kitchen when he heard them enter. He dropped the towel he was holding and walked into the dining room. Father Giovanni was not surprised by the entourage that confronted him. He had been expecting them for some time. One of the men stepped forward.

"Father Giovanni?"

"Yes... How can I help you?"

"We are here to shut you down. As I'm sure you are well aware, this facility is in violation of many, many health, safety, building, zoning, child care, and social services laws. As a courtesy to you, we have representatives from the affected municipal, county, and state agencies who will be happy to answer your questions. And the officers are here to make sure you comply... now... today."

Although Father Giovanni had expected to be censured, he was startled and angered by the horribly insensitive attitude of the speaker.

"Do you have any paper work?"

The speaker pulled out a sheaf of papers and handed it to Father Giovanni. They all looked very official. Father Giovanni had no doubt they had been checked, and then checked again, for all the finer points of law.

"I need to study these…"

"You can do that some other time. Right now you need to inform your residents," the man almost spat out the words "They have to leave… today…before 3PM. We have vans to haul away their things"

Father Giovanni tried logic.

"But where will they go? Where will the children go? …. Most of these people came from the street. They will be homeless."

One of the women spoke up.

"We will make an attempt to see they have a suitable place to go. And the children belong in a government approved child care facility."

"And where would that be?" Father Giovanni said to the woman in a somber voice.

She hesitated for a moment. "We'll take them to Child Services. They can attend to their proper placement."

"In other words you have no place for them to go."

The woman only scowled. She was there to enforce the rules and regulations of her government agency. What happened to the residents was someone else's problem.

Father Giovanni felt helpless. He knew he was outnumbered. If he resisted, there would be a scuffle… He would surely lose. His residents were doomed… no matter what he did. He turned and summoned two members of his kitchen staff.

"Go and round up everyone you can find. Bring them here so these people – he waved his hand with an air of disgust - can explain what's happening to them."

The two women had been listening to the exchange between Father Giovanni and the agency representatives. Stunned and apprehensive, they went to find as many residents as they could. In 20 minutes some 35 adults and several children were collected in the dining room. There were sounds of anger and protest. Two of the children began to cry. The unwelcome agency visitors began to feel uneasy. The two policemen placed themselves between the entourage of bureaucrats and the outraged residents. Father Giovanni spoke to the agency representatives.

"That's all the residents we can find. The rest are out. Some are working to earn a few dollars… Most of the children are down at the playground… You'll have to find the rest of my residents, or wait for them to come home."

The word "Home" stuck in Father Giovanni's throat. But somehow he managed to continue.

"Go ahead… Tell them what is in store for them… What you plan to do…Where they will go… Go ahead… Tell them."

The man who led the procession of bureaucrats into the NC drew himself up as though to look as official and important as possible. He was beginning to speak when Harry Kieslowski burst into the room, saw what was happening, and sprinted as fast as he could toward the speaker.

"You can't do this!" he shouted at the man. "You have no right to hurt these people."

Harry grabbed the man's suit jacket by the lapels and began to shake him violently with all of the frustration and anger he had accumulated since he lost Alice. The man staggered back and fell to the floor. The two officers rushed to intervene. One drew his gun and pointed it at Harry. But Harry was beyond fear. He lunged at the officer and pushed him so hard the man fell backward to the dining room wall. They scuffled. The gun went off. Harry gave out an anguished cry and fell to the floor.

"Stand back!" yelled the other officer. "Stand back all of you!"

Father Giovanni crumpled against a wall and slid into a sitting position on the floor, his face deformed by a mixture of anguish and anger. Suddenly Clarise emerged from the kitchen brandishing a large soup spoon dripping with vegetable stew. She charged the other officer with such ferocity she was able to knock him against the wall.

She screamed at the him in a shrill voice: "Get out... get out... get out of our home!"

Clarise hit the policeman on the head with her spoon. He cried out in pain. Then several of the residents charged the two bewildered officers, disarmed them, dragged them to the big oak front doors, and threw them into a heap on the parking lot apron. The contingent of bureaucrats, who by now were petrified for their own safety, left the building as fast as they could, eyes wide with fear. By now, every resident had joined into the chant. The noise was deafening:

"Get out...get out... get out of our home!"

Then they closed the big oak doors with a loud thud, and began to stack tables and chairs against the door handles. Other residents barricaded the rear entrance. Pandemonium gripped the Neighborhood Community.

Father Giovanni crawled to Harry's side. His heart sunk as he surveyed Harry's limp body. Blood was still oozing from the gunshot wound in Harry's stomach. Clarise knelt down by Harry, checked for a pulse, and shook her head. Tears welled up in Father Giovanni's eyes. He looked down at this lonely little man who had never hurt anyone. His was a struggle to survive, to overcome the odds that were stacked against him, and to care for the woman who was his life.

Clarise gently drew down Harry's eyelids. His face was still contorted by the excruciating pain and sudden surprise of being shot. Father Giovanni took Harry's hand. Clarise sat down on the floor next to Harry, lifted his head so that it lay in her lap, and began to stroke his hair with great compassion. They patiently waited for the change that would tell them Harry had completed his journey to the Spiritual Universe. And in a little while, it happened. Harry's face began to relax. A look of serene bliss swept ever so slowly over his face. Father Giovanni knew in his heart, Harry was on the angels' path. His transformation would soon be complete. Harry was at peace. Then in a few moments Father Giovanni detected an aura of joy on Harry's face. He had joined his beloved Alice.

***

They were on the evening news. A video had been made of the residents as they threw the policemen out of the building. Then came the hasty and unceremonious exit of four more people as they scrambled for safety. The TV news anchor described the event as an insurrection against civil authority by a renegade Priest who refused to conform to the rules and regulations of state and county agencies, thus endangering the lives of over 80 adults and children. The anchor interviewed a spokeswomen from the Police Department who said they would try to bring some sense of order to the situation tomorrow morning. She confirmed they would employ a SWAT team if necessary to subdue the renegades. In another brief interview, Congresswoman Belle Gunness told the anchor:

"This incident is just another reason why the Federal Government should place civil limitations on the politically incorrect teachings of the Catholic Church. Thanks to the hard work of the California delegation, Congress has given $297 million dollars to the Department of Public and Personal Safety to develop a Book of Rules to replace the outdated mythology of the Bible and the anti-progressive theology of the Koran."

At the conclusion of the video story, a printed message appeared on the screen:

"This presentation has been approved by the Department of Public Information"

***

"You have to leave," Clarise said reluctantly to Father Giovanni. "This has been an extreme embarrassment to the civil agencies, not to mention the county authorities. They are going to want revenge, and people like Belle Gunness will parade you through the courts like a mud covered beast to slaughter. No one will care you aren't actually a priest. But they will use your trial as an excuse to hurt the Catholic Church... and all Christians... or anyone else who dares believe in God."

Father Giovanni wanted to wretch. A cascade of violent emotions swept over him... threatened to consume his very being. But he slowly... ever so slowly... calmed himself. *"Patience... I must have patience,"* he thought. Father Giovanni looked at Clarise.

"You're right. I better leave tonight, after everyone has gone to bed. The trouble is, I don't know where to go. It never occurred to me I would be branded as a fugitive... an enemy of the State."

Clarise gently took Father Giovanni's arm, and placed a slip of paper in his hand. It had a name and address in Northern California on the Eel River. She had known for some time the state would close down the NC, and she had guessed Father Giovanni would need to leave San Jose. Clarise had arranged a place of safety for him at her cousin's farm. He could stay there until things cooled down.
    "You'll always be Father Giovanni to these people.... and to the people you helped in the past with food, shelter, and hope. You have done a magnificent job, the kind of work God would want from anyone who follows His teachings.... And," she said bowing her head, "you'll always be Father Giovanni to me."
    It did not take long for Father Giovanni to pack. He had few possessions. Clarise collected enough food to last for several meals and put it into an old backpack. Nothing fancy. Mostly dry food that could be combined with water and cooked over a camp fire. They both knew Father Giovanni would have to avoid any public areas – shopping centers, trains, busses, towns – where he might be seen. She reminded him he could not use his cell phone because that would give the authorities a way to locate where he was. Father Giovanni thought for a moment, and then gave her the instrument. He told her to go to the San Jose railroad station as soon as she could, and to put the cell phone in an envelope on a train going to Los Angeles.
    "Put a fictitious address in LA on the envelope," he said.
    Clarise smiled at the thought of the state trying to find him in the human chaos of Southern California. She stayed with Father Giovanni until it was time to go. A few minutes after 2AM, he slipped out the back door of the NC. As he trudged away, Father Giovanni turned for one last look at his little community, the jewel of his tireless effort for more than 17 years. Then he disappeared into the night.

***

    The next day, Clarise had the men place pipes out the windows of the NC. When the police came, they were sure the pipes were guns. A negotiator was called in. Clarise made two simple demands: the residents were to be treated with respect, and the county must find a home for everyone living at the Neighborhood Community. The negotiator passed the demands on to the County bureaucracy. Several state agencies were contacted. No one was sure what to do. After a very protracted discussion, it was decided to keep all of the residents at the NC until the county could find a place for them. Clarise agreed. And the siege was ended. She had the men remove the barricades and open the big oak doors. Then 35 adults and 43 children walked out of the building, singing a hymn, and smiling at the video cameras. Although the tension of the siege was shown on the nightly news broadcast accompanied by the inflammatory comments of a thoroughly biased reporter, that moment of human triumph was banned from the nightly news broadcast by the Department of Public Information.

***

Rick played or talked with his children almost every day. The hot days of July gave them plenty of time to sit under a tree next to Putah Creek, tossing an occasional stone into the water, or going for a swim. At 15, Adonica was already becoming a young lady. Intelligent and serious by nature, she was also very protective of her brother and sister. Serafina was a slender, very bright, and strikingly beautiful 12 year old girl. Although she had her mother's lovely eyes and quiet demeanor, Serafina seemed to have developed an incredible inner strength. At 7, Ramon was all boy, a robust edition of his father who loved to spend as much time as he could with his grandfather, Josue. They could often be seen working side by side in the fields or tending to the farm animals. Josue was also teaching Ramon how to use the tools of a farm machinery mechanic.

On a sultry evening in early July, Rick decided it was time to propose to Neema. They strolled together, hand in hand, to the pathway over the old Vaca Valley Railroad trestle that crosses Putah Creek. Gazing down at the water as it flowed lazily under the bridge, Rick put his arm around Neema, drew her close to him, and whispered softly in her ear.

"I love you... please.... I want you to be my wife... forever."

Neema looked up at him with an expression of love and wonder. Tears of happiness welled in her eyes. Her voice trembled when she spoke. "I was beginning to think you would never ask."

She snuggled into his arms, and hugged him with intense emotion. Neema had patiently waited for Rick to deal with his emotions and commitment to Rosalinda. It had taken a long time for him to resolve his feelings. But now it was done. Neema could be joined with him as one person. A feeling of quiet joy swept over her.

"I... I can't give you much," Rick stammered. "Right now I'm just an unemployed..."

Neema looked up at the man she loved with all her heart. With a tender smile she put her finger to his lips to silence him and said one word.

"Hush...."

***

From time to time Rick would take a morning walk through the woods to the farm house next door. More often than not, Micah would have a cup of coffee ready for him. They talked about religion, politics, humanity, theology, space, time, the Cosmos, and just about anything else that happened to pop into Rick's head. Micah seemed to know everything. He could speak eloquently about the stars, or give an equally knowledgeable dissertation about atoms. Ricardo could only wonder at the man's knowledge. He soaked it up with great interest.

Early in the morning of a beautiful July day, Rick again ventured to Micah's home. As the two men quietly talked, Rick told Micah about his proposal to Neema, her acceptance, and his call to Phillip to tell him the news. Rick chuckled as he told Micah about the call. He had been in the middle of telling Phillip about Neema, when Phillip interrupted to exclaim with great energy he had proposed to Lydia. The two men had laughed together about their sudden commitment to the institution of marriage. Then Phillip proposed they have a double wedding. Before Rick could say anything, Lydia came on the phone with Phillip and shrieked her obvious enthusiasm for the idea.

"And what are you going to do?" Micah asked.

"It's all out of my hands. Lydia called Neema and they planned the whole thing. I suspect those two had already decided on a double wedding... Anyway we will have the service in two weeks."

Micah could only smile. He had a special place in his heart for these two couples. Micah was pleased they would stand before God and take their vows.

"Can I come?" he asked.

"Of course... you must come...and everyone else we know in Winters. It will be a day of commitment and joy."

Micah sat back in his chair and looked at the flowers that seemed to bloom with such perfection in his garden. His face became more solemn. He looked Rick straight in the eye to hold his attention.

"Rick... you will be leaving us soon... leaving Winters... and before you go, I have one thing to add to our conversations."

Rick sat back in his chair. Micah was very solemn.

"The Church is in trouble. Conventional theology is under attack from several directions at the same time. Although most people want to believe in the spiritual, theology has lost its way. Old explanations of the Cosmos collide with the discoveries of science. The more we know about the physical universe, the greater our rejection of the Spiritual Universe. Theology has not kept pace with man's knowledge. If the human race is to survive, that has to change. Mankind must rediscover the wonders of the spiritual. The message must be simple and unambiguous. I have given you the tools to understand the relationship of the physical with the spiritual. You have learned a new theology. Now you must carry that message to others."

Rick was very perplexed by what he heard. "But why me? I have no religious training... I am not an expert on the Bible... Surely there must be others who are more qualified."

"Rick, you have the best of qualifications. You have experienced all the human emotions: love, great sorrow, frustration, triumph, failure, joy and so on. These provide the basis for your understanding of the human condition. There has always been a connection between you and the spiritual. You have developed a great compassion and sensitivity for those around you. Abigail took a great interest in your intellectual development, and you responded to her enthusiasm. In our many conversations over the years, I have given you the basis of a new theology. That is your preparation. It is more than enough."

"But how can I make a difference? Who needs this message you describe?"

"Christianity is at a crossroads. Socialist cultural democracy clashes with ancient doctrine. There has been a significant fragmentation of theology. Absent charismatic leadership, the Christian experience mostly centers around ancient tradition and doctrine. Humanity is hurting. Confusion. Distrust. Fear. Hurt. Economic deprivation. Psychological trauma. Millions are going to need the comfort of a stable and re-assuring spiritual experience. Humanity desperately needs an enlightened vision of the Spiritual Universe. That is where you come in. In whatever you do, you must promote, practice, teach and encourage high moral values and loving compassion. Encourage honesty and integrity. Seek to elevate human interaction. Confirm the nobility of human existence. Comfort those in distress with person-to-person contact. Focus on those who honestly seek the help of God and for whom the Holy Trinity can make a real difference. Provide a path for those who seek the Spiritual Universe. Deliver a positive message. Preserve a sense of family among those you meet."

Rick was still doubtful. "I still don't understand....why me?"

"You have been chosen for this task from the day you were conceived. Everything that has happened before, is preparation for what is to come."

Although Rick was astonished by Micah's assertion, he decided not to challenge him again.

"What happens next?"

"Only God knows for the moment," said Micah. "Your confusion is understandable. But I have great faith in you. Find your way. Let it come. Your understanding of your role will increase as you come closer to God."

***

In two weeks, Neema and Rick were married in a double wedding that joined Phillip with Lydia. It was a simple ceremony. Over in a few minutes. Serafina and Adonica were pretty flower girls. Ramon pretended he was an usher. Phillip was nervous. Lydia entranced. Neema joyful. Rick especially calm. After the service, Mari and Josue hosted a quiet garden party. Neema and the girls carried on a lively conversation. Ramon never left his father's side. Phillip looked like he was still nervous about his new status, - a married man. Lydia was radiant with happiness. As the sun set behind the hills, Rick turned to Phillip and said:

"This is a moment of great joy for both of us. Let us never forget the happiness of this day."

***

    Peter was jubilant. He could hardly contain himself as he dialed the number to call Rick. The cell phone rang several times before a voice answered. It was Neema. Then Peter remembered the precautions they were taking to avoid calling attention to themselves. He constrained his enthusiasm and simply asked Neema: "Could I come to visit with you?"
    For Rick and Neema, those words had another meaning. They meant Peter had good news. Neema responded with another question.
"Do we need to discuss your arrival?"
    "Yes.... I'll be on tomorrow's AM schedule."
    Neema indicated she understood, and they hung up.
    Peter was still energized by the events of the day. He had secured a rural ISP license from the NIS for all of Humboldt, Trinity, Del Norte, and Siskiyou Counties. They had even given him a grant to fund the business. Peter suddenly realized he had much to do before boarding the first train from Santa Clara to Davis tomorrow morning. He had to contact John and James, make arrangements for a bank to receive the funds the NIS had promised, and pack for his trip to Winters.

***

    Somewhere in San Jose, in a gleaming gold multistory office building, the District Manager for the National Internet Service sat back in the comfort of his big leather office chair and smiled with satisfaction. He had made his quota. Met his schedule. That accomplishment would look good on his annual performance review. His superiors would be impressed.
    He looked at the five files on his desk. Five successful requests for a license. The NIS had processed over 1300 requests. His staff had painstakingly gone through each one. Held hundreds of committee meetings. Long hours arguing about every detail of each proposal, months of office politics, and then finally recommending 15 for his consideration. At the last minute... this man... what was his name? ... Peter... Yes... Peter... had appeared out of nowhere with a breathless request for a license and the funding to start his business. The District Manager decided Peter was so audacious he must have political connections. He couldn't be sure of course, but Peter seemed to be so positive and passionate the District Manager decided he'd better help the man. Peter's request was open ended. After approving four license requests, the manager had one left. But he needed to be able to prove the grant would create 120 jobs. Peter had been creative. Over 14 initial employees. Then they would be selling something over the Internet. The District Manager couldn't remember what they were going to sell. All he could remember is that it was something like Amazon. That was enough for him. Without Peter's knowledge, the District Manager changed the number of "Probable New

Jobs" from 36 to 120. And to make sure the venture was a success, he had given this guy Peter the balance of the funds his District had been instructed to spend on the Rural ISP program. Just over $3 million dollars.

Yes... it had been a good day... the District Manager had given someone else the Internet Service responsibility for four rural counties in the middle of nowhere, and made his quota - on schedule.

***

By mid-August, Rick, Neema, Phillip, Lydia and Antonio were ready to move North to a town Rick had picked on the Eel River. Rick and Phillip had gone up to the area to look for homes, apartments, and industrial space in late July. After consultation with Neema, Rick had signed the papers for a modest farm house nestled on a hillside. The 15 acre property included an industrial building the former owner had used for a machine shop. Not a pretty building, but sturdy and well insulated. It would serve as the home of their new ISP business.

Neema and Lydia had been collecting odds and ends of used furniture. Beds, chests, chairs, couches, tables, and kitchen paraphernalia.... The Mitchell's barn bulged with stuff. George joked it looked like a giant rummage sale.

They decided James, Peter and John would follow as soon as Peter completed his arrangements with the NIS in San Jose. Sarah and Christina would stay in Winters until Rick found them a suitable apartment. Days of preparation. Lots of hard work. But finally they were ready.

It was an emotional day when Rick left Winters. Josue hugged his son and wished him well. Mari gave him a bag of freshly baked pastries, and with tears in her eyes she whispered to Neema:

"Please take care of my son."

Abigail and George worried excessively about the small details of moving. Antonio held hands with Sarah until the last possible moment. It was a very human reaction to a separation of unknown length and a venture of great risk. But they all managed to be very brave and they were determined to be optimistic about the future.

And so ... after many hugs and some tears, they left in three passenger vehicles and two heavily loaded moving vans, headed West over the hills to Route 101, and turned North. By nightfall, they would arrive in the town that would become their new home.

***

In this town, if you were a farmer, every other farmer was your friend. Automatically. No questions asked. And all the farmers helped each other with the big projects: planting, harvest, livestock roundup, and sending their products south to the big markets in Sacramento and San Francisco. Most farmers were up at 5AM, tending to the animals and milking the cows. Then get cleaned up for breakfast, eat in a hurry, and leave the house to work through a long list of daily chores. Come 5PM they returned to feed the animals and milk the cows. Summers they might work after dinner until 8 or 9PM. The life of a farmer's wife includes making big breakfasts, hearty lunches, and three course dinners, along with washing, cleaning, tending to the children, caring for domestic animals, working in the family vegetable garden, helping her husband on really busy days, and .... having babies. There is a division of labor because that is the only way all the daily chores will get done.

Although farming is hard work, most of these farm families were satisfied with their life-style, and they were certainly glad to be isolated by distance from the human chaos that had erupted in the urban areas of California. Daily life centered around the farm, family, friends, animals and occasional trips to town. Town life centered around the little non-denominational but mostly Protestant Church. The elderly Pastor acted as minister, counselor, friend, law giver, event coordinator, and part time Assistant County Clerk.

There was, therefore, some disappointment when it was learned these new people in town were not going to be farmers. (A vegetable garden and a few animals you raise to eat but can't bring yourself to slaughter don't count). Nosey neighbors soon learned Rick and Neema were opening an Internet business of some kind, she was sweet and he was charismatic, they had three kids all by his previous wife who had died, they came from Santa Clara, were born in Winters, and had arrived with two friends who were also born in Winters. The other couple worked for Rick in some capacity they didn't understand, and had no children (why not?). The wife was a bit pushy, and with his pony tail the man was an "original character."

Somehow, Antonio was able to slip into town under the gossip radar.

***

Rick and Neema made lists. Things they needed to buy when they went into town. Things they needed to do. People they needed to see. If it wasn't on a list, it probably would be forgotten. Rick had three lists when he went into town on the third day after moving. He went to the bank to establish a checking account, walked over to the real estate office to sign some papers, purchased a long list of groceries at a rather small sized "super market" and then looked for the hardware store to buy some fixtures. That's where he met Kato.

The ramshackle building seemed to be divided into two sections. About three fourths of the structure was hardware store, and the remainder was home to the local newspaper, printer and bookstore. When Rick entered the building, he immediately noticed the two parts of the building were connected by an open doorway. Although the bell on the door tinkled merrily when he entered, no one seemed to be in the building. Rick called.

"Hello?"

No answer. He called again.

"Is anyone here?"

A voice from somewhere in the newspaper office responded, obviously annoyed by Rick's interruption.

"Just a darn minute... I have to finish this paragraph," said the voice.

Rick ventured to the open doorway and peered into the newspaper, bookstore and printer establishment. In the corner was an old roll top desk, almost lost in a sea of papers and books. Sitting at the desk was a muscular man with black bushy hair and brown skin. He finished scribbling something on a pad of paper and looked up at Rick.

"Printing or hardware?"

"Hardware .... if you got what I need."

The man struggled to his feet. He was taller than Rick, with piercing brown eyes. He squinted at Rick as though trying to understand him. He walked to the doorway and stuck out his hand.

"Welcome to our little town... My name's Kato"

Rick grasped Kato's beefy hand, returned the man's handshake, and held his hand for a brief moment.

"UCLA. ... I'm impressed. What is a college graduate doing in this little spot on the map?"

Kato was startled by the revelation.

"How'd you know I went to UCLA?"

Rick stammered a bit. "*How do I get out of this*?" he thought.

"I say that to everyone. Once in a while I'm right," he grinned.

Kato looked at him suspiciously.

"You from the NSS?"

"No... you might say I'm not on good terms with the NSS."

"Kill somebody? ... Steal their goodies?"

Rick was beginning to feel uncomfortable.

"Nothing like that.... We just moved here ... Bought a farm."

Kato brightened. "You the guy who just purchased the Smather's place?"

"Yes... and I need a few fixtures."

"I heard about you. Going to start a business here. The gossip mill has been going full steam. Lost your wife, three kids, remarried..... or is it married to three wives with one kid," Kato said mischievously. "I heard both ways."

"One wife, three children, and a new business."

"Well now, around here... that passes for news.... Sit down while I write it all up for the paper... Best way to get the facts straight..."

"Please... I.... we ... have to remain low key. We would prefer to go about our own business without any fuss."

"Son... you're in a little rural town. Everybody knows everybody and everybody knows everybody's business... If you don't want them spinning yarns about you, we best write you up for the paper."

167

Rick looked Kato straight in the eye. His stare was so intense, Kato was taken back.

"Can I trust you?"

Kato could only stammer "Sure... but I don't understand... Are you sure you're not on the lam?"

Rick ignored the question. "Give me your hands," he demanded, and before Kato could react, he took the big man's hands in his own. Rick continued to look intently at Kato for a few moments, and then let his hands go.

"I can trust you, I can see you are a man of integrity and good judgment."

Kato was flabbergasted.

"You can see that just by holding hands with me?"

"It helps... Now once again... No newspaper story about me, my family or my team."

"Team?"

"The people who will come here to work with me..... Agreed?"

Kato just shook his head in wonder. This was a very strange conversation. Then he had an idea.

"I'll agree to keep you people out of the paper if you will tell me what the hell is going on."

"We... my company... had a run in with a local Congresswoman... I refused to give her a bribe. Our business was closed by the Department of Public Information. We hacked into the NSS files to get jobs.... They know we hacked their files... By shear luck we got out of a serious mess... I ... we .. chose this town to start over... but we can't attract attention... understand?"

Kato stared at Rick. "I'm glad you trust me... that is a whopper of a story."

Kato motioned Rick to go with him into the newspaper, bookstore and printer establishment, handed Rick a chair, and the two of them sat down. Kato looked at Rick for a moment before speaking, and then said in a very low voice.

"Isabel and I came here because we needed to disappear. Same problem as you. Some fool thing happened. I still don't understand it all.... But they were hot on our tail when we left LA."

Kato leaned back and smiled.

"And now, my new friend, you know something about me that no one else around here knows... and I trust you."

The two men began to laugh. The tension in the office dissolved. They understood each other. They would indeed become close friends. Kato looked at Rick thoughtfully.

"We need to find a way to introduce you to the community.... so no one can start any silly stories.... and so you and your wife can get closer to the community. These are good people. They just need a little hand holding once in a while."

"I'll leave it in your capable hands," Rick said. "We should plan to have a long talk...."

A woman's voice interrupted them from the hardware store.

"And now," said Kato, "you'll get to meet my much better half."

He looked at Rick with a gleam in his eye.

"Just so you know... she's a UCLA grad too... Cheerleader ... Best looking Hispanic girl on the planet ... Every football game I used to look at her through my binoculars. My roommate told me I was a pervert.. When I told him I was going to marry her, he said I was hopeless."

Kato began to laugh at himself with a wide mischievous grin.

"And I did..... I married her right after she graduated."

A woman poked her head into the newspaper, bookstore and printer establishment. Isabel looked to be a year or two younger than Kato, and although she had put on a few pounds, she was still a very attractive woman with flawless olive skin and beautiful brown hair.

"Is he my customer or your customer?" she asked.

Kato smiled at his wife. "Just one more minute and he's all yours.... We're trying to figure out a way to introduce him and his wife to the community."

"Put it in the paper... You ain't got nothing else to write about."

"No," Kato said. "I can't do that... I'll explain later. Can't you think of something else?"

Isabel looked at the two men for a long moment and then her face brightened.

"We can introduce them at church... on Sunday... before the service."

***

Neema and Rick had planned to bring the children up to live with them just before school opened in September. Sarah and Christina offered to come up with them when they moved into the apartment Phillip had reserved for them. But the call Neema received in late August galvanized her into action. It was about 4:30 in the afternoon when the call came. Neema picked up the phone. It was Mari.

"Something terrible has happened."

Neema's heart jumped and a dull thud hit her in the chest.

"Has anyone been hurt?"

"No, nothing like that.... But we had a visit today from the Department of Social Services, Division of Child Abuse.... They asked for our adoption papers. We never signed anything with Rick. The woman said we were in violation of the law because we had no legal right to care for Adonica, Serafina or Ramon."

"But you're their grandparents. How can they say that?"

"She said it doesn't matter. Without the proper paper work they can't live with us. She said it was for their protection. The State of California considers them to be wards of the State."

"What can we do to help? What happens next?" The questions tumbled out of Neema's mouth.

"They gave us 15 days to get the proper paper work approved by the Department of Social Services. But when we asked how long the approvals would take, they said it normally takes several months.... They assign a case worker... hold hearings... and go to court. In the meantime the children will be put in a foster home. It's hopeless.... I just know they will show up and take them from us."

Neema thought frantically about their options. Then she gathered her strength and spoke as calmly as she could to Mari.

"We planned for them to come here in September. Let's just do it this week."

"But how will we get them to you?" Mari was clearly worried.

"I'll see if Sarah is willing to move sooner than planned. Let me talk to her and call you back."

The two women exchanged a few more words about the proposed move, how Rick and Phillip were doing, the renovation of the machine shop into a computer center, and then said goodbye. By the end of the call, Mari had calmed down and Neema was feeling better. *"Why does the State have to come between parents and grandparents?"* she thought. *"It's just more oppressive bureaucratic interference with family life."*

She called Sarah. After telling Sarah the story, Sarah asked Christina to come to the phone. Sarah put her cell phone on the docking cradle, and switched to the speakerphone function. Christina was appalled and had a few choice words about bureaucratic interference with family life. Both women agreed to move as soon as they could. They would bring the children with them. Satisfied she had things under control, Neema called Mari and relayed the plan. Mari had only one comment:

"Oh... Thank God!"

***

Sarah and Christina arrived with the children the first week of September. It was both a tearful and a joyous reunion. Neema and Rick would be together with the children at long last. They quickly unloaded the children's things from the rental moving van and said goodbye to Sarah and Christina as they drove back into town to see their new apartment for the first time. Adonica, Serafina and Ramon were thrilled with the farm. Adonica immediately decided she wanted two cows, a horse, and a goat. Serafina talked about kittens. Ramon wanted a dog. Rick and Neema smiled with the joy of the day.

When the State Social Worker visited Mari and Josue the following week, they told him the children had moved in with their parents. They gave him an address and a telephone number to verify where the children were. He only grunted in response and left the house. He never bothered checking on the whereabouts of the children.

***

They went to church the very next Sunday as a family. All dressed up and smiling. The people of the congregation were very friendly – and a little nosey. But Neema and Rick had not yet lost the euphoria of being together as a family, so they took all the questions in stride. Just before the service, the Pastor asked if there were any new faces in the congregation. Kato stood up and told everyone – in an overly loud voice – "Yes... We have 5 new neighbors!"

Kato, accompanied by Isabel, walked up to the front of the hall and introduced Rick, Neema and the children – one by one. Adonica was mesmerized by the introductions. Serafina could only give a shy smile. Ramon grinned broadly and said "hello" to everyone when his turn came. Then Kato gave a few details of Rick's new business venture. When he finished, the Pastor asked those seated near Rick's family to shake hands. Everyone clapped. Rick was impressed with the openness and genuinely friendly nature of the congregation. These were good people. They all sat down and joined together in the opening hymns, prayers and announcements of the service. The ushers took a collection. The Pastor prayed again, and then mounted the pulpit to speak.

"As you know, on the first Sunday of the month I turn the pulpit over to someone in the congregation. We have had the benefit of several inspirational and informative sermons. Now... normally... I inform the speaker so he or she can prepare in advance.... But today..."

The Pastor looked directly at Rick. All eyes in the congregation seemed to follow his gaze.

"We have among us a man who has new wisdom... something different to teach us... and this is a wonderful way to get to know our new neighbors."

Rick was astonished. Neema began to laugh. The children were puzzled. The congregation began to clap. Many urged him to take the pulpit. The Pastor motioned for Rick to come up. He hesitated. Then he felt a gentle push in the small of his back. Some unknown force was urging him to walk up to the front of the church. He slowly made his way to the pulpit. The Pastor smiled benignly, as though he knew what to expect. Rick mounted the steps to the pulpit, cleared his throat, and waited for the congregation to take their seats.

"As unaccustomed as I am to public speaking," he began. He stopped. The congregation waited expectantly. *"A bad start... try again... quick.. what did you discuss with Micah or Father Giovanni?"* Then he again felt a reassuring hand, this time on his shoulder. He had an inspiration.

"I'd like to tell you a story... a story about love... and about sharing."

Rick began to tell the congregation about his experiences at the Neighborhood Community in San Jose, what it was, how it worked, what he did, and the tragic death of Alice and Harry. He spoke for about 25 minutes. When he finished there was stunned silence in the hall. Several people were in tears. Rick led them in a brief prayer and stepped down from the pulpit. The Pastor was at a loss for words. He motioned to the organist who promptly launched into the closing hymn. The congregation sang with deep heartfelt emotion.

Neema was smiling with great happiness. There were tears in her eyes. She was so proud of her man, the emotion of the moment almost overwhelmed her. The children were astonished... Their father. .. A preacher?

After the hymn the congregation swarmed around Rick and his family. Lots of hugs and handshakes. Adonica was a rock, smiled with a light in her eye, returned every greeting and best wishes she received. Serafina was a little more reserved – shy – but she soon warmed up to all the attention. Animated by all the commotion, Ramon stuck out his hand and gave a lively handshake to every person he could contact. Neema could only look at Rick. She never took her eyes from him as she acknowledged the greetings that swirled around them.

After most of the congregation left the church, they walked out to Neema's CR-V, a happy family, hand in hand. Neema's hand closed firmly over Rick's fingers. She never wanted to let go. After they helped the children into the CR-V, he turned to her and whispered. "Did I do OK?"

Neema looked up at him, spoke in a voice broken with emotion, and said:

"You are magnificent."

**

A week later John, James with his wife Renita, and Peter with his wife Jocelyn, made their move northward. They settled into the same apartment complex where Antonio had taken refuge. Peter and James planned to buy a house when the opportunity presented itself. John was quite content with his surroundings and soon had all manner of electronics hooked up in the living room of his apartment.

As soon as he was mostly settled, Peter came to see Rick and the industrial building they would be using for a computer center. He liked the building. It had enough power and they could rig a radio link to an Internet access point. There was much to do. He and Rick developed a plan of action, made a long list of things to do, and started an even longer list of hardware to buy. Peter soon had everyone working on projects. Wiring, setting up servers, installing software.... there were a million details. Lydia began a set of books to keep track of the ISP's expenses, took charge of the lists, and acted as project coordinator. Christina pitched right in to help with the work. She pulled wire, unpacked boxes of electronics, and whatever else she could do to be useful. By the end of September, they were somewhat operational. It would be another 6 weeks, however, before they could start to solicit business.

Rick and Peter were regular customers at the hardware store. Kato was delighted to have the business. The store was an organized mess of confusion. It had everything from fishing worms for 5 cents (the sign said: "Best Fat Worms in Humboldt County"), to a large selection of tools and implements for the farmers. Rick noticed Kato had set aside a considerable amount of space for "Indoor Gardening", with plant stands, lights, timers, meters, plant trays, watering systems and a hundred other items. But no seeds. When Phillip asked where the seeds were kept, Kato replied the growers had other sources for the seeds they needed. When Phillip pressed Kato on that point, he replied in a circumspect way:

"When the Greenies put the lumber companies out of business, unemployment around here was a terrible strain on everyone. Families suffered. Marriages broke up. Kids went hungry. The Greenies went back to San Francisco and congratulated themselves on what a great thing they did for the environment. Our neighbors were left to rot. No one gave a damn about them. Some of them – he waved his hand toward the hills – started a new trend in farming. It was either that or starve."

Kato started to fidget with several bins of nuts and bolts. His bitterness and disgust was only too obvious.

"I suppose it's a big irony…. You might say… Those same people who screwed up our lumber business are among the best customers we have for the stuff our shadow farmers grow."

And that's all he would say.

***

Rick got into the habit of spending time with Kato whenever he went into town. He would usually find him in the newspaper, bookstore and printer establishment. Rick would go through the hardware side of the building, say "Hello" to Isabel, give her a list of things he needed, and then look for Kato. By October, he had the routine down to a science. That gave him 20 or 30 minutes to spend with Kato.

It was a particularly chilly day. The October sun was almost hidden from view by clouds of fog and the mist of light drizzle. Shaking himself as though to cast away the cold, Rick sat down next to Kato's ancient desk. He happened to glance at Kato's PC monitor and saw a disturbing news headline. "Renegade Priest Preaches Revolution". There, in the center of the screen, was a picture of Father Giovanni. Rick looked at the screen and began to read the story.

"Friend of yours? Kato asked with some curiosity.

"That's the man who managed the Neighborhood Community in San Jose."

"Oh… so that's the Priest you spoke about in church"

Rick waved Kato off until he had finished the article.

"He's here… Father Giovanni has a place on the Eel River," Rick said.

"I don't think he's too popular with the powers that be."

"If I know Father Giovanni, he's preaching a reformed version of Christianity. Those beliefs don't sit well with the establishment."

Kato looked at Rick with increased curiosity. "Would you like to see him?"

Rick thought about his answer for several moments. "Yes ... But how could I find him?"

Kato chuckled. "I can fix that for you... We have people around here who usually know where everything and everyone is hiding."

"Then let's make the arrangements."

***

The October sun broke through the haze of fog and mist about 11AM. Rick and Antonio had just finished running a power wire to a server when Neema appeared at the door of the building.

"I've got mail for you," she called across the room, "and a message."

Rick smiled at his wife. Even in her grubby work clothes, she stirred the sensation of love within him. He walked to the door, took the envelope, and started to open it.

"First the message," Neema said. "Before I forget... the Pastor from our church called and asked if you would please speak again next month."

Rick nodded his agreement as he read the letter. It was from a church in the next town, inviting him to preach a sermon the second week of November. Rick showed the letter to Neema. Surprised and delighted with the invitation, she gave Rick a pretty little smile and coyly asked: "Will you go?"

"Do you think I should?"

"Of course... I've always wanted to be married to someone who is famous... Three sermons within a month... What would my father say?"

"Neema, it's nice to be asked to participate in a service. But I think they are probably just curious... or perhaps bored with their Pastor's sermons."

Rick chuckled and smiled at Neema.

"On the other hand, it would be nice to meet these people. And I ..." Rick stopped, deep in thought. "Let's talk about this later."

***

The fuel riots in San Jose and Sacramento had motivated the California Legislature to relax the restrictions on oil refining. Although very expensive, gasoline was becoming more readily available. People within the community were relieved. They needed the additional supplies of gasoline, diesel and propane fuels if they were to survive the winter. For Rick and Neema, it meant they could visit other towns with more freedom.

Rick gave another sermon at his church the first week of November. He spoke on two fundamental characteristics of the universe. Neema could not believe his depth of compassion and wide range of knowledge.

"*Where does he get all this?*" she asked herself.

After the service, several people surrounded Rick, asking him questions and thanking him for the sermon. The Pastor was very gracious. He also thanked Rick for the sermon and then walked with Rick and his family to the church door.

"Look at them," he said as he waved his arm toward the parking lot. "There are more people here than any other Sunday this month."

The following Sunday Rick drove his family to the next town to give the sermon as he had promised. Several people greeted them in the church parking lot, gave them all a warm welcome, and escorted them into the sanctuary. Rick was puzzled by the large number of teenagers and young adults in the seated congregation. One of the hosts explained that each year the local Future Farmers of America held an annual day of thanksgiving by going to church. Challenged by the opportunity to speak to them Rick decided to change his topic. He thought about the many discussions he had with Micah when he was a teenager. An idea began to form in his mind. When the time for the sermon came, he climbed to the pulpit, carefully surveyed each young face in the audience, and then announced his subject.

"Today... I am going to talk about love... and lust."

A ripple of giggles swept through the younger members of the congregation. Some of the adults gasped. Rick then began to describe the differences between love and lust. He closed by showing how both affect the quality of a relationship. It was a good lesson for the young people, and timely reminder for the adults. After the service was over, Rick was again mobbed by people with questions and comments. Neema could not help but notice he seemed to love them all, answered almost every question with care, and hugged many of the parishioners with genuine empathy. He was, she decided, going through some kind of transformation.

The Pastor was very happy with the outcome of his invitation. Allowing a stranger to speak to his congregation involved a certain amount of risk, but the result had been well worth the gamble. As they were leaving, he tugged gently on Neema's sleeve.

"Where did you find him?" he asked. "When he is speaking, he projects a gentle persona, ... a natural charisma that encourages trust... I was watching my parishioners... They want to believe in him."

Neema was both flattered and taken back by the comment.

"So you agree I chose a good husband?"

"Yes, and a good messenger."

***

It was a beautiful sunny day, and Rick decided he would like to take his family for a walk through the little seaside town. They stopped and looked in the store windows, talked and laughed about the day's events, and found a little restaurant where they could have lunch. Ramon was, as usual, starved. He could have eaten everything on the menu. Adonica picked out a dish that promised to have a limited number of calories. Serafina fussed over her choice until Neema coaxed her to make a decision. Rick and Neema both chose fish. Then they all settled back to wait for their lunch. Although Neema was very happy, she was also perplexed.

"When you made the decision to come to this parish, you seemed somewhat indecisive. And you told me we should talk about your reasoning at a later time."

"Yes... I did."

"Well... is now a good time?"

Rick sighed. He was not yet sure of what he wanted to say. He also thought it would be best if he shared his thoughts with Neema, inconclusive or not. He wanted her counsel. Rick looked at his wife and smiled.

"Can we talk later this afternoon?"

***

After lunch they walked through the town, visited the park, read the memorial, and gazed over the little harbor. Three badly weathered fishing boats were tied to the town wharf. Seagulls and sandpipers cried out as they walked along a path that would take them to a rocky point. The children ran on ahead to explore an inlet.

"Now... ?" Neema asked.

"I guess so... But I'll warn you... my thoughts are still a little jumbled."

Neema lovingly squeezed Rick's arm.

"That's OK... We can work on this together."

He didn't respond right away. Rick was deep in thought. When he finally did speak, his manner was both calm and deliberate.

"I'm not sure where all this is going.... or where it may end.... or how it affects us... but I feel like I'm being pushed in a new direction. I was totally at ease speaking in church. It was a wonderful experience. The words just came to me.

"Where did you get your ideas?" Neema asked.

"From Abigail... from Mari... from Josue... from Micah... from Father Giovanni... and even from you." Rick smiled tenderly at Neema. "I once heard a man say we are the sum of all our experiences. Every person we talk to, every word we read, and every experience we have contributes to who we are... and who we will become."

"Who do you think had the greatest influence on your religious ideas?"

"Micah... I used to visit him two or three times a week when I was a teenager. He loved to talk about humanity, theology, the universe and just about anything I could think of.... He is a fascinating man."

"What about Father Giovanni. You talk about him as though he's something special."

"I learned from Father Giovanni... He is a good teacher... It's as though our conversations were an extension of the ones I used to have with Micah... and of course my experiences at the NC were ...."

Rick stopped talking for a moment, collecting his thoughts as they continued to walk toward the inlet where Adonica was pointing to a sea urchin at the bottom of a tidal pool. Ramon and Serafina were picking their way across the rocks to get a better look.

"It's all coming together. Ideas about God, science, evolution, the universe, theology... the role of religion in government... Micah and Father Giovanni had ideas that are a little different from those you and I learned in Sunday school, but it all makes sense to me."

Neema took Rick's arm again and stopped him. He turned to her and looked into her eyes. He sensed her love and devotion. He also saw a question.

"Where do you intend to go with this?"

Rick pondered his answer for a moment.

"What I have learned is really a message. I believe they gave me a message that is worth delivering to others... Christians, Jews, Muslims, Liberals, atheists, anyone willing to listen. These are hard times. The economy doesn't seem to improve. People... good men and women... nice people... are out of work... and there is talk of revolution."

Neema winced at the word revolution. Things were bad enough without the chaos of a terrible political confrontation. Rick sensed her dismay.

"The sophisticated explanations of science have failed us. They can only describe things that are physical... People desperately need a message that will bring them closer to the spiritual... a message of hope... a trust that exists outside our physical existence. I would like to believe... in some small way... I can make a positive contribution."

Rick took Neema into his arms.

"This is a journey we take together. I won't do it unless you are with me every step of the way. I will not do this unless you are by my side.... You are my friend... My constant companion... and the woman I love."

***

True to his word, Kato made contact with a man, who knew a woman, who had a friend that knew where to find Father Giovanni. In late October Rick made the arduous journey into the hills where the Eel River lazily saunters through a large grassy meadow. He drove to the end of an old dirt logging road, parked beside several other cars, and found the trail to the meadow. Rick followed a well worn footpath through a forest of pine and cedar as it climbed up and up for at least three miles. Despite the season, it was still a warm afternoon when he at last emerged from the forest and surveyed the meadow. Far in the distance, down by the river, he could see the figure of a man who appeared to be talking to a small group of people. He started down the gentle slop toward them.

Father Giovanni was speaking in a loud voice to several men and women with vigorous sweeping motions of his hands. He had just performed a baptism and was urging them all to follow the word of God. Then – out of the corner of his eye - he noticed Ricardo coming toward him. He was both surprised and full of joy.

"Behold!" he called in a loud voice. "It is he who approaches."

The people all turned to look at Rick as he made his way to where Father Giovanni was standing. The two men embraced and shook hands. Father Giovanni was very glad to see Rick, and Rick was relieved his mentor appeared to be in good health. Father Giovanni introduced Rick to his little congregation.

"They have come to be baptized," he said. "Some from as far away as Bakersfield."

His arm swept upward toward a young couple standing next to Rick.

"We have just completed our little exercise. They are with God now... and all of the blessings of the Holy Trinity."

Father Giovanni smiled at the assembled group and asked if they had any questions. There were a few murmurs, but no one spoke. Although Rick had only come to see if his old friend was OK, he had a sudden thought. He looked at Father Giovanni.

"Would you baptize me?"

Father Giovanni looked a bit surprised at the suggestion.

"Perhaps it is you who should be baptizing me," he said with a warm smile.

"No... you are my inspiration... and you are close to God."

Rick knelt down next to Father Giovanni and gazed out over the river and meadow. Father Giovanni wet his hand with a few drops of water from a basin, placed his hand on Rick's head and said a prayer. He then performed the baptism, finishing with the words:

"I baptize thee in the name of God the Holy Father, God the Holy Mother and God the Holy Spirit."

Everyone murmured "Amen."

***

After the others left the meadow, Father Giovanni led Rick up a hill to his little cabin. He stirred the coals of a fire he had going in a cast iron stove, threw on another piece of wood, and reached up for a rather rusty tin box perched precariously on a shelf above the stove. He carefully removed a fresh teabag from the tin and proceeded to make two cups of tea. They talked for about an hour about Rick's experiences since leaving the NC in San Jose. Rick made sure Father Giovanni had the food he needed to sustain himself until winter, and urged him to spend the winter months at Rick's farm. They talked at length about the sermons Father Giovanni was preaching. Rick was concerned the Christian community would consider his friend's ideas too radical, and the NSS would think they were dangerously anti-government. But Father Giovanni made it clear he would not change one word of his sermons. Not for anyone.

At about 3:30 Father Giovanni suggested Rick should leave for the trailhead because it would soon be dark. They shook hands and walked to the door of the cabin. Father Giovanni had a few last words for Rick:

"Your transformation is nearly complete. You must become a leader. At this point in human history, the world needs direction... political and spiritual... It will be a rough road. You will make mistakes. But I have faith in you. I sensed your destiny the first day you entered my little community in San Jose... God bless your journey."

Chapter 7   Ministry

It was a spectacular sunset. Banks of gray clouds tinged with streaks of bright red, orange and yellow set against the pale blue sky. Snow had fallen over the hills, providing a backdrop of crisp white snow for the outlines of trees that populated the slopes all the way up to the top of the ridge. The cold of winter had already established an icy grip on the valley. The air was filled with the pungent smell of the smoke that lazily rose from wood stove chimneys. Rick and Neema were making dinner when the telephone rang. Adonica rushed to answer the call, hopeful it might be the boy who had squeezed her hand at school that day. But when she picked up the telephone, her looked quickly turned from excitement to alarm.

"Daddy, it's for you. Some man says there has been an accident… and the driver is asking for you."

A feeling of dread swept over Rick. Who could it be? How bad were the injuries? He took the instrument from Adonica.

"Hello… this is Rick"

The voice on the telephone explained he was calling from the hospital. A woman had been brought in from an accident on Route 101. Her car had skidded off the road on a patch of black ice, and careened down a ravine. She had multiple injuries.

"What's her name?"

"Clarise," the man answered.

Rick was both shocked and alarmed. He paused a moment to think and then responded to the man on the telephone.

"I'll be there as soon as I can. The roads are icy in spots, so it may take awhile."

He hung up the instrument and turned to Neema.

"It's Clarise, Father Giovanni's friend at the NC in San Jose. She's been in an accident and she's asking for me."

Neema's eyes widened with a mixture of distress and compassion. Rick had often talked about Father Giovanni and the people at the NC. The confrontation between Clarise and the police at the NC had been a victory for the residents.

"What on earth?" Neema burst out. "Why is she all the way up here?"

Rick turned to Adonica.

"I have to go to the hospital and I want to take your mother with me… Can you and Serafina finish with dinner… and clean up… and get yourselves and Ramon to bed?"

Adonica nodded her agreement. Serafina grasped her sister's hand as if to assure herself that everything would be OK. Ramon was in his bedroom. They called for him to come down to the kitchen. Rick and Neema made preparations to leave, ate a few hurried bites of dinner, and put on their winter coats. They kissed the girls on the cheek, hugged Ramon, opened the kitchen door and rushed off into the twilight.

Rick instantly felt the sting of the bitter cold on his cheeks and nose. They got into Neema's CR-V, shivered with cold as Rick started the engine, and plunged down the hill to town.

***

When Rick and Neema got to the hospital, they were surprised to find Peter in the lobby. Rick shook off the cold and removed his coat.

"What brings you to the hospital?"

"I've just been released from post op care. I had some minor surgery done today as an outpatient..... and why are you here?"

"Remember Clarise? She's here. She has been in an auto accident."

Peter looked with sympathy at Rick. He knew the people at the NC were all a very important part of Rick's life.

"Can I help? I can stay. Perhaps give you some moral support."

"By all means," responded Rick. "Let's go find Clarise."

The three friends walked to the admissions counter, identified the room where Clarise had been taken, and started down the hall. A doctor intercepted them and placed his hand on Rick's chest to stop him. Rick quickly sensed the Doctor's concern. He didn't expect Clarise to live.

"Are you here to see Clarise? the Doctor asked. "Are you Rick?"

"I'm Rick. This is my wife Neema, and my friend Peter."

The Doctor frowned. "I should only let one of you go in at a time.... but it won't make any difference to her condition. I don't expect her to live the night. She has internal bleeding from multiple internal injuries. There is nothing we can do. I'm so sorry."

Rick and Neema thanked the Doctor for his help. Then they apprehensively walked down the hall to a room in the critical care unit. Clarise was a round faced, matronly woman in her fifties. Pale and suffering from her injuries, Clarise's bandaged body was framed by the white sheets of the hospital bed. A pair of needles had been inserted into her arm, each one connected by a long tube to a pouch of fluid. Her eyes were closed.

Rick whispered in her ear. "Clarise... it's Rick... Ricardo... I have Neema with me... and Peter my friend."

Clarise stirred as though in a dream state and looked up at him.

"I have to tell you....."

Clarise choked, coughed and cleared her throat.

"I have to tell you.... Father Giovanni is in great danger... The NSS is going to send agents to arrest him.... I drove up here to find him..... to warn him."

Rick looked upon Clarise with sympathy. Neema and Peter moved closer to the bed. Rick took the woman's hand and clasped it in his own. Her feeble hand was ice cold. Rick knew life was draining from her body.

"We can warn Father Giovanni. Do you know when the NSS agents are coming?"

Clarise lay motionless. Her eyes closed again. Then after a few moments, she spoke in a whisper.

"No... soon.... next week... next month... but soon."

Clarise abruptly opened her eyes in terror. She had to tell Rick. Make him understand.

"Oh Rick... they'll torture him... They will be merciless... His escape from San Jose was an embarrassment to the NSS... They hate him for what he did at the NC.... and... they hate him because he is a man of God.... The NSS doesn't like any theology that conflicts with government policy... Especially Christianity."

Peter looked at Clarise with astonishment and shock. He thought he knew all about the government's anti-Christian policies, but somehow he had been oblivious to their importance. Now these words were coming from a woman on her deathbed. A feeling of dread began to sweep over him. It was as though he had discovered the horror of Hell for the first time. But his thoughts were nothing compared to what he was about to witness.

Rick bent over and tenderly kissed Clarise on the forehead.

"Go to sleep Clarise... Rest your eyes.... Let your soul be at peace."

Clarise was sure Rick would get a message to Father Giovanni. She had accomplished her mission. She could rest in peace. Clarise wanted to join her family. She let herself slip into a deep trance. Images of her life swept through her semi-conscious state. After several minutes, she felt a surge of new energy. Clarise found herself on a footpath that wandered through a beautiful wooded garden. She could smell the delightful fragrance of flowers and hear the restless waters of the ocean. At the end of the footpath rays of sunlight cascaded through a portal. The sunlight seemed to summon her. Here - come to me. But Clarise was afraid. The fear of the unknown had always haunted her. Then she felt a gentle hand on her arm. It was Rick. He took her hand and walked with her down the footpath toward the sunlight. He seemed very calm... serene... confident.... loving.

"Let's take this walk together... Be not afraid, Clarise... for soon God will be at your side."

They walked slowly, hand in hand, down the footpath toward a portal bathed in the soft glow of sunlight. She was aware of the woods, the fragrance of flowers, and the footpath under her feet. Clarise no longer felt any of the pain that had coursed through her body since the accident. Instead, she was experiencing the serene warmth of a new found spiritual energy. Clarise was at peace.

Then Rick released her hand, stopped, and turned to look at her.

"Goodbye Clarise... and God bless you for being the wonderful woman you are."

Clarise smiled at Rick and continued her walk on the angels' footpath. She was unafraid. Rick had given her new found self confidence. An angel beckoned to her from beyond the portal. It gently took her hand and led her into a different dimension. And then she was gone. Gone into the sunlight. Gone from this physical universe. Clarise was with God the Holy Spirit.

Peter was watching Rick as he closed his eyes and took the woman's hand. Rick shut himself off from everything else that was going on in the room. His spirit seemed to be totally detached from his physical body. Rick murmured something in a whisper so faint Peter could not understand what he said. Peter watched Clarise with astonishment. The expression on her face softened from the contortion of pain to a look of sweet contentment.

"*She is no longer with us....,*" he thought. "*And where is Rick?.... he ... he's not here... he's somewhere else!*"

Peter's heart began to pound. His hands began to shake. What had he just witnessed?

Neema placed her hand on Rick's arm.

"It's OK... Rick... you've completed your task... Come back to us," she whispered tenderly.

Rick began to stir. He slowly opened his eyes. A tear made its way down his cheek.

"She's with God... Neema. It's a shame she had to go so soon... But God will care for her."

***

They made arrangements to have Clarise cremated, pending notification of next of kin. Rick did not think Clarise had anyone else in this world, except Father Giovanni and a few friends. There were forms to fill out. Conversations with the hospital staff. And then three very tired people headed for the front door. But before they got there, Peter took Rick's arm and held him back.

"Do you do this very often?" Peter asked in wonder.

"I will do it whenever someone needs me who is close to my heart," Rick responded with a friendly smile.

Neema came back to them and looked at Peter.

"All people who seek to be with God are close to Rick's heart. He brings them to the Spiritual Universe."

Peter looked thoughtfully at Rick. He was still trembling and he suddenly felt very warm. Peter didn't understand what he had witnessed, or Neema's comment about a Spiritual Universe. But whatever was happening with Rick, he wanted to be with him.

"You are taking a journey... aren't you?" Peter asked with some passion.

"Yes.. it is a road I must travel."

"I'd like to come with you on this journey... wherever it takes us."

"It will not be an easy road to follow," Rick said with a frown.

"I think I understand the risk, and I still want to join you."

"Then by all means my friend... you are most welcome."

***

Phillip closed the door of his car and walked toward the ramshackle building that was home to Kato's hardware, newspaper, printer and bookstore. He found Isabel just inside the door of the hardware section, busily arranging a display of Christmas ornaments. He handed her a list of things he wanted to buy.

"Good morning..... Here's a list... Just a few things... Mostly for Lydia," he said.

"Well a cool good morning to you Phillip and how is Lydia?"

"She's fine. Trying to make apple sauce to put away for the winter. She's really gotten into canning.... I don't know what half this stuff is for, but she says she needs it."

Isabel looked over the list. "No problem. Give me a few minutes to finish here. Go into the newspaper office and say hello to Kato."

Phillip smiled at Isabel and turned to go into Kato's office. "Don't break the bank," he called back over his shoulder. We're just poor people.... like everybody else."

Isabel chuckled and went back to her work. Phillip entered the newspaper, printer and bookstore part of the building to look for Kato. He found the big man sitting at his desk, holding a letter in his beefy hands. Kato looked up at Phillip.

"Will you look at this?" he said with some disgust. "Big Sister has ordered everyone to be tagged for identification."

"Big Sister?" Phillip asked.

"Rose O'Brien... our beloved President. She wants everyone to have an embedded Radio Frequency Identification tag so the Department of Public and Personal Safety can monitor our whereabouts."

Phillip frowned his disagreement with the news. The tiny RFID tags were already in use all over the world. They were embedded in clothing, food, furniture, tires... Just about every product sold in America. Whenever a product with an RFID tag passed a scanner, the information on the tag could be detected and relayed over the Internet to a computer data base.

"I'm dead set against this," Kato fumed. "Our activity on the Internet has been recorded and stored for several years. Location technology, combined with network monitoring systems, tracks and records our activity and thoughts. Information on us is being kept in multiple data bases that can be cross linked and cross referenced for the collection of personal information. Big Sister knows our financial information, political affiliations, political outlook, and personal attitudes. Every time we make a purchase with a credit card, debit card, or personal check, it is recorded and stored for future use..... Where the hell is our personal privacy anymore?"

"It's probably worse than you can imagine," Phillip said. "These data bases can be hacked. Stored data can be stolen, altered, or deleted. Our personal data is already being sold, traded, sorted, and searched without regard for our privacy or civil rights."

Kato's face showed his obvious revulsion. "We live in a brave new world, Phillip.... Where is this all going?"

"We are all connected to the network. With this last piece in place, Rose will be able to make us objects for network monitoring and behavior management."

"Damn," Kato said. "I don't think people around here will take too kindly to all that monitoring and control."

"Behavior management... all backed by the police power of the State... It's for our safety and security," Phillip intoned with mock seriousness.

Kato was about to respond when Isabel poked her head through the door.

"I have everything ready. Just come to the cash register... and bring your wallet," she chuckled. Then Isabel realized the two men were very unhappy.

"Good Lord," she said. "You two been talking politics again?"

***

Peter was very pleased with their progress. In a few short weeks they had been able to set up their computers and communications equipment, establish their Internet business, and start the challenging process of building a stream of revenue. Peter had been able to get 95 people from all over Northern California to come to a business meeting. He made a proposal to them. When the NIS took over the Internet, thousands of independent software and service entrepreneurs had been put out of business. These were the people who developed Web sites for small business owners and municipalities, managed local ISPs, and sold products through their own Web stores. Peter believed he could use Rick's Internet license as a tool to help them restart their Internet business ventures.

Anxious to network with their peers, curious about Peter's proposal, and elated at the prospect of making some money, they had come to the meeting with great expectations. Peter didn't let them down. Before they left, he had established several important business contacts, and persuaded several people to be a potential conduit for the dissemination of information, a sort of news underground that would collect and share information with everyone else on the network. Peter was determined his network would spread throughout America.

Several days after the meeting, Peter decided it was time for a little celebration. So on the Wednesday morning before Thanksgiving, he arrived at work with several bags filled with all kinds of cheese, crackers, deli meats, sour dough bread, potato chips, and nuts. Peter even brought in a mixed case of wine. And sure enough, by noon, everyone was anxious to get started with the party.

It was a wonderful, relaxing, time. Quiet conversations. Occasional laughter. A little kidding. By 2PM the consumption of wine had elevated the noise level in the ISP office area to a happy cacophony of boisterous sounds. It was a relief to be working again, and they were grateful to be safe from the uncompromising threats of the NSS.

Rick, Neema and Lydia joined the party around 2:30PM. Peter immediately made sure each of them had a glass of wine and invited them to enjoy the food he had brought – or at least the odds and ends that were left. Rick smiled good naturedly and joined in the conversations. By 3:00PM the party had quieted down again and they all gathered in a circle on the floor around Rick. The conversation dwindled away, and Phillip decided to ask a bold philosophical question. He spoke up in a voice loud enough to get everyone's attention.

"Rick... you've given maybe 12 sermons so far... and your fame is spreading far and wide."

There was a little twitter of chuckles and comments from the assembled group. Rick was not that famous. Yet they all had heard about his session with Clarise from Peter, and they knew Rick was able to make a connection they really did not understand. They were curious to hear more. Phillip continued to press his question.

"You've been preaching about the word of God.... and your success is impressive. But I'd like to know... we'd all like to know... who or what is this guy?"

Rick gave Phillip a gentle smile and sighed. He had put Phillip off once before. He might as well take this opportunity to explain his theology.

"Are you all sure you want to hear this?" he asked the group.

They all nodded in agreement, and settled back to hear what he had to say.

"First of all, let us recognize we all have our own interpretations of the nature of God. Peter's beliefs have a Bavarian cultural background, Sarah draws her thoughts from her Hebrew heritage, Antonio's faith is based on the Hispanic Catholic tradition, and my own.... are drawn from my mother, my father and my neighbor... Micah. Although there are many similarities in our basic beliefs, we each have our own thoughts about who or what God is, and I urge you to retain those beliefs if you are comfortable with them."

Rick paused to survey the group. They were his friends, as much as they were his employees. He was lucky to have them as companions.

"What I am going to tell you today.... is a little different from what you may have learned in the past. If you like what you hear, then I urge you to rethink your beliefs. But don't rush the process. It will take time to absorb all the implications."

Rick paused again, looked at each person in the group, and then continued.

"We have searched for God since the beginning of human intelligence. We have been very creative in our interpretation of what and who is a God. Our explanations have typically been drawn from current experience, our fears, and our desires. God is a woman. God is a man. God is an animal. God is a star, the sun, or the moon. God is an invisible being. God exists in the earth, in the sky, or outside our universe. God is good, God is fickle, God is a firm ruler.

"The list of ideas about God is very long. Gradually, however, most humans have come to perceive God as a supernatural being, creator of all that exists, the source of moral values, and the judge of human activity. For many, faith in the message and character of this God provides life with its intrinsic value.

"In order to fully understand God, we must abandon the requirement that all phenomena has a physical material explanation. As human science has proven over and over again, phenomena which we cannot see today is often tomorrow's new discovery. Atoms did not exist, until man had the tools to find them. Electrons did not exist until man had the means to identify their existence. DNA was only a theory until the end of the 20th century. Unfortunately, our quest to understand the physical has not been accompanied by an equally intense search for spiritual truth. That means we will not understand the Spiritual Universe until we have the intellectual and emotional tools to realize its wondrous beauty. For every individual, this quest for faith can not be fruitful until we are ready to accept the answer.

"We can start our search for God by developing a better understanding of our universe. We know our physical universe was created at a single point of space-time. Although there are several theories about the events that occurred, they all acknowledge a moment of creation. .... and here is the point to remember... If there is creation, then there must be a mechanism for creation.

"All physical matter, energy, and living organisms are governed by natural laws that give unity and order to our physical universe. The easiest explanation of their existence is that they were created by design ... which infers creative intelligence.

"People all over our planet, throughout human history, have experienced the supernatural. Although it is not well understood, it will not go away. Even science admits experience of the supernatural has occurred. This suggests spiritual phenomena are real. One explanation involves the recognition of a power that exists in another dimension or universe.

"Our human identification of a moral code and our empathy for other living organisms suggests a set of natural laws that come from a spiritual source. They certainly do not come from our sensation of the competitive physical universe. They have been discovered by the inspired revelations of philosophers and theologians for over 3000 years. They have been verified by enlightened thought, intellect and introspection. The universality of these concepts in cultures all over our planet suggests they were created and communicated to us by an intelligence outside the experience of our physical universe.

"One can ponder these thoughts endlessly. But to no avail if the mind is closed to the enlightened exploration of the spiritual. If we wish to know

God, we must be willing to discover and embrace that which is revealed to us.

"It is time for us to rethink our perception of God. That understanding which has served us in the past will not suffice for our future. We have lived long enough on this planet to comprehend a more sophisticated belief system.

"In Christian tradition the Holy Trinity brings together God the Father, God the Son and God the Holy Ghost. It shows us that the spirit of God can exist in human flesh, as it did in the person of Jesus Christ. It also suggests a personal God in the form of a fatherly figure, and a spiritual God that governs the universe. If you are comfortable with this concept, then keep it close to your heart."

Again Rick paused to scan the faces seated before him. They were receptive to his teaching.

"Our Christian and Muslim concept of God followed in the tradition of Eastern Mediterranean religious beliefs. God was powerful and God was male. If however, we are willing to observe the evidence of our EcoSystem, our perception of God must include that which we can experience. The pattern of family organization for almost all animals, including humans, suggests God is three persons. It is this triad that forms The Holy Trinity. It is a fundamental model of life. There is God the Holy Father, creator and sovereign of the physical Cosmos. He governs material matter. God the Holy Father can be discovered through the sciences of physics, chemistry, geology, and mathematics. He created the Temporal Universe which is the physical environment of our existence. God the Holy Father is order, judgment and love. There is also God the Holy Mother, creator and sovereign of all living things in the Cosmos. She governs all forms of energy. God the Holy Mother can be discovered through the sciences of physics, chemistry, biology and mathematics. She is life, nurture, compassion and love. And finally, there is God the Holy Spirit, creator and sovereign of the spiritual. God the Holy Spirit brings together God the Holy Mother and God the Holy Father to create and sustain the moral life-force that exists throughout the Cosmos. Spiritual energy influences our understanding of honor, integrity, compassion, justice, and love. It encourages moral behavior, personal responsibility, and loving procreation. God as the Holy Spirit can be discovered through introspection and communication with the Spiritual Universe. This form of the Holy Trinity enables transformation and is the path to heaven.

"God the Holy Father, God the Holy Mother and God the Holy Spirit are one in the persona of a supreme being, a force that creates, observes, guides, assists, and judges our person within a framework of time and space. We are able to connect with the Spiritual Universe, and the Holy Trinity, through prayer and heightened sensory awareness.

"God exists in another dimension of our universe. That means God is everywhere, surrounding us at all times with compassion, love, and the energy of life. The more open we are to God, the closer we get to the moral life-force that exists throughout the Cosmos. If we make an honest, sincere and humble attempt to seek God, He will listen, counsel, and judge. We must be aware, however, God rarely interferes with natural events because He prefers to preserve natural law. I emphasize this point because you will want to... need to ... connect with God. He is there, you only need to take the time... and make the effort ... to talk with Him.

"So there you have it. God is the Holy Trinity.... It will take time for you to understand what I mean by this, but there is God the Father, God the Mother, and God the Spirit. They are all one and the same, the life force that flows through the Cosmos."

"But that's not what I learned as a child..." Phillip said slowly.

"And now you are an adult. You have the knowledge and wisdom to evaluate new ideas. Take the time to understand this basic concept. It is more complex than the simple theology you learned as a child. But new knowledge always challenges our intellectual power to reason. Don't fight it. Consider my judgment."

John spoke up. "Have you put these thoughts down on a piece of paper?"

Rick thought for a moment. "Yes, John. I have started to write my thoughts down so that I can review them from time to time. When I have something put together, I'll give you a copy."

***

After Rick's presentation, Antonio drove Sarah back to her apartment. Perhaps it was the wine. Or maybe she was just feeling mellow. But in any event, Sarah felt very comfortable with him. "*He's an idealist,*" she thought. "*Rick's presentation made a big impression on him.*"

She studied him for a moment. Antonio was a bit chunky, she decided. But definitely cute with his curly black hair and black eyes. Sarah's face turned crimson with the realization she found Antonio attractive. She didn't want him to see her face this way, so she turned to look out the passenger window.

When they arrived at her apartment, she did something she had never done before. Sarah invited Antonio to come with her. Antonio was immediately flustered.

"*This can't be happening.... She's never given me the time of day... Just that one time in Winters when she felt sorry for me,*" he thought. But he managed to recover enough to stammer a response to Sarah.

"Sure... I can stay for a few moments."

Then he shrugged with another thought. "*Princess... I can stay all night if you want me to.*"

Sarah only gave him one of her enigmatic smiles and turned to open the door of the car.

Antonio rushed around the car to join her on the sidewalk. In his haste, he slipped on a patch of ice. Swinging his arms like a wild man, he lunged toward Sarah as he tried to recover his balance. He almost knocked her down. Antonio cursed beneath his breath.

"Clumsy... nutcase.. she's going to think you're a klutz."

Sarah cheerfully took his arm and walked with him to the door of her apartment. She unlocked the door and let them both into her living room. She helped Antonio with his coat, and then removed her own coat and scarf.

"I'll make us some tea.... black or cream?"

"Black... straight... with a little sugar ... please."

Sarah went into her kitchen to make the tea, leaving the baffled Antonio alone on the coach to ponder his feelings. It took forever for her to make the tea. Antonio began to fidget. When she finally returned with a tray, she was very formal, carefully measuring out the sugar, stirring each cup, and serving one to him. Antonio became even more anguished. He didn't know what to say.

Sarah sat down beside him on the coach. "Have you finished your applications project?" she asked.

"*Oh great... ,*" thought Antonio. "*She wants to talk about work.*"

Disappointed by the turn of the conversation and still baffled by the invitation to come into her apartment... her life, he responded with a long explanation of the system he was working on. Sarah daintily sipped her tea, dried her lips with a napkin from time to time, and listened to him with deliberate attention. When he finished, she put down the cup and turned to him, her brown eyes searching every inch of his face. "*Rick is right,*" she thought. "*The person I marry will be my constant partner, my best friend, and my trusted companion for a long, long time. Of all the men I've met, Antonio is the only one I can talk to without feeling self-conscious. He's so easy to get along with...*"

Sarah looked at Antonio with a growing passion. "Do you think I'm shy?"

Antonio didn't know how to answer her. He thought "*If I say yes, she might think I'm criticizing her.... If I say no, she'll probably decide I don't think about her.*"

But before Antonio could search his mind for just the right answer, Sarah spoke again in a hushed voice.

"We are two shy people," she said. "But together we can be one strong person."

She suddenly realized she was in love with him. It swept over her with such intensity she felt a little lightheaded. On an impulse, Sarah grabbed the lapels of his shirt and pulled him to her. She took his face in her hands and gave him a long warm passionate kiss. Antonio's heart leapt as the heat of the moment swept over him. He wrapped his arms around her and eagerly returned her kiss. Sarah's face was radiant with excitement. They were both shaking with the sudden exhilaration of shared love. Then she leaned back just enough to speak to him.

"You can be my shy guy," she said softly. "And I'll be your guardian angel."

***

John smiled with some satisfaction. He had found a way to publish radio broadcasts over the Internet without being detected. They could be received by anyone who knew the broadcast URL. But he was sure no one could identify where they came from. He tested his theory several times. John even had three of his buddies try to track his broadcasts to the source. They all failed. When he had finished his testing, he called Rick over to his desk.

"You've been asking if I could devise a way to broadcast radio programs over the Internet without being detected," John said with a touch of obvious pride in his voice. "Well.. Phillip and I have done it. You can now take to the airways without fear of Gestapo retaliation."

Broadcasting a radio ministry had been a dream for Rick. He could send a message of hope and love to anyone who cared to listen. The radio transmissions could also be used to convey uncensored news and current events as they happened, without interference from the Department of Public Information or the NSS. For months all news and information had been censored or created by the Department of Public Information. If people wanted to hear any other viewpoint, they had to get it from the rumor mill, usually passed from town to town by truck drivers and travelers, or from rogue Internet sites. Most of the rumors were wildly inaccurate.

"This will be a blessing for those who want the truth," Rick said. "We have many sources of information. Now we can publish what we learn. Hopefully our version of the truth will be more accurate than the carefully fabricated reports that come from the Government."

John nodded in agreement. "When do you want to start?"

"Let's try a one hour program tomorrow. If that goes well, we can increase our programming time by an hour or two each week."

"I'll set up a recording station for you in your office."

Rick was still cautious. "Are you sure we can't be detected? If they find us, John, we'll all be in more hot water than we can handle. The NSS will make an example of us for sure."

John was very solemn when he responded. "I know the risks. ... So far, anyone caught trying to bypass the censorship process has either been shot or confined to a re-education camp... But I think we can fool them."

Rick thought for a few moments, considering the risks. He felt compelled to spread the word of God by any means at his disposal, and he knew there was a surge of anti-government resentment developing all over the nation. People needed reliable information. On the other hand, he knew he had to get all of his people to agree that challenging the DPI and NSS was worth the risk.

"Let me talk to Peter and call a meeting of our people... I need to know how they all feel. If anyone objects, we will not do it.... I can't ask them to take the risk just because you and I think it's a good idea."

"I've already talked to Peter. He thinks the others will agree to go ahead with the broadcasts. But I'll wait for your decision."

Rick frowned. "If we do agree to start the Internet radio broadcasts, you've got to remember... in everything you do.... our lives are in your hands."

***

As the weather service promised, December was ushered in with a blast of cold air and showers of snow. Driving on icy roads became a daily challenge. Fortunately, Rick's employees all lived reasonably close to the building they had converted into an Internet service center. Getting to and from work was a minor problem. The team continued to make rapid progress toward a fully operational system.

Every Friday afternoon, Rick and Peter assembled the ISP team to go over plans for the following week, and to discuss any questions or comments they might have about work. The first meeting in December was very short. Only 15 minutes or so. Peter had become a skilled manager, stayed on top of the work, and was close to each member of the ISP team. As the meeting broke up, James, Antonio, and John stopped Rick in the hall. John spoke first.

"Can we talk with you?" he asked. "Peter thinks you could use some help."

Puzzled by the question and John's comment, Rick nodded to the three men. They followed him into the small cubicle that served as his office, and found a place to sit down. Rick eyed them one by one and sensed they were intent on making a decision.

"How can I help you?" Rick said pleasantly. "And what mischief is Peter up to?"

John looked at the other two men before responding, as though not sure what he should say.

"Peter told us about your sermons... and we heard you talk about God... and then there is the incident with Clarise at the hospital and... well we would like to know where this is all going... I mean Peter told us he will follow your lead... No matter where it takes you... We're kind of wondering if we should too."

Rick sat back in his chair to think about his answer. *"This is a surprise,"* he thought. *"And a welcome turn of events... What should I say."* Rick sat forward in his chair.

"I'm not sure where this is all going. My plan ... if you can call it that ... is to formalize my thoughts on paper, and preach a sermon whenever asked. I think Peter will soon be ready to preach in my place if he wants too... We've had two inquiries from congregations in the Sacramento River valley. I can't be in two places at once, so I'll have to let him fill in for me from time to time... Where we go from there.... I don't know... I don't detect there is any lack of interest... If people want us, we will go."

James began to fidget with his fingers. He was clearly puzzled by the change in Rick's persona. "Why are people asking for you?" he asked.

Rick pondered the question for a moment. "I'm not sure... I haven't performed any miracles. I'm not a magician... and my message is quite different from traditional Christian theology... Perhaps it is the manner of my presentation. That's what Neema tells me... But then it must be more then that."

"I think it's because Christianity is under attack," James interrupted. "Rose O'Brien is just itching to find an excuse to shut down our religious institutions. There is a rumor she even plans to ban the Bible and the Koran as terrorist manuscripts."

Rick could only roll his eyes toward the ceiling. There were rampant rumors of Rose O'Brien's tirades against Christianity. But then, she was angry with just about everything and anything that she believed were detrimental to her complete domination of American life. Mostly her screams went nowhere. But with a useless Congress, anything was possible.

"Why would she do that?" Rick asked innocently.

"Because...," John responded. "Because she has her own theology and she doesn't like disagreement. She believes Christian theology serves no purpose... It's just a collection of ignorant myths that stand in her way. In her mind, the very core of the Christian belief system is evaporating because it can't survive scientific analysis or objective scholarship."

"Many knowledgeable people believe Jesus never existed, and even if he did, his presence can't account for the rapid rise of Christianity," James added.

Rick smiled a gentle smile he usually reserved for those times when he was called upon to give a children's sermon.

"It's true the church has been forced to abandon many of its theological positions. The basis of our Christian belief system rests on the status of our human knowledge as it was some 2,000 years ago. But to dismiss Christianity because many of these stories and beliefs are based on a mythological understanding of our Cosmos doesn't change the historical importance of Christianity, nor does it change the nature of God.... So yes, we do have a more sophisticated grasp of physics, chemistry, mathematics, biology, and so on. But do you know what that really means?"

Neither John nor James could respond. They shifted uncomfortably in their seats. But Antonio had a sudden flash of insight.

"That only means we also have to develop a more sophisticated understanding of God."

Rick was very pleased with Antonio's answer.

"Yes... that is precisely what it means... We must have a belief system that rests on credible knowledge... else it will perish... and that gentlemen... is what I'm about."

James grinned at the implications. "A second Christian Reformation!" he exclaimed. "A Renaissance of Christian beliefs!"

John became equally enthusiastic. "Now we know why your sermons have received such great attention. People are desperate for a better interpretation of Christian theology."

Rick's composure became intensely serious.

"There is a God... If we don't fully understand the nature of God, that's our fault.... To say God doesn't exist because a skeptic cannot see God is foolish nonsense.... There are many scientific discoveries that skeptics derided before they were revealed....They did exist. The fact we could not understand them was a human weakness. And Jesus did exist. He was the greatest human ever to walk the face of this earth... and God selected Jesus to deliver a message to humanity... One which we humans have – unfortunately – often ignored. But it is there nonetheless."

Rick paused to give weight to his words. Then he went on.

"Christianity didn't flourish among the Jews because they already had a well developed theology of their own. What really happened was that Christianity thrived and gathered unstoppable strength within lands dominated by Rome.... and that's because the underlying Pagan theologies of the Roman Empire had little credibility. Rome had become a cesspool of putrid immorality, irresponsible sexual behavior, sordid bloodthirsty entertainment, and murder as a means of gaining political power... Lying had become an art form.... Politicians were treated with cynical contempt.... Treachery was expected behavior... Corruption was a way of life."

Rick again paused for a moment. He wanted to drive home a few more points.

"Human life had no significance. The structural worth of an individual was based on one's current - and often temporary - utility value. One was a slave, a concubine, a senator, a gladiator, a farmer, or a soldier... But outside this occupation the individual had little value.... And then into this quagmire of personal desolation came the message of Christianity. Remember this... People need a spiritual experience.... They need to know they have a personal value within the Cosmos that transcends the limitations of mere physical existence. Else life loses its meaning. Think of the concepts you associate with a civilized culture - integrity, love, truth, charity, compassion, personal responsibility, and so on. People need to live within a cultural ecosystem that reinforces the importance of these values. Christianity was the right theology, at the right time, in Roman history."

"And what is your mission?" asked John.

"My mission is to clarify the message of Christ, the message of love.... and to add one other... the existence of a Spiritual Universe."

"But what can we do?" James asked. "We'd like to help you with your mission, but we don't know much about that stuff."

Rick thought about his answer for almost a minute. Then he quietly spoke.

"You can learn... I'll teach you.... Peter will help... and then you can teach others by deed and sermon."

"But we're not preachers," Antonio protested. "We're programmers."

Rick smiled contentedly at the three men.

"I will make you programmers of good thoughts."

***

Josue and Mari drove up from Winters to spend Christmas with Rick and his family. Adonica, Serafina and Ramon could hardly contain their excitement. The bond of love between them and their grandparents was very deep, and they hadn't seen them since moving into their new home. Ramon cheerfully agreed to give up his room so Mari and Josue could have a quiet place of their own, and Adonica promised to stay close to Mari in case she needed something. Each day of the visit had been carefully planned. There was so much to tell Josue and Mari, and there was so much to show them.

The day of their arrival seemed to drag on and on, each hour passing more slowly than the last. Finally, after what seemed to be hours of anxious waiting, a car appeared in the driveway. Ramon announced the arrival with a boisterous yell. Adonica, Serafina and Ramon rushed out of the house to greet Josue and Mari, all talking at once with animated gestures. Rick and Neema happily followed their children out to the car. Josue got out, arched his back to relieve the stiffness, and stretched his arms.

"Boy!" exclaimed Josue. "That was a tough drive.... it took longer than I thought."

"Welcome to our little house," Rick said.

There were hugs and kisses all around. Josue unpacked what seemed to be an unlimited number of bags, boxes and suitcases from the car. Everyone took two or three items into the house. The presents were carefully arranged under the tree. Ramon dragged and carried the bags to his room. Adonica carried three boxes of breads, cakes, pies, cookies and cans into the kitchen. Serafina helped Josue and Mari with their coats. And then they all took a quick tour of the house.

Tired from the long drive, but happy to be with his grandchildren, Josue settled down into a big overstuffed easy chair. Rick, Mari and Neema made themselves comfortable on the couch. The children gathered around their grandparents on the floor.

"Now...," said Josue. "Tell us the news."

***

They went to church on Christmas eve to celebrate the birth of Christ. A thousand bright stars filled the icy cold night sky as they walked through the parking lot to the church door. Sixteen year old Adonica stayed beside her grandmother to make sure she didn't slip on the ice and snow. Ramon playfully tried to make a snowball, but the snow was too fluffy to pack. Once inside, several friendly parishioners welcomed them with Christmas greetings as they made their way to a pew. The service was both warm and exhilarating. They sang Christmas carols, bowed their heads in prayer, heard a beautiful tribute from the church choir, listened to a brief sermon, and closed the service with a very enthusiastic "Joy To The World."

After the ceremony, most of the congregation gathered around Rick and Neema to wish them a Merry Christmas. Josue and Mari were both amazed at the attention given to Rick. Mari was filled with the pride of a loving mother as she watched her son greet each person by name, and she was very pleased Neema seemed to be in the middle of the animated conversations that surrounded the family. After the throng of parishioners had thinned out, Serafina came over and grasped her grandfather's hand. She leaned her head against his arm.

"I wish everyday could be like this, grandpa."

"So do I," said Josue in a low voice. "So do I."

***

"You tell him," said Rick. "You tell him just like you told me."

Josue was somewhat reluctant to take on the chore. "That was over 30 years ago," he said. "I've forgotten what I told you."

"But you did a great job…. Tell him about the real meaning of Christmas."

Josue thought for a moment and then nodded his head. "OK…," he sighed. "I'll talk to Ramon."

The two girls giggled. This was a big deal. Ramon had been asking for all sorts of things he wanted for Christmas. They were sure he would be disappointed. Rick called Ramon.

"Ramon… Ramon come sit with your grandfather. He has something to tell you."

Rick turned to the girls. "And you two scoot…. This is between Ramon and his grandfather."

Adonica and Serafina giggled again and left the room. Rick winked at Neema and they went into the kitchen. Alone in the warm living room with seven year old Ramon, a crackling fire in the fireplace, the delightful scent of a Christmas tree, and the glow of Christmas lights, Josue began to talk about Santa Claus - just as he had when Rick was Ramon's age. He hoisted Ramon onto his knee and put his arm around the boy's shoulders. With great affection he carefully explained about the true meaning of Christmas. Josue started by explaining the significance of the service they had just attended. He went on to talk about the spiritual value of Christmas, and how the birth of Jesus changed the world. Josue finished by telling his grandson about Santa Claus. After he finished he asked Ramon: "Do you have any questions you would like to ask me?"

"No…. I understand."

"You mean… it's not a surprise?"

"No…. I know all that stuff… I just wanted to see what you would say."

***

Christmas morning was filled with good smells from the kitchen, many happy conversations, the excitement of opening presents, a feeling of great joy, and plenty of hugs. They had a big Christmas ham for dinner with all the trimmings, and a choice of pies and cakes for dessert. Mari had brought much too much food from Winters. Adonica complained it would all do terrible things to her figure. But Serafina and Ramon were all too happy to have a taste of every dessert.

After the dishes had been cleared from the table, Josue and Rick sat together in the living room. Each man was alone with his pleasant thoughts. It had been a delightful family Christmas. Nothing could happen to ruin the day.

But they made the mistake of turning on the TV. Rick was searching the channels for a football game. One of the channels was carrying the national news. He was shocked to see a picture of a burned Church. A news reporter was explaining the Church had been firebombed late Christmas Eve. Although confined to one side of the building, the fire had extensively damaged a wall and several stained glass windows. Two fascist swastikas had been painted on the front doors. It was not known who was responsible. The report included two interviews with local politicians. One condemned the incident as an obvious hate crime, but added some people in the congregation understood the motivation for the assault on the Church. The other politician was obviously hostile. He blamed the congregation for aggravating the community, and perpetuating theological myths that are no longer appropriate.

"What does he mean – no longer appropriate?" asked Josue.

Rick frowned. "I think he means the teachings of this Church are not politically correct."

"Doesn't that restriction violate the Church's First Amendment rights under our Constitution?"

"I don't think these people care... In their eyes being politically correct is more important than being morally right... Political theology trumps religious philosophy. They believe if any church gets involved in a political activity, then the church must expect to become a target of political protest."

"Including arson?"

"By whatever means is socially acceptable."

"But what constitutes political activity?"

"Any discussion or statement of morality that upsets any group..."

"Including the beliefs of Christianity?"

Rick frowned... he hated the answer he was about to make.

"If you're a Christian, if you're strong in your religious beliefs, you're deemed a loser."

Josue paused a minute or more before speaking again.

"Where is this all leading.... What good can come from all this?"

"I believe that if government rejects the existence of God, then its spiritual connection with universal moral values is broken. As we have witnessed so many times in human history, the ethical conduct of government inevitably deteriorates. That leads to a deterioration of public trust. The decline of public trust compromises the moral obligations of the family and the individual. The social contract that binds us to the political establishment ceases to exist..... So to answer your question, nothing good can come from this.... nothing good at all."

***

Josue and Mari stayed for another six days. They toured the town, visited with Kato and Isabel at the newspaper, stood in rapt wonder while Phillip explained all the hardware and software they were working on at the ISP, and had an informal luncheon with everyone who worked at the ISP.

Mostly, however, they spent as much time as they could with their grandchildren. Days of animated conversation, evenings of quiet talk. When it came time to say goodbye, there were a few tears accompanied by many affectionate hugs. Just before she got into the car, Mari turned to Neema.

"You have a wonderful family, Neema. Adonica is well on her way to becoming a young woman. Serafina is developing a strong will of her own, and Ramon is such a pleasure... But I'm concerned about Rick. Although we are very proud of him, he seems to be totally immersed in a new calling that contradicts government social policy. We worry something will happen to him."

"I worry too, Mari. I'll keep an eye on him for both of us."

***

Staying warm became a challenge. Winter storms with freezing rain and heavy snow plagued them all January. Temperatures were well below normal. By a stroke of good fortune, residents in the more populous areas of Humboldt County had access to lower cost natural gas. For everyone else, it was a miserable winter. Propane had become very expensive, and so it was not unusual to see pickup trucks loaded with tree trunks and branches on the road into town. The air was often filled with the pungent odor and lazy haze of woodstove fires. By mid-January some families were also using coal smuggled in from the Rocky Mountain states for heat and cooking. Despite government attempts to intervene, and over the objections of those who could afford to burn the more expensive propane or heating oil, the consumption of coal was spreading throughout the west.

In some communities, government attempts to stop the transportation of coal were met with armed resistance.

Rick and Peter were able to keep the ISP warm with the heat from the servers and a propane furnace that blew warm air into the programmers work area. Rick kept the wood stove at home stoked with fuel almost every day. Members of the church congregation organized a "Keep Us Warm" campaign to collect money for families who were too poor to buy the natural gas, propane or coal they needed to stay alive. Unfortunately, despite everyone's best efforts, there were several deaths attributed to exposure and exposure related diseases.

Despite the reality of colder winters and cooler summers, government officials continued to deny there was a global cooling trend.

***

Phillip could hear the tires of his car spinning on the ice and snow that covered the driveway to the ISP building. The car's speed slowly declined until it lost all foreword momentum. Tires spinning, the car began to slide backward down the icy slope. Phillip cursed under his breath and tried to gently brake the car's backward progress. But to no avail. The car slid sideways off the road. When he tried to pull ahead, the tires spun furiously, but the car didn't move. He was stuck.

With great patience he stoically removed the chains from the trunk and laid them out on the ice. One set of links on each side. The chains on the uphill side were not hard to wrap around the tire. But when he tried to wrap the chains on the downhill tire, his foot slipped on the ice and he went sprawling into the snow. Hands freezing, fingers numb from the cold steel and icy snow, he again struggled to arrange the chains around the tire. It took at least ten minutes to complete the job, and by then the cold had begun to seep into his winter jacket and wrapped its icy grip around his legs. Cold and miserable, he got into the car and carefully touched the accelerator just enough to drag the chains a quarter turn around the tires. He got out, latched the chains, and put on the tensioners. Satisfied everything was ready, he got into the car and applied just enough pressure on the accelerator to turn the tires. Mercifully, they grabbed and scratched their way out of the ditch and gave him enough traction to move the car up the driveway into a parking space.

Phillip got out of his car and carefully examined his chains for loose links or tensioners. Satisfied they were as tight as he could get them, he went up the walk toward the front door. Just as he reached for the doorknob, his left foot slipped on the ice, and he fell to the ground with a heavy thud. He banged his elbow on the ice. Phillip groaned with pain. This time he cursed out loud.

***

"It was awful!" Philip exclaimed to Rick later that morning. "Winter is out to get me... I went through hell just to get to work."

"An apt description of hell," said Rick. "Hell is often characterized as overwhelming misery."

"The spirits are out to get me."

"Umm... I think we make our own hell," Rick intoned philosophically.

"You don't think there is a place of fire and brimstone overrun with wicked demons who find great pleasure in torturing us humans?"

"No.... I learned a long time ago that place doesn't exist."

"Then where is hell?"

Rick took a sip of his coffee and motioned Phillip to the overstuffed easy chair in his office.

"Think of your experience this morning... You just described it as hell... You were probably not alone when you were confronted with bad roads, chains, and cars that slip and slide on the ice. It's happening all over America. We humans frequently experience hell. But mostly it is of our own making.... You knew the roads would be icy, but you didn't put on your chains until you got into trouble."

"But where is this place?"

"Hell is often described as a place of great suffering, continuous torture, the screaming agony of being scorched by fire, being eaten by wild beasts, and so on. When describing hell, we humans have been very creative.... Fire, pain, humiliation, and horror. Our literature is littered with ghosts and devils. But that's not the real hell.... Think of a place where people suffer from disease... a place where innocent children are abused... where millions die from hunger... where there is the slaughter of war... where there is endemic corruption... where there is murder... where there is unrelenting hatred... where nice people die and cruel people thrive."

"I get the picture," Phillip interrupted. "This is hell... here... on this earth... in this life... we experience hell."

"Yes, that is the right answer. Here on earth, in this physical universe, we humans have the intellectual capability of producing an existence that is closer to paradise, or nearer to hell. There is an infinite continuum of existence from one pole to the other. We humans have, unfortunately, been more inclined to create the conditions of hell.

"Years ago, it was assumed we must live by a strict moral code. The Church told us that if we failed to abide by the rules, we would go to Hell. The Bible, the Koran and the Buddhist Scripture all take the same approach to enforcement. Obey or be punished..... It continues to be true. We cannot break the natural laws of the Cosmos without exposing ourselves to physical or emotional injury. We do it when we ignore the rules of common sense. If we defile our bodies with drugs or alcohol, if we debilitate ourselves with too much stress, or if we ignore the wisdom of experience, we are doomed to suffer the consequences. In so doing, we create our own self-inflicted Hell.... That's the way the system works... Phillip... Hell does exist. It is here... On this earth. We make our own, we humans. ... With our words and thoughts, and our often irrational behavior."

Phillip was thoughtful. He wanted to sum it all up. " So.. We are the creators of our own personal Hell... Like I did this morning when I got stuck."

"Like kids in high school or college do when they participate in perversion, drink too much, or take drugs. It all seems so innocent at first. But they create their own Hell by doing so... and the result is always unhappiness and despair, along with declining physical and mental health. Sometimes even injury or death."

Phillip became cynical. "And where is God in all this?"

"God is dismayed by our creation of Hell on earth. She gave us an ability to think and reason that is far superior to her other creations. ... He gave us commandments to follow, that we might create God's Kingdom on Earth... God the Holy Spirit gives us counsel. If we create our own Hell, we risk being punished in this life."

"God doesn't interfere?"

"God does not usually intercede in our affairs. We make life what it is. Just remember what I teach in church. We humans have the intellectual capability of producing an existence that is closer to paradise, or nearer to Hell.... It's up to us."

***

Peter carefully put the telephone down in its cradle and covered his face with his hands. He turned to look at his wife, Jocelyn. "She's in trouble... I just know it."

Jocelyn looked up from her needle work. "What kind of trouble?"

"I don't really know... There was just something in her voice... She tried to assure me everything was OK... But I have a terrible feeling she is not doing well."

"Does she have a roof over her head?... Plenty to eat?"

Peter gave his wife a blank look. "I really don't know... Since her divorce she has been in a haze... Wandering from one relationship to the next. She doesn't seem to have any problem attracting men... But she keeps making bad choices."

"What's she doing?"

Peter thought a moment. "She seems to be working at some bad job that doesn't pay much... I guess my biggest concern is she seems depressed."

Jocelyn put her work down on the living room coffee table and looked at her husband. She could see he was worried about his niece. He had always been a big brother to her since the death of her parents. She knew he cared for his niece with an emotional intensity.... "*But then,*" she thought, "*that's how he does everything.*"

Peter looked to be deep in his own thoughts. Jocelyn had the greatest sympathy for his distress. Although Peter's niece was usually a practical, no nonsense person, she tended to be emotionally intense.... just like her Uncle. Jocelyn spoke up.

"Why don't you invite Anika up for a visit," she said. "You haven't seen her for several months. It would do you both good to catch up on the news."

Peter nodded his agreement. If he could talk to Anika in person, he could do a better job of understanding her physical and emotional condition. Peter reached for the telephone.

"I'll call her to come up as soon as she can get away. We can put her in the spare bedroom... And thank you for being so thoughtful."

Jocelyn gave him a gentle smile. She liked Anika. Peter's niece had stayed with them through the early days of her messy divorce. Then Jocelyn sighed. *Now I'll have two intense personalities in the house.*

***

Phillip and Rick were in the process of closing the ISP for the day. When the chores were done, Phillip walked into Rick's office with a bottle of red wine and two glasses.

"Want to be philosophical for awhile?"

Rick smiled at his old friend and sat down in his office chair.

"Sure... take a seat... It's time to relax."

Phillip poured two glasses of wine and toasted Rick. They took a sip and settled back in their chairs. Phillip looked at the ceiling... and then at Rick.

"Am I your friend?" Phillip asked.

The question surprised Rick. He decided Philip was testing him.

"Of course, we have been friends since we were kids," he replied.

"But what is friendship?"

"Friendships are an expression of love. 'I love you' can be translated as: 'I am your friend.' Therefore: Be a true friend of those you love."

"And how do we find friends?" Phillip challenged Rick again.

"If you want to have a friend, then be one. Start by learning to be a good friend to yourself. As my father Josue has said: If you do not like who you are, how can you love someone else?"

Phillip had one more question. "Is God your friend?"

"My friendship with God is a loving spiritual relationship that flows through the physical universe and fills me with the energy of life. .... As God has said: I love those who love me. If you seek to be my friend, you will find me."

"But that assumes there is a God. ... OK...OK...You've convinced me of that... But where do we find out about God... In the Bible?"

"Are you asking me if the Bible is the word of God?"

Phillip nodded his head. He knew he was in for a lecture, but it was an answer he wanted to hear from his friend.

"There are three basic ways to perceive the text of the Bible.... Conservative Christians believe the Bible is – word for word – the work of God. In essence, God caused every word to be written. Even the revisions and translations are the work of God. ... Many contemporary Christians choose to believe, however, that God used the stories and scripture we find in the Bible as a way of conveying his message to us. God left the specific interpretation and text to human authors.... And then there are the skeptics. They like to point out the Bible's errors, weaknesses, and contradictions. For them, the Bible is nothing more than a collection of fables."

"So. Who is right?" Phillip asked.

"God encourages us to embrace a constructive theology. The path to these beliefs is spelled out in the Bible. They encourage us to have a compassion for others, to follow the wisdom of God's law, and to seek the reward of everlasting life... Many contemporary Christians prefer to believe that although the Bible was written and revised by human authors over a period of years, it does reveal the word of God. There is inspiration. There is hope. We come to understand the truth of God's wisdom, the benefits of sustaining a positive faith, and the elation of compassion. We are challenged to adopt a constructive interpretation of Christian theology, one that brings us closer to God."

Rick paused to take another sip of his wine.

"In a sense, the Bible's critics and skeptics are right. The theology is not always consistent. There are contradictions in the description of persons, places, and events. It is difficult or impossible to identify when many of the Bible's most important characters were born. We are unable to document when or where they died. It's obvious most of the Bible's authors want us to believe their story, even when it appears to contradict the words of other authors. One can reasonably ask, if this is the word of God, then why is it so disorganized and inconsistent?"

Rick paused again. Phillip was intently listening to everything Rick was saying.

"To answer this question, we must take a thoughtful holistic view of the Bible.... Since the Bible is a collection of books, it should not be surprising that the number of books included in various versions of the Bible vary from religion to religion, and from period to period in human history. Because Christians are human by intellect and emotion, it should also not be surprising theologians continue to interpret both the Old and New Testaments in different ways. For example, there is no universal consensus on the nature of God, the divinity of Jesus, concept of original sin, or the characterization of hell. But our search for truth confirms we humans are concerned about these concepts. The more we learn, the closer we are to the Spiritual Universe. Think of the Bible as a footpath to God. It has many sign posts. There are many messages of faith to guide humanity. Our footpath has hills to climb that test our strength, and to descend with a sense of divine exhilaration. We are challenged to find and understand spiritual truth."

Rick paused briefly for another sip of wine.

"Think about it. If you were God, how would you reach out to humanity? When the content of the Bible was created; radio, television, newspaper, magazine, telephone, and Internet media did not exist. The materials for creating written records were difficult to use. Making copies was a laborious manual task. Most of the people you want to reach can not read or write. So how do you convey your message to humanity? ... By inspiring selected humans to create a story that incorporates your message, and then having it repeated over and over again as people travel from land to land. Eventually, your message is converted into a written form that can be copied and sent everywhere your messengers go. By this means, you are able to teach and guide humanity. It's not perfect. But it works....

"Although the Bible presents us with content drawn from another age, it's lessons are timeless, the people we meet are authentic, and the drama is ageless. There is a unity of purpose. There are prophecies and the lessons of history. There is moral right and wrong, the best and worst of human behavior, and the experience of both pain and joy. The Bible is a book about tribes, families and individuals. The Bible's authors tell us about marriage, divorce, adultery, obedience, authority, honesty, parenting, nature, revelation, behavior, God, and much more. It presents us with real life stories of spiritual vision, high ideals, and great moral depth."

Phillip spoke up. "And that's its value?"

"No other book has had a greater influence on humanity because in its essence, this book is about us. ... We are the people in the Bible... It connects us with the compassion and wisdom of God. ...And that is why it has endured."

***

Rick closed and locked the door of the ISP building. He began to walk very carefully over the icy driveway to his house. Phillip started for his car. Then he stopped and called to Rick.

"How the hell ... err.. how the heck do you know all this religious stuff?"

Rick stopped, and then carefully made his way back to where Phillip was standing.

"From your mother."

"From my mother!" Phillip exclaimed. "She is an atheist!"

Rick could only smile at his friend's consternation.

"Your mother is a remarkable woman, Phillip... When we were growing up, you showed an interest in computers. So she made sure you had all the toys and every piece of software you really wanted .... and you excelled in Computer Science at Davis.... For me, my interests were more to philosophy and history. So she made sure I read several of the key texts on philosophy and religion... The Bible was one of them... as was the Koran. Your mother was determined we both would have the best possible education according to our interests.... Her personal beliefs didn't matter to her... Her objective was education."

Phillip was stunned. But then he began to ponder. "Yes, I remember now. She insisted I follow my interest in computers and that made me happy.... I guess for you it was the same dedication to philosophy... and you're right, my mom is a terrific woman."

Rick smiled as he recalled many fond memories of their parents.

"I sometimes think your mother and Mari were in cahoots... Working together... It always seemed once I got a book from Abigail, Mari would start asking questions about it."

"We've been had," Phillip grinned.

Rick enjoyed the moment of humor with his friend. They were lucky... They had great parents.

"And then there's my father Josue. I think it sort of set him back when he realized I wouldn't grow up to be the world's greatest farm machinery mechanic. But he soon adjusted... Mari made sure of that.... And so Josue started reading the same stuff I was. Just to prompt my interest... I don't think either of us fully understood all the stuff we were reading. But some has stuck with me all these years... and it was a big help when Rosalinda passed away."

"Was there anyone else?"

"Sure... Your father was a rock. We could always depend on him for advice and a little extra change. Remember when he gave you gas money so we could use your car for a date with Rosalinda and Lydia? I guess he didn't want us to get stuck somewhere... He didn't want to be called in the middle of the night to come and rescue us."

Phillip chuckled at the memory. "Anyone else?" he asked.

"There are teachers and coaches and people who have been good to me. But I guess the other two men who influenced me the most were my next door neighbor Micah and Father Giovanni. I spent many hours with Micah when I was a teenager. He was a great teacher. He taught me about spiritual evolution. And from Father Giovanni I learned a great deal about truth and compassion. Both men are good friends."

***

The call came in at about 1PM on Monday afternoon. Lydia took the call and immediately switched it to Rick.

"Can you come right away?" the woman's voice asked. "My husband just died and... I don't think he's going to make it into heaven."

Rick asked the woman a few questions and then reassured her he would get to the funeral home as soon as he could. After he hung up the telephone, Rick had an inspiration. He went to the door of his little office and called out: "Does anyone know where Sarah is?"

James answered. "She and Christina are working on our taxes .... over there."

He pointed to a cubicle in the back of the open office area. Sarah poked her head up above the partition.

"What do you need?"

"Could you and Christina come to my office, please?"

"Sure... anything to get out of this stuff... it's a real drudge."

Sarah and Christina quickly appeared at the door of Rick's office. "What's up?" Christina asked.

"Kato and Isabel are at the funeral parlor with a friend. Her husband has passed away and they asked if I could go down to console the poor woman... I'd like you to come with me."

Puzzled by the request, but willing to help, Sarah and Christina went to get their coats. In a few moments they were on their way to the funeral home.

***

The funeral home was located in a modest structure with a snow covered lawn, a partially cleared parking area, and a few forlorn shrubs struggling to stay alive through a tough winter. Rick parked the car and walked with Sarah and Christina to a weathered entrance door. The interior of the funeral home was damp, dark, and depressing. A few desolate candles surrounded a casket in the middle of the viewing room. Three people were off to the side, having a discussion. Rick immediately recognized Kato and Isabel.

"Well... here we are... Kato and Isabel, you know Sarah and Christina I think."

Isabel gave them a friendly smile as she shook hands. Kato seemed relieved someone else was here to help console his friend. He took Rick by the arm and introduced them.

"Sheila, this is Ricardo Vasquez. ... He is the man I told you about."

Sheila looked at Rick and began to cry. Through her sobs, Rick could make out only a few words. Christina and Sarah were confused by what she was saying. Rick held up his hand.

"Stop.. Just stop and relax... I can help you... But I need you to give me your hand."

Although the woman was puzzled by Rick's request and uncertain about what would happen, she shyly offered her hand to Rick. He took it in his two hands, placing one on the back of her hand, and one on the palm. He looked at her intently. The woman began to relax and regain her composure. Christina and Isabel noticed Sheila looked stronger, as though some new found energy was flowing through her body. Rick released Sheila's hand and began to speak.

"Your husband died yesterday morning. You are afraid he won't make it into heaven because he was a drunkard and has probably committed numerous sins against man and God."

Sheila was dumbfounded. "How did you know that?" she asked.

"That's my little secret... I need to know the answer to three questions... Are you willing to answer them?"

Sheila was even more uncertain of what to expect. But Kato stepped forward and took her arm.

"Sheila, answer the man... he won't bite."

A small – almost imperceptible – smile crossed everyone's face. Even Sheila saw the humor in Kato's remark. "Ok... I guess... What do you want to know?"

Rick looked at her intently, as though trying to divine some great truth.

"Did Harold ever kill anyone?"

At first Sheila didn't want to answer Rick's question. "*How does he know Harold's name?*" she thought. But she collected her thoughts, and said "No one, Harold never hurt anyone... ever."

"Did Harold ever deliberately try to hurt someone?"

"No... I don't think so?"

"Has he ever tried to deceive someone for personal gain?"

"No... Harold was just a plain old drunk... That's his biggest crime... That I know of..."

Rick already knew the answers to his questions. But it was good psychology to have Sheila tell him about her husband. Any damage he did, he did to himself. Harold created his own personal Hell and lived in it for more than 15 years. First his liver failed. Then his heart couldn't take the strain of keeping his body alive. Fifteen years of shame and fifteen days to die. Not much to say about a man.

"Do you mind if I touch Harold?"

"No... not if you think it will help."

Rick went up to the open casket and looked at the sallow, bloated face of a man in his fifties. Someone joined him at the casket. It was the undertaker.

"I couldn't do much with his face... He was real sick when he died."

Rick nodded and took Harold's hand in his two hands. He placed them the same way he had when he communicated with Sheila. One on the back, and one on the palm. Rick prayed for a few minutes and then carefully placed Harold's hand back into the coffin. He turned to Sheila.

"I can do nothing for him."

Sheila's face contorted into confusion. She looked as though she would cry again.

"I can do nothing for Harold because he is already with God.... He made the transformation last night at about 6:45PM. He is safely in the Spiritual Universe."

Sheila almost fainted. Isabel and Sarah rushed to support her weight and helped her to a chair.

"I don't understand...," Sheila moaned. "He's gone? ... He made it?"

"He is with God," Rick said with a reassuring smile.

The room began to swirl around Sheila. Her eyes glazed with a blank stare and she fainted.

Isabel, Sarah and Christina took turns trying to revive the stricken woman. It took about 5 minutes, but she finally opened her eyes and looked up at a startled Christina.

"Oh my God... Oh my God... Six forty five PM. ... That's when I kissed him on the cheek and said goodbye."

Sheila searched out Rick's face and looked at him with an expression of wonder and relief.

"I don't know how you knew all this.... I don't understand what just happened... But I do know you are a good man Ricardo Juan Sanchez Vasquez... Thank you."

It was Rick's turn to be surprised. Sheila knew his full name. But then he remembered. For some people, spiritual communication is a two way conversation.

The undertaker interrupted them. Very business like. Obtuse. He had seen this spooky stuff before. It didn't impress him because he didn't know what was happening. He never would.

"Shall we ready Harold for a full burial or prepare him for cremation?"

Sheila looked tearfully at Rick. "What should I do?"

"It doesn't matter. If you prefer a full burial in a plot, then do that.... If you prefer a cremation, then that is OK."

"But doesn't he need his body?" Sheila asked.

"Harold is no longer in his body. His physical presence in this universe had ended. His energy ... his spiritual being ... left his body and has gone into the Spiritual Universe. His physical body is of no further use to him. The choice of burial or cremation is a personal one. Only you can make that choice."

Rick leaned over Sheila's chair and touched her arm. He said a few quiet words in her ear. She seemed to relax and then smiled bravely.

"I can make that decision. It will be easier knowing Harold is all right."

Rick turned to Isabel and Kato. "You may want to stay a few more minutes. But I think Sheila will be strong enough to handle things from now on."

Rick turned and walked toward the door of the funeral home's parlor. He motioned for Sarah and Christina to follow.

Isabel was indecisive. She looked uneasily at her husband, then at Christina and Sarah. She motioned for them to come closer.

"Did you see what I just saw?" she whispered.

The others nodded. It had been a very moving demonstration of Rick's ability to communicate with the spiritual.

"And I have some questions," Kato responded.

Mystified by the exchange between Rick and Sheila, and Rick's ability to communicate with Harold, they all turned to look at Rick with a look of wonder and disbelief. Somewhat embarrassed by all the attention, he again beckoned for them to follow him.

Kato, Isabel, Sarah and Christina walked behind Rick into the funeral home's parlor. They found several chairs and sat down in a semi-circle. Kato spoke first.

"You came here to help a woman you never met, correctly described a man you never met, understood what had happened between them, and assured her he was in the Spiritual Universe. And then ... even though you are a total stranger, she knew your full name..... How do you do that?"

"The short answer is... I have a gift... It can be described as spiritual communication. I am aware of a person's thoughts. Clasping her hand in mine made the communication easier... We had a quiet conversation... my thoughts to her... her thoughts to me."

Christina was skeptical. "You never knew anything about Sheila?"

"No.... She does not go to church. I never met her."

Rick frowned when he looked at Christina. "Personal communication on this level is not unusual. Many people have experienced it through the ages. I just have a better sensitivity than most humans."

But Sarah was not convinced Rick was just more sensitive than most people.

"I've heard stories about your ... sessions or whatever you call them... from Peter, and then from Antonio, and I know what I just saw.... Your capability is above the ordinary."

Rick looked at Sarah and then at Christina.

"I brought you here to show you spiritual communication is real... As real as that chair you're sitting on and because if you are willing to believe in the spiritual, then you can help me with my work."

Rick turned to look at Isabel and Kato.

"Meeting you two at this funeral home is a bonus. If you are willing to believe, then by all means... do join us."

Kato looked uncertain. "I want to know more about this... Spiritual Universe... Does everyone get to go there?"

Rick thought for a moment before answering.

"No... the transformation from the physical to the spiritual happens to everyone, a person's energy ... spiritual energy ... is released from the physical body. But in order to find the Spiritual Universe, one must first believe it is real.... Does it not seem logical?... We are unlikely to find something if we do not believe it exists."

Isabel raised her hand and spoke.

"But what happens to those who do not make it into the Spiritual Universe?"

"Redemption is possible... for a period of time. Many spirits find their way to the angels' footpath because they become believers... The reality of death changes their mind..... But eventually the spiritual energy of non-believers dissipates into the Cosmos... like your breath does on a cold morning. The soul ceases to exist.... Souls that refuse to believe disappear."

Kato had another question.

"What about murderers, crooks and nasty people... ?"

Rick looked from face to face. They were all curious..

"Redemption is always possible.... Even the fallen may find their way.... But first they must repent and truly believe in the Spiritual Universe and the ways of the Holy Spirit.... Those that refuse to do so.... disappear into the Cosmos as random waves of energy."

"If a person's spiritual energy has not found the angels' footpath, does it stay with the physical body?"

"It can.... and usually does for a time.... It is hard to accept the physical body has ceased to function... that physical life is over.... They yearn for their physical being to be alive again. But the reality of death eventually becomes impossible to deny."

Rick stood up and stretched his arms above his head.

"Most people make the transformation and find the angels' footpath right away... Many even experience it before they die.... That's why some people seem to be so serene at the moment of death.... For them, it is a moment of joy."

Kato had one last question.

"Do these people ever connect with us... these spiritual beings?"

"After spending some time in the Spiritual Universe, the spiritual energy of some souls does find its way into the spiritual dimension which surrounds us... but that is a topic for another day."

Rick looked each person in the eye. One by one.

"Now I have two questions for you... Do you believe what you have witnessed today reveals a divine message that all should hear?"

Still awed by the experience they had just witnessed, they nodded in agreement.

"Will you help me to bring this message to others?"

Kato looked at Isabel, Sarah looked at Christina, and then they all looked at each other as though to assure themselves they were making the right decision.

Kato spoke for them... "Yes," he said solemnly. "We want to be included in whatever you do and wherever you go."

***

When Anika arrived at the door of their home, Jocelyn and Peter were both shocked to see how exhausted and disheveled she looked. They were used to seeing an attractive, blue eyed blond with a great figure. The woman at their door looked like she had been run over by a truck. Peter gathered his decorum and welcomed his niece.

"Anika!" he exclaimed with more enthusiasm than he felt. "It's so nice to see you."

Anika managed a faint smile. "Good to see you Uncle... and you too Jocelyn."

Both Jocelyn and Peter gave Anika a warm hug.

"Can I help you with your luggage?"

Anika looked forlornly at her Uncle.

"Everything I own is in that car.... It's stuffed.... and the car's a wreck looking for a place to die."

Jocelyn was again shocked by what she saw and heard.

"Well come on in, we'll find somewhere for your belongings. Your clothes and personal items will go in your room."

There was something final about the term "your room" and Jocelyn knew it. Peter looked incredulous.

"You'll have plenty of time to tell us all the news. ... Let's get you located."

And with that, both he and Jocelyn busied themselves with the task of helping Anika get settled. Peter found some extra space in a room next to the kitchen pantry. Anika was able to get most of her clothing and personal items into the spare bedroom. Jocelyn made tea for them and found some cookies for a treat. The three of them settled down in the living room to have a chat.

"I'm sorry to do this to you... I really am," Anika began. "I had an affair with a guy who was very nice... Good looking... He turned out to be an NSS agent... When he discovered I was related to you Peter, he started pestering me to tell him all about you and your group.... I tried to break it off but he kept after me for information and then threatened to have me arrested if I didn't cooperate."

Peter was alarmed at the news. "And what did you tell him?"

"Nothing... because I don't know what the hell you are doing... The guy seems to think you're part of some kind of conspiracy... A religious hate group... The NSS would like to put you out of business."

"Did he mention the Internet?"

"I'm not sure... Something about radio broadcasts."

Peter frowned at Anika's revelation. Apparently John's attempts to hide the source of Rick's Internet radio broadcasts wasn't working. He had to find out how much the NSS really knew.

"Anika... do you remember anything else he said?"

"No... I'm sorry... But when I wouldn't cooperate, he started leaning on me.... I lost my job... I couldn't land another."

Anika looked at Jocelyn. She was obviously ashamed.

"Except at a sex club... stripping... But I was even kicked out of that job... These guys are merciless."

Peter studied Anika. "Do they know where you went?"

"No. I made sure I left in the dead of night without saying goodbye to my friends... I'm exhausted from the driving. The roads are in terrible shape... Doesn't anybody care?"

Peter chuckled. "The Federal Government is broke... and so is the State of California... They can't afford to fix the roads anymore.... or fund the NSS to chase us up here."

He paused a moment. "I suppose that's the good part."

Jocelyn was openly sympathetic.

"As soon as you finish your tea, I'll show you where the extra towels are... You look like you need a shower."

"At least… and then can I please get some sleep?"

***

That same day, Phillip and Lydia had supper with Rick and Neema at Rick's house. Afterward, Phillip and Rick retired to the living room to have a chat. Neema and Lydia were carrying on a lively conversation in the kitchen. The kids were busy with their homework. Phillip started the conversation with a question.

"You tell a great story, Rick…. But I still don't get this stuff about a Spiritual Universe… Can you explain it to me?"

Rick looked at his friend with some compassion. "Always challenging me… keeps me honest." Then he cleared his throat and tried to put it all together for Phillip.

"We have talked about physical reality, and you have agreed we live in a bipolar Cosmos. You have also agreed that although the Cosmos is in constant change, there is order underlying the interaction of all that occurs in the Cosmos… A set of rules by which things work…. We may not understand them all. But they exist."

"Sure," Phillip responded. "So keep going."

"The order of the Cosmos includes three important principles. First, there are two realities, in a unity of opposites. Each one produces the possibility of the other. All phenomena is the compliment of its opposite. If there is up, there must be down. If there is right, there must be left. If there is forward, then there is also backward. The light of the sun alternates with the darkness of night. We may be healthy while having the potential of illness. Rest and motion are relative forms of the same event. Matter and energy are forms of the same unity. Life and death are inseparable. Male and female are opposite versions of the same life form. Our physical bodies are interdependent with our spiritual life force. Both equilibrium and instability are bipolar realities of the same natural states of being. There are many examples of bipolar existence. There is unity because each state of being is related to its opposite."

Rick paused to let Phillip contemplate these ideas. Then he continued.

"If there is a physical universe, then there must be a Spiritual Universe. Each is an expression of the same reality. If there is matter, then there is energy. Both are forms of the same quantum reality. Thus. If there is life, then there is not life. Life and not life are opposite versions of the same reality. If life exists in the physical universe as energy and matter, then not life exists in a Spiritual Universe as energy and mass. Since energy and matter can not be created or destroyed, the event which we call death is merely a transformation from one state to another. Each is an expression of the same bipolar reality.

The fact that neither matter nor energy can be created or destroyed leaves open the possibility that we humans can be transformed into the matter and energy of another dimension. For most of us, our human form remains in this dimension and our energy is transformed into the stuff of another dimension. Many people have been able to experience their being as energy in another dimension.

"For people like Jesus, human matter and energy were both transformed into a figure that can appear as mass in any dimension. God followed the rules of physics. Neither the body (matter) nor spirit (energy) were destroyed. God's power made the space-time conversion. After that Jesus could appear in our physical dimension whenever he wanted to be with us.

"And what of God? Energy exists in many forms, in multiple dimensions, throughout the Cosmos. Since God is a form of energy, God exists everywhere in the Cosmos."

"Can people be transformed into a figure that can appear as mass in any dimension?" Phillip asked.

"Yes... But I must confess I don't understand the rules. Who gets transformed, why they are selected, and how it gets done are still a mystery to me."

Phillip acknowledged Rick's comment with a frown. Then he continued to probe.

"So according to you, a bipolar Cosmos includes the possibility of a Spiritual Universe."

"Sure... If there is a physical universe, then there must be its opposite: a Spiritual Universe. These two complimentary realities co-exist in the Cosmos. There is a boundary between them where the physical dimension intersects with the Spiritual Dimension of our existence. Both dimensions are all around us. We humans have trained ourselves to identify the evidence of the physical universe through our five physical senses: hearing, seeing, smelling, tasting and touching. We are able to experience the presence of the Spiritual Dimension with our sixth sense when we seek to become one with the energy that flows throughout the Cosmos.

"We all benefit from having a sense of contact with the Spiritual Universe. We yearn for faith without doubt. To achieve this state of bliss, we must have a faith which rests on a foundation of credible beliefs. It is on this single point that much of current religious philosophy has failed us all. Many popular beliefs are tied to archaic perceptions of reality. If today's knowledge is tomorrow's ignorance, then it follows that theological values must be drawn from universal truths that can not be challenged by evolving scientific knowledge. There is no need for religion to describe the mechanics of a physical universe. Leave them for science to discover. Instead, let us seek the knowledge that flows from God's spiritual reality."

"So it's like you said," Phillip interjected. "The Spiritual Universe exists in a plane that is parallel with its physical counterpart throughout the Cosmos. God the Father, God the Mother and God the Holy Spirit come together as a unity within this plane, creating the energy of the Holy Trinity."

" Of course. Good conclusion. ... Death, meditation, and sudden mental stress may give us an opportunity to experience the consciousness, existence and reality of the Spiritual Dimension. We drift into another space and time. People who are very ill may have the sensation of floating back and forth between physical and spiritual reality. For them, the boundary that separates the physical universe from the Spiritual Universe becomes transparent. Physically, they are in this universe. Spiritually, they may be elsewhere.

"Phillip, our pursuit of the spiritual will lead us to God and the Spiritual Universe. Never underestimate the power this passion can release within us. Faith in the spiritual can be a source of great personal strength and joy. In truth, most of us are pursuing the same quest. We want to be sure that life has meaning. We are, in a sense, always searching for a truth that is greater than ourselves, even if we are unable to fully comprehend the meaning of our discovery."

"So where are you going with all this knowledge?"

Rick thought about his answer for perhaps a full 5 minutes. Phillip began to get nervous. But Rick brought Phillip's thoughts together.

"A spiritual awakening is coming. It will occur within most human cultures, all over our earth. Hundreds, then thousands, and finally millions of individuals will awaken to the reality of the Spiritual Dimension. They will seek to become one with the energy of the Spiritual Universe. The continuing deterioration of physical life on our planet will force a dramatic change in what is regarded as acceptable social behavior. There will be a widespread rejection of pseudo sophisticated belief systems, and a growing disgust with decadent moral behavior. These individuals will seek to replace the emotional and intellectual Hell of barren ideology with the joyful contentment that can only be found through the energy of a spiritual union with universal truth. Most will experience a spiritual sensation of love and peace. With each spiritual awakening comes a greater sense of personal awareness. We know who we are and what we can do. We reject the stress of trying to be something which we are not. Instead, we are free to focus our energy on doing that which is positive and constructive."

Phillip was obviously impressed and moved by Rick's summation.

"And again I ask you... what are you about?"

"Each awakening is accompanied by many troubling questions. Over time the answers will come to us through quiet prayer, moments of inspired intuition, whispers that come in dreams, and words of wisdom that may be written or spoken by another human. Individuals who have experienced a spiritual awakening are able to uplift those around them by seeing that which is worthy in every soul. People who quietly come into contact with the spiritually awakened are able to experience the radiance of loving energy.

"Phillip....When the time of death is near, a spiritual awakening enables the soul to make a seamless transition from the physical universe to the Spiritual Universe. The energy of the body is transformed into a spiritual manifestation of our personal being... And that is my message... my mission.... is to bring us all closer to the Spiritual... and to tie the physical with the spiritual through natural experience."

***

The next morning, Peter told Rick the bad news: according to his analysis of Anika's comments, it was highly probable the NSS knew who was behind the Internet radio broadcasts Phillip and John were publishing. Rick's face became extremely grim. He and his team were in trouble. Rick called a staff meeting for 9:00AM.

After they were assembled, Rick had Peter share his analysis of Anika's comments. John and Phillip were stunned. They had been sure no one could detect where their broadcasts were originating. Antonio, Sarah and James were confused by the revelation. Lydia rolled her eyes in resignation. She had known in her heart this would happen.

"What material are we broadcasting now?" asked Rick.

"We're doing about 3 hours a day," John responded. "There's your stuff, some material the other ISPs have relayed to us, a regular transmission from Father Giovanni, and repeats. We could do more, but the programming the other ISPs are sending to us is pretty tough – they want to start a revolution."

Rick's heart sank. It was one thing to send out theological dissertations, sermons and prayers. But he knew some of the ISPs were itching for a fight and Father Giovanni would be vociferously anti-government.

"Do you have any recordings of Father Giovanni?"

"Sure," Phillip responded. "We have a whole stack of his stuff on DVDs."

"OK," Rick said. "Pick one and let's listen to what he has been saying."

Phillip went to his cubicle and picked up a DVD. He inserted it into his PC and set up the loud speakers. In a moment, Father Giovanni's husky voice filled the room. As usual, he spoke with great energy.

"Why should we tolerate a corrupt and dysfunctional government? The halls of power are filled with men and women who lust for power, caring not for the fortunes of ordinary people. Lies and deceit are the tools of politicians."

Rick signaled Phillip to turn it off.

"Well... that should put us on the map," Rick said dryly.

"And in the gun sights of the NSS," added James.

Rick looked at John and Philip.

"We are in more trouble than we can handle. Don't broadcast anything except my material until we get this sorted out. At least we can claim our Constitutional rights ... if we have any left... under the Freedom of Religion clause."

"Do you want me to check on our links?" John asked. "Maybe I can find out how much they know."

Rick thought for a moment and then responded.

"John, see what you can find out....And James, I want you to pretend you're the NSS... Try to track down the origination of John's broadcasts."

James grinned broadly. "Sort of a good guy, bad guy game. He tries to hide and I try to find him."

"That just about sums it up… You'll have to work overtime. There's a lot of hours ahead for all of us."

***

Later that day, Peter walked into Rick's office and pounded his fist on Rick's desk.

"Damn it, we've lost touch with Father Giovanni. Something has gone wrong. He should have listened to the message we gave him from Clarise… She died trying to warn him… But no, he wouldn't stop. No one seems to know where he is."

The ring tone of the telephone on Rick's desk interrupted Peter's exasperated outburst. Rick motioned Peter to a chair and picked up the instrument. He recognized the voice on the other end of the line. It belonged to one of the former NC residents in San Jose. The voice spoke for about 30 seconds and then hung up.

Rick suddenly felt very despondent. He looked at Peter with a sense of dread.

"The call was about Father Giovanni.… He's been arrested by the NSS."

Chapter 8   Rebellion

The ice and snow of January was replaced by the ice and slush of February. The roads would often be wet with rain or slush during mid-day. By late afternoon, the water and slush would freeze into a treacherous ice that would not melt again until late the next morning. Walking or driving was a challenge. Raw cold winds, dreary gray clouds, and constant misty rain or snow made things even more depressing. Most people described the weather as "miserable." Everyone hoped March would bring the welcome relief of sunshine.

Peter had carefully negotiated the icy roads into town to purchase groceries and a few items of hardware. His last stop was at the hardware store. As soon as he entered, he heard Kato's angry voice blasting through the store from the newspaper office. Peter walked through the door and grinned at his friend.

"What in heck has you all riled up?"

"This is worse than censorship," Kato responded loudly. "We are being told what to say and what to do!"

"Who is doing that?"

"The Department of Public Information.... Those bureaucrats will stop at nothing to control our lives,... our thoughts,... our relationships,... the food we eat,... and even our sex life."

Kato tossed a small book to Peter. "Here, see for yourself. It's chock full of rules and regulations."

Peter caught the volume and looked at the cover. The title of the book alarmed him. He read:

"Citizen's Manual of Personal and Social Responsibility."

Peter thumbed open the introduction.

"The purpose of this book is to create a social environment of peace and harmony for all citizens. It describes the rules, expected behavior, and laws that govern our daily life. All citizens are expected to comply. It is recommended you read and remember the entire contents of this book."

Peter whistled. "They can't be serious."

"They are," bellowed Kato. "Read the bottom paragraph."

Peter scanned down the page to the last paragraph.

"In order to assure the harmonious adoption of these codes, the study of alternate religious or political works is discouraged. All forms of media, and the contents therein, must receive prior approval from the Department of Public Information before publication or use. Exceptions will not be tolerated."

Peter was astonished. "Does this mean all unapproved media is banned?

"That's the way I read it," Kato fumed. "All unapproved information is considered subversive. Authors and publishers are subject to arrest, trial and punishment if they fail to get the DPI's approval."

"Doesn't that violate our Constitutional rights."

Kato's answer dripped with cynicism. "Do you think they give a damn?"

"No, I guess not," Peter said. "Our government routinely ignores the Constitution. This is just one more example... But wait. Won't Christians and Muslims object?"

"They don't say it, but the way I read the introduction and the rules, they are banning both the Bible and the Koran. You know they think those books are nothing but a bunch of mindless mythology."

"They want everyone to think the same way... Well, that's a form of harmony... I guess."

"But not one most people will like. This time they've gone too far... This Book Of Rules will get challenged for sure."

"May I have a copy?" Peter asked. "I think Rick will be most interested to see this little book."

***

Antonio was frustrated. He had fallen in love with Sarah, and after several months of flirting, she had responded. They had an affectionate relationship. Call it love with a light touch. But every time he asked her to move in with him, she would coyly avoid giving him an answer. And that only served to increase his frustration. Of course he wanted to marry Sarah, but he never even allowed himself to believe it would be possible. Her family would not approve, and he had decided that without their blessing, Sarah would never marry him. Besides, he was unsure if she was ready to make a long term commitment.

On a very cold Saturday night in February, she had him over for dinner. It was all very loving and affectionate. Candlelight, real linen napkins, her best china, and Sarah was an excellent cook. Conversation over dinner was mostly about the people they knew, the weather, and Rick's growing popularity. After dinner, she cleared the table and did the dishes. Antonio offered to dry them for her, but Sarah pushed him out of the kitchen and into the living room. In a few minutes she joined him on the sofa. Sarah seemed eager to engage in a little after dinner love making. Antonio suddenly got the courage to ask her again.

"Sarah... why don't you move in with me? We enjoy being together and with only one apartment to pay for, we could save the rent money for other things we both want."

Sarah squirmed on the sofa and coyly said, "You know I'm not that kind of girl."

"*Oh God... she's teasing me again,*" Antonio thought. "*We've done everything there is to do... What's she afraid of?*"

Sarah began to massage his arm with the fingers of her left hand. She abruptly reached around him with her right hand and roughly pulled him to her. Sarah gave him a warm, passionate kiss and then searched

Antonio's eyes, as though trying to reassure herself of something. Then... in a quiet, loving voice, she asked him a question:

"Will you marry me?"

Antonio was both astounded and flustered. But here she was, holding him close to her, asking him to get married! Antonio decided this was the moment he would take command. Show his real feelings. He spoke with authority.

"The question, Sarah... Will you marry me?"

"Of course, Antonio... It's time," she said quietly.

"When?" he demanded.

"Just as soon as we can."

Sarah smiled shyly at him.

"Antonio... I'm pregnant."

Antonio was astonished, speechless, and thrilled - all at the same time. The words just tumbled out of his mouth.

"Now will you move in with me?"

***

The Commander of the San Jose NSS District fumbled through the files on his desk. He read and then reread a report. His empty office was cold and damp. He was uncomfortable. And he was furious.

"These people are idiots. The National Internet Service has funded our enemy!" he shouted to an empty office. Then he pushed a button on his pager.

"Get me the Legal Officer!" he demanded.

After several minutes, a young woman appeared at the door. Without acknowledging her presence, the Commander growled his displeasure.

"First these people hack our files, then they get away, and then they have the audacity to apply for a grant to start a business.... And then... these idiots at the National Internet Service not only give them a territory... they give them over $2 million dollars!"

He angrily thumbed again through the report.

"Wait!" he exclaimed. "They got over $3 million dollars!"

The Commander looked up at the Legal Officer.

"What can we do to these idiots? They never bothered to check with us for a security clearance. Can we arrest the idiot who approved the grant?"

The woman gave him a contemptuous look. She hated her boss.

"Give me the report. I'll look in to it."

She took the report from the Commander's shaking hands and started for the door. Before she left, she turned to look at the Commander. She already knew the answer to the question she was going to ask.

"If you want these people so badly, why don't you just arrest them?"

The woman's sarcastic question only served to increase the Commander's anger.

"Because they are out of our jurisdiction… and we can't pursue them in another District's territory."

A wicked gleam appeared in the Commander's eyes.

"But if I get my chance, I'll ignore that little protocol…. These people the NIS funded have been making illegal broadcasts over the Internet… They have been disseminating some kind of terrorist philosophy. As soon as I have conclusive proof, I'll go after them… with or without Sacramento's approval."

A nasty smile swept over the Commander's face.

"And if Sacramento objects, we can tell Washington they're incompetent. They should have made the arrest. When they didn't, we had to do it for them, and that will impress the National Commander."

The Commander was obviously relishing the prospect of sticking it to Sacramento.

"And after that, we will be able to go anywhere and do anything we damn well please."

***

Anika was impressed with Rick the very first time she met him. Peter and Jocelyn brought her with them to church on Sunday. It was a mercifully sunny day. The air was clear, crisp and cold. They met Rick, Neema and their children in the parking lot, and walked with them into the church. All through the service, Anika kept stealing little glances at Rick. When he got up to speak, she listened with rapt attention to every word. Rick's persona and message resonated with Anika. She felt a rush of happiness flow through her body. He was everything Peter had described to her. Rick was a man with a message. He had spiritual power.

After the service, she went with Peter to meet Rick again. As soon as he took her hand, she knew for sure. Rick was no ordinary mortal. There was a strong flow of energy flowing from him that shook her very being. His calm reassurance gave her emotional strength. Anika didn't want to let go. She wanted to hold his hand. But then – suddenly aware of Neema – she backed away.

"Peter told me so much about you," she stammered. "Now that we've met, I'm impressed even more."

Rick smiled at her and put his arm around Neema.

"I'm glad you decided to come to church. And you should be equally impressed with Peter. He is also a teacher, and a good one. Come Spring, he will be touring the Sacramento River Valley carrying our message to all who will listen."

Anika thought for a moment, and then spoke with great resolve.

"And I shall go with him. I want to help you in any way I can."

Neema smiled uneasily. It was not unusual for people to react to Rick with Anika's passion. But few had her…. charms.

***

After they drove away from the church and turned onto the highway, Anika turned and looked intently at her Uncle.

"I want to do whatever it is you do. Will you teach me?"

Jocelyn smiled, mostly to herself. Anika tended to be volatile. Emotional. And she had been depressed ever since her arrival. It was good to see her change of mood. Jocelyn hoped it would last.

Peter was also happy to see Anika's enthusiasm. It would brighten things at home. He sensed, however, Anika saw something in Rick he had missed. Peter began to ponder on the meaning of that thought.

"You can come with me to our team meetings," Peter said. "We share our experiences and knowledge."

"There are others?" Anika asked with surprise.

"Yes… If you decide to stay with us, you'll be in good company."

Anika suddenly began to pout.

"Rick won't like me… I have a… mixed past."

"When you learn Rick's theology, you'll find he is far more concerned with how you treat other people than your …. illustrious past. He'll be more interested in what you have in your heart. What you choose to believe… and your faith in the spiritual."

They rode in silence all the way home. Peter realized he now had two issues to resolve. Anika had seen something in Rick he had overlooked… And there was the issue of theology. He realized he had just used the word for the first time. Rick did have a theology… and a message. Peter wanted to piece it all together.

***

"Eureka! I did it!" James exclaimed. "Renita, come and see."

James sat back in his chair with a great sense of satisfaction. He had just figured out how to track John's Internet broadcasts back to John's PC. He had won his bet. He had triumphed over one of the best programmers on the planet.

Renita came into the bedroom of their apartment where James had established a part time office. She was both happy and curious to see what her husband had accomplished.

"You did what?" she asked.

James pointed at his screen. There, among the jumble of letters and numbers, was an address. James pointed to it.

"That's John's Internet address. I picked up one of his broadcasts, just like anyone else, and then began backtracking through the hops to the source and bingo! I recognized John's address. It's his PC. He can't deny it."

"Are we going to be rich?" Renita asked. "I mean, what did you bet?"

James got up from the chair and stretched his tall, thin frame.

"Just a cup of coffee," he said sheepishly. "I should have bet him money."

Renita smiled at the thought of the bet. She knew these two were always betting on something. They had a friendly competition. Who was the better programmer? But more often than not, they helped each other with intricate code and procedures. It was nice to have a friend with John's genial persona and intellectual capability.

"When will you tell John?" she asked.

"As soon as I get to work tomorrow, I'll make him get me a cup of coffee... just to rub it in."

"And what will John say?"

James was suddenly struck with the dreadful implications of what he had done. If he could track John's broadcasts, then so could the NSS. By now, they probably knew all about John's activity and where he was located. Where they were all located. James turned to his wife with a look of fear and distress that frightened her.

"This is terrible!"

***

By the end of February, warmer weather had returned to Northern California. At least it had stopped snowing along the coast and in the valleys. Days of blustery weather, with cold rain and gray clouds were occasionally punctuated with a day of partly cloudy skies. Here and there a daffodil struggled to emerge from the cold hard ground. Driving into town to shop was less hazardous. Rick would occasionally take Ramon with him to the hardware store because his son loved to play with all the tools and gadgets. Isabel soon became attached to Ramon and would take extra time with him on each visit. Together they would wander through the store, Ramon asking question after question. Rick admired Isabel for her good natured patience.

When Rick and Ramon arrived at the hardware store, Isabel quickly took Ramon under her wing and motioned for Rick to go into the newspaper, printer and bookstore part of the building to look for Kato. A devoted Christian, she was obviously upset about something. Rick said goodbye to Ramon and walked through the door. He found Kato bent over his desk, furiously writing something on his PC.

"What's up?" Rick asked as he walked toward Kato's cluttered desk.

"You're not going to like this... Here, I just got this over the wire service from the Department of Public Information... It's pretty straight... considering the source."

Rick took the article from Kato and began to read it. It was about a trial for the men who had set fire to the church last Christmas Eve. Rick frowned when he read the text.

"It says the Church aggravated the community by making unpopular political statements. The prosecutor presented a case based on the assumption the community had a right to respond."

"He's more concerned about being politically correct than the facts of the case."

Rick read further. "In a courtroom filled with a hostile crowd.... Hostile to whom?"

"Hostile toward the Church.... The defendant's lawyers say their clients were merely exercising their right to freedom of speech when they set fire to the Church," Kato responded.

Rick finished reading the article and gave it back to Kato. "The Judge ruled the Church was in violation of the law according to The Citizen's Manual of Personal and Social Responsibility. He called the fire a spontaneous reaction, and gave the defendants a 30 day suspended sentence for vandalism."

Kato was very unhappy. "A slap on the wrist... or less."

Rick became despondent. "Does this mean it's OK to set fire to your political opponent's house."

"So long as the court believes it's politically correct," Kato responded.

Rick thought for a moment. Then forced himself to be more cheerful. "I think this will backfire... No pun intended... Anyone can claim what they did is politically correct. That means justice is becoming the province of the politically strong. The weak will suffer and continue to suffer until they rebel."

"Justice is only fair if it is based on the rule of law," Kato murmured. "That's the foundation of our nation's legal system.... or at least it used to be.... In this case the rule of law is contained in that damn book, that incredibly repressive Citizen's Manual of Personal and Social Responsibility.... Most people call it The Book Of Rules."

***

Although at first skeptical, John reluctantly agreed with James. It was possible to trace the Internet broadcasts back to their ISP and John's PC. It was therefore highly likely the NSS knew who they were and what they were doing. When they gave this information to Rick, he called the team together and led a candid discussion of the risks. After a lively debate, they took a vote. It was unanimous. The Internet broadcasts would continue because they were a success. It was also a matter of personal pride. Working on the broadcasts had given them a magnificent purpose in life. They were bringing hope and comfort to millions. Rick closed the meeting with a prayer. He asked God to protect their humble efforts.

The blustery winds of March brought with them warmer temperatures. The snow and ice that had plagued the valleys and coastal areas was gone. Here and there, patches of green began to appear. It was time to convey Rick's teaching to a personal audience through the use of teaching sessions and sermons. Christina and Sarah were assigned to go north into Oregon. They would visit established congregations along Route 101 as far as the Washington border. Peter and James would do a tour of Washington up to the Canadian border. Isabel would keep an eye on the store while Kato and Antonio ventured into Nevada. Rick had to be careful to schedule the missions so that only two people were gone from the ISP at one time. They still had a business to manage.

Rick selected Phillip and John to do a tour of the Sacramento River valley. Although John would do most of the teaching, Rick believed it would be good for Phillip to witness the effect John would have on his audience. As it turned out, they also received an invitation to visit a congregation in Fresno. Plans were made, advice was given, and bags were packed. In early March Phillip and John traveled the narrow roads that wind their way over the mountains to Redding. From there they traveled South, visiting additional congregations in Red Bluff, Chico, Oroville and Marysville. Against Rick's counsel they even stayed overnight in Pleasant Grove, just north of Sacramento.

The next day they drove south and had a rousing service with an enthusiastic congregation in Centerville. After the service a young man named Haben brought his mother to meet John and Phillip. They shook hands and exchanged greetings. Then Haben asked the two men a question.

"How do I become one of you?" he asked with enthusiasm. "You seem to be on a mission."

Haben's mother smiled and nodded her approval. A Christian of great faith, she was sure Haben was destined to do great things for the Lord. Phillip and John were uncertain. No one had ever asked to work for Rick. After a moment's thought, John answered.

"We are just regular guys, Haben…. We work for a living… This activity takes up almost all of our spare time. How would you support yourself?"

"My Mom and I are going to San Jose. We are going to help our uncle with his grocery store. It will be long hours for me, but I think I will still have time to help you out."

"I'll make sure he has the time," his mother interjected. Then she grinned and chuckled.

"When he isn't chasing girls."

Haben was mortified at his mother's remark. He was ready to make a commitment to a cause. He needed a sense of mission and these people were obviously doing great things.

"How can I prove my worth to you?"

Phillip placed his hand on the young man's shoulder.

"When you get to San Jose, keep an eye on things for us. Our teaching is not very popular with the NSS just now, and we need to know what they are up to."

John nodded in agreement.

"Don't get into trouble. Mostly what you can do is listen to what others are saying. If you think you have important information, just give us a call."

John handed Haben a card with his telephone number on it.

"Please don't share this number with anyone. It connects to our workplace. Mostly we use it to manage our business, but I'll give it to you because I believe you are sincere."

Haben eagerly took the card. "This is great, you can count on me."

Haben and his mother said goodbye and walked out of the church. Phillip turned to John.

"Do you think he will sustain his enthusiasm for us?"

"Perhaps he will do great things for Rick," John responded. "Only God knows."

***

Word of their mission spread throughout the San Joaquin Valley and they were able to make productive stops in Madera, Modesto, and Stockton on their way back home. Thus far, they had moved so fast through the valleys they had been able to evade the NSS. Phillip guessed the Sacramento District, for reasons he could not understand, had no interest in arresting him or John. But the San Jose District would be willing to breach jurisdictional district lines if they thought they could get away with it. They might not be willing to go north or east of Sacramento, but Winters was an easy drive from San Jose.

Despite the risk, Phillip was determined to stop in Winters to see his parents. They turned West on 80 from Sacramento, went through Davis, and soon were on the driveway of the house that had been his home for most of his life. It was a sunny, but cool afternoon. A few flowers had managed to struggle up from the cold ground. When they got out of the car, Phillip was troubled by what he saw. The fields were still too wet to plough. Only sporadic patches of green vegetation dotted the landscape. He knew that by now the fields should have been covered with new grass. It would be a short planting season.

Phillip and John walked up the concrete steps to the front porch and rang the doorbell. They heard noises inside, the shuffling of chairs, and George's voice. Phillip guessed he had been taking a nap. When George finally opened the door, he was both annoyed at the intrusion and delighted to see his son. George managed a broad but unconvincing smile. Behind him a voice called out. Phillip recognized the voice of his older sister, Josephine. He shook his father's hand, and then gave him a spontaneous hug. Although George was somewhat surprised by his son's sudden affection, he returned the hug with equal energy. Phillip was delighted to see his sister, and she was only too happy to give him a warm welcome. Phillip introduced John as they went into the living room.

"Where's Mom?" Phillip asked.

George looked depressed. "She's in bed... She's not well... not well at all."

Alarmed, Phillip looked at his sister for an explanation. "What's wrong?"

Josephine gave him a carefully worded response.

"Abigail has been confined to bed for about a week.... We've had the doctor come to the house... He did it as a favor to George... The doctor doesn't think Abigail will be with us too much longer."

Phillip did a quick calculation in his head. Both Abigail and George were 73. A sudden illness should not be unexpected. Although George looked to be rumpled with age, he seemed to be relatively healthy.

"Can I see her?"

"Of course," said Josephine, and she turned to lead the way upstairs.

John found himself a comfortable stuffed chair and sat down. George decided to stay with John. He hated seeing Abigail in this condition, and his knees hurt when he climbed the stairs.

When they reached the second floor landing, Josephine turned to Phillip.

"Respiratory infection, then two strokes. Abigail can't digest her food and she has refused tube feeding. Her health has gone downhill very fast."

"Why wasn't I told?"

"Phillip, you had enough problems of your own, and there was nothing you could do to help her."

Phillip grumbled something under his breath. He suddenly felt guilty. Embarrassed. He had been so self-centered. He had forgotten about his parents. Phillip wanted to believe Abigail was a healthy, active, and assertive woman. That's how he always pictured her in his mind. He had ignored the reality of his mother's aging.

Josephine knocked on the bedroom door and went into the room. Phillip tried to smile for his mother, but what he saw horrified him. In the middle of the bed was a thin, emaciated woman with sunken eyes and splotchy gray skin. Phillip approached the bed.

"Hi Mom," he said with as much cheerfulness as he could muster. "John and I have been touring the valleys ... Giving talks...... You'd be proud of us. We have accomplished a lot."

The woman on the bed seemed like a stranger. Someone he did not know. Phillip could not understand why she had declined so fast. Abigail slowly responded.

"Phillip!.... So nice of you to come.... Did Josephine put you up to this?"

"No Mom, John and I were on our way home... You know... to Humboldt County, and we thought we'd stop in to see how you and Dad were."

"Not too damn well." Abigail retorted. "The Doctor says I don't have much time."

The frail woman on the bed shifted her body ever so slightly and closed her eyes. Phillip waited for her to speak again, but she didn't move.

"We'd better let her sleep," said Josephine. "She'll be awake again about 4:30. You can talk to her then."

Phillip walked despondently down the stairs with his sister. When he saw his father, George refused to look at him. Josephine just shook her head.

"He always wanted to die first... He's already a lonely old man."

Phillip was shocked by Josephine's comment. He had an image of his father as a healthy, robust, highly intelligent man. But now here he was, his health seeping away from his body, emotionally withdrawn, physically weak, and obviously very depressed. George wanted to die. Phillip was badly shaken.

"Are you going to stay?" he asked.

"Yes... I'll stay until they both pass away."

***

Phillip was torn. On the one hand, he wanted to stay with his parents. But he also knew he and John were in serious danger if he lingered in Winters. So the next morning he held his mother's hand for several minutes and then kissed her tenderly on the forehead. He almost broke down when he hugged his father goodbye. The tears wanted to come, but he managed to choke them back. As he got into the car, he looked back at his sister.

"I'll bring Rick with me next time... He can help them both."

Then he threw the car into gear and backed out of the driveway onto the county road. He waved goodbye to Josephine and drove away.

Rick had been right. Stopping in Winters was a big risk. About two hours later, a big black SUV drove slowly past the house. Three men gazed at every inch of the property, hoping to see evidence Phillip and John were there. Disappointed, they drove away. But a few moments later, the SUV reappeared. This time it came into the driveway. The three men got out and walked boldly up to the front door. One of them rapped sharply on the door with a club. When Josephine answered, the man demanded to know where Phillip was hiding. Although Josephine was terrified, she managed to steady her nerves and pointed to the barn.

"Look for yourself."

"He's not here, is he?" the man growled.

"No."

"Has he been here?"

"He left this morning after a very short visit."

"Where'd he go?" another agent demanded.

"I don't really know," Josephine answered sweetly. "You know how brothers are. He comes and goes without telling us much of anything."

The agents conferred among themselves. They would have preferred to arrest Josephine, but that meant taking her all the way back to Sunnyvale for interrogation. They decided the information she would give them wasn't worth the effort. Besides, they were not ready to challenge the Sacramento District's jurisdiction over Winters. They started for the SUV. Before getting in, one of the agents turned and snarled a warning to Josephine.

"You'd better not tell anyone we were here, or you'll be in big trouble."

And after that nasty threat, they drove off again.

As the SUV approached the freeway entrance, one of the agents spoke up.

"We'll get him next time."

***

It was a long, boring and occasionally frustrating drive from Winters to Humboldt County. Neither Phillip nor John were very talkative. Both men were still tired from the hectic activity of the last week. But as they passed through the Redwoods at Myers Flat, John asked Phillip a question.

"Are you feeling guilty about your mother?"

Phillip scowled for a moment, and then allowed himself to release his grief.

"How could I do that?... How could I see my parents and not notice their deteriorating health?"... I was so wrapped up in myself, I ignored what was going on.... My sister must think I'm a real fool. She probably thinks I have no respect for my mother and father."

"Do you?"

"Of course... I love them both... and I respect them!"

"Isn't that what Rick is teaching us... Honor thy father and respect thy mother... or something like that?"

"Yes... But I just didn't make the connection... Those are good words... But damn it, I failed to apply them to my own parents."

"What will you do now.... Now that you feel very guilty?"

Philip thought for a moment.

"I'll live what you teach.... I'll call Josephine every day... I think I'll write a letter to my Dad and tell him I love him."

"Now you're on the right track. We can't just teach this stuff. We have to live it... Set the example for others... and ourselves."

***

Word gets around. The NSS is holding Father Giovanni. At first, no one cared. Who the hell is Father Giovanni? But details began to filter through the confusion. Former residents of the NC went out of their way to spread rumors and information. Father Giovanni was a beloved apostle and prophet, a man who cared about the homeless and the victims of an unfeeling public welfare system. Father Giovanni loved children. There were posters of him holding a baby in his arms, and a little girl on his lap. All very benevolent. Within the space of 30 days, Father Giovanni became a folk hero. Champion of the downtrodden. Victim of the hated NSS.

Then came the ultimate insult. The NSS announced it would try Father Giovanni for preaching sedition. They said he failed to obey the law as set out in the Citizen's Manual of Personal and Social Responsibility. Everyone was sure it would be a mock trial. Father Giovanni was doomed. And what had he done? Nothing. Absolutely nothing. Father Giovanni was a good guy. A hero. His release became a cause on the San Jose State campus. More posters. A rally with several speeches. By now the information was wildly incorrect. But no one cared. Except the NSS. They were furious.

Then one of the former residents of the NC started talking to the media about a guy who worked with Father Giovanni. A miracle worker. A prophet. A man who had a direct connection to something called the Spiritual Universe. He could read your mind. He could feel your emotions. Gossip about his powers resonated through Santa Clara valley. The students at San Jose State picked up the idea. Rumor was he had been exiled to Northern California by the NSS. More bad guy, good guy rhetoric. Rick became a folk hero almost overnight.

All that attention didn't go unnoticed. The NSS was livid. Media people expressed surprise. Most of the local politicians were sympathetic. Congresswoman Belle Gunness was outraged.

And then there was the leader of a local Muslim congregation, Omar Jones. He had a very different interest in Rick and Father Giovanni.

Omar Jones, alias Mohammed Ahriman Abu, had been brought up in an African American ghetto in Los Angeles. As a teenager he went looking for a hero to emulate. He picked Colin Powell. He started going to church with his grandmother. A big kid, he found a place as a full back on his high school football team. That led to a college scholarship. He excelled as a player and as a student. After graduation there was a four year stint in the army. He went overseas, was impressed by the local people he met, and converted to Islam. Twenty years later he was functioning as the Imam for a Muslim congregation in San Jose.

Omar hated the Book Of Rules because it was a secular, Godless document, created by non-believers who wanted to force it on the Muslim community as a substitute for the Qur'an. He also noticed the Book Of Rules was being quoted as the primary source of moral law for Christians, Hindus, Buddhists and other faiths. Omar believed it was time for people of faith to unite against the secular forces that were imposing the will of government on traditional religious theology. In order to accomplish his objective, he wanted to enlist the support of the Christian community. In March, just before the trial of Father Giovanni was scheduled to begin, he decided to act. Omar would ask members of the Muslim community to join in the protests that were building against the trial. That would show how Muslims objected to the mock trial and persecution of a Christian. In order to further reinforce a united Muslim-Christian front against the NSS, he would also seek an alliance with the emerging leader of Christianity in

Northern California. On a cool gray day in March, he called his best friend and most trusted aid into his office.

Omar looked solemnly at the big man who was sitting next to him. "I have a job for you."

Jimar shifted his tall muscular frame in the easy chair.

"Does it pay real money?"

Omar smiled. "No, but it has other rewards."

Jimar grinned at his friend. "Your jobs always do."

"I want you to take a message from me to this prophet.. Rick ... in upstate California. I want to arrange a meeting.... In any town he picks."

Jimar was puzzled. He didn't particularly like Hispanics. Most of them, if they had any religion at all, were Catholics.

"You want to meet him... this man?"

"Yes, and as soon as you can arrange a secret meeting."

"Why a special meeting? Why not just go up there and see him?"

"I can't be seen as going to him, and I doubt he would see me without an introduction. I want to establish a partnership with him if I can."

Jimar was still mystified.

"But why make partnership with this guy? From what I hear, he isn't a true Catholic. And besides why make a deal with someone who is not a Muslim?"

"Catholic or not, he has gathered a large following wherever he goes, and now his friends are spreading his philosophy all over the State. We can't argue with success."

Jimar was still not convinced. "But why do we need his help?"

"Because my friend, before going into battle against your enemies, it is wise to make as many friends as you can."

***

It was a rare show of solidarity. Christians, Muslims, Hindus and a dozen other religious organizations marched together in front of the Santa Clara County Court House, all chanting slogans and waving banners. Even a few agnostics and atheists joined in the protest. Everyone believed Father Giovanni was innocent of any crime. For the demonstrators, this was not prosecution, it was persecution. The police cars came with flashing lights and screaming sirens. It took over 50 cops to restore a minimum of order. Although there was no violence, the Department of Public Information promptly labeled the protest as the work of theological criminals.

The trial was all prosecution and no defense. The NSS prevailed without much effort. The outcome of the trial had been preordained. In a little less than two hours, Father Giovanni was remanded to the custody of NSS. He would be sentenced at a later date.

The protestors went home and back to school, frustrated by the day's events. Although they had failed to help Father Giovanni, many were determined to escalate the scope of the protest. The people of Santa Clara

Valley were repelled by the fraudulent circumstances of the trial. They felt vulnerable. The NSS could arrest anyone. With or without a good reason. Fear replaced complacency. The seeds of rebellion had been planted.

***

Of all the things Rick did, he seemed to be the happiest when he was surrounded by people. Whenever he preached, he would close his service with a prayer and then call for a hymn. He would ask the congregation to stand, sing with them for a few stanzas, and then walk down from the pulpit into the pew area. As they were singing, he would shake hands and exchange hugs with as many people as he could. He genuinely enjoyed the fellowship. Talking, smiling, and being himself. Neema adored him when he was swept up in the enthusiasm of these moments. Here was the man she loved.

Rick had been invited to speak before a very large congregation near Sacramento. At first, he refused, fearing he would be arrested by the NSS. But when the minister of the church contacted the local NSS District Commander, he was very cooperative. He even sent Rick a personal note, assuring him the NSS would not interfere with his participation in a service. The Sacramento District Commander was convinced his superiors in Washington were thinking of making an alliance with Rick. The NSS didn't want to arrest him, he reasoned, because the Washington political establishment wanted to control Rick's activity and message.

The service for the congregation near Sacramento had ended with a traditional hymn. Once again, Rick walked into the pew area, obviously pleased with the affectionate response of the congregation. After the hymn ended, most of the congregation filed out of the church. Rick was still talking with a small group of people when he was approached by a dark-skinned woman, and a blond teenage girl. The woman seemed to be outspoken, strong in her opinions. The girl was equally passionate. After speaking to them for a moment, Rick motioned Neema. She walked the few steps to his side.

"Neema, this is Gabriela and Amanda. They both tell me they enjoyed the sermon and would like to hear more. Gabriela lives here in Sacramento. Amanda is on a break from her high school in... where was that?"

Amanda spoke with enthusiasm. "Albuquerque, New Mexico."

Neema smiled at the girl. "You're a long way from home."

"Oh my family has been friends with Gabriela forever... My Dad insisted I come to visit with her during spring break."

"I think he sent her to spy on me," Gabriela grinned. "I haven't been writing to him as often as I should... Amanda should be skiing or sitting on some beach. Not cooped up with me in Sacramento."

"That's not true, Gabriela," Amanda retorted. "I've wanted to visit with you since Junior High. This was just the first chance I got."

Rick took both of Gabriela's hands in his own, and closed his eyes.

"You're a devote Christian, Gabriela. Why bother with me?"

"I didn't think much about it before today. But you have really inspired me. Given me a new energy for Christ."

Rick smiled at Gabriela, and then took Amanda's hands.

"We have a daughter about your age. Her name is Adonica...."

Then Rick stopped. A look of surprise swept over his face.

"Your last name is Taylor," he said in a matter of fact manner.

"Why yes," Amanda responded. "How did you know?"

"It's a gift... and your father's name is George Kincade Taylor!"

Amanda grinned at Rick with great surprise. "Do you know my father?"

Rick rolled his shoulder. It still ached from time to time. A football injury Rick would never forget.

"You might say we met at Stanford.... When you see him, say hello."

Gabriela was mesmerized by Rick. *"How did he know so much about Amanda?"* she thought, *"and what does he know about me?... It must be true...He can see into your mind.... Well, all he saw in Amanda was the sweet innocence of youth.... But when he looked into my thoughts.... What did he see?.... Oh my.. Oh my!"*

***

That afternoon Gabriela took Amanda to the airport, helped her with the luggage, and watched as she disappeared into the secure passenger area. Satisfied Amanda was safely on her way back home to New Mexico, Gabriela walked out of the terminal and headed for the parking lot. She pulled out her cell phone and dialed a familiar number in Washington, DC. A woman's voice answered. She immediately recognized Gabriela's voice and went to look for her boss. George Kincaid Taylor came to the phone.

"Hello, Gabriela... How's my daughter."

"She's fine. Amanda is on her way back to Albuquerque. She should be there on the 7:30 flight from Sacramento."

"That's great, Gabriela. We can't thank you enough for watching over Amanda this last week. I'll make sure she gets picked up on her arrival. Did you have any problems?"

"She's a bright, lovely teenager, George. Very passionate about everything. At first she was upset about coming here instead of going down to Mexico for Spring break, but she soon adjusted."

"Well... you know we have to be careful with her. She's very vulnerable at that age. And we were worried she would be kidnapped if she went to any of the usual party places."

"We had a nice visit, George. I didn't remember how pretty she was. I haven't seen her since the company Christmas party.... just over 5 years ago."

"Yes... she attracts boys like bees to honey."

"I took her to church with me this morning. She immediately fell in love with the preacher."

"Really? What's his name?"

"He was a guest speaker from up Northern California. Very inspirational. His name is Ricardo Vasquez. But everyone calls him Rick."

George began to laugh, and the laughter grew louder. Gabriela could imagine him sitting back in his chair and staring at the ceiling when he had a good laugh, just like he did when she worked for him.

"OK... What's funny about him? ... He seemed like a real nice guy."

"Oh I know Mr. Vasquez. I tackled him in a football game my senior year at Stanford. I'll bet he still remembers me."

Gabriela was surprised. "You played football against him?

"Yes... If I remember right he was a wide receiver for San Jose State. I decked him good. I still don't think he saw me coming."

George chuckled again. It was a sweet memory.

"Can we trust him?" Gabriela asked.

"Absolutely. He's a first class guy. I heard about a preacher named Rick, but I never made the connection. What a small world."

"I see you're still working on Sunday. Just like you did when you were my boss in Albuquerque. Don't you ever take any time off?"

"No... I'm afraid not... We have so much to do. Our party's still a mess. Everyday brings a new challenge."

"Well bless you for your efforts, George. Our nation needs you now more than ever."

"You're very kind, Gabriela... I guess that's what I appreciated most when you were my Executive Assistant."

"And I miss working with you." Gabriela paused. She had worked with George Kincaid Taylor for almost 15 years. Tough times and good times. He built his contracting business up from nothing, and eventually became a prime operations and maintenance contractor for the Department of Energy. A man of dignity, authority, humility and patience, he had also risen within the ranks of the Conservative Party to a position of national leadership. But now he was having second thoughts about his future. Gabriela understood his anguish.

By now, she had walked all the way to her car. As she turned the key in the lock, she spoke again.

"If I can help .... Just holler."

"Thank you, Gabriela. And again, Helen and I are most grateful for keeping Amanda occupied this last week. We could rest easy knowing she was with you."

After George hung up, Gabriela made a decision. Come June, she would drive up to Northern California. Whatever Rick was doing, she wanted to help him.

***

The Commander of the San Jose NSS District was unsure what to do. His Internet software experts had just confirmed they could locate the source of the Internet radio ministry. He was sure it was Ricardo. But the programs were always about some religious nonsense. He could enforce the law as he saw fit according to the Book Of Rules, but that gave him three problems. First, the enforcement of religious speech rules had never been tested in Federal Court. Hence, the outcome of a trial was uncertain. He didn't want to proceed unless he could be sure of winning. Second, Father Giovanni's trial had produced a nasty anti-NSS demonstration. If he arrested Rick, he would risk making that situation worse. And third, Rick was seldom within his jurisdiction. Trapping him in the San Jose District would be a challenge for which he did not have enough resources. On the other hand, if he went up north to find Ricardo, he would technically not have the authority to arrest him. That was certain to annoy the Sacramento Commander.

"And besides," the San Jose District Commander fumed out loud, "Sacramento's up to something."

Frustrated and angry, he decided to wait to make his move.

***

The call came just as Phillip and Lydia were closing up the ISP for the night. It was Phillip's sister, Josephine.

"Abigail," Josephine said sadly, "is very ill. The Doctor doesn't think she will last 24 hours."

Phillip struggled with his feelings. The call was not unexpected. Abigail had been failing for some time. But it still shook him.

"I'm coming down... I'll bring Lydia with me. We should be there before midnight."

"I don't think that's a good idea," Josephine retorted. "Someone is watching the house."

"Doesn't matter, I'm coming.... Do they watch the house at night?"

"No, a man shows up in a black car and parks outside our gate. He scans the place with his binoculars, and then leaves."

"I'll put the car in the barn, he'll never see me."

"Phillip, I still don't think this is a good idea," Josephine interjected. She was clearly alarmed.

"I'm coming. Make sure the back door is open so I can drive in without waking everyone up."

"Oh Phillip, this is very risky... But I'll make sure you can get into the barn."

"See you later, Josephine... and I love you."

Phillip hung up the instrument and turned to Lydia. She had listened to most of the conversation.

"If you're going, I'm going," she said with great resolution.

"Going where?" a voice called out from Rick's office. He appeared at the door, smiling as he put on his winter coat.

"It's Abigail," Phillip said. "She's failing. Lydia and I are going down tonight... if that's OK with you."

Rick's smile turned into a frown. "I'm coming with you," he said with solemn resolve.

Phillip protested. "You can't come... They want you worse than me. So far the San Jose NSS District has been unwilling to come this far north, but they can show up in Winters on short notice. Your trip to Sacramento was carefully planned and the Sacramento NSS agreed to let you come. If you show up in Winters without political protection, the San Jose District Commander will leap at the chance to catch us."

Rick walked over to his friends and gave each of them a hug.

"I'm going... and Neema will want to come. Abigail is too important to us all. We have to be with her."

***

Although a blustery March had brought a hint of warmer weather, the roads could still be icy at night. Phillip had to slow down several times to avoid the black ice that can turn a road surface into a skating rink. It was 1AM when he finally turned into the driveway of his parent's house and slowly drove around to the barn. Once inside, he quickly turned off the lights, got out of the car, and walked to the barn doors. With some effort he got them closed and locked the latch. Then they trudged around the barn to the back door of the house. Josephine was waiting for them in the kitchen.

Rick and Lydia waited patiently while Phillip and his two sisters exchanged hugs and a few words of welcome. Then Josephine came over to Rick and gave him a warm embrace.

"I'm so glad you came," she said quietly. "Mom has been asking for you all afternoon.... She seems so strange... It's like she's not in this world.... Come on up to her bedroom. Come and see for yourself."

"But it's in the middle of the night," protested Neema. "Shouldn't we wait until morning?"

Josephine consoled her sister.

"Time no longer has any meaning for Abigail... She's probably awake... She sleeps in little catnaps... and I know she wants to see Rick. Just be quiet. We don't want to wake George up."

Josephine turned and started for the stairs. Neema, Phillip, Rick and Lydia obediently followed, walking as quietly as they could. When they entered the master bedroom, Abigail was asleep, her eyes and face a picture of contentment. A lone lamp on the nightstand revealed the faint outline of her thin body under the blankets. Josephine gently touched Abigail's arm.

"Mom... Mom... we have company."

Abigail barely stirred. It took a few moments for her to recognize Josephine.

"Who?"

"It's Neema and Phillip... They've come to say hello and they brought Lydia and Rick with them."

The old woman tried to focus on the human shapes grouped around her bed. She seemed unable to recognize anyone. Then Rick stepped closer and took her hand. Abigail immediately knew who it was. She grasped his arm with withered fingers.

"So ... you've come to see an old woman die," she said in a whisper.

"I've come to see a wonderful woman make her way into the Spiritual Universe," Rick responded.

Abigail's voice became a feeble murmur. Rick had difficulty understanding her words.

"Oh rubbish... You know I never believed in all that stuff," she said.

Rick knew better. He could feel she had already drifted closer to God. Her spirit was somewhere between this universe and the next.

"Perhaps, Abigail.... But you lived your life as though you did. Phillip and I owe so much to you ... and you were a good mother to your girls."

"Oh pooh..."

"Abigail, you are surrounded by love. Can you feel it?"

The old woman shifted her body and looked around the room. But her eyes could no longer focus. She could see only shapes in the shadows. Frustrated, she dropped her head back on the pillow.

"Feel the love," Rick said again.

Abigail closed her eyes and let her thoughts drift away. A feeling of sweet energy began to flow through her body. It was the energy of love. It was energy from those around her. She began to dream. She found herself in a beautiful garden. It was filled with beautiful flowers, tall flowering shrubs, deep green grass and lovely birch trees. Here and there the light of the warm sun filtered through the leaves of the trees. Golden beams fell on a footpath of stone that beckoned her to a portal bathed in soft white light. A gentle voice penetrated her dream. It was Rick.

"What do you see, Abigail?"

Abigail began to feel she was no longer bound by this earth. She was sure she could fly. Her feet barely touched the footpath as she walked slowly toward the portal. Then as she entered, Abigail was overcome with happiness.

"Oh Rick.... I believe... it's wonderful!"

***

Neema and Josephine took their mother's death with calm resignation. Phillip, however, was thoroughly shaken by what he had just witnessed. After his sisters left the room, he gave Rick a spontaneous hug.

"That was magnificent. I can't deny myself any longer. I believe, Rick. You can count on me to help you in any way I can."

Rick smiled, his heart filled with the delight of affectionate friendship. "And you shall have the opportunity."

***

The next morning Neema, Josephine and Phillip waited patiently for George to wake up. When he finally opened his eyes, they gathered around his bed to tell him about Abigail's death. But he already knew she was gone from this earth. George had dreamed of her passing. He had shared her moment of ultimate peace. Abigail told him to come with her as soon as he could. So when he finally spoke, he calmly announced his own death would take place in a few days.

***

The hastily arranged funeral was a family affair. Mari and Josue joined them for the brief service, Rick said a simple prayer, and Phillip placed a rose on Abigail's shroud. Tears in his eyes, George clearly wanted to be with his beloved Abigail. He walked with hesitation up to the casket, looked at his wife for several minutes, and then sighed.

"Goodbye, Abigail… Peace be with you my love… We shall be together again… It will not be long."

Firmly, but gently, Phillip led his father out of the funeral home, and helped him into the car. As he stood up to close the door, he saw a man through the window of a black car. The man was busily taking pictures of them all. Phillip motioned to Rick and pointed at the black car. Rick nodded he understood. Rick and Neema went home with Mari and Josue. Phillip took Lydia, Josephine and his father back to his parent's house. As they drove out of Winters, he had Lydia call Rick. When she made the connection, Phillip took the instrument from his wife.

"I'll pick you up in 45 minutes."

Rick quickly agreed. In a few more minutes he drove into the driveway of his parent's house. He brought the car to a stop and turned to Josue.

"Phillip will be here in less than 45 minutes. We have to get out of here or risk arrest."

Josue understood. Mari was alarmed.

"Why are they still after you?" she asked.

"I don't know, Mari…. and I don't want to find out…. In a few months I think everything will either blow over or I will have enough influence to avoid a confrontation. Until then we just have to keep out of their way."

Mari was distressed. "Can't a lawyer help you?"

"The NSS operates outside the law. Very few lawyers are willing to take the risk."

They got out of the car and stood in the driveway, waiting for Phillip to pick them up.

"I'm so proud of you," Mari said. "We try to listen to your Internet services. You bring hope to so many people."

Rick looked at his mother with compassion.

"We have been lucky, so far. They seem to be well received. We get e-mail from all over the world."

Then he noticed his mother was shivering from the cold.

"Let's go inside. We can watch for Phillip from the front room."

**

They were able to get over the mountains and head north on 101 before the informant in the black car was able to mobilize the NSS agents from San Jose. After some confusion, they decided not to pursue Rick. This time.

Night had fallen before Rick and his friends finally made their way to Humboldt County. After the fear of possible confrontation with the NSS, Neema and Rick were especially happy to see their children. All three were asleep when Neema and Rick tip toed into the house. They went upstairs and peeked into each bedroom. One by one they looked upon the sleeping faces of their children. After closing the last door, Neema turned to Rick and gave him a little kiss on the cheek.

"Now I feel safe," she said.

The following week Jimar found his way to the ISP building. At first, Lydia was reluctant to tell the big man where he could find Rick because Jimar seemed to be harboring some kind of resentment. But Peter intervened and invited Jimar to have a cup of coffee while they waited for Rick to return from town. When Jimar asked several questions about Rick and Rick's family, Peter became more guarded in his comments. He changed the subject and asked Jimar if he had heard of Father Giovanni. It was then Jimar revealed that Father Giovanni's arrest had motivated his friend Omar to arrange a meeting with Rick. Peter encouraged Jimar to tell him about Omar, and the Muslim Mosque in San Jose. After twenty minutes of discussion, Peter was satisfied Jimar could become a trusted friend. When Rick returned from town, he introduced him to Jimar.

"Well... this is certainly a surprise," Rick said. "I'm flattered you came all the way from San Jose to see us."

"You might say, I'm on a mission. My friend Omar sent me. He would like to know if you would be willing to meet with him to discuss a possible working partnership."

"Friends are always a greater asset than enemies," Rick responded.

Jimar was surprised at the remark. "That's what Omar told me before I left. You two must think alike."

Rick came closer to Jimar and started to take the man's hand as he did with so many others. He placed one hand on top of Jimar's fingers, palm down and one underneath, palm up. Jimar recoiled at Rick's touch, and took a step back. He had heard about Rick's sensitivity. Rick smiled and continued to offer his hand. After a moment of uncertainty, Jimar again extended his hand. The two men shook hands, and then Rick motioned Jimar to a chair.

"And so... You are on a mission.... Sent by Omar Jones, alias Mohammed Ahriman Abu, to arrange a meeting at a neutral place where we can talk about theology, partnership, and reformation."

"How did you know his Muslim name?" Jimar asked.

"You told me," Rick responded. "When you shook my hand."

Jimar was stunned. "And what else do you know?"

"You both converted from Christianity to Islam. Omar was raised by his grandmother. He has a great affection for her. And you were raised by your parents. You don't get along with your father. Shall I go on?"

Jimar settled back into his chair and thought for a moment.

"No... I'm convinced you do have the gift everyone talks about.... I sometimes get the same feeling from Omar... You two should get together. There is much to talk about."

"If Omar would like to spend some time with me, that would be most welcome. Where would he like to have this meeting?"

"I have no place in mind. I think Omar is willing to leave that up to you. The NSS seems to limit your movements."

Rick thought for a moment. Then he made his decision.

"May I suggest Davis? It's far enough from San Jose to give us some measure of security. The Sacramento NSS District Commander seems more tolerant of our work. I don't think he will bother us if we do this without attracting attention."

Jimar shook his head in agreement.

"There is some kind of conflict between Sacramento and San Jose. At least that's the word on the street.... Perhaps I can work that to our advantage. I'll take your suggestion to Omar. He will be pleased you agreed to work with him."

Jimar stood up as though to leave. He was taller than Rick, with a heavy frame and muscular arms. Rick motioned for him to sit down.

"Have you had dinner?"

"No. Just a sandwich in Ukiah."

"Then you must come home with me for dinner. I'd like you to meet my family."

After some protest, Jimar agreed have dinner with Rick, Neema and the children. They made him welcome, and he was soon at ease in their home. Jimar marveled at the obvious friendship and consideration the members of Rick's family extended to each other and to him. When he left later that evening, the girls gave him a hug and Ramon shook his hand. For Jimar, it was a refreshing experience. The next day, as he drove back to San Jose, he vowed to help them if he got the chance.

***

    The spark of energy that ignites spontaneous demonstrations is often hard to identify. Was it the crushing hardship of chronic economic recession? Was it the oppressive regulation of a restrictive government? Was it the ignorance of blind ideology? Or was it simply the loss of personal freedom? Whatever the cause, spontaneous demonstrations did break out on the first day of April at three California university campuses. Students blocked building entrances, disrupted classes, and marched in the streets. There were strident speeches and emotional songs. The failures of an autocratic government were forcefully condemned. The NSS was vilified. Ineffective political processes were described with much sarcasm. Whatever happened, they asked, to the promises of life, liberty, and the pursuit of happiness?

    By the afternoon of the second day, there was much talk of moral mission. Terms such as independence, industry, fidelity, caring, charity, honesty, and integrity became more common in the noisy rhetoric. And then someone mentioned Father Giovanni. The name resonated with campus crowds. Within hours he became a symbol of the oppressed and defenseless. Hundreds of students descended on the NSS compound in Sunnyvale, demanding his release. The NSS responded with tear gas and troopers carrying clubs. It was a bloody confrontation that took hours to suppress.

    When the demonstrations finally subsided, the students returned to their classrooms. The NSS, badly shaken by the energy of the assault on the Sunnyvale compound, began to look for someone to punish. They arrested several students. They resolved to make Father Giovanni a symbol of their authority. And they placed the blame for the demonstrations on Rick.

***

    Less than four weeks after Abigail died, Josephine called Phillip. George was failing fast. Although they knew the NSS informant would be in the area, Phillip and Lydia immediately left for Winters. They arrived just as the April sun was casting long shadows over the green forests and grasses of the western mountains. Phillip drove the car into the barn, got out, and closed the big barn door with a satisfying thud. As he and Lydia walked silently to the house, Phillip carefully surveyed the county road. There was no one in sight.

    They gave Josephine an affectionate hug, and then she led them upstairs to the master bedroom. George appeared to be sleeping. His face almost serene.

"He's been like that for two days," Josephine said. "I'm not sure where he is, but I don't think he is here among us. He mumbles from time to time, but I can't make out the words.... I know he desperately wants to be with Abigail... They were so much in love... Perhaps he is looking for her."

Philip knelt down by the bed and took his father's hand. The old man seemed to be at peace with the world, his chest rising and falling in long easy breaths. Although he didn't stir when Phillip touched his hand, Phillip could sense George was aware of his presence. Phillip carefully placed his father's hand on the blanket and stood up.

"There is nothing to do but wait," he said. "Why don't we make supper and have a talk."

Josephine and Lydia nodded in agreement and the three of them went downstairs to the kitchen.

"I'm disappointed Rick couldn't come," Josephine said.

"He was out of town when you called.... speaking in Seattle. Otherwise he would be here. He loved George and Abigail. They were a second family for him. And Neema didn't want to leave the children alone. She wanted to come. But it didn't work out."

Lydia began to put out the dishes for supper. Josephine opened the refrigerator and pulled out the salad drawer. In less than an hour, they had a light supper ready and sat down to eat.

"Have you seen anything of the NSS?" Lydia asked.

"Only that annoying informant in his black car," Josephine responded.

"Does he come by here often?"

"Probably once or twice a day.... I think he would come in to search the house if I wasn't here."

Phillip thought about the NSS and the informant. After supper, he picked up the telephone and called the local police station. After a brief conversation, he hung up. They were clearing the dishes when the telephone rang again. Lydia answered.

"It's for you," she said to Phillip.

Phillip had a guarded conversation with someone, thanked them for their help, and hung up.

"What was that all about?" Lydia demanded.

"You'll see," Phillip smiled and winked at his sister. "You'll see."

They went upstairs after doing the dishes to see if George was OK. They found him in almost the same position on the bed. He was still resting comfortably. Satisfied they could do nothing for him, they went downstairs again. Phillip wanted to talk to his sister about the house, her financial situation, and her plans.

The next morning was the start of a perfect day. A few fleecy clouds playfully raced across a pure blue sky. The air was moist and cool. There was the smell of wet grass, and the sound of birds. Hand in hand, Phillip and Lydia took a short walk around the house before breakfast. Then they went inside, beckoned by the smell of freshly brewed coffee and cinnamon buns Josephine was heating for breakfast. The breakfast conversation was light and occasionally humorous.

After breakfast, Josephine went upstairs to wake George. When she saw him, she shuddered and returned to the upstairs landing.

"Phillip!.. Lydia!... Come quick!"

Phillip and Lydia rushed upstairs to join Josephine. Inside the bedroom, they found George thrashing about on the white sheets. Then he abruptly stopped, and settled back on his pillow. Phillip knelt down beside the bed and took George's hand. He could sense his father was slowly slipping away from them. Phillip spoke in a low voice.

"I'm here with you Dad."

Phillip closed his eyes and began to pray. He desperately wanted to connect with his father. George whispered something Phillip could not hear. He leaned over and put his ear closer to George's lips.

"I found it," his father whispered joyfully. "I found the Angels' Footpath."

A rush of warmth swept over Phillip. Overwhelmed by love, he began to form a deep spiritual connection with his father. He found himself in a forest. They were together on a footpath. He remembered Rick's words and whispered them to his father.

"Let's take this walk together."

George seemed to be at peace as they walked down the forest path toward the soft light that marked the entrance to another dimension. When they reached the portal, George turned and solemnly shook his son's hand.

"Thank you, Phillip," he said with a gentle smile.

Then he disappeared into the light. A moment later, in a voice filled with joyful emotion, he clearly said one word.

"Abigail!"

***

They attended the funeral two days later. Josephine read a touching eulogy. Phillip said a prayer that honored both his parents. Mari and Josue both cried because they had lost their two best friends in the space of less than a month. As they left the church, Phillip spotted the informant's black car. The man inside was busily watching them with a video camera and microphone. Phillip decided to ignore him. He quickly guided Lydia and Josephine to his car. They drove home in silence, each of them absorbed by their own thoughts. When they arrived at the house, Phillip deliberately parked in the driveway.

***

The NSS informant had called the San Jose District Commander three times in two days, but the man always seemed to be out of the office.

Frustrated by his failure to rouse San Jose, he followed Phillip's car back to the Mitchell's house after the funeral, and parked on the side of the road where he could keep an eye on the property. He dialed the Commander's phone again. There was still no answer. The informant cursed and was about to try another number in Sunnyvale when he was startled by the flashing lights of a police car that had pulled up behind him. Annoyed by the disruption, he started to get out to confront the dumb policeman who dared to challenge his authority. But his movements were interrupted by a voice that blared out over the police car's loudspeaker.

"Stay in your car... Put your hands on the wheel where I can see them," the voice demanded.

Although very angry, the informant did as he was told. He peered at the police car behind him.

"That," he sneered, "must be the world's oldest police car."

It was Officer Johnson. He took his time. He wanted to annoy the informant. Before he got out of the police car, he counted to 100....twice. Then he opened the door, and walked slowly to the informant's car. The informant rolled down the window.

"Do you know who I am!" he shouted. "You have no right to stop me!"

"May I please see your registration and driver's license," Officer Johnson responded casually.

"I'm with the NSS you idiot. On assignment... I can have you arrested!"

Officer Johnson took several moments to respond. Then he said in a calm voice.

"Do I look like Mickey Mouse?"

"But you have no authority over me!"

Officer Johnson placed his hand on his hip, next to his gun. He leisurely unbuttoned the flap that covered his holster.

"And guess what I have."

The informant's face turned bright red with hatred, but he complied with Officer Johnson's request. He took the license from his wallet, along with his NSS identification, and handed them to Officer Johnson. Then he retrieved the vehicle registration from the glove compartment. He toyed with lunging for the gun he kept there, but decided Officer Johnson was in a better position to take a shot. He felt powerless, and that only served to increase his frustration.

Officer Johnson took his time, carefully studying each document with deliberate care. The informant continued to fume. Then Officer Johnson handed the documents back to the informant.

"You don't live around here, do you?"

"No... Of course not."

"Well I'll tell you about this town.... It's a nice place... with nice people... and I plan to keep it that way... So I'm going to be nice to you... Nicer than you NSS people know how to be... I'm going to escort you out to the freeway. You can go north or you can go south. But if I ever see you in this town again, you'll have to deal with me.... personally.... man to man...

and just so there's no mistake, I don't like you... I don't like your kind... understood?"

The NSS informant nodded, his face contorted with anger. He was being kicked out of Winters by a two bit cop. The thought made him livid. Officer Johnson spoke again.

"I'll be watching for you. I'll know if you come back."

Officer Johnson stood up and looked at the informant in the eye.

"Now... Friend... Turn around and drive to the Interstate."

With that remark, Officer Johnson walked back to his police car, his hand resting easily on his holster. The informant got the message. He started his car, turned it around on the county road, and started toward the freeway. Officer Johnson watched the informant drive away, and then turned toward the house. He saw Phillip in the driveway. A faint smile crossed Officer Johnson's face. He gave Phillip an informal salute, got into his car, turned it around, and followed the informant to the freeway.

***

After being kicked out of Winters, the NSS informant didn't tell his superiors about the confrontation with Officer Johnson. He certainly didn't want that episode on his record. Instead, he told them he was bored, and asked for a new assignment.

His superiors were both confused and embarrassed. No one seemed to know who the informant was, or why he had been sent to Winters. Meetings were held. Memos were written. Blame was placed. After several weeks of bureaucratic stupor, it was finally decided the informant would be assigned to spy on troublemakers at the University of California in Berkeley. Once again, however, no one was assigned to manage his activities.

Chapter 9   Revolution

As soon as Haben and his mother were settled in San Jose, he set out to explore the City. The Cinco de Mayo celebration was in full swing and provided the young man with an enjoyable leisure activity. On Sunday he wandered aimlessly through the many booths of the street fair, admiring the pretty girls and occasionally sampling the food. By four o'clock he was tired and thirsty. He decided to stop for a beer at a tavern on First Street. As soon as he walked in, he spotted a muscular man in his early thirties, sitting alone at the long mahogany bar. He sat down by the man and ordered a beer.

"Nice day, but I'm tired of walking."

The man turned to look at Haben. Then he smiled.

"Then take a load off, brother."

Although the man had black hair and brown eyes, he was lighter in color than Haben. He sipped his beer slowly, as though hoping to make it last a long time.

"My name's Haben. I just moved here from Fresno with my Mom."

"Well welcome to San Jose," the man said. "I'm called Jimar and I've lived here four ... no five years... What do you do for work?"

"I work in a grocery store for my Uncle... How about you?"

Jimar thought for a moment before answering.

"I guess you might call me a handyman.... Odd jobs... Here and there... And anything that needs doing at the Mosque."

Haben was surprised.

"You're a Muslim?"

Jimar looked around him and then answered.

"Yes... But don't tell anyone I'm here... I'm not supposed to drink."

Haben chuckled.

"OK. But only if you promise not to tell anyone I'm here... I'm a Christian and I'm not supposed to drink."

The two men laughed briefly at their revelation. Their conversation continued for another 20 minutes before Jimar had to leave. As they shook hands, Jimar invited Haben to visit the Mosque. Curious, Haben agreed to stop by the following Saturday after midday prayers.

***

At first, Haben was a little nervous. But his youthful curiosity overcame his fear. He entered the unpretentious Mosque and waited for Jimar. In a few minutes, the big man ambled out of an office. He immediately recognized Haben.

"Hello my friend. Welcome to our humble home."

Haben approached Jimar and shook his hand.

"Come with me," Jimar said. "I want you to meet my best friend."

Jimar led the way into the office. Smiling, he pointed to Haben and said to the man behind the desk: "We have a new convert."

Omar stood up and greeted Haben warmly. "Come, sit down and tell us about yourself."

Haben told them he was born and raised in Fresno. His father, a Sergeant in the Army reserves, had been killed while on duty overseas. He and his mother had come to San Jose to work for his uncle.

"But I'm not a convert," Haben said. "I want to follow Pastor Rick. I heard one of his team speak in Fresno. Have you heard of him?"

"Ah yes," replied Omar. "The Prophet of Humboldt County. Although we have much in common, I have not yet had the pleasure of meeting him."

Omar pointed to Jimar. "My friend met him. He was a most gracious host. When do you plan to see him?"

"I'm not sure. The man who spoke... John I think... and his friend Phillip, asked me to help them keep track of the NSS."

Haben abruptly stopped talking and looked at the two men. He was very afraid he had said too much. What would they do?

Omar understood Haben's fear. He grinned and looked at Haben.

"Your secret is safe with us," he teased. "We won't tell on you."

Grateful he was among friends, Haben could only return a sheepish smile.

"Have you heard about his special gifts?" Jimar asked.

"Only a little bit. I know he demonstrated them when he was here in San Jose with Father.... Father..."

"Father Giovanni," Omar added.

"Yes... But I heard Father Giovanni was in prison."

Omar looked sadly at Jimar. He paused for a moment before he spoke.

"Can you keep a secret?... I mean better than you just did when you told us you were spying on the NSS."

Haben blushed. He was extremely embarrassed by his mistake.

"We are trying to figure out a way to see Father Giovanni in prison. We know the people of San Jose are angry with the NSS. They would like to get him out of prison. But no one has been able to talk with Father Giovanni."

Haben was stunned by Omar's revelation. "But why are you interested in helping a Christian?"

"When Jimar was in Humboldt County, Rick asked him if we could do something to help Father Giovanni," Omar replied. "We do it to prove our friendship, and because we dislike the NSS for both political and religious reasons."

"For the moment," said Jimar, "we can do nothing. Then Jimar had an idea. "If we get a chance to visit him in prison, would you like to come?"

Haben thought about what he had just heard, and the implications for him. This was way over his head. Yet he wanted to prove to Rick he could be a loyal friend.

"I'm in," Haben said. "God help us all."

***

The house was filled with the fresh sweet air of an early May morning. Rick was just coming down the stairs for breakfast when Neema called to him from the kitchen.

"Your friend Taylor has done it now!" she exclaimed.

"Done what?" Rick asked.

"He's starting a new political party... They just had a big press conference in Washington. He's joined up with his pal Robert Wells from Arizona."

"What's it called... his new party?"

"The American Constitution Party. He wants to appeal to moderate voters from middle America. George has three heavy weights behind him... Babcock, Davis, and Marshall."

Rick sat down at the kitchen table and poured milk on his cereal. He watched the TV while he ate his breakfast. The news again shifted to the Taylor news conference. A very attractive woman with olive skin and a regal carriage was talking to the press.

"Who's that?" Neema asked.

"I don't know."

Then a character display crossed the screen. It identified the woman as Hannah Zane, a political consultant to George Kincade Taylor. The programming changed again to an ad. Neema shut off the sound.

"George will stir up the political pot, that's for sure," Neema said. Then she noticed Rick seemed to be preoccupied.

"What are you thinking about?"

"Old memories," Rick replied. "A few memories of another time."

***

Haben was stacking boxes of pasta on a shelf in his uncle's grocery store when his cell phone rang a short musical tune. He clicked it on and answered. It was Jimar. He told Haben he had been given permission to visit Father Giovanni in prison, and asked if Haben would like to come with him. Although Haben hesitated at first, he agreed. Jimar told him he would pick him up later that day. After he hung up, Haben had a feeling of dread. There were many rumors about Father Giovanni. He was a religious icon. He was a political prisoner. Although there was an upwelling of support for him, going to the Sunnyvale prison was nevertheless a frightening proposition.

***

The guards at the prison gate were expecting them, and after a brief inspection for bombs or contraband, they were allowed to drive into the compound. Even though it was late May, the barren guardroom where they waited to be escorted to Father Giovanni's cell was unpleasantly cold. Haben was nervous. He trembled from the cold and his growing apprehension. Jimar seemed unconcerned. In a few minutes a guard appeared and beckoned them to follow him into the cell block. Neither Haben nor Jimar were prepared for what they were about to experience.

Cold gray walls, dimly lit passage ways, and the musty smell of decomposing cement assaulted their senses. The rows of ugly cells were filled with despairing men and women. Sallow faces turned to look at them, pitiful eyes pleading for help. The stench of vomit, urine and feces grew stronger as they approached Father Giovanni's cell. The guard paused at a cell door, opened it, and motioned for them to go inside. There, on a steel mesh cot covered with filthy bedding, lay the man they had come to see. Jimar summoned his courage.

"Father Giovanni?"

A bruised and battered man tried to lift his head. He hadn't been allowed to shave. His unkempt salt and pepper colored beard was soiled with streaks of blood and scraps of food.

Jimar tried again. "Father Giovanni?"

The man looked very tired and very old. He opened his bleary eyes and tried to focus them on Jimar.

"I am the one you seek."

"Father Giovanni, my name is Jimar and this is Haben. We've come to talk to you."

Father Giovanni tried to sit up, but he was in too much pain. He somehow managed to turn over on his back so he could see both of his visitors.

"Well at least you haven't come to torture me.... But God only knows why you are here."

Jimar took Father Giovanni's cold hand. It had no energy. No life.

"Do you know why they are holding you? Is it because of your broadcasts?"

Father Giovanni swallowed with some difficulty.

"They didn't like what I said about the NSS... or the Book Of Rules... or the Government.... or anything else."

Haben found a dirty glass, poured some water from a metal pitcher, and handed it to Father Giovanni. Jimar propped the man's head up so he could drink. Father Giovanni only took a few sips before falling back on his pillow.

"People are angry with the NSS," Haben said. "There's even talk of a demonstration to secure your release."

"No.. No...it won't do any good," Father Giovanni protested. "They will kill me…. The hatred of these people is unlimited by time or space…. They are the devils of hell… I will be here until I die…. The protestors will only get hurt…. It won't do any good."

"But then can we help you?" Jimar said. "Are we allowed to bring you food and water? Can we shave you? Bring you clean bedding?"

"No…. The NSS won't allow that."

Father Giovanni's eyes seemed to glaze over, as though he were far away.

"I only want to know one thing."

"What?" both men said almost simultaneously.

"I baptized a man some months ago… in the Eel River…. I believe he is the one…. His name is Ricardo… Have you heard of him?"

"Why yes!" exclaimed Jimar. "I met him and his team. And I had supper with Rick and his family… They were very nice to me."

Haben's eyes flashed with excitement.

"And I met two of his people in Fresno. They are preaching a new theology…. It is becoming very popular…. and I hear he has a special gift."

Haben stopped and looked with surprise at Father Giovanni's face. The look of pain and despair was gone. It had been replaced by a veil of peace. Despite the filth that covered his face, Father Giovanni looked almost angelic.

"Then he is the one," murmured Father Giovanni. "He is the one we have been expecting…. Now go away before the NSS gets too curious. There's no reason for you two to get into trouble."

Jimar was frustrated. He was a powerful man, tall and strong. He could stare down any man on the planet, but he could do nothing to help the wretched figure on the bed before him. A tear began to well in his right eye. Jimar turned to Haben.

"He's right… We'd better leave."

As they made their way back to the guardroom, their escort leered at Haben and Jimar. The smirk on his face sent a clear message. "We have the power and you don't."

It took all of Jimar's will power to keep from punching the man in the face. He wanted to wipe away that arrogant display of ignorance. But instead he muttered a few words to Haben.

"This place stinks of evil."

***

By now, Phillip and John were inseparable friends. Although they spent much of their time on software development and maintenance, they did it with an easy banter that made the difficult and demanding work more fun. Just before Memorial Day they went into town to see Kato and his wife Isabel. The four of them were very devoted to their missionary work. Like everyone else on Rick's team, they spent much of their spare time broadcasting Rick's message over the Internet. They all contributed to the content, keeping it fresh and lively. Their Internet broadcasts had also been picked up by several Christian radio stations for retransmission.

But Phillip was uneasy. He knew he had avoided the NSS by a narrow margin on at least two occasions. It was only a matter of time before someone in Washington decided it was politically expedient to arrest them all for violating the regulations printed in The Book Of Rules. If that happened, their efforts would have to go underground. Unregulated Christian religious activity would have to become invisible to the NSS.

As usual, they found Isabel in the hardware store, and Kato in the newspaper, printer and bookstore part of the building, fuming over a dispatch from the Department of Public Information newswire.

"All lies!" Kato bellowed. "Even when they screw up, they find someone else to blame... Always find a scapegoat for failure... That's what they do. Who can trust them any more?"

"The entire Federal Government?" asked John.

"And the State of California, and the County, and the locals... It's become a habit. No one wants to take any responsibility any more."

Isabel poked her head through the hardware store door.

"Hush, Kato you'll have a stroke."

Kato settled back in his chair. The look on his face was still one of disgust.

"And to what do I owe this visit?" he asked.

"Is Isabel busy?" asked Phillip.

"She's always busy," replied Kato. "But no one's in the store... Want me to ask her?"

"Yes... Please see if she can join us."

Kato called Isabel, and after some fuss, she joined the men.

"This whole thing with the government is coming to a head," said Phillip. "My fear is that we will get caught in the middle... We will become some kind of scapegoat when the powers that be get really angry... And it's going to happen. This cool wet weather has screwed up the production of food. There is talk of shortages. The Government keeps promoting a form of class warfare in order to divide us. The economy has never recovered. Fuel is expensive. It all adds up to a great deal of personal stress... This can't go on.. At some point the pot is going to boil over and when it does, the Government is going to be looking for someone to blame."

"And we could easily be caught in the middle," added John.

"So what do we do?" asked Isabel.

"Peter is concerned we will be forced to go underground for our own safety. We need to work out a way to communicate among the surviving congregations in a way that doesn't attract attention."

Kato sighed. "I agree... I knew it was going to come to this."

***

"How did it go?' Omar asked.

"About as I expected," Jimar answered. "I am determined to stop the NSS in any way I can. You wouldn't believe the filth, the smells, the inhumane conditions, the..."

"And how did Haben take it?" Omar asked, turning to the young man.

Jimar looked at Haben, and then back at Omar.

"Very well... Although if we had stayed any longer, I do believe he would have puked."

Haben looked a little embarrassed. His stomach was still upset. Omar studied Haben's face.

"Do you know why we asked you to go with Jimar?"

"I think so. But I'm..."

Omar impatiently interrupted Haben's hesitant response.

"We wanted you to see for yourself... what we are up against. You have seen the worst of human behavior. These people have created a special kind of Hell."

"This is not the kind of government we want," added Jimar. "These are disciples of the devil. They will devour Rick and his team... including you... if they decide to get really nasty."

Haben shuddered at the thought. But he was resolute. He wanted to prove his worth to Phillip and John.

"Are you with us?' asked Omar.

"Yes. of course. But I don't understand. Why would a Muslim Imam want to work with a Christian leader?"

Omar looked intently at Haben.

"Soon I will travel to have a conversation with your Prophet. For obvious reasons, the location is a secret. In the meantime I want to prove to my people, and to him, that we can work together. We must work together. We have a common enemy. If we can set an example for others to follow, we can accomplish great things."

***

Memorial Day was a day of spontaneous rebellion. Students swapped personal ID cards and Radio Frequency Identification Tags to screw up the NSS tracking system. RFID tags for auto parts were sewn into sweaters. RFID tags for meat were enclosed in boxes of software. Dog IDs were substituted for human IDs, and vice versa. Students even exchanged bags of tags with students on campuses in other states. Acts of ID tag sabotage became very creative.

In San Jose, students protested the continuing imprisonment of Father Giovanni, and the existence of the NSS. Elsewhere the rebellion was more focused on the hated Book Of Rules. The rebellion spread to campuses across America. Frustration and anger energized the volume of the rhetoric. Sporadic violence broke out. That evening, huge bonfires lit up the sky in multiple cities across the nation. Students chanted anti-establishment slogans.

The National Security Service was furious. Agents began arresting people at random for interrogation and imprisonment in re-education camps. Political leaders and media hacks called the demonstrations irresponsible, racist, and reactionary. Many wondered openly about national security and whether or not stronger measures against protest were justified.

Peter had a different opinion.

"You can't blame them," he said to his wife Jocelyn. "Most graduates have bleak employment prospects, many believe they no longer have the freedom to be successful, and most face a life of grinding hardship. They have an education. But they know it will do them no good."

Jocelyn frowned. "It can't be that bad."

"Yes it is," Peter replied. "Our government's response is politically correct and politically expedient.... Which means it's worthless.... Satan has acquired the force of reason. Insidious logic without a trace of compassion. Corruption without end. Lies masquerading as truth. The arrogance of entrenched political power. All shrouded in the cloak of intellectual self-righteousness."

Peter paused for a moment.

"I'm sorry to say this, Jocelyn.... But things are destined to get far worse for America."

***

In mid June Rick, Neema and the children traveled down the coast and crossed the mountains into Winters. At first, the plan was to stay for two days with Josue and Mari. But when Josue told them Officer Johnson had kicked the NSS informant out of town, Rick decided it would be safe to stay a little longer. Mari and Josue were delighted to see their grandchildren. Adonica had become a very intelligent 16 year old teenager. Serafina was a pretty 13 year old struggling with her new found emotions. Eight year old Ramon immediately bonded once again with his grandfather. It would be three days of happy laughter, animated conversations, and heartfelt love.

The next afternoon, Rick went into Davis for his meeting with Omar. They met in the outdoor patio of a local restaurant after the lunch hour. Omar had Jimar and Haben with him. After shaking hands and exchanging cordial greetings, the four men found comfortable seats around a restaurant table. Except for the waitress, they had the patio to themselves.

"Where shall we start?" asked Omar.

Rick looked at each of his three new companions, and then back at Omar.

"We're both interested in God. Let's start with religion."

Omar nodded in agreement. Haben and Jimar sat back to observe the conversation.

"I have felt for some time," Omar began, "that we have much in common... Muslims and Christians... and if we try, we can find a common ground from which we can work together."

"I can sense the influence of your grandmother. She brought you up as a Christian, did she not?" Rick responded.

Omar was surprised by Rick's remark. Then he smiled. He understood how Rick knew about his grandmother. Omar guessed Rick knew much more about him than he would have liked. But once he shook hands with Rick, Omar no longer had any secrets. He accepted Rick's ability with a shrug. It really didn't make any difference.

"I've heard about your gift," he said. "And you are right. She was a wonderful woman. My grandmother never gave up on me. And yes, I converted to Islam several years ago.... But to my point. Do you agree?"

"Of course. If a theology fails to bring people together, it has no moral value."

"Then I would like to ask you a few questions."

Rick nodded in agreement. He sensed Omar was looking for closure, and his questions would help him to find his way.

"Do you believe there is only one God?"

"Yes... of course."

"Do you believe our God has a special relationship with mankind?"

"Yes."

"Do you believe God created everything?"

"I believe God created the Cosmos... That includes everything we experience in the physical universe."

"Is your God loving and forgiving?"

"That is what we teach."

"Does your God have a special relationship with humans?"

"I believe we humans were created in God's image, and that means God wants a special relationship with humanity."

"I am troubled by your concept of the Holy Trinity. Does that not mean you worship three Gods?"

"No... God is three persons. God the Holy Father, God the Holy Mother and God the Holy Spirit... All three exist in one being. For me, it is the Holy Trinity."

"How can that be?"

"You and I are single persons, are we not?"

Omar was puzzled. He frowned at the thought.

"How does this relate to God?"

"You and I are alike," Rick replied. "We are both male and female, as are all humans. Men are usually more male than female. Women are usually more female than male. But we all have both elements within our one frame. And no matter how boorish our perception may be, we all experience the spiritual. Every one of us, man or woman. We are three things in one person... God is no different."

Omar thought for a moment. He was trying to compare Islam with Christianity.

"I need to think about your answers. But I will say this. Your God is my God. We are brothers in our beliefs. And like brothers, we may differ in how we look at things, but we have much in common. Christianity and Islam share a common beginning with the teachings of Abraham, perhaps 1800 years BC. Both Jesus and Mohammed drew upon these laws when they created the concept of a single God. Both religions incorporate theology from the words of the Old Testament. We both believe our founders were infallible and sinless. Both men were Prophets. Both men were raised up by God through resurrection and transported to heaven."

Omar paused. He waited for Rick to respond.

"Muhammad was both a political and a religious leader," Rick said. "Jesus refused to become a political leader. For Him, the Kingdom of Heaven was a place of peace to which we could all ascend."

Omar looked quizzically at Rick.

"But I hear you do not believe Jesus was God... In that you agree with us."

"Although many Christians choose to believe God and Jesus are one person, I prefer to believe God dwelled in the body and spirit of Jesus from time to time, just as he dwelled in the body of Muhammad... and as he dwells in all of us when we are one with the Spiritual Universe.... In that we are very close, you and I, in our interpretation of the nature of Jesus and Muhammad. Or to put it another way, our differences are too trivial to argue over."

Omar nodded his agreement and challenged Rick again.

"We believe man is born sinless, a belief you evidently share.... But I thought all Christians believe babies are sinful when they are born, and must be redeemed by God in order to get into heaven."

Rick thought about his answer for a moment.

"I think I am closer to your beliefs on the concept of sin. I have seen too many babies.. healthy, happy, lively, curious, creative children.. to believe they are somehow burdened with a sin for which they are not responsible.... It is more logical, is it not, to believe children are born sinless?... Then we adults teach them to sin and they become corrupted by their social environment. Do you agree?"

"Yes... I do... What sins I have done....."

A slight smile crossed Omar's face. He knew he could hide nothing from Rick.

"My sins are many .... as you know. I learned them in this life from those around me. I have come to believe as most Muslims do. Each of us is responsible to avoid sin throughout our life."

Omar seemed to be relieved, as though a great weight had been lifted from his shoulders. Rick sensed Omar had been worried they would not get along, and was now beginning to feel more positive about their relationship. He asked another question.

"My people tell me you believe this is Hell... This physical dimension around us... this world. But neither Muslims nor Christians share your concept of Hell. I do not propose to let that stand between us, but can you explain it to me?"

"I have observed we humans make our own Hell, often by committing a sin against the teachings of the Holy Spirit... and then we suffer the consequences. Therefore if there is a Hell, it is our own fault... We can choose... we humans... to move closer to the paradise God offers, or closer to the Hell of human failure. Have you not seen this yourself?"

Omar enthusiastically pounded his fist on the table. He was satisfied with Rick's remarks.

"Enough... Our differences are trivial. It would be a sin against God to let them come between us. Together we can be strong. Together we can do God's work. We have a common enemy, Rick... and it is written in our history ... the enemy of my enemy is my friend."

"And who is our enemy?"

Omar spoke with a great passion.

"There is an arrogant conspiracy between financial power and political leadership, devious legal opinion has more value than compassion and love, the poor are being marginalized by a system of Government that only pretends to care for them, corruption is endemic in most of our institutions, those who do not believe in God have become insufferably patronizing and cynical, and worst of all ... worst of all too many people do not feel the need to believe in God, or the moral value God brings into their lives. Instead they seek the mindless self-serving sludge of Godless philosophies and ideologies. Rick, our common enemy is unbelief."

"I agree," Rick said quietly. Omar continued with his thoughts.

"Our common enemy is aggressive atheism. It seeks to destroy Muslim and Christian alike. It alienates us from our common source of spiritual and moral values... and it is leading us to a cynical, immoral, intemperate, and thoroughly corrupt society."

Rick was surprised by Omar's passion. After a pause, Omar offered another thought.

"And people will suffer... The weak become slaves to those in power and to those who control human knowledge... Lies become truth... Armageddon beckons humanity to perish."

Rick gently responded to Omar's assertion.

"Omar... You are a wise and passionate philosopher... What can we do?"

Omar seemed to be at a loss for words, so Rick challenged him.

"If I can get Christianity to separate itself from some of its favorite superstitions, then it would be a stronger voice versus naturalist philosophy. This can be a positive and constructive activity."

Omar looked thoughtfully at Rick.

"I believe corruption has made us cynical of government. Immoral behavior has poisoned our self esteem. Contemptuous attitudes have devastated our good manners... Do you agree?"

Rick paused before answering the question. Then he chose his words carefully.

"I agree humanity is always in danger of slipping backward... Closer to Hell... Micah once told me .... dying cultures have no civility."

"And that's our challenge," Omar interrupted. "We must teach a worthy, positive, and constructive religious philosophy that encourages people to have a loving personal relationship with God. With this foundation, believers will be able to restore their faith in the possibilities of humanity."

Rick leaned back in his chair and smiled. He was very comfortable with Omar. This was a good man, a man he could trust.

"Enough of philosophy," Omar said. "What do you plan to do about California?"

"I'll leave that up to the civil authorities."

"But it's a mess... Street gangs control whole neighborhoods, infrastructure is crumbling, healthcare is deteriorating. The government has no money to help the poor."

"All true... and more. But fixing those problems belongs to the people through their choice of Government."

"That's where you and I differ," Omar said with some passion. "If I had enough people, I'd go to Sacramento and clean house."

"With acts of terrorism?"

No... protests and strikes can be used to force change. A thousand voices are far more effective than a bomb because they have a positive influence on public opinion. If we want to encourage change, we need more friends ... not more enemies."

Rick understood Omar's frustration. But he wanted to make this particular distinction between Islam and Christianity very clear.

"You believe religion and government are two faces of the same entity. Religion is inseparable from government. They are one and the same. Unfortunately, if the institution of a religious government becomes corrupt, then religion is used to justify the acts of bad Government, no matter how evil they may be. .... I believe our role as Christians is to provide the moral ecosystem for Government. It's a sort of checks and balances. Government takes its political authority from the people. It takes its moral authority from a religion with high moral standards. As long as they remain separate, religion can have a positive influence on the morality of the political establishment."

"That's separation of Church and State," Omar interjected.

"Yes... and the basis for the provisions of our original Constitution. The men and women who were instrumental in the creation of the Constitution were well aware religion was often implicitly involved in the corruption and immoral acts of governments all over Europe. They wanted to use religious theology as a moral influence over the political system. That's why you see 'In God We Trust' and other references to the Spiritual in the physical representations of our political institutions. A belief in the spiritual is always present as a constructive influence, but religion has no political authority. The assumption was, of course, that if the activities of government became morally corrupt, the people would protest. They would demand government conduct itself according to the commandments of a higher moral authority. Don't you agree?"

"That is what some of our Prophets believe."

"Then if you can help Islamic tradition to do the same, we would come closer to a compatible theology, would we not?"

Omar saw the synergy. He believed religious competition serves no useful purpose.

"As you have said, together we can accomplish great things... We believe in the spiritual importance of Prophets, including your Jesus. Prophets bring us God's message. Our Prophet Said Nursi told us that Muslims and Christians can work together to build a true civilization of dignity, justice and fellowship...."

"The most important message from God is the one about love. That is, and should be, the central thesis of any constructive theology," Rick added.

"But all too many people chase lust in the mistaken belief it is love."

"Then we must show the difference between animal lust and the spiritual value of love."

Omar pondered his next question. "So you see yourself as a moral influence?"

"If we are successful, we can help to restore the higher principles of our theology to the functions and operations of government," Rick replied. "But I will not lead a revolution."

"In that effort, I will work with you," said Omar. "I just wish we could be more aggressive."

"You can still give moral support and advice to the protestors. You can work to subvert the operations of the NSS. You can help to elevate a new breed of leaders who will be strong enough to have a positive impact on our future.... There are many things you can do."

"And how about you?' asked Omar.

"I will focus on delivering the message God has given to me. It is a message of love, responsibility, and spiritual renaissance. Jesus brought forth the message of love and responsibility 2000 years ago. God has now added the message of spiritual renaissance. I am compelled to bring this message to all who will listen."

"Enough of philosophy," Omar said emphatically. "Who do you like in Washington?"

"I believe what George Taylor is trying to do will be good for America."

"Do you know him?"

"I've met him twice."

Omar was surprised. "Where?"

"The first time, he tackled me at a college football game... The second time was at a bar in Santa Clara."

Omar's eyes brightened with wonder. "You played football?"

"Yes... I was a wide receiver for San Jose State. I was tackled by George Taylor in a game against Stanford."

"And I played football!" Omar interjected.

"Yes, I know," Rick responded. "You were a fullback at San Diego State."

Then Rick chuckled. "A fullback who majored in Philosophy."

Omar was taken back. He had no secrets from this man. Rick knew everything about him.

***

The two men talked for another half hour. Then Omar brought Jimar and Haben into the conversation. Haben told Rick about visiting with Father Giovanni at the NSS prison in Sunnyvale. It was the one part of the conversation that angered Rick. Sad and frustrated, he knew he was powerless to help his friend. On the other hand, Rick was impressed by Haben's honesty and enthusiasm. He invited the young man to visit with his team in Humboldt County.

After the meeting, Rick drove back to Winters. He said a brief hello to his family and then walked the familiar footpath to visit with Micah. They talked until dinner time about Rick's mission. Although Rick didn't understand why, Micah appeared to be very interested in Rick's ministry. Micah wanted to know every detail. And then he further confused Rick by appearing to be unconcerned about the fate of Father Giovanni. When Rick questioned him, Micah would only say:

"Don't worry about Father Giovanni. His imprisonment has a purpose."

***

July brought hot days, cool nights and the return of the familiar coastal fog. Rick and Neema would often have a morning cup of coffee in the gazebo Rick had constructed behind the house. Here they could enjoy the beauty and fresh scents of their flower garden, and watch the antics of the many birds that came to Neema's feeders. They were just finishing their coffee on a Friday morning when Rick's cell phone rang. He switched to talk and answered. The voice on the other end was tense with concern. It was Helen Taylor.

"There is a lot of opposition to what George is doing," she said. "We are concerned for Amanda's safety. George thinks it's best if we can reduce her exposure to our enemies. We'd like to send her with Gabriela to Northern California for the summer. Could you help find them a place to stay.... and could you keep an eye on Amanda?"

Rick was startled by the request. But he wanted to assure Helen of Amanda's safety.

"Of course you can send them here. Neema and I can make a few inquiries about a place to stay. It should not be difficult to find a nice place for them. We can even find something for Amanda and Gabriela to do at our ISP. It's just down the hill from our house."

"Oh thank you, Rick... George and I are most grateful for your help. I'll call Gabriela. She should be in touch with you by tonight."

"That's fine. And by the way, just how is George doing?"

"He's gathering a number of influential people around him. The support for his plan is gathering momentum. But the old guard is defiant and getting nasty. It will take awhile for this all to work out."

"Well, you tell George he has our support. If we can help in any way, just give us a call."

Rick exchanged a few more words with Helen and then gave the cell phone to Neema. The two women carried on a lengthy conversation. Rick smiled as he kissed Neema on the cheek and started down the hill to the ISP.

***

The Commander of the San Jose NSS District was furious. He had just received word of yet another protest against The Book Of Rules, and it was insufferably hot in his office. He began to pace back and forth, like a caged animal.

"Get me the Legal Officer!" he bellowed to his assistant.

In a few moments the young woman appeared.

"Once again these idiots are protesting our authority and once again I don't have enough men to arrest them all... It's a disgrace I tell you. A damn disgrace."

"And what," said the Legal Officer, "do you plan to do?"

The District Commander continued to pace back and forth, deep in thought. He was consumed by his frustration. Then he had an idea. Turning to the Legal Officer he narrowed his eyes and gave her an evil smile.

"I'm going to make an example of that Father Giovanni.... I'll kill their hero.. That should stop them cold... They won't have anything to yowl about if he's dead."

"But he hasn't been properly tried," the Legal Officer responded. "The trail you held last March didn't follow procedure. You can't condemn him to die without a legal trial."

The District Commander looked at her, his eyes filled with hatred.

"Oh yes... the ritual of a trial. Some window dressing before we hang him... Well, he's had all the trial he's going to get. Prepare the necessary papers for his execution."

***

By late July Gabriela and Amanda found a nice place to stay near Rick and Neema. Amanda and Adonica soon became friends. Amanda was already enrolled at a small college in Arizona, and she planned to start her freshman year in the fall. Adonica wanted to find a university where she could pursue her growing interest in medicine. She was still sending out requests for applications and information. The two girls shared a happy summer, flirting with the boys they met, hiking the local mountain trails, and making endless shopping trips to towns along the coast.

Gabriela took an immediate interest in the missionary work the team was doing over the Internet, and began composing short stories to illustrate Rick's message. She was a good writer. Everyone welcomed her warmhearted text. Although they suspected the stories drew upon her own life experiences, she insisted they were all fiction.

"A good story," she said one time, "conveys a message that strengthens our values."

John would take Gabriela's work and post it on various blogs. He also created a place for her stories on Rick's Web site. They worked together on several projects and by late July, John had developed a crush on Gabriela. It did not take long for her to notice his interest. Flattered by the attention, she encouraged his interest by inventing reasons for them to be together. On a very warm afternoon in late July, the ever assertive Gabriela finally challenged him.

"I think you and I have much in common, John," she said. "Do you think you could find a 60 year old woman of mixed heritage and a not so great figure attractive?"

John stood up and studied Gabriela's face. She was almost as tall as he was, and he could look her right in the eye.

"Do you find anything you like about me?"

"I think you are a very intelligent man. You have the manners of a real gentleman, and ....."

Gabriela stopped talking for a moment and came closer to John's face. "Of course I do."

John drew her closer and they hugged each other like old friends. In his moment of happiness, John decided he needed to lose some weight. And so did Gabriela.

***

Peter happened to be walking down the hall when he saw them embrace. A happy smile crossed his face. His heart was glad these two lonely people had found someone to love. They would not have any illusions about their romance. They would be good companions and loyal friends. They would share their daily experiences. And they would find contentment in a compassionate relationship.

"*Gabriela was definitely a strong woman*," Peter thought. "*She will stand with him in his work. They are a natural team.*"

It was then, Peter decided to ask Gabriela if she would like to become a permanent member of their team. He knew she would say yes. Gabriela was already involved in their daily broadcasts, and she understood Rick's message.

***

The Commander of the San Jose NSS District openly ridiculed the protestors. He wanted to show everyone he was in total control of Santa Clara County. In order to assert his authority, the District Commander decided to make a public spectacle of an anti-government criminal. He would put Father Giovanni on display as an enemy of the State, and then hang him.

A thick layer of dreary fog covered the Bay on the morning of the NSS event. Most people were wearing coats or sweaters to fend off the raw chill of the cool damp air. Despite the risk of arrest, there were many who came to protest the hanging. But the NSS was well prepared. They assembled a crowd of supporters and paid rabble rousers to make sure the hanging appeared to have plenty of popular support.

Haben was determined to witness the hanging. He held a very thin hope that Father Giovanni would receive a last minute reprieve. As he walked slowly toward the Plaza where the hanging was scheduled to be held, two goons from the assembled crowd confronted him.

"Where's your sign?" said a big man. "You can't get any closer unless you have one of these."

He held up a placard on a stick with the words "Hang The Criminal." Then he showed Haben another one which read "Justice for the People."

Haben backed away in disgust. The two men sneered at him and walked back toward the stage where Father Giovanni would be hung.

Haben resolved to get as close as he could without having to confront another NSS goon. He walked up the block and then crossed the street to where he could have a better view of the proceedings. He didn't have to wait long. Three black SUVs suddenly appeared. Their flashing lights and wailing sirens stirred the crowd. They cheered lustily when two NSS agents pulled Father Giovanni from the back seat of the second SUV and shoved him toward the stage.

Haben almost retched when he saw Father Giovanni's ghostly pallid and blood stained face. He had obviously been beaten that morning. The poor man could hardly walk. The crowd jeered, calling him several nasty names. He stumbled on the bottom steps of the stage. Father Giovanni recovered, and then carefully placed each foot on the next step as he slowly ascended to the gallows. No one made any attempt to help him. Haben's heart ached as the NSS agent placed the rope around Father Giovanni's neck. The District Commander stepped forward and read a short list of crimes to the crowd. A signal was given, and the crowd started chanting "Hang Him, Hang Him." Someone pulled a lever, and Father Giovanni dropped through a trap door. He didn't struggle. Haben guessed he was too weak to protest. The rope made an ugly burn mark on his neck. He shuddered briefly, and then was still. His body hung in the air. The crowd cheered. Haben looked down at the cold gray cement of the curb in disgust.

Haben was about to walk away when he noticed another uniformed NSS officer, a rather nice looking young woman who was watching the brutal murder with great interest. Her grim face was a piece of stone. At first Haben thought she was just as mean as the District Commander, but as he watched her, he thought he saw a tear rolling down her cheek. She briefly turned to him, and then quickly looked down at the pavement.

Haben felt a hand on his shoulder. Startled, he turned quickly and found himself face to face with Jimar. The big man scowled at the crowd surrounding the stage.

"Now you are witness to the religion of hate."

The press came on queue. The District Commander had Father Giovanni's body hoisted back up so he could stand next to it on the stage. Pictures were taken. One was particularly gruesome. It showed the cruel face of the District Commander, proudly dressed in the formal uniform of the NSS, standing next to the bloody lifeless body of a man hanging from the gallows.

It was the picture that would spark a revolution.

***

Despite the risk, Rick was determined to attend Father Giovanni's funeral. He said a cheerless goodbye to Neema, kissed each of his three children on the cheek, and started the long drive to San Jose. As he passed through Marin County, he called Omar on his cell phone to ask where the funeral service would be held. Omar was stunned by the call. He could not believe Rick would risk everything to attend Father Giovanni's funeral. At first he could only stammer in his disbelief. Then he recovered sufficiently to tell Rick where to find the funeral home in South San Jose. Rick thanked Omar for the information and hung up. As night fell over the City, Rick drove into San Jose. He stopped by Omar's Mosque on the chance Omar would still be there. The lights were still on. Rick drove into the rear parking lot and parked behind the building. From this location, his car could not be seen from the street. Rick got out of his car and walked the few steps to the back door of the building. As he entered the Mosque, he was greeted by Haben and Jimar.

"What the heck are you doing here?" the surprised young man demanded in a loud voice.

Jimar could only shake his head in disbelief.

"You have no street smarts," he said with solemn authority. "You shouldn't be here."

Rick could only smile with compassion at their concern.

"I know it's a big risk," he said. "But this man means far too much to me to leave this earth without my saying goodbye."

"If the NSS catches you, you'll both be making that journey!" exclaimed Haben.

Omar heard the commotion and came out of his office. He gestured to Haben.

"OK... That's enough... We all know the risk."

Omar walked over to Rick and welcomed him with a kiss on both cheeks. It was a sign of respect. Rick shook Omar's hand and he offered his hand to Jimar and Haben.

"We have to hide your car," Jimar said. "We can put it in the garage."

Omar nodded his head in agreement.

"You must stay with me tonight," he said. "You will be my honored guest."

"Thank you for your offer. But are you up to the risk of harboring a fugitive?"

"Hospitality is a custom I wish to keep," Omar said. "You would do the same for me without hesitation."

Omar turned to Jimar.

"Tomorrow morning, you can pick up Rick and take him to the funeral home. After the funeral, bring him back here. Tomorrow night, after it is dark, Rick should be able to drive out of San Jose without detection."

Jimar began to smile. "It will be a pleasure to fool the NSS."

***

The next morning Jimar took Rick to the funeral home. The service was scheduled for 11AM. Several mourners were already there when he arrived. They all knew him. Some had been at the NC. Others had listened to his Internet radio broadcasts. Rick cordially shook hands with each person and thanked them for coming. Then he knelt down at the side of Father Giovanni's casket and offered a brief prayer to his old friend.

About 10:45AM the funeral home director came into the room. He announced the Priest would not be coming to conduct the funeral service because he had been threatened by the NSS. Rick frowned. These people had no respect for either life or death. A murmur of bewilderment rippled through the small group that had gathered to say goodbye to Father Giovanni. The funeral director shrugged his shoulders and left the room. As soon as he was gone, Rick stepped forward.

"I'll do it," he said emphatically. "It is the least I can do for this wonderful man."

And so the funeral service began. Although Rick had said goodbye to the dying several times, he had never conducted a funeral service. He improvised, mixing prayer with short passages from the Bible. One of the women stepped forward and said she would like to read a tribute to Father

Giovanni. Rick recognized her from the NC. He warmly welcomed her. The tribute was both loving and compassionate. Rick closed the service with a prayer. Then he walked up to the casket and looked down upon Father Giovanni's face.

"Goodbye, my friend... May God grant you the peace you so well deserve."

Just as he stepped back from the casket, Jimar shouted out a single word.

"Damn!"

"What's the matter?" Rick called.

"It's the NSS."

Rick was not surprised. He had expected the NSS would make an appearance.

"Attention everyone, just remain calm and walk slowly out of the building. Leave the parking lot as soon as you can."

The small group of mourners immediately headed for the funeral home door. Rick walked over to the widow where Jimar was watching the parking lot. He was clearly puzzled.

"There's only one SUV," Jimar said. "And usually they check the license plate of any car parked near the building before a raid."

As they watched, there was a flurry of activity as people exited the building and hastily got into their cars. After the last car had departed, the door of the SUV slowly opened and out stepped a young woman dressed in the uniform of the NSS.

"It's the District Legal Officer!" Jimar hissed. He hated that uniform and anyone who wore it

By contrast, Rick was very calm.

"Let's step into the storage room. From there we can watch her when she comes into the building."

The two men quickly walked into the small storage room. They left the door open just enough so they could see the casket. In a moment the NSS officer came into the room. She hesitated, looked around to see if she was alone, and then proceeded to the casket. She looked with some sympathy at Father Giovanni, and then knelt down beside the casket as though to pray.

Rick was surprised and compassionate. Then he thoroughly rattled Jimar by slowly opening the storage room door. He walked over to the NSS officer and put his hand on her shoulder. Startled by the touch of his hand, she flinched and turned to look up at Rick. Her eyes widened with surprise and wonder.

"You!" she exclaimed.

"Yes... I am the one you seek," Rick answered.

Rick tenderly took her hand and helped the Legal Officer to her feet. She was obviously flustered.

"I recognize you from your pictures.... You shouldn't be here.... You're in great danger."

Rick smiled at the young woman. He spoke to her in a low voice.

"And I know you shouldn't be here... at least not as a worshipper... You should be among those who hate."

The young woman narrowed her eyes and frowned at Rick. She became defensive.

"I've known about Father Giovanni for some time... He deserved better treatment. But there was nothing I could do... We aren't all nasty people."

"I know... And I know you are doing what you can to help the victims."

The Legal Officer was suddenly alarmed.

"You won't tell... will you?"

"Of course not," Rick replied. "In another circumstance you would rebel at what the NSS is doing... Come to think of it, you are rebelling.... Frankly, I don't understand why we haven't all been arrested for sedition. Our teaching conflicts with The Book Of Rules, and the NSS should hate our Internet ministry. I'm guessing you had something to do with our being able to avoid prosecution."

Rick had already sensed what the young woman had done for his team. But he wanted to hear her explanation.

"I changed your file... I've done it several times.... On several occasions, when the NSS was about to go up to Humboldt County to arrest you, I fabricated an emergency of greater priority. So they would go do something else instead.... And since this rebellion began, it hasn't been hard to divert their attention to some disturbance here in Santa Clara County."

"And so... it would seem I owe our freedom to you, young lady. I do thank you from the bottom of my heart."

"You should leave San Jose, however... There is only so much I can do to protect you."

"I plan to leave after dark."

"That's fine. They won't be able to recognize you in the dark and don't worry about your car... I changed the description and license number we have on file. I substituted a record that belongs to one of our clerks."

Rick chuckled... He was about to speak again when the NSS Legal Officer became very serious. She appeared to be unsure of herself. She appealed to Rick.

"Will God forgive me?"

Rick smiled gently, took her hands in his own, and looked into her eyes.

"You are closer to the Holy Spirit than you think. Please... Keep on being the compassionate person you want to be."

The young woman smiled shyly, squeezed Rick's hands, and turned to walk away. When she reached the door, she turned and said in a quiet voice "Thank you." And then she was gone.

Jimar came out of his hiding place and looked at Rick with wonder.

"And so ... now you have made friends with the devil."

Rick responded without looking at Jimar. "I have friends in many places."

***

They had a quiet supper at the Mosque. Haben joined them and was astonished by the story Jimar told them with great pleasure. Omar grinned with satisfaction. They had someone on the inside of the NSS who would help them. That was good. He knew, however, it was a link he could only use with great caution. He didn't want to jeopardize the Legal Officer's safety.

After supper, Haben talked privately with Rick for some time. He wanted to join Rick's team. Rick was impressed with his earnest plea to work with them.

"Well... OK... Haben. You will be the youngest member of our team. Your commitment to our work will demand dedication and resolve. I expect great things from you."

Haben gave him an enthusiastic grin. He had just joined a team that was doing something really important. They would be his family. He was getting closer to God. Haben decided he wanted to live in Humboldt County. His mother would be very happy.

***

Peter walked into Rick's office and placed a sheet of paper on his desk. Peter was jubilant.

"Our audience keeps growing," he said. "Over a million hits a day. People from all over the world. We must be doing something right."

Rick smiled. He was pleased they had been able to accomplish so much in a short time.

"We have used the Internet well," he said. "In 1455 Gutenberg printed the first Bible using moveable type. Volume printing revolutionized the way the word of God was spread among people of limited income. In 1517 Martin Luther posted his 95 theses on the door of a Catholic Cathedral, and by the end of 1519 he had begun a new era of biblical scholarship. He started a reformation that changed Christian theology.... So here we are today, using the Internet to once again revolutionize the way the word of God is spread, and we have been able to introduce our own new era of Christian teaching."

Peter sat down in a big stuffed chair, and looked out the window. His eyes scanned the hills outside the ISP building for the dwindling rays of September sun that filtered through the trees.

"Why... why have we been so successful?"

Rick paused a moment before responding. He searched for the right words.

"We teach a positive and constructive theology... It has rational credibility even among most scientists... To that we can add a fundamental fact. We humans crave a link to the Cosmos. That need is built into the mechanisms that drive our emotions. We yearn to experience the spiritual.... something outside our personal ecosystem to which we can attach our deepest feelings, our hopes, our dreams, and our need for reassurance. We all need to belong to something outside ourselves. The sense of wanting to belong to something greater than our person is a fundamental construct of our social self."

"Do you really believe we can start a Christian Reformation?"

"Most religions are continually changing. Christianity is no different. There is a great diversity of Christian theology from congregation to congregation. But in the final analysis, people are attracted to a religious experience that places emphasis on a direct personal experience of God. We seek to find peace and comfort from a troubled world. A good religious experience encourages us to establish a spiritual union with the Holy Trinity and Jesus Christ. Within this experience, we are able to find the personal sanctuary of the Spiritual Universe. Jesus gave us God's message about love and personal responsibility. We have added new concepts about our spiritual link to the Cosmos."

Rick paused to take a sip of coffee.

"With inspiration and determination, the human spirit is magnificent. We have planted a seed. It will flourish in the soul of humanity. ... A Christian Reformation is inevitable because we humans want to believe.... We will learn to use our knowledge.... God will guide our thoughts."

***

On most Sunday mornings the ISP office was humming with apostolic activity. As a matter of personal safety, and as a practical matter, the team could be more effective if they worked on Internet content rather than traveling from place to place in California. By mid-September, they had established a comfortable routine. Rick and Peter were focused on broadcasting a universal message of friendship, love, hope and compassion. Every member of the team was able to make a contribution to that effort. Their Reformation was gaining momentum among people of all kinds in many nations.

On this particular Sunday, Sarah was working with an Italian friend who wanted to translate Rick's sermons and verses into Italian. Gabriela was having a lively messaging exchange with someone in Spain. Christina was busily converting English to Mandarin, and Haben was struggling to help someone in France. Amanda, Adonica and Serafina were exchanging text messages with other young people on the Internet.

Then it happened. Sarah gave out a loud exclamation.

"Oh God... My water's broken!"

Amanda looked over at Adonica and began to giggle. Serafina's eyes were wide with wonder. Christina closed the file she was working on, got up from her chair, and walked over to where Sarah was sitting. The girls regained their composure and gathered around the now panting Sarah. Gabriela looked over at Sarah, and then quickly typed a message to her Spanish contact.

"Excuse me, I have to go deliver a baby."

Sarah had all the help she needed. The girls helped Sarah to the floor. Gabriela called to Antonio.

"Antonio!... Come here... Your wife's having a baby!"

Antonio was completely flustered. He had been expecting Sarah to have her baby in a week or two. But the baby had other plans. The contractions began. Sarah gave out a cry.

Peter heard the commotion and came over to where Sarah was lying on the floor. He immediately grasped the situation.

"Gabriela, you stay with Sarah. I'll bring the car around," he directed as he went out the door.

In a few moments Peter returned. With Gabriela's help, he was able to assist Sarah to her feet and they began to walk toward the door. Peter looked at the now thoroughly shaken Antonio.

"I'll drive... You get into the back seat."

Antonio looked fearfully at his wife, and then climbed into the rear seat. Peter started the engine and waved everyone goodbye. The car roared off in a cloud of dust down the driveway to the county road.

"I'll call the Doctor and the hospital," Gabriela said. "You girls see if you can clean up the mess."

Rick, who had been up at the house with Neema, appeared at the door. Adonica breathlessly filled him in on every detail.

"Well.. now it happens... new life... new blessings," he said.

About two hours later they got the call. Sarah had given birth to a beautiful baby girl. Sarah was fine. Antonio was a wreck.

***

Rick was busy with a composition he was writing for his blog when Christina knocked on the door of his office. He looked up to see an unusually shy Christina smiling at him.

"May I come in?" she asked.

"Of course. You're always welcome."

Christina came in and sat down in a chair next to Rick's desk. She sat stiffly upright, as though trying to look absolutely prim and proper. Normally an assertive person, Christina was a bit hesitant. Rick sensed she had come to ask something very important.

"Relax, Christina," he said with a smile. "I think I know why you are here."

Christina didn't reply right away. She fidgeted with her fingers for a moment and then spoke.

"You and Neema, and everyone else... you've been so good to me, ... a lost soul in need of refuge... I have learned a lot from you and the others."

"But now you want to leave us," Rick interrupted.

Christina was still hesitant. She stared at the floor for a moment, and then abruptly looked up at Rick.

"As you know, I graduated from Stanford and I have a Masters Degree from The Chicago School of Economics. Although it has been very nice to be here, I want to use my education and the things you taught me somewhere else. My father found a job for me with a consulting firm in Washington. They are right in the middle of all the action... the revolution... a new constitution... it's a dream job for me."

Rick didn't answer right way. He was sorry to see Christina go.

"I am only concerned about two thing, your safety and your commitment to teach our theology to others."

"It is a risk... The revolution is just getting started and there will be confrontation. But my father assures me he can arrange for safe passage by air, a nice place in a peaceful neighborhood, and all the help I need to get settled.... As for my work, I promise I will keep on doing what I can to teach others. Sarah will keep me posted on what you are doing, and she will keep me updated on our mission. I've already contacted a Christian congregation outside of Washington and they want me to help them. The pastor is a big fan of yours."

Christina smiled and became more assertive.

"But before I go, I would like to have your blessing."

Rick stroked his hair and grinned at Christina.

"How could I refuse?" he asked. "You're smart and organized. Your intelligence and education will serve you well. This is a good move for you. When do you leave?"

"Next week, I start my new job October 2."

"I have one request... Take Amanda with you. It's time for her to join her father."

"Sure!" Christina responded. "I'll make sure she gets there safely. Taylor's American Constitution Party is gaining popularity. He has enough political power to protect his family now."

"We must support his effort in any way we can," Rick said solemnly. "Constitutional democracy can only survive if the governed are moral. That's our challenge.... All of us... Taylor's political efforts must be linked to a virtuous sense of moral behavior."

***

October would be a month most Christians would remember with bitterness and revulsion. President Mary Rose Chartres O'Brien ordered the destruction of all religious books that failed to meet Federal Government publication criteria. The objective, she said, was to prevent the dissemination of treacherous lies and myths. American moral standards were best served by the behavior criteria described by the

Citizen's Manual of Personal and Social Responsibility, also known, she acknowledged, as The Book Of Rules.

Several NSS Districts immediately took the President's order as a directive to seize and destroy all copies of the Bible and The Book of Mormon. The San Jose NSS District Commander was especially delighted with the order. It would give him an excuse to suppress the political opposition of the Christian and Mormon communities. He immediately arranged to stage a public book burning, complete with a parade and a night of festivities.

Posters appeared all over San Jose the day before the event. Lawful citizens were urged to bring copies of the offending books to the bonfire.

"We must purify moral thought," the poster text exclaimed. "The Citizen's Manual of Personal and Social Responsibility is the only legal source of moral belief and conduct. All other books of moral theology must be destroyed in order to prevent confusion."

Late that night a mob gathered in the square. Uniformed NSS agents were everywhere. They carried heavy wood nightsticks to subdue any protest against the burning. The gold lettering on their green arm bands proclaimed their mission "To Protect America." Goons with green arm bands circulated among the crowd, looking for someone to assault. A pale thin man with long gray hair and rimless spectacles climbed slowly onto the podium platform. He was soon joined by the NSS District Commander. The mob gathered around the platform to hear them speak.

"The Bible is an empty-headed labyrinth of contradictions and nonsense," the thin man screamed. "It was written by uneducated religious fanatics. It is a synthesis of bizarre myths, fictional characters, ignorant folklore, and pagan rituals. God is a delusion of the weak. The life of Jesus is nothing more than a rehash of ancient Jewish and Pagan legends. The prophecies are absurd. The doctrines are bizarre. The Bible is useless as a moral guide."

The Commander of the San Jose NSS District placed his hands on his hips and thrust out his chest in a pose of defiance.

"We must," the Commander shouted, "burn all books with un-American ideas. We must eliminate all criminal opposition to The Book Of Rules. The era of extreme religious intellectualism is now at an end, and thus you do well in this midnight hour to commit to the flames the evil spirit of the past. This is a strong, great and symbolic cleansing you do here tonight."

The NSS District Commander gave a signal to his assembled agents. They waved copies of the unwanted books in the air and then threw them into the bonfire. The mob joined in with enthusiasm. The band began to play marching songs. There were cheers and chants. The NSS District Commander was very pleased.

Two blocks from the square, Omar and Jimar watched the bonfire with disgust. The mob began to chant obscenities. Omar turned away. He had seen enough.

"This is the work of Satan," he said to Jimar. "It is evil. These are the gatekeepers of Hell..."

"Why do you care if they burn Bibles and Mormon books?" asked Jimar.

"Because my friend, we have a common enemy. If they are bold enough to burn the Bible, the Qur'an is next."

***

Public reaction to the book burning was swift and passionate. The Internet was alive with protest. The Christian community had nothing but scathing comments about the NSS. Mobs closed down freeways and blocked access to state capitols. They briefly closed both the Golden Gate and Bay bridges. There was rampant civil disobedience. Students flooded college and university campuses with protest marches. Civil authority evaporated in some parts of San Francisco, Oakland and Los Angeles. Frightened politicians rushed to denounce the bonfire. The reaction was so intense, President Mary Rose Chartres O'Brien was forced to issue a statement, condemning the NSS action as the work of a few zealots who would be reprimanded.

But she refused to back down on her condemnation of any religious work that contradicted the moral theology of her Citizen's Manual of Personal and Social Responsibility. She was still focused and determined to reshape America according to her vision.

Then a picture appeared on the Internet. It was swiftly copied for street posters and protest signs. Copies suddenly materialized throughout America. The subject of the picture galvanized public opposition to the administration in Washington and escalated its abusive ridicule of America's useless Congress. The picture had been taken by a media photographer hired by the NSS. It showed the Commander of the San Jose NSS District standing on a platform beside the lifeless body of Father Giovanni, his battered corpse still hanging by a rope from the gallows.

It became the symbol of revolution.

Chapter 10   Renaissance

These were the worst of times. Increased poverty was a major cause of the revolution. Chronic recession continued to cause high rates of unemployment. Family incomes declined. Food and fuel prices continued to increase. Millions of families suffered the privation of inadequate heat or nourishment. The Federal Government was unable to finance its obligations. Congress was useless. Many state, county and local governments were forced to declare bankruptcy. The public healthcare system steadily deteriorated. Medicare was no longer available. Social Security payments were reduced. Funding for education and welfare were woefully inadequate. Bureaucratic bungling prevented the efficient provision of government services. There was endemic corruption, frequent strikes, and occasional riots. The primary role of the National Security Service was to enforce civil obedience.

Through all this turmoil, Rick and his team quietly went about their work with dedication and determination. Working with several local church groups, they were able to establish soup kitchens, food distribution centers, clothing swaps, and temporary shelters. A fuel fund was set up to provide emergency cash to buy heating and cooking fuel for impoverished families. But no matter how hard they worked, there was always a need for more help.

Rick was true to his beliefs. He lived his convictions. Peter, Sarah, Kato and Gabriela proved to be especially good at transcribing Rick's thoughts into text that could be posted on their Internet blog. Phillip and John maintained the blog with dogged determination and, despite the risk, they continued to send out Rick's Internet radio broadcasts. Anika, James, Antonio, Haben and Isabel maintained contact with the hundreds of people who sent e-mails to Rick and his team. Christina had established a mission near Washington. She exchanged e-mails with Sarah almost every day. They were very busy.

Rick and his team, along with other Christian organizations all over the world, were trying to redefine the fundamental belief system upon which Christianity rested. Call it the Christian Renaissance. It was stimulating a reformation of Christian theology. Fierce debates occurred as people sought to understand the meaning of new ideas. Old religious beliefs frequently clashed with renaissance theology. Religious institutions were shaken and divided by the collision of ideas. Existing organizations were forced to change or risk being swept into the dustbin of theological history. The debate was not always civil.

But the hard work was paying off. Interest in Rick and his theology was growing day by day. We humans yearn for the solace of a satisfying religious faith. Hardship encourages people to look outside their physical environment for spiritual support. Ricardo Juan Sanchez Vasquez provided a credible foundation. Many came to view him as a good shepherd and the holy messenger of God. Thus, the team made a lot of friends. In many lands.

They also made a lot of enemies. Both unbelievers and believers. We humans can be very tenacious when it comes to protecting our established beliefs. New ideas invite confrontation.

***

Neema, Rick and the children enjoyed a pleasant Christmas with Mari and Josue in Winters. Eight year old Ramon once again delighted his grandfather with his interest in finding out how things work. For Christmas, Josue gave Ramon a tool box and an electric drill. Mari gave 13 year old Serafina a soccer ball, and this stimulated a lively conversation about her school's participation in the state championships. Because she was developing a great interest in medicine, Mari gave sixteen year old Adonica a book on anatomy and they talked about picking the right university to study biology. The rest of the presents were a mix of sweaters, socks, dresses, pants and other practical things the children could use when they got back to Humboldt County.

But mostly Christmas wasn't about presents, it was about sharing the warmth of love. Mari and Josue were very proud of their son's accomplishments and demeanor. He obviously had an affectionate and fulfilling relationship with Neema. Their grandchildren were a constant source of joy. With loving anticipation of Christmas, Mari had spent two mornings baking her wonderful breads and pastries for them. Although Rick and Neema lightheartedly complained about the weight they would put on, they all enjoyed them with enthusiasm.

The day after Christmas, Rick paid a visit to Micah. The old man was in a solemn mood. They talked at length about Rick's ministry and the effect his internet efforts were having on the emerging Christian renaissance. Micah was worried economic privation was demoralizing the nation. He believed, however, the revolution would bring about a better government in Washington. If state and county governments were forced to follow the same political model, there was hope for the future. Then the conversation turned to Rick's safety.

"Don't you fear for your safety, coming all the way down here for Christmas?" Micah asked.

"Not any more," replied Rick. "The NSS has its hands full with the revolution. To them, I'm small potatoes. They won't bother me. Besides, the word on the street is that they are under pressure to lighten up on their arrests."

"Never trust a rabid animal," said Micah. "They will bite without reason."

***

The cold, damp air of January penetrated the walls of the White House, sending chills through everyone who worked there. Even with her wool sweater, President Mary Rose Chartres O'Brien shivered as her cold fingers sifted through the dispatches in her office. Then she came upon a familiar and unwelcome name.

"He's still in business!" Mary Rose shouted to her assistant. "That asshole continues to defy me!"

The President's Assistant came into the office and looked expectantly at the President for direction. Mary Rose continued to fume.

"These Prophet broadcasts must be stopped once and for all. This guy Rick has stirred up the whole nation against me!"

"I don't think he's into politics, Madam President. He's just a preacher of some kind. Rick has never advocated the overthrow of the government. In fact, he seems to distance himself from taking sides in any political movement."

"I don't give a damn!" Mary Rose shouted. "Have that jerk of a general write an order. Tell the California National Guard to restore order. Shoot the damn dissidents. And find this asshole. Have the NSS arrest him."

"I don't think that would be wise," chirped her assistant. "He's quite popular. If the NSS arrests him, that will add fuel to the revolution…"

Mary Rose's face turned beet red with anger.

"Find the bastard!" she screamed, "and kill him!"

The President's Assistant quickly left the President's office and scurried down the hall to her desk. She picked up the telephone and dialed a familiar number. The phone rang once and she hung up.

***

Spying works both ways. George Kincade Taylor believed in an old revolutionary adage: "They have spies that watch us, and we have spies that watch them". When the special telephone in his office rang once, he knew it was the President's Assistant, asking for a meeting. The location and the time were prearranged according to the calendar. George called Robert Wells into his office.

"Something's up. I just had a call."

Robert looked at the calendar. "Today at 4PM, at the Lincoln Memorial…. I'll go."

"No, You've been too often. I'll send Helen."

"Your wife is much too easy to recognize," Robert said. "I don't think that's wise."

George thought for a moment.

"I'll send Amanda."

***

Amanda was both thrilled and uneasy about her role as a spy. Although her meeting with the President's Assistant was very brief, she brought back valuable information. As soon as he read the text of the message from the President's Assistant, George sent an encrypted message to three men. The general who ran the California National Guard agreed with Taylor. He would refuse to obey the order he received from President Mary Rose because it didn't make any sense to pit National Guard troops against civilians. The Pentagon Army General took a wait and see attitude, agreeing to delay any action indefinitely. Fearing retaliation from Taylor, the NSS National Commander ordered the California District Commanders to leave Rick alone.

George Kincade Taylor was gradually taking charge of America.

***

The San Jose NSS District Commander paced back and forth in his office. His face revealed a mixture of anger and confusion as he read the e-mail text for the fifth time. One paragraph was particularly annoying. It was very short. "The San Jose NSS District Office is to be closed, effective immediately. Representatives from the National Office will manage the closure process. They are expected to arrive tomorrow afternoon."

"All my work," the District Commander fumed, "is for nothing."

He continued to pace back and forth in his office, trying to understand what happened.

"It's those bastards from Sacramento," he raged. "They did this to me!"

He was suddenly aware the District Legal Officer was standing in the doorway of his office. There was the slightest of smiles on her lips.

"What the hell do you want!" demanded the District Commander.

"I understand most of us have been laid off... or perhaps it should be called... fired. The scuttlebutt from Washington is that Mary Rose has decided you have become a symbol of repression. She had to shut down the San Jose Office to save face. But she probably will not stop there. She's fighting for her political life... There is so much hatred for the NSS she may shut the whole service down.... You should be proud of yourself," she smirked. "You are famous. You started a revolution that will bring down our government."

"Get out! Get out of my sight you sniveling broad!" the District Commander shouted.

***

Dying regimes lose touch with reality. There is confusion. The functions of management are corrupted by the personal survival demands of political expediency. The natural course of bureaucratic behavior creates an unworkable system of regulations backed by the stupid, overbearing and arrogant use of police power. Personal freedom evaporates. Individuals can only survive by acting outside the system.

By the first week of March, patches of sunlight had begun to penetrate the thick layer of clouds that hung like the gloom of death over Santa Clara County. Bureaucrats from Washington had closed the NSS San Jose District Office. There was a street celebration with huge bonfires and dancing in front of the gold building. Only a skeleton staff remained at the Sunnyvale compound. The NSS Commander had been ordered to destroy his uniforms and NSS paraphernalia. Without them, he had become just another unemployed citizen. But his humiliation wasn't over. On the fifth of March, there was a sharp knock on his apartment door. When he opened the door, the Commander was confronted by four men in Army Military Police uniforms.

"Commander, you are under arrest for crimes against the people of the United States," one of the men said. "We are here to take you to Sunnyvale for interrogation and confinement."

***

The pale thin man with long gray hair and rimless spectacles remained cold and impassive throughout the interrogation. His questions were both confrontational and demeaning. The Commander was furious. Two weeks ago, this sniveling idiot worked for him. After the interrogator was finished, armed guards took the Commander back to his dreary cell. Although the Army had taken some pains to clean it up, it still smelled of urine and vomit. Patches of faded blood stains blotched the concrete floor. The Commander fumed at the irony. He was a prisoner in his own prison. The Commander sat down on the stinking bed and glowered with revulsion at the cold gray walls around him. Then he saw it. A thin line of scratches on the wall. He stood up to get a closer look. The words were unmistakable. They spelled out a name.

Father Giovanni.

***

Morning sunlight managed to penetrate the bluster of March to warm Rick's office. Green grass had replaced white snow on the lawn. Here and there, the green stems of flowers reached upward toward the welcome rays of the sun. Rick was a happy man. The team understood and was able to teach Rick's theology. His children were happily engaged with all the activities of school. And Neema, dear sweet Neema, was the joy of his life. Even the news article he saw on the Internet failed to diminish his sense of contentment. "The former Commander of the NSS District in San Jose," it read, "has escaped from the Sunnyvale compound where he was being kept for trial. His escape was aided by several former NSS agents."

Rick frowned as he read the last sentence. But he put it all aside. *"They will find him soon enough,"* he thought.

He picked up a letter from his desk. It was from a religious group in Sacramento. He slit the envelope and removed a single sheet of paper. Rick read the text with increasing interest. Then he called Phillip and Peter.

"What's up," asked Phillip as he and Peter came into Rick's office.

"I've been invited to speak at a Christian rally in Sacramento."

"When?" asked Peter.

"Early April. They also want to have a conference to discuss our theology."

Phillip looked puzzled. "Who is the sponsor?"

"A council of ministers and priests. I've heard of them. They often bring in people who have alternative ideas about theology for a presentation and discussion."

"We have their attention," said Peter. "It could be very productive."

"Yes… I suppose so… But I'm not sure if it is the right time. There are food riots, unemployment protests, and political confrontations in Sacramento. The public employees are on strike. It has disrupted the whole city… I think I'll wait until things have settled down before going to our state capitol."

Peter looked thoughtfully at Rick.

"Your popularity as a prophet is growing. Perhaps they will also look upon you as a political leader. It is but a short step from one to the other."

"Peter… you know my feelings about the separation of Church and State. I have no interest in being a political leader."

"But many hold you in high esteem as a venerated religious teacher. It would only be a short step to political greatness."

Rick smiled kindheartedly at his friend.

"You know that's not my mission. Although the moral authority for political leadership must come from a strong sense of the spiritual, the State must always be separate from the Church. Behave yourself."

"Well," said Phillip. "If you do decide to go, then we'll go with you… We can't trust you to be alone in that crowd…. You need protection."

***

That night Rick had a dream about meeting with Father Giovanni. It was a lethargic kind of dream. Images came and went in a swirl of clouds. But just before he woke up, Rick clearly heard Father Giovanni's words.

"You have planted the seed of a new theology. You have conveyed the message of God to all who would listen. Now it is time for you to prove the truth of your teaching."

When he awakened, Rick resolved to accept the invitation.

***

It was a strange conversation. As they drove down to Winters with the children on Sunday morning, Rick began to outline his plan for the team. The more he talked, the greater Neema's anxiety. Rick was assuming she would be the one to fulfill his vision. But that begged a question: "What would he be doing?"

"Some members of our team are better suited to missionary work than others. But each one has a place in our effort," Rick was saying. "You must encourage them to do what they do best."

"Are you breaking up the team?" Neema asked.

"No.. Of course not. But if one is a great speaker, then let that person speak. Others can write. So let them write. And we need technicians to run the ISP so our message will continue to be heard everywhere."

"Then who goes where?"

"Peter is a very passionate speaker, and a natural leader. He must go to Washington to support Christina. Phillip and Lydia should be encouraged to go to New York. They should fit right in with the Christian community there. John and Gabriela could do a great deal of good if they spent some time in the Southeast. The remainder of the team would make their best contribution if they stayed in Humboldt County. They can respond to e-mails, manage the blogs and keep the ISP running. The core theology of our belief system is in our computer files. Protect them from harm."

"And what are you going to do, ... while I'm doing all this management?"

Rick smiled and gently placed his hand on her arm.

"I am going to love you with all my heart."

***

After dropping the children off with Mari and Josue, Rick and Neema continued on to Sacramento. The warmth of the mid-afternoon sun was accompanied by a cooling breeze that blew gently across the delta grasslands as they crossed the causeway and turned toward the downtown area. Once there Rick parked the car and escorted Neema to the Cathedral. The walk leading to the Cathedral door was lined with hundreds of fragrant flowers. The walk itself was covered with red, yellow and white petals. An usher appeared in the doorway, smiled with delight to see Rick, and turned to announce his coming to the congregation. People spilled out of the church to greet Rick and Neema, everybody talking at once. They were able to shake hands with almost everyone. The Priest appeared and gave them both a spontaneous hug.

"Welcome," he said. "We have been waiting with great anticipation for your arrival. There are people here from several congregations... Catholics, Methodists, Presbyterians... even some members of our local Synagogue. You have become very famous."

Peter and Phillip had been following Rick's car down from Humboldt County. They were determined to protect their friends from harm. But by the time they arrived a few moments later, the jubilant crowd had already accompanied Rick and Neema into the sanctuary. The two men hastily walked up the steps to the Cathedral door.

Once inside, Rick was greeted by an enthusiastic Haben who had been visiting with his mother in San Jose. They exchanged greetings as the congregation gathered around them. Although at first Peter and Phillip were alarmed by the zeal of the adulation, they soon realized Rick was among friends. Peter relaxed and watched the crowd.

"God is here," he said to Phillip. "I can feel his presence."

The Priest led Rick to a lectern.

"We'll sing one hymn," he said to Rick over the din. "Just to get things going... You know how the Methodists love to sing... Then I'll say a prayer and turn the lectern over to you."

He raised his hands to quiet the congregation.

"We can begin now... Let us begin our Palm Sunday service with a hymn of joy."

***

On Monday Rick met with the council of ministers and priests to discuss his theology. They met in the Cathedral office. When Rick entered the building, he was greeted by eight men. They shook hands and were very cordial. But Rick sensed three of them were unreceptive to his theology. After taking his seat in a semi-circle of chairs, he addressed them first.

"I can understand your reluctance to accept my gift. Although it is not unusual for a person to sense or know what someone else is thinking, my capability appears to exceed anything you have experienced."

Rick looked directly at the man who appeared to have the deepest doubts.

"For example, you believe I am a charlatan. A fake. Isn't that right?"

The minister was suddenly embarrassed.

"Well, it is certainly unusual."

"Give me your hands."

The minister reluctantly came to Rick's chair and opened his two hands, palm up. Rick took them into his own hands and closed his eyes.

"Think about your childhood," he ordered.

The minister thought for a moment and then murmured: "Anything in particular?"

"It doesn't matter. Think of anything you wish."

After a few moments, Rick let the minister's hands go, and motioned for him to return to his seat.

"You were born in San Diego. When you were three, your parents moved to Mill Valley so your father could take a job in San Francisco."

The minister was disturbed by the revelation, but remained unconvinced.

"You could have found that out from my church secretary."

"That's true, but I did not. You can check with her... Judith.... Am I right?"

"Yes."

"Would Judith know anything about your childhood?"

"No... I don't think so."

"At age seven, you found a lost dog. You took her home and pleaded with your mother to keep her. The dog's name was.... Raffles, was it not?... And she was a black and white poodle shepherd mix."

The minister began to feel awkward. He knew his church secretary would not know much about his boyhood dog.

"Yes... Listen.. I don't know how you do it ... But I'm willing to hear what you have to say."

Rick stared at the other two unbelievers.

"Who's next?"

The two men looked away. Rick's gift was well known. Now they had seen a demonstration of his ability. One minister quietly said: "We are ready to hear you speak."

The Cathedral Priest asked the first question.

"Was Jesus God?"

Rick didn't respond right away. Instead he looked from man to man, weighing the gravity of his answer. Then he spoke with deliberation.

"First, please allow me to apologize for what I have just done. My gift has been given to me to help those who seek a better understanding of the spiritual, and to assist those who are making the transformation from this universe to the next.... And that is how it should always be used."

Rick paused. The other men felt more at ease. He waited for a moment, and continued.

"Jesus was not God.... Although God dwelled within Jesus, He and God are two different beings. If we are virtuous, honest, and receptive in our quest to be at one with the Holy Spirit, God can reside within any person."

"Then you have a different interpretation of the Holy Trinity."

"My model is the natural order of things. There is the male and the female in most of God's kingdom, there is also the physical and the spiritual, creation and destruction, life and death, and so on. I choose to believe these things follow the natural order of the Cosmos. There are both physical and spiritual laws that govern the conduct of all things. Since these laws are the work of a creator, and there is both female and male, as well as the spiritual and the physical, then they must be a reflection of a Holy Trinity... God the Holy Mother is the creator of life, God the Holy Father is the creator of the physical Cosmos, and God the Holy Spirit is the creator of values, ... including love, ... which is the most important value of all... There is a discussion of the Holy Trinity on my Blog."

"I have read your blog and listened to your sermons ... Quite impressive," the Priest said.

One of the ministers spoke up.

"What about the separation of Church and State?"

"Good government is always truly devoted to the health and welfare of those who are governed. Its political authority comes from the people. Its moral values come from God. Political corruption always occurs if government fails to embrace both of these truths."

"But can't people provide high moral standards? Why do we need God?"

"We need God's inspiration and guidance because we humans don't have the ability to maintain high ethical standards. We always fail. Greed, privation, fear, hatred, conceit.... there are a million excuses for our failure. Thus if we want to sustain a high sense of right versus wrong, we must look to the word of God for counsel. Our Cosmos operates by a set of physical and spiritual rules. We need to sustain our connection with the creator who put them in place."

And so it went. For almost two hours Rick answered each question as best he could. By then he was worn out.

"Enough gentlemen... I must end our session because I am exhausted... I'll take one last question... and that has to be it for today."

The Priest looked up at Rick, raised his hand to silence the others, and asked the last question.

"Are you a prophet sent by God?"

The question embarrassed Rick. He had never given his persona much thought.

"I'm just a guy," he said. "I'm just a guy who has been inspired to teach."

The men looked at each other and then – stiff from sitting so long – got up and began to chat among themselves. They were again very cordial as they left the Cathedral office, shaking Rick's hand, and urging him to continue his mission. After the Priest said goodbye to the others, he returned to his chair. With great deliberation, he slowly sat down and gazed at Rick.

"You articulate a comprehensive theology," he said. "You project confidence and sincerity... You have given me much to think about."

The Priest looked at Rick for a moment, and stroked his chin as though pondering something he could not understand.

"Actually, there is one answer I completely disagree with."

"And which question troubles you?"

"The last one."

***

As he was leaving the Cathedral, Rick was stopped on the sidewalk by a television reporter and a camera crew. She immediately confronted him with a question.

"Are you going to lead a revolution against our government?" the reporter demanded.

She thrust the microphone in Rick's face. There was a smirk on her face that clearly conveyed her disdain for him. Rick stopped and gave her a benevolent smile.

"No... If you have read my Internet text, you know I believe in the separation of Church and State."

"But you are preaching sedition!" she exclaimed. "You are defying the Book of Rules!"

"I preach from the heart," Rick said quietly.

"There is a rumor that President Rose O'Brien has declared you to be an enemy of the state," the reporter said. "How do you respond to her charge?"

Rick was about to respond when Phillip stepped in between him and the reporter. He smiled at her and pushed the microphone away from Rick's face.

"Here," he said taking control of the microphone. "Allow me to help you. I'll be happy to answer your questions."

While this was happening, Peter grabbed Rick's arm and pulled him away to his car. He opened the door and pushed Rick into the vehicle. Phillip left the reporter and got into the rear seat. The reporter screamed another question at Rick.

"Who gave you the right to do this?"

***

The confrontation with the reporter was on the Tuesday morning news. It opened with a rather long condemnation of terrorist groups who were defying civil authority. Although the Department of Public Information refrained from accusing Christian groups of sedition, the Catholic Cathedral was used as a backdrop for the entire piece. The brief interview between Rick and the reporter was cut and edited to make it look like a violent confrontation. After Rick, Phillip and Peter got into their car, the reporter added:

"And there they go, the leader of a Christian terrorist group and his two thugs."

There was of course, the obligatory text on the screen at the end of the piece:

"This News Item has been approved by the Department of Public Information."

***

Despite media hostility, Rick elected to attend a Fellowship Rally at the Sacramento Fair Grounds on Wednesday afternoon. At first, the reception was cordial. Several people shook his hand and praised his work. They asked good questions and listened attentively to his answers. But Rick sensed the media piece had made everyone nervous. People were genuinely apprehensive about the looming possibility of a bloody revolution. Many were frustrated by the events of the previous day. Rick knew frustration usually leads to anger.

During the rally, one of the speakers expressed disappointment that Rick and his followers were unwilling to lead a revolution. Then another speaker said that Rick's lack of leadership had left the Christian community in a precarious position. He read the text of the TV piece and then turned to look directly at Rick.

"You led us down the path of revolution but then left us without the leadership we need to overcome our enemies."

There were murmurs of agreement from the crowd. Someone produced a sign: "Myths and Lies Will Not Save Us."

A man near the stage shouted, "We get nothing but empty promises from these people!"

The sound of unhappy voices rippled through the crowd. The dissent became louder. When Rick tried to respond, his words were drowned out by catcalls and insults. Rather than challenge them, Rick walked away from the stage and left the rally.

***

Thursday evening Rick and Neema took Mari, Josue, Peter, Phillip, and Haben out to dinner. Neema arranged for them to have a private room. Although everyone was relaxed and in a good mood, Phillip was uneasy that Rick had gone to the fellowship rally by himself.

We should have been there with you," he said. "Peter and I could have helped you overcome the crowd's criticism."

"That was the wrong place and the wrong time for a confrontation," Rick replied. "It would have done no good.... These people need to realize we believe in separation of Church and State. If they want to fix their political problems, they will have to develop their own political solution. If they want to come closer to the spiritual, we can help them... Our message must be one of peace and hope, else it will not endure. That is something Jesus understood. We should follow His example."

"The Cathedral Priest called," said Neema. "He was most apologetic. He asked if we would like to join with him at services tomorrow afternoon. Then he chuckled ... He said he thinks he can guarantee a better reception."

Rick thought about the invitation. Most of the people he had met over the last few days were compassionate Christians, happy to hear his message, and willing to engage him in conversation. He decided to accept the Priest's invitation.

"And now," Rick said with some enthusiasm, let's have a glass of wine before supper."

He reached for a decanter of red wine sitting on the table and removed the cap. Then he carefully poured a glass for them all.

"A toast," Rick proclaimed. "A toast to what we have accomplished and to the future of our mission. May God be with us."

***

Friday morning dawned warmer than usual in Washington. President Mary Rose Chartres O'Brien paced back and forth in the Oval Office. Despite intelligence to the contrary, she was convinced Rick and his movement were out to get her. The hatred and paranoia were so intense, she was beginning to feel ill.

There was a ring on her in-house telephone. It was her assistant.

"There is a man on the telephone. The switchboard let him through to me. He's very insistent. He claims to have been the NSS Commander in San Jose. Isn't he the one who sparked the rebellion against you?"

Those thoughts only served to make Mary Rose even more agitated.

"Put the bastard on!" she exclaimed. "I'll make him wish he never heard of me."

Her assistant put through the call. President Mary Rose picked up the instrument.

"What the hell do you want!"

The man's voice was soft in a lethal sort of way. He calmly explained the reason for his call.

"We have a common enemy. His name is Ricardo Juan Sanchez Vasquez. He is an enemy of the State and a threat to your rule. But .... I can eliminate him for you."

Mary Rose replied with a mixture of disgust for the man on the telephone and hatred for the man who was trying to overthrow her administration. She could barely speak.

"And how do you propose to do that?"

"My informants tell me Ricardo has been invited to attend a special service this afternoon in Sacramento. I can wait until he leaves at about 4:30PM. I can assassinate him as he comes out of the church. I want to make a deal with you. You pay me, and protect me from prosecution, and I will eliminate him. Without his leadership, his little group will disintegrate."

"Why do I believe you can do this?" Mary Rose demanded.

"You can check my record. I am an excellent shot. When the church service breaks up, the people will not be expecting any trouble. They will be filled with their silly affection for one another and most of them will be too busy with their children to even notice me. It will be easy to get close enough to him to do the job."

"How much?" Mary Rose demanded suspiciously.

"Two million."

Rose thought for a moment. The price was cheap. Petty cash. For 2 million she would be free of that rebel and his goons. Then a plan began to form in her mind.

"OK, we have a deal. Kill Rick and the money will be waiting for you in Washington... And I'll dream up a reason to circumvent prosecution."

"Thank you Madam President. It is a pleasure doing business with you."

President Mary Rose hung up the telephone. A sly smile crossed her lips as she thought about her options. *"If he is unsuccessful, I can have him arrested for attempted murder. That will please the Christians. ... But if he succeeds, I can have him arrested and tried for murder. My followers will be happy Rick is dead. The Christians will be happy I caught the killer. Either way I come out ahead."*

Mary Rose sat down behind the ornate desk. *"I hope that little weasel is successful."*

She pushed a button on the intercom. "Get me the Director of the Department of Public Information."

In a few moments a man's voice came on the line. In a very solicitous voice dripping with phony friendliness, he asked how he could help her. President Mary Rose ignored his babbling.

"There is a church service in Sacramento this afternoon. It's at the Catholic Cathedral. I want you to assign a TV crew to cover the parishioners as they exit the service at about 4:30. Keep broadcasting until I tell you to stop. I want this piece to be on every TV screen in America... Do you understand?... Every moment on every TV screen in America!"

"But this will be raw and live. We will not have any chance to edit the broadcast," the Director whined.

"It doesn't matter. I want the people to see everything that happens." Mary Rose stopped herself from saying what she thought, *"when the bastard gets killed and we arrest the killer."*

"As you say Madam President... We will broadcast the entire event. I'll instruct the programming outlets to keep broadcasting until you give us other instructions."

The Director of the Department of Public Information asked a few more questions and then hung up. Mary Rose smiled as she returned to pacing back and forth in the oval office.

Outside the President's office, the President's Assistant put down her telephone, carefully placing it in the cradle to avoid any noise. Her face was pale with shock. After looking up and down the empty hall, she dialed a special number and let it ring twice.

The Director of the Department of Public Information immediately called the Western Regional Director in San Francisco to set up the broadcast. The Western Regional Director called the District Deputy in San Jose to relay the instructions. The District Deputy in San Jose then called the Sacramento Bureau Chief. Although the Sacramento staff were dumbfounded by the request, they did as they were told. A TV crew was immediately dispatched to cover the service.

***

"Daddy, the special telephone rang twice. What does that mean?"

George Kincade Taylor looked at his daughter with some alarm.

"It means your White House contact wants a meeting right now. Go to the location she gave you last time and stay there until she arrives. Try to look as innocent as you can. We never know how long it will take her to arrive."

Amanda felt a rush of the excitement. For a second time, she was playing spy. She quickly put on her coat, kissed her father on the cheek, and walked out of the building. It was a short walk to the bus line and the bus she needed came within a few minutes. As the bus moved along the avenue toward the Lincoln Memorial, Amanda looked at the reflection in her window to see if anyone was following her. Satisfied she was alone, Amanda got off the bus and began to walk slowly toward the monument. Then she saw her contact behind a pillar. Amanda walked as though taking in the sights until she was close to the woman.

"Amanda?" the woman asked.

"Don't you recognize me from the last time?"

The President's Assistant peered at Amanda.

"Oh... Now I do," she said in a hushed voice.

"Amanda, you must tell your father. There is a plot to assassinate Rick this afternoon in Sacramento. It's supposed to happen as he leaves a service at the Catholic Cathedral. The assassin is the former District Commander of the NSS in San Jose."

Amanda was stunned by the revelation. Eyes wide with excitement, she could only stammer a response.

"Are you sure?"

"Yes, I heard it on a telephone call. You must tell your father right away."

"But what can he do?"

"Your father is a resourceful man.... Now go."

The President's Assistant turned and walked away, leaving Amanda frightened and confused. She loved Rick's team. They were nice people. They needed her father's protection. Amanda abruptly turned away from the memorial and walked quickly back to a bus stop. A little over 30 minutes later, she walked into George Taylor's office.

"They plan to assassinate Rick," she panted breathlessly. "The President's Assistant told me it will happen this afternoon at the Cathedral in Sacramento."

George Taylor frowned and quickly reached for a secure telephone. He asked the person who answered to talk to Amanda.

"Tell him everything," George said.

***

Friday afternoon, Rick and Neema went to the Cathedral in Sacramento. Phillip, Peter and Haben followed them in another car. Phillip was determined he would not let Rick out of his sight again. As they were driving across the causeway into the city, Phillip turned to Haben.

"Would you be willing to help us with Rick's protection? There should be a large crowd at the Cathedral and we don't know what to expect."

"Sure!" Haben responded with enthusiasm. "Just tell me what to do."

Once again the walkway to the Cathedral was lined with fragrant flowers. Rick and Neema arrived just in time for the service. The Priest was very gracious. Once again he apologized for the bad interview and the problems Rick encountered at the rally.

"Those things happen," Rick responded. "We live in an imperfect universe."

"Please do join me in conducting the service," the Priest said as they walked into the building. "We have people here from several denominations. It will help to make this a service for all people of faith."

"Thank you for the invitation. It will be my pleasure," Rick replied.

Before the doors closed behind them, Rick looked back to see if Phillip, Peter and Haben had arrived. Out of the corner of his eye, he saw what looked to be a big white TV studio van parked across the street. He shrugged off the nagging feeling the van meant trouble.

***

Phillip, Peter and Haben arrived shortly after Rick and Neema. They exchanged greetings with several very friendly people and took their seats in a pew at the rear of the Cathedral. As was their custom, they earnestly participated in the service. Although he was troubled by the TV studio van parked outside the building, Phillip could at least relax while he watched the activity in the Cathedral.

After the last prayer, Rick immersed himself in the congregation. He shook hands and hugged as many people as he could. Neema followed him as he gradually made his way to the Cathedral door. The congregation began to spill out of the building onto the sidewalk. It was such a nice day, few people were in any hurry to leave the area. The Priest caught up with them and drew Rick aside.

"Thank you for coming. I know it is a long trip for you to come all the way down from Humboldt County, but you are always welcome to visit with us. I would especially like to spend more time with you on theological subjects, but for now we'll just have to say goodbye."

"You have been a gracious host, Father. It would be a privilege to visit with you again... And rest assured, if you come our way, please plan to stay with us for awhile."

The two men shook hands. They understood each other and they both welcomed the friendship that had emerged between them these last few days.

Rick turned to go out of the building, arm in arm with a very happy Neema. For her, it was a perfect day. Phillip fell in behind his sister. He motioned for Haben to walk behind Rick. Peter walked down the sidewalk ahead of them. As soon as the TV studio crew spotted Rick, they focused three cameras on him. The reporter didn't know what to say. She had no carefully written and politically sanitized script. So she just said into her microphone: "We have been waiting for Ricardo to leave the sanctuary with his wife and friends. They are making their way down the steps and into the throng of people who are still here."

Then she shut up.

Phillip spotted a man coming toward them, head turned down as though he wanted to look at the sidewalk – or perhaps hide his face. Phillip thought there was something familiar about the man. Instinctively he quickly stepped around Neema and started toward the man. Alarmed by Phillip's sudden move, Haben came to Rick's side. The man looked up. Phillip found himself staring into the eyes of the San Jose NSS Commander as he raised his arm. The Commander shifted his gaze to look directly at Rick as he pointed a gun at him. Phillip lunged for the gun just as it went off. He heard a shriek of pain behind him. Phillip threw the Commander to the ground and grabbed the Commander's arm. The gun went off three more times. There were screams of fear, children crying, and the sound of people running. Peter rushed to help Phillip. Together they subdued the cursing Commander and disarmed him.

"Oh God," Phillip thought, "Rick has been killed."

He was afraid to look. Phillip had to physically force himself to turn his head. He saw a body on the sidewalk, blood pooling around a man's head. Neema was kneeling over him, tears in her eyes. Then Phillip was almost overcome with a sensation of joyful relief mixed with intense grief. It was Haben. He had been shot through the neck. Blood was gushing from an artery.

Rick knelt down beside Haben with a mixture of shock and sorrow. He grasped Haben's hand. The young man looked up at him.

"Did I do OK," he asked. "Did I keep you safe?"

"You have done more than I can ever thank you for...."

Rick tried to stop the bleeding by placing his hand over the wound. But it was no use. The pool of blood spread ever larger over the sidewalk. Life began to fade from Haben's eyes. The Priest appeared and knelt down beside Rick.

"We've called for an ambulance and the police... It won't take long for them to get here."

"Everything is getting hazy," Haben moaned. "What is happening to me?"

Rick quietly grasped Haben's hands in his own.

"Father, will you give this man the Last Rights?"

"Of course," the Priest replied. His voice shaken by Haben's condition, and with great sadness, he solemnly began to repeat the words he knew only too well. Haben was close to losing consciousness. Several people gathered around to offer sympathy. Neema was sobbing. She grasped her brother's shirt collar and buried her head against his chest. The TV crew used a boom microphone to catch every word Rick and the Priest were saying to Haben. Three cameras recorded the pathos of the scene. The reporter was speechless.

After the Priest finished, Rick spoke to Haben.

"Where are you, Haben?"

"I can't see anything."

Haben blinked his eyes several times and tried to sit up. Rick and the Priest gently restrained him. Haben lay back on the walk. He was terrified by what was happening to him. Rick spoke to him again.

"Haben... keep your eyes closed... so you can see the way to God... Let the images come into your mind."

The Priest looked at Rick with curiosity and wonder. Rick seemed to be slipping away from them. The Priest looked up at Peter.

"What's happening?"

"Rick is with Haben," Peter replied. "He is guiding Haben into a garden. From there they will walk down a footpath to a portal filled with sunlight."

"You mean he is not actually here?"

"Physically, his form is as you see it. But his soul is in the Spiritual Dimension."

Neema withdrew from her brother's protective arms and came to kneel beside Rick. She placed her hand on his shoulder.

Rick began to whisper words of reassurance into Haben's ear.

"Come Haben, Let's take this walk together...."

Haben's face slowly relaxed. The terror of the moment was replaced by an aura of serenity.

"It's just as you described it," he murmured. "A beautiful garden... A footpath lined with flowers... sunlight shining through a portal and ... I see him.... Coming through the portal to greet me... It's Father Giovanni!"

Haben breathed his last breath. A faint smile appeared on his lips. The Priest crossed himself.

"I wanted to believe this could happen... But I was skeptical... Now I have seen it with my own eyes... This is a wonderful demonstration of God's presence among us."

Neema began to gently massage Rick's neck and shoulders.

"Come back," she whispered. "Rick... come back to us."

Rick began to stir. The Priest took Rick's blood stained hand and gently squeezed it.

Slowly. Ever so slowly. Rick recovered his composure.

"Haben is with God now. Father Giovanni was there to walk with him through the portal."

They slowly stood up. Rick turned to the Priest.

"May I wash my hands?"

"Of course," said the Priest, "come with me."

As they walked into the Cathedral, they could hear the sound of police car and ambulance sirens. The vehicles slid to a stop on the street. Two officers jumped out of the police car and ran to where Peter still had the cursing Commander pinned to the sidewalk. The ambulance crew rushed to Haben's side. The medic simply shook his head. He motioned for his partner to bring the body bag.

After Rick washed his hands, he sat down on a pew with Phillip, Neema and the Priest. Peter was still giving a statement to the police officers. The commander was securely chained inside the police car. People were still milling around the blood stain on the sidewalk. Some were thoroughly shaken by what they had just witnessed. The TV studio crew was broadcasting every action and most of the comments. After she regained her composure, the reporter began to interview witnesses.

Rick looked at the Priest.

"We make a good team... You provided a traditional Christian response. I'm sure you connected with God."

The Priest was still a bit shaken by the experience. Although unsure of what to think, he felt a surge of exhilaration.

"And you, my friend, have given us all a moment of spiritual inspiration."

***

The Sacramento Bureau Chief was becoming nervous. He was still broadcasting the scene at the Cathedral as instructed, but he began to worry that somehow he had missed the President's instruction to stop. So he called District Deputy in San Jose. It being late in the afternoon, the District Deputy had already departed for the day. The question confused the Shift Supervisor, so she called the Western Regional Director in San Francisco. He had also gone for the day. Sensing something was definitely wrong, the Western Regional Shift Supervisor tried to call the Department of Public Information in Washington. The Director, he was informed by a third level bureaucrat, could not be reached until Monday.

The President's Assistant locked her desk and stood up. She was tired, she needed some rest, and she was deeply moved by the incident in Sacramento. The President's Assistant had stayed at her desk until late in the evening because she expected President Mary Rose to burst out of the Oval Office at any moment, demanding the programming from Sacramento be stopped. But with the exception of a few staff members going about their chores, there was nothing but silence in the White House. The TV monitor in the hall continued to show the scene at the Cathedral. By now however, everyone had gone. The TV crew could do nothing but focus their cameras on the now darkened Cathedral. The text on the bottom of the screen read:

"This programming has been approved by the Department of Public Information"

Unable to contain her curiosity any longer, the President's Assistant carefully opened the office door and looked in. She was shocked by what she saw. President Mary Rose Chartres O'Brien was laying on the couch, body in disarray, unseeing eyes staring at the ceiling. Her face revealed a mixture of spastic shock and wicked disbelief. Apparently, the President had suffered a stroke.

***

George Kincade Taylor chuckled as he clicked the TV remote. It was early Saturday morning and every channel was still showing the front of the Sacramento Cathedral. Every hour, on the hour, the Sacramento studio crew had been replaying the scene of Haben's death.

"This is unbelievable," George said to Helen as he sat down to breakfast. "No one wants to risk the President's wrath. So they are broadcasting the same thing over and over again. They won't stop until Mary Rose tells them to do so."

"Why doesn't she do that?" asked Helen.

"My friends at the hospital say she is still in a semi-conscious state. She can't speak."

"But surely someone has the authority."

"You keep forgetting, Helen. These people have created a bureaucratic dictatorship. Decisions are made top down. Personal initiative is discouraged. Creative thinking is not allowed. Public employees have become robotic drones. That's why this government is no longer effective."

George chuckled again. Helen sat down to join him for breakfast.

"You seem very pleased."

"I can't help it. The irony is just too sweet. Rick has just been given hours of free programming to millions of people who will now understand who he is and what he can do. His work has even been endorsed by the Department of Public Information."

Helen was surprised. "How do you figure that?"

"Because the text message on the bottom of the screen.... See it?"

Helen read the text aloud. *"This programming has been approved by the Department of Public Information."*

She looked very puzzled.

"But why would they do that? I thought they regarded Rick as an enemy of the State."

"For the same reason I gave you before. The message is there because someone is supposed to put it there. They just follow the Department's procedures and rules. Although they probably have figured out by now the endorsement is a huge mistake for the O'Brien Administration, they don't have to take any responsibility. They can hide behind the autocratic procedures and rules of their bureaucracy."

"After Mary Rose wakes up, they'll probably publish a retraction."

"It's too late for that. Most Americans are naturally curious. They will be motivated to learn a lot more about Rick's renaissance theology."

"But they won't be quick to throw out traditional theology," said Helen. "The scene where he and the Priest worked together to pray over a dying man tells me the traditional and the renaissance can work together."

"That's because they are both Christians. They have much in common."

Amanda came downstairs to join her parents for breakfast.

"That program still on?"

"Yes," Helen responded. "Your father thinks it will stay on until Mary Rose recovers enough to speak."

"When will that be?"

"No one knows. The radio news has been saying it could be any time now."

George began to frown. "This incident could easily spark public protests across the nation. I'd better get to the office to keep tabs on what is happening."

"But won't your staff be out for the weekend?" Helen asked.

"Yes, but when they see this, they will know this whole situation could become very unstable. And my people," George smiled, "are not afraid to take the initiative. They will come in as soon as they can."

Amanda changed the subject. "Does anyone know where Rick is now?"

"The radio news broadcast said he plans to attend Haben's funeral and then go home."

Amanda looked at her father.

"The man you had me talk to on the telephone said he would rush to the Cathedral as fast as he could. But what happened?"

"He got there too late. By the time he arrived, the police had secured the area."

Amanda was depressed. She was deeply touched by Haben's death. Then her thoughts shifted to Rick.

"Daddy, how will this affect Rick?"

George thought for a moment, and took a sip of coffee before answering.

"Rick has suddenly become a very important spiritual icon in America. Maybe all over the world. Thanks to President Mary Rose O'Brien he could develop into an influential religious leader.... I would like to have him work with us. He seems to understand the purpose of theology better than any person I know. He could have a great moral influence on the revolution."

"When I was in California, I made friends with Christina Leung," Amanda said. "She's very smart. I think she's started a mission in Virginia or Maryland. Anyway, she can tell you all about Rick's mission and his team."

"Can you get in touch with her?"

"Sure. I'll call Sarah in California for Christina's telephone number."

George Kincade Taylor looked thoughtfully at his daughter. Then he smiled.

"Call her. Perhaps we can find a way to work together."

Chapter 11   Angels

Sitting in a gazebo surrounded by a lovely garden of flowers, shrubs and trees, Father Giovanni and Haben were having a quiet conversation.

"I have a special treat for you," Father Giovanni said. "Someone is coming to see you."

"Someone is coming to see me?" asked Haben.

"Yes… Just look down the garden footpath… Do you see him?"

Haben looked intently where Father Giovanni pointed. A lone figure gradually appeared. Father Giovanni stood up. "Come with me, I'll introduce you."

Haben followed Father Giovanni a short distance on the garden footpath. Father Giovanni shook hands with the man, and said a few words of welcome. Then he turned to Haben.

"Haben, meet Micah, Rick's neighbor in Winters."

Haben was astonished. Rick had described Micah and talked about Micah's counsel. But Haben could not understand how Micah could be on this side of the portal.

"Aren't you still alive… I mean in the physical universe?" Haben stammered as he shook Micah's hand.

"Father Giovanni and I get that a lot," Micah replied with a genial smile. "You might say we are special people. We are able to live on both sides of the portal."

"But how do you do that?" Haben asked.

Micah looked at Haben thoughtfully. "It is a gift. It is a gift God gives to those who are special. Someone like you, Haben…. You will soon learn how to live on both sides of the portal. Father Giovanni will show you how when he teaches you the finer points of being an angel."

Haben's eyes filled with wonder. "Me… An angel?"

Father Giovanni put his hand on Haben's shoulder. "All in good time my young friend," he said. "For now, it is important you get to know Micah."

Father Giovanni and Micah started to walk toward the gazebo. Micah changed the subject.

"Well Haben," Micah said. "How do you like it here?"

"It's very nice, but I miss the excitement of the physical universe."

"Another young man who likes the challenge of hell," Micah smiled. He understood Haben's feelings. There were many like him.

"We will find something for you to do in the physical universe. Let Father Giovanni teach you how to be an angel. When he says you're ready, I will send you back."

"Just like that?"

"As soon as Father Giovanni tells me you're ready."

"Can I go to work for Rick?"

"Work for the Good Shepherd? Probably not. It is better if you have a different assignment."

Haben was disappointed. Micah sought to console him.

"Whatever you do, it will be important, and I will keep in touch with you."

Haben was puzzled. "What happens next?"

Micah motioned them to a gazebo bench. He smiled again at the young man.

"I'll leave that up to Father Giovanni.... Patience my friend. Angels must learn to have patience.... In the meantime, you should focus your attention on the job at hand... These people ... the ones you just left... face many challenges."

Haben became thoughtful. "What will happen to them?"

"We have given them a choice... These humans.... They have heard about the lessons of love from Jesus and the Angels' Footpath to here from Rick. It's up to them. They can continue on the destructive course they have established or they can experience a renaissance of belief. The present course will lead them to the ravages of Hell. They still have, on the other hand, a chance to turn their planet into paradise... Hatred or love. ... That's their choice."

"A footpath?" Haben asked.

"Yes. It is the footpath of the angels. We put it there for people to follow. The Angels' Footpath is a place of love, faith and hope. If people look for it, they will find their way to heaven."

"And what's my job?"

"When you're ready," said Father Giovanni, "you will help us. Our job is to give them a chance to make the right choice. We try to nudge them in the right direction."

Haben became more enthusiastic about his prospects. He would be doing something important. His mother could be proud of his work.

"What about Rick's team? ... Will I be replaced?" Haben asked.

"They have already elected Lydia to replace you. She knows she has a big responsibility. You're a tough act to follow. You made a totally unselfish sacrifice."

Haben was proud of his accomplishment.

"But what about Rick and Rick's family?... What will happen to them?"

"Neema and Rick have much to do. Adonica will most certainly pursue her interest in medicine. Ramon will follow in his grandfather's footsteps."

Micah paused for a moment, and winked at Father Giovanni.

"And I do believe Serafina has inherited Rick's gift."

The Beginning

******

Made in the USA
Charleston, SC
09 September 2010